The editor gratefully acknowledges permission to print the following material:

"Mangoes," by Vivian Leal. © 1996. Printed by permission of the author.

"Emoria at the Tracks," by James López. © 1996. Printed by permission of the author.

"Angie Luna," by Sergio Troncoso. © 1996. Printed by permission of the author.

"The Kiss," by Ilan Stavans. © 1996. Printed by permission of the author.

"Through the Raw Meat," by Verónica González. © 1996. Printed by permission of the author.

"The Economy of Virtue," by Daniel Cooper Alarcón. © 1996. Printed by permission of the author.

"Babies," by Abraham Rodríguez, Jr. © 1992 by Abraham Rodríguez, Jr. Originally published in *The Boy Without a Flag: Tales of the South Bronx.* Milkweed Editions, 1992. Reprinted by permission of Milkweed Editions.

"Daddy," by Lisa Y. Garibay. © 1996. Printed by permission of the author.

"Chinese Memories," by Armando F. Gutiérrez. © 1996. Printed by permission of the author.

"The Circumstances Surrounding My Penis," by David Rice. © 1996. Originally published in *Give the Pig a Chance,* Arizona, Bilingual Press, 1996. Reprinted by permission of the author.

"The Next Big Thing," by Michele M. Serros. © 1996. Printed by permission of the author.

"Last Words," by Erasmo Guerra. © 1996. Printed by permission of the author.

"Soldier," by Anthony Castro. © 1996. Printed by permission of the author.

"Drizzle of Moths," by Ricardo Armijo. © 1996. Printed by permission of the author.

"Mark," by Demetria Martínez. © 1996. Printed by permission of the author.

"We Don't Need No Stinking Maps," by Catherine Loya. © 1996. Printed by permission of the author.

"Crime," by Danny Romero. © 1996. Printed by permission of the author.

"Abuela Marielita," by Cecilia Rodríguez Milanés. ©1992. Originally pub-

Contents

ILAN STAVANS

Introduction

The genealogy of Latino letters is finally being established. We are learning to recognize that the literary renaissance that swept the country at the end of the eighties and in the early nineties didn't come out of nowhere; instead it was the result of a long process of assimilation and acculturation and a struggle to find homogeneity in the very heterogeneous Hispanic population of the United States. To a large extent the renaissance was the result of an ever expanding influence of a growing Hispanic middle class, from which there triumphantly emerged a lucid assembly of literary critics, memorialists, social scientists, poets, and fiction writers, from thirty-eight to fifty years old, some of them stationed at highbrow academic institutions. Their signature was increasingly recognizable: Campus organizations competed to have them as lecturers, magazines published their polemical work, radio and TV interviews multiplied, and intense discussions of their work swept through educated milieus and reverberated across the border. But at the doorsteps of the next millennium and with their work canonized, the need for dissent, for a different perspective and a new intellectual expansion is already being felt. Hispanics have replaced Asians as the fastest-growing minority in the nation, and it is estimated that by 2010 they will number more than forty-five million, many moving to secure jobs in government, academia, and the media industry. So a renewed collective self-portrait is already necessary.

The term *renaissance* appropriately described the flood of writing by Hispanics in the late 1980s. After all, Latino artists and intellectuals were active north of the Rio Grande even before the Treaty of Guadalupe Hidalgo, signed in 1848. But for years Spanish remained the main language of use among Mexicans in the Southwest, and it wasn't until the middle of the twentieth century that literature in English began to appear. In my previous book *The Hispanic Condition: Reflections on Culture and Identity in America*, I explored in full the labyrinthine history of Hispanics north of the Rio Grande and the ups and downs of their cultural upheaval. The community traces its intellectual roots to Cabeza de Vaca's *Shipwreck* and to other chronicles by Spanish *exploradores* in Florida and the Southwest, written for an Iberian audience. The first attempts at addressing a native constituency belong to Cuban poet and activist José Martí, who lived in exile in New York and Key West, as well as to the militancy of Puerto Rican intellectual Eugenio María de Hostos, whose role in favor of Puerto Rico's independence during the Spanish-American War in 1898 made him a cultural ambassador in the eyes of many.

The very first novel by a Latino written in English was Felipe Alfau's amazing *Locos: A Comedy of Gestures*. Drafted in 1928, it wasn't published by Farrar & Rinehart, until 1936. This modernist—or, more accurately, protopostmodernist—book, similar in spirit to Nabokov's *Pale Fire* and to Pirandello's plays, often makes critics uncomfortable, if anything because it was written by a Spaniard, who traditionally was seen in Latin America and by Hispanics in the United States as an aggressor. And not only was its author, born in 1902, from Barcelona, but he was also a fervent conservative, pro-Franco during the Spanish Civil War and an acknowledged Republican in U.S. politics. Still, it's unquestionable that Alfau was among the very first to switch languages successfully, from Spanish to English, north of the border. No matter what ideological viewpoint one professes, he stands as a titanic innovator and a door opener.

Simultaneously, the tobacco workers Bernardo Vega and Jesús Colón, stationed in New York before World War II, began reflecting on Puerto Rican and Afro-Caribbean culture in the United States, as did the erudite Harlem Renaissance scholar Arthur Alfonso Schomburg. Some three decades later came José Antonio Villarreal's *Pocho*, about a Mexican-American young man, published by Doubleday in 1959 and considered by critics the first Chicano novel produced for a non-Hispanic audience. (The term *Chicano*, first used by the writer Mario Suárez in the forties, wasn't in vogue yet.) A plethora of autobiographical and fiction narratives, short and long, followed it during the late sixties and in the seventies, in most part by Mexican-Americans writing about rural settings, like Tomás Rivera (*And the Earth Did Not Part* . . .), Rudolfo A. Anaya (*Bless Me, Ultima*), and the younger Ron Arias (*The Road to Tamazunchale*). Their works frequently portrayed Mexican-Americans as rural citizens, poor, exploited, and disliked, forced to migrate to the city. These narratives were accompanied by the New York urban stories of Puerto Ricans, such as Nicholasa Mohr, Piri Thomas, and Edward Rivera, set in the Bronx, Manhattan, and Spanish Harlem. Altogether more humorous and lighthearted, these works presented Hispanics as alienated and ghettoized, a forgotten community living within the belly of a capitalist beast.

In spite of their talent and commercial appeal, these Latino writers flourished thanks to the effort and goodwill of small presses. This doesn't mean that a prestigious New York house wouldn't occasionally bring out a novel or collection of stories by a Cuban-American, a Chicano, or a Puerto Rican on the mainland, but it wasn't in any consistent way, at least not until the late eighties, when the Anglo establishment took the Latino voices more seriously. It is generally agreed that the renaissance was ignited by Oscar Hijuelos's winning the Pulitzer Prize in 1990 for *The Mambo Kings Play Songs of Love*. The award was preceded by enormous interest in the book, published almost a year earlier, and was followed by numerous translations and a Hollywood film. Almost immediately writers like Sandra Cisneros, Julia Alvarez, and Cristina García were embraced by the

New York establishment, and recognized marginal voices, such as the best-selling Chicano novelist Rudolfo A. Anaya, moved to center stage by signing handsome contracts with prestigious houses. What followed was a new readership, which in turn gave way to new writers, and so on. One can claim of course that a substantial number of the Latino books that appeared in the early nineties were junk, but that is to be expected in our society, bound as we are to excess.

Among the concerns of this renaissance was the attempt to find common ground linking heterogeneous Latino groups. Not surprisingly the attempt at building the canon, an act that unavoidably seeks to honor the past, was anything but peaceful. Some thinkers vociferously opposed the idea of unified Latino history, claiming that Hispanics were not, and would never be, a single throng. Instead they should be addressed as independent entities only loosely related: Cuban-Americans, Puerto Ricans on the mainland, Chicanos, et al.—each with a unique perspective and a distinct joie de vivre. After all, these critics claimed, does anybody address Italians, Germans, and French under the rubric of Europeans? Others (like myself) sought a more harmonious, less tribal future, suggesting that in spite of the many cultural differences, Latin Americans south of the border more or less share a history (and a *her*story as well), a cuisine, and, more than anything else, a worldview, and since Latinos are, as comedian John Leguizamo states, "recovering Latin Americans," the common ground they share ought to be highlighted. After all, African-Americans, Asians, and even Jews are also heterogeneous groups, made up of various national backgrounds, often disconnected from one another.

Other contested issues brought along by the renaissance dealt with language and appellation. A solid number of Hispanics in the United States still live and write *en español* and feel oppressed by their English-speaking, attention-seeking peers. Which *is* the mother tongue? As for appellation, the debate pondered to exhaustion the many names used to identify the community: Hispanic, Latino and Latina, *mestizo* and *mestiza*—or simply Cuban-American, Chicano, Puerto Rican, and so on. Tired of the polemic, Manuel Ramos, the Denver lawyer and mystery writer, suggested an endearing solution, the name *María*. "It's the best name for all of us," he claimed. "It's beautiful, and most of us already have it somewhere in our names, male and female. So, from now on, I propose that we simply say María People of the United States, and everyone will know what we mean. It has the advantage of not being loaded with any political baggage, no hint of political correctness, and it's currently relevant to just about every group that could be included."

The renaissance had as its target the ancient stereotypes of Hispanics, seen for ages as impulsive, undemocratic, lazy, lusty, and even barbarous, that help explain why Benjamin Franklin in 1767 marked Mexico and Cuba for future expansion; why Anglo-Americans justified their invasion of Texas in 1836 as a battle against Mexican intruders and for self-determination; and why Teddy Roosevelt felt no remorse when he brought his Rough Riders to Cuba during the Spanish-American War of 1898, as if he were just stepping out into his own backyard and not into his neighbor's house. These preconceived ideas obviously could not disappear from one day to the next, but questioning them was the duty of the day.

But by the mid-nineties this literary renaissance was clearly growing too cozy, too comfortable with itself. Being applauded has its risks; it can make you complacent and uncritical. Some moved away from so-called ethnic literature; others began to experiment with plots much like the historical novels produced by Latin Americans like Gabriel García Márquez and Mario Vargas Llosa. Cisneros's *The House on Mango Street* became required reading in numerous high schools and colleges across the country, as did García's *Dreaming in Cuban*. Simultaneously, a well-stocked bookshelf of Latino classics came to be recognizable in addition to Martí, Schomburg, Alfau, Colón, and Villarreal, Américo Paredes's *With His Pistol in His Hand*, about the Mexican-American border outlaw Gregorio Cortés, was approached as a cultural landmark, as were Gloria Anzaldúa's *Borderlands / La Frontera: The New Mestiza*, a pastiche on race and gender; Piri Thomas's *Down These Mean Streets*, a memoir on

Puerto Rican life in the fifties in New York, complete with ingredients on drug addiction, crime, prison, and religious redemption; and Juan Gómez-Quiñones's "On Culture," an incisive anthropological essay with a Marxist perspective, on Mexican culture north of the Rio Grande. They were not alone. The outlaw Joaquín Murrieta and the Chicano activists Rubén Salazar and Oscar "Zeta" Acosta, acquired a legendary status, and Tony Montana, the violent hero of Brian De Palma's film *Scarface*, and the rock and roll singer Ritchie Valens, and Selena, the assassinated *tejana* star, became, for better or worse, community icons.

If it seems as if I'm discussing ancient history, it's because these changes occurred at an astonishing speed, equal only to the rapid entrance of Latinos to mainstream culture. The banquet to which they were denied entrance for decades suddenly became tangible. And the next wave of literati is already pushing its way in, a generation of up-and-coming *soñadores* born in 1960 or after—the Latino Generation X. In spite of their tender ages (many are between twenty-three and twenty-six), some are already well-known writers with solid followings. Demetria Martínez, a native of El Salvador, won the 1994 Western States Book Award for Fiction with her first novel, *Mother Tongue*, recently reissued by a mainstream press. A convert to Judaism and a former journalist, Martínez often lectures in colleges and universities and is a well-known poet. David Rice is responsible for a compelling collection of stories, *Give the Pig a Chance*, and Abraham Rodríguez, Jr., a Puerto Rican-American raised in the South Bronx, is the author of *The Boy Without a Flag*, a well-received collection of Latino stories, and *Spidertown*, a novel about drugs among alienated adolescents. Danny Romero's stories have appeared in respected anthologies and journals, and Michele M. Serros is a community activist and performance activist in California, best known for her book *Chicana Falsa*. Finally, Virgil Suárez, a longtime personal friend, is a prolific Cuban-American editor and fiction writer whose books include *Latin Jazz, The Cutter*, and *Welcome to the Oasis and Other Stories*, as well as a couple of anthologies: *Iguana Dreams* (coedited with his wife, Delia Poey) and *Paper Dance* (coedited with Victor Hernández Cruz and Leroy V. Quintana). While some of them were approached as members of the Latino renaissance, their inclusion in this volume is a signal of the age-group they belong to.

The remaining seventeen are "discoveries." While for years they have devoted their energy to literature, many are seeing their names in print for the first time. Bringing to light these many debutantes is of course a gamble, both personal and editorial. In preparing an anthology of new voices, one needs to have a sharp critical eye but also to keep in mind how prophetic a short story can be. My reading habits have led me back to works (of yuppie fiction, of southwestern literature, of post–civil rights African-American voices) published over the last thirty years. At least two-thirds of those included in those dusty volumes were never heard of again, as I'm sure will happen with some of the more than two dozen selected for this one. No professional career is without obstacles.

Yet as a group they display an astonishing talent and a variety of styles and technics. What they have in common is youth and an invigorating approach to literature. They are Catholic, Jewish, Protestant, and atheist; Puerto Ricans, Chicanos, Cuban-Americans, and Dominicans, of Iberian and Central American blood; they live in inner cities, suburbs, and college towns; and they come from Denver, Los Angeles, New York City, Miami, East Lansing, San Antonio, Teaneck, Seattle, Tallahassee, and Boston. They all have watched the same episodes of *Star Trek* and would know what to say should Hijuelos or Cisneros show up for dinner. A handful of them, including Verónica González, Daniel Cooper Alarcón, Vivian Leal, and James López, have a powerful control of language, often turning it into narrative. Others, such as Sergio Troncoso, Cecilia Rodríguez Milanés, and Catherine Loya, are capable of re-creating powerful cinematic images, of showing how the speed of life can massacre emotions.

They will take us to a love scene in the Tex-Mex *frontera* and to the household of a broken marriage, to a TV set that connects the present with memories long gone and to a subway train leading to a future of independence. But beyond these illusory bridges, nothing is sure. Do these writers make up a compact literary generation? Obviously it's too early to say. What is clear is their urgent need to go beyond the nostalgia that flavored the prose of their literary parents, which explains why they are so rough, so sharp-edged, so akin to low, hard-boiled culture, so determined to get things down in their own style. They are the kind of people who, to paraphrase W. H. Auden, know what they think only when they see what they say. What they aren't is immigrants with a Spanish accent; instead they are proud to perceive themselves as hyphenated people perfectly fluent in the language of the American dream. More than any literary generation before them, they are incredibly well read in Latino letters and know that to succeed, they must go beyond quotas. In short, these are open-eyed mythmakers of the future, a young generation of Latino writers fully aware of their immense possibilities—a New World discovering itself anew.

VIVIAN LEAL
Mangoes

Ah, to bite into the ticklish flesh of a ripe red and yellow mango. One has to be careful with mangoes: If they ripen too long on the tree, birds will come and peck at them. The trick is to pluck them from the tree a hot day away from their lusty red ardor. Left unrefrigerated, they remember their tree-bound passion so that their light pink blush continues to deepen into full embarrassment. If you don't eat them then, they rot.

Margarita

Very early, before anyone else is up, Margarita hears a mango drop to the ground in the yard. The sound has not woken her directly. She has woken to wait for it. She rises slowly from her bed, still impatient at the deliberateness with which she must will her muscles to respond. *"¡Qué horror!"* she sighs. She looks to see if he still sleeps. He will get up any minute now and realize she has left her bed. He will yell for the nurse to go find her. But perhaps today she will have time enough to make it out to the yard, to lay her hands on her own piece of fruit.

The hallway needs paint, she notes, as she advances through it.

Her fingertips tap the walls, more for direction than for support. She leaves a trail of gray paint chips. They shimmer on the floor of the darkened house. Everything has been shifted and moved, supposedly to accommodate her illness. It makes her angry, the mess they have made of her beautiful furniture. Since the day he said he would move his office home so that he could take over her daily care, Margarita has been slowly cornered into her bedroom. Her terrace overlooking the garden with her towering mango tree is strewn with desks, file cabinets, and copy machines. Her wrought-iron armchairs, made to withstand any weather, have been shoved into safe, sheltered corners where they age, unused. Her mahogany dining ensemble is a worktable. Only his vanity has saved the elegant sitting room. There hangs the fortuitous portrait of her mother, the one that looks so much like Margarita that the young who never knew Carlota mistake her for Margarita. But it is not Margarita, could never be. The woman in the picture stands tall, arrogantly, all the prestige of a large hacienda holding up her vertebrae. Her shoulders angle away from her hips so that the green satin fabric of her dress is stretched taut; its creases shine in the warm light of an afternoon sun. Behind her a man rushes past in a horse-drawn carriage. The breeze he creates billows through her hair, but softly.

"All the brides in the family used to come to our sala to take their picture before this portrait. They knew ours was the most elegant sitting room. This portrait of my Tita's mother, I wept when it was lost," Fausto always bragged, still brags.

True enough. There on her Chippendale table stands silver-framed picture after picture of taffeta-, silk- or organza-clad brides posing before a marble mantelpiece above which hangs Carlota. Margarita stills finds it incredible that it is here, that after such long journeys for each of them, they both are here, together again in this rotting house.

Fausto needs this room, this attempt at a re-creation of their old Havana salón. Its faded dignity allows him to pretend that he has disassembled their home for her, that were it not for her illness, their residence would be a place of magnificence. She finally understands his need for this. The day she returned from the hospital he needed her to pick up the heavy French silver fork and eat her diced chicken. She, who had not picked up anything for two months, picked up that fork and brought the trembling little cube to the only side of her mouth she could then open. How he had banged his fist on that table! How he had glared at that first of so many nurses! "See! What do you know? I told you she could do it!" Proud that his wife, his Margarita, could still demonstrate that refinement, that elegance of wealth for which he had married her.

By now she has mastered the terrace gate that foreshortened her first solo forays past her bedroom. She can slide it by throwing her weight against it. The flagstones at the edge of the yard are harder to negotiate. The little Japanese grass he had planted between them (how many years ago?) died, so the stones have slid and tilted into the rich brown dirt. Since her latest fall out here, her heart beats faster as she steps from one stone to the next, each crack between them a chasm to her. There! She has crossed over the rocks. Margarita passes the incestuous potted plants all lined up in a row, their branches hopelessly tangled as they steal water from one another, die together. At last she walks free toward her mango tree.

But halfway to the fallen piece of fruit that first compelled her to rise from her bed, she smiles and, still smiling, sighs a disappointed "*¡Qué horror!*"

"*¡Doña Margarita, Doña Margarita! Espere, que voy. Por favor, Doña Margarita!*" Breathless and frightened, Luz comes to her rescue. "Here, here, Doña Margarita, you sit down on this chair and just tell me which one you want." It is hopeless to resist, so Margarita sits and points, while plump Luz in her red polka-dot blouse darts around the yard as if connected by a long string to Margarita's pointing finger. One by one she delivers the retrieved mangoes into Margarita's lap. Luz walks to the left. Luz walks backward, away from the trunk. Luz climbs up the rusty ladder and thrusts with the clawed wooden pole, a basket on its end, into that stubbornly prudish foliage that refuses to be penetrated. Luz pulls and ducks and chases the falling fruit until

Margarita's lap is so full that Luz has to run to the kitchen to get a plastic shopping bag to carry all the mangoes inside.

Margarita enjoys this—very much. The mangoes are one thing, of course, the best thing. Second best is being outdoors in the air other people have breathed and exhaled through open windows. But there is no denying that watching Luz maneuvering to please her, pleases her—deliciously, maliciously.

Waiting for Luz to return, Margarita surveys her land. The yard is barren. Nothing organic, not even a weed, grows out of the ground except for the tree. It shakes its vast green mane in the wind, infinite tresses catching the sunlight above, leaving the yard in shadow. Sprouting at an angle from the dirt, three copper pipes crisscross the now-empty spaces; they are the only remnant of his plan to irrigate the yard, its long-dead banana trees, fig trees, and avocado trees. All those muddy-booted men trampling through her house to transform her vast sunny lawn into a veritable plantation. "Just like Torrecillas, Tita. Look at that little mango tree. Eh? Never be as good, I know, but close. Pretty close." Fausto had grabbed her by the waist and shaken her to the tune of that guajiro refrain of her old country and long-ago youth "*¡Manguito mangué, de Torrecilla é!*"

Her family's trees were indeed famed for their mangoes. The best in the country, much smoother than the ones Luz so frantically collected, sliced, and serves to her now for breakfast.

Fausto

Fausto inspects his face in the mirror carefully, clinically. He is surprised, repulsed. Just yesterday, as he left his business lunch, a very *guapa* young lady had stepped aside and held the elevator door for him. How in God's name had he not seen it before? Sure, he'd known he was getting older, slower, less vigorous than he had always been. But somehow he hadn't really thought of this as an outward change, something that could be seen by others, by strange, attractive women even. From now on, he decides, he will wear one of his beautiful silk handkerchiefs

around his neck and tuck it inside his shirt *a la euro*[
at least hide some of the horrid wrinkles around h[

He walks out of his bedroom toward the little r[
kitchen where Luz has set up a small table for meals. *[*
past the used-to-be-dining-room—now-file-room and __ sala,
he, as always, bids a *buenos días* to his regal mother-in-law. She
warns him, as always, to be prudent or to at least to be discreet.
"Fausto, Margarita may not know what she is dealing with, but I
know you. People talk to me; they are not afraid of hurting *my*
feelings. Don't you delude that sharp legal mind of yours into
thinking there are no limits. Yes, the Irizarry firm is yours, but
there are conditions."

Fausto thought he should have felt relief at her early death.
After that he had free rein over the firm, over the lands, and over
Margarita. He felt Carlota's death, before exile, before Alicia,
had been the first disappointment of his married life. When
Carlota died, instead of relief, he had felt regret, as if he had been
unfairly denied a challenge, one indeed worthy of him. The
other "men" in the family were just too diluted, too disorga-
nized to do more than register their complaints. Yes, he had
missed Carlota. Still, she had put up a considerable fight beyond
the grave: the conditions in her will, her deathbed confidences,
and, most of all, those knowing eyes staring at him every day in
his very own sala.

"I think Abuelita was angry at the painter," his granddaughter
Clara observed on the occasion of her sixth feast day, the Day of
Santa Clara. The entire family had gathered to drink cider and
eat chocolate cake, there in the most elegant room in the house.
Fausto had made sure Clara had the best, always. The firstborn
of his firstborn. As a child she had indeed been a creature of his
dreams. Quick, articulate, beautiful, and with a keen sense of the
drama to be found, and profited from, in life. She had sat on the
divan, dressed like a princess, in Swiss lace and Spanish linen,
graciously accepting her Ladro figurines: a ballerina; *La
Cenicienta* and her prince; a young girl holding a candle, peering
out into the dark. Last, she had opened Fausto's gift: a gold-braid
ring with an inlaid ruby flanked by two pearls. She had wept

.arge tears from those green eyes so much like her great-grand-mother's at times and so deceptively like Margarita's at others. She had wept fully and gratefully, as if she instinctively had known this was the best response to his largess. Fausto was pleased. Yet he remembers thinking how green is an endlessly hued color. It can be Carlota deep or Margarita soft and still look identically clear in certain shades of light.

"No, not Abuelita—" her worthless mother had corrected her—"that is Abuelita's mother." How his son could have married such a cunning spendthrift still pained him. Just thinking about the way she controlled Andrés's life made Fausto's ulcer burn. Why, she had dared ban him from his own son's house, a house he had helped put the down payment on. All these years, all these fights, and she was still mistress of Andrés's home!

These memories help Fausto decide to have a scotch before sitting down to breakfast. He glowers when he looks at the table. Would these *imbeciles* never get it straight? The knives were on the left again.

"The señora would like some more mangoes, Luz. . . . Get your strength up, Tita. Clara remembered. She's coming for lunch . . . finally."

Margarita

Margarita suspects Luz. Worn and humble when she arrived, she has flowered into quite a fleshy woman. Her dry, blotchy skin has softened into a smooth, creamy brown. Her hair falls softly over her face. No more cheap dye jobs and ponytails. But the giveaway, that snake-link gold necklace, is unmistakable. Just what he would purchase. Just what he thought her worth.

Now as Luz labors to get Margarita dressed for lunch, *la dama de la casa* points to her full-carat ruby ring, to her Tiffany bracelet, to her gold earrings with diamonds that move inside their settings to shine all the more. She wants them on. Sometimes when she is not in a hurry, Margarita lets her body become limp. She ceases sending those powerful messages to her limbs to hold firm, to bear her weight. It makes dressing her quite a chore. Still, she is careful not to make it too hard; she does not want to return to her previous wardrobe of varying states of deshabille. For months they dressed her in nothing but pajamas, the soft, lacy outfits her tireless daughter-in-law brought over. Margarita would gesture and push away the gowns and robes in a childish tug-of-war that at first she always lost. "Now, Doña Margarita, won't we be more comfortable wearing this in this heat," Luz would say as she forced yet one more laced gown over Margarita's body.

Finally, as her strength returned and her anger increased, she grew less dignified in her protestations. Grabbing on to Luz's hair and letting herself hang from those dyed pieces of straw was not beyond her. Once Luz shoved her and let her drop. For once Margarita was glad of the huge bruises that formed on her arms from the slightest contact with any solid object. Usually she felt disgusted by this unsightly side effect of the blood-thinning medications. But Fausto's wrath at Luz had made the marks well worth it. Now all the nurses dressed her in her old silk dresses in the morning. They knew she liked her hair set, her nails painted. This physical vanity at the end of her life surprised her. These things had seemed like such an effort to her before.

In Cuba Fausto had urged her to host "ladies of society" teas. He expected her to visit and receive these wives of past, present, and possible clients. It was, he said, her contribution to their livelihood. Back then she wanted to please Fausto any way she could, to make up for all she could not give him and, especially, for Alicia.

Walking toward the waiting tea guests in her sala, she had overheard a conversation regarding her fatal lack of attention to her appearance.

"She's just not *presumida*; she doesn't work at it at all."

"But she is so beautiful. I don't understand."

"It makes Fausto crazy, you know. He tells her all the time. She forgets, she says, to wear the jewels he buys her. I mean, did you see her at the country club the other night? She was wearing the same dress she had on at the nun's luncheon that afternoon. Why, she must have perspired in it all day!"

"Well, *está bien* if that is what she wants for herself. You know where Fausto's going to go if she keeps this up . . ."

"Oh, Fausto, he'd go that way anyway. *El se le correría a Grace Kelly.*"

"Well, I'm not so sure, but what truly concerns me, what is really *criminal*, is that she dresses Alicia the same way. *La pobrecita infeliz*, she's not to blame. It's hard enough on her being around normal people without having to look so *desfachatada*."

On that day she became aware that the jewels in her safety-deposit box were a subject of public discussion. She understood them to be a kind of payment from Fausto, regularly and dutifully made. From then on, whatever magnificent ring, pendant, bracelet, watch Fausto gave her, she made sure to wear once, somewhere very public, then never again. She made exceptions for family occasions, for something that required a church ceremony. This discipline gave her strength. She began to feel that the voice that echoed back when she spoke to herself inside her head, spoke in deeper, harsher tones than the tentative hums she had heretofore been used to. This altered inner speech described to her all those women who pitied and judged her, all of them distraught by the idea of that hoarded treasure sitting unworn in a cold safety-deposit box. She could see their necks itch, their fingers throb.

She is ready now for one more meal with Fausto and her family. One more opportunity for disaster. At least, she thinks, no one holds her responsible anymore. No one expects her to step in, to intercede and smooth things over. She can just watch them sit tensely at the table, passing around their lies, chewing their pride, drinking their scorn.

Poor Fausto. Now that he can no longer vent his anger at anyone, or anything on her, at least not directly and certainly not in public, he seems to be eating himself alive. A bleeding ulcer, the doctor said, but Margarita thinks differently.

★ ★ ★

Sitting at the dinner table, Fausto looked disgusted. It was the same look of disgust he had heretofore reserved for her on social occasions, especially if Margarita tried to tell a story. That was not the way it went at all, he would announce. His wife never got stories straight.

"Mami, for God's sake, be quiet. You know nothing. What do you know?"

When this happened, she simply remembered who she was, repeated her name to herself, "Margarita Teresita del Niño Jesús Irizarry Ponce de León, Margarita Teresita del Niño Jesús Irizarry Ponce de León." She huddled herself up in the memory of Torrecillas, mansion of thirty-two rooms, fragrant wicker, silver and crystal, inherited jewels, and ceremony. Torrecillas of the many servants, the large fields, large stables, large chapel, of the gorged pantry, of the *abuelo*'s reign. It was there she had shared the old nursery with her girl cousins. The *abuelo* had ordered them up there, away from the boys, when the first of them had become a "señorita." She remembered the late nights after the nannies gave up and went to bed, there where no one in the house could hear them, even if they screamed. "Even if we screamed." How they would relish the fear in that! What if a crazy *guajiro* with a machete crept up the ironwork and through their window? What would he do to them? And what if the boys crept in, scissors in hand, and, while they slept, cut their hair or worse? And what if they woke in the night to find everyone else below dead? Oh, the *gritos* they had spewed into the tall, echoing cement ceiling, knowing no one could hear. She remembered their raids on the pantry that had nothing to do with hunger and the night she first sat at the adult table in the vast, curtained dining room.

But all this was gone. And Fausto would never let her forget it, as he couldn't. Gone her father's law firm, which Fausto, hoping to inherit it, had joined upon their marriage. She heard that Raúl Castro had Torrecillas now. That always got Fausto angry when she said it.

Who were they now? And what had she learned in this long life? What did she know?

Alicia

Alicia's father has ordered a special lunch brought from La Caoba, the Spanish *panadería* he bought last year. There are *croquetas* stuffed with chicken or ham paste, a delicious *arroz con pollo*, and little *pastelillitos* stuffed with guava or cream cheese for dessert—if they make it to dessert this time. Somehow one of them always manages to spoil everything so that Alicia has to eat dessert for breakfast the next day while she reads her newspapers.

But it would go well this time, Alicia thought. She wanted to see people, more people, to give a party with a big, noisy band. Everyone would stay late, really late, perhaps until after midnight. Then she would make them her breakfast specialty: eggs scrambled with cream cheese.

She has called her goddaughter Clara ahead of time, to make sure she stays calm. Clara is so *fuerte*. She will not let anything go. She always has to say what she thinks. Clara is so beautiful. Her current fiancé looks like Ricardo José, the handsome *galán* on *Ansias de Vivir*, Alicia's current soap opera. She has begun to dream of Clara's boyfriend. It is the kind of dream she has often had about Andrés's childhood friend Fernando Rodríguez, who once sat her on his lap and kissed her on the lips, who married in 1966 and had two kids, one of whom died in a car accident in 1978. In her dream they are in bed, kissing and touching and moving up and down against each other, just like on *Ansias de Vivir*.

She felt so guilty after that first dream that she confessed to Clara; Alicia did not want her to be jealous. Clara hugged her and said, "Well, Madrina, I also must confess: I dream of him too." They laughed and ate turkey sandwiches on crusty bread. The next time Clara brought him over he was very nice to Alicia. He held her chair for her when they sat down to eat. Alicia even dared ask him for a picture of himself, with Clara, of course.

He and Clara would be married soon. They would have babies; they would sleep in the same bed at night. These were things Alicia understood she would never have.

She wishes God had made her "problem" either much better or much worse. Then, she thinks, she would not care about these things. But her problem just will not let her say what she means, what she feels. An idea will feel solid, real when she thinks it, but if she tries to speak it, it gets all confused. She becomes nervous and weepy, and then she can never say what she was going to say. Sometimes she can't even remember what it was, not even inside her head. It is like living inside that plain-walled carpeted room in Philadelphia, U.S.A., where the doctors made her crawl around and around, in one direction and then in the other. She always winds up in the same empty, wordless space.

At times like these she can only repeat the words she long ago heard her father say about her brother's wife. She had known instantly, from the way he said them, that they were exactly what she felt when she could not speak. "*Me da una rabia.*" That is all she can say. "*Me da una rabia.*" Suddenly that is all she can feel. She hates herself; she hates her family; she hates God.

Sometimes, with Clara, if Clara speaks slowly and holds her hand, she can talk for a while. But in the end Clara always tries to get Alicia to make up her mind. She pushes Alicia to finish her thought. But by then Clara is hanging on to Alicia's hand instead of the other way around, dragging Alicia to the end. Alicia's head hurts from the effort. By the time she gets the words out, she doesn't like what she has said. She does not think it is what she meant. She wishes Clara would not make her say things.

"Well, *feliz santo*, Abuelo!" Clara announces, as if she were toasting the bride and groom at a big wedding.

"Thank you, thank you." Fausto smiles. Then his face turns a bit more serious. "Now confess to me, Clara. Did our little Alicia remind you? You usually don't remember. You don't even call."

"Ay, Papi, no—" Alicia interrupts. But her father raises his palm in the air with great authority, as if signaling traffic to stop at a busy intersection in one of the frequent island-wide blackouts. It is his signal for Alicia to shut up.

"Honestly, Abuelo, Alicia did call, but I know your feast day is important to you."

"And feast days, they are not important to you anymore, is that it?"

"We celebrate birthdays."

"Birthdays! What are birthdays? It's an American notion, Clara. Don't betray your heritage. What do I want to celebrate another birth-day for? Each one just brings me closer to death."

Clara looks angry, but she looks at Alicia and winks. "Well, Madrina, what have you been up to?"

"That's right, change the subject, Clara. You know you are in the wrong."

"The Red Sox have a game on TV tonight," Alicia answers Clara. She is nervous and wants everyone to calm down. She gets up her courage and gives her father an exact replication of his own "halt" signal. Her body stiffens, locks into position. She lets out an involuntary "hum!," her body releasing some of her pentup tension.

Her father sighs and says, "Our little Chuchi is in love with an American baseball player."

Alicia relaxes and feels herself turning red. But it feels good, this red, somewhat soft and giggly.

"Luz! Luz, bring me another *quimbombó*!" her father commands.

Clara and Andrés look at each other. Alicia pleads with Clara silently.

"That's number four, Grandfather, don't you think it is a bit early?"

Alicia has also been counting. It is actually number five. Clara did not see the breakfast *quimbombó*. She closes her eyes, and thinks, "*Por favor, por favor*, please let it not start again," and waits for the shouts and insults. But they don't come. He must not have heard.

To everyone's surprise, Alicia's mother gets up. She insists on getting Fausto's beverage herself. The nurses rush to her side, but she swats them off. Andrés gets up and goes to the kitchen to help their mother. She must not mind his help because he does not come back until she does. Andrés hands his father his drink. Clara glares at him.

Alicia thinks her mother is "agitated." That is the word Dr. Cintrón uses when he sees her with all this energy, when she keeps escaping into the yard or hiding in the darkened *sala*. Maybe, Alicia thinks, she has not taken the blue pill for her nerves. Maybe Luz forgot. Alicia personally gave her the red and yellow pill for the blood and the triangular white one for the heart. She is not due for anything else for another four hours. Fausto, however, needs to take the big white pill for his ulcer with his meal.

Since her mother's second, most debilitating stroke, Alicia has slept almost every night in her parents' bed with her father. She rests more easily there, listening to her mother's breathing and giving Margarita her late-night medications herself. She doesn't have to worry about anything. She can just cuddle up to her father's warm body and sleep until seven, when the nurses arrive. Then she returns to her room, climbs in her bed, and sleeps for another three hours.

They have made it to the *pastelillitos*. Alicia chooses one with guava paste and cream cheese. Everyone eats dessert. No one leaves angry. Clara asks Alicia to walk her to the door, where the lunch's completion prompts Alicia to say, "I'm happy as a crocodile, my dear. Tonight when I go to bed I'm going to kiss your picture."

Clara

Clara bore yet another of her grandfather's passionate good-bye hugs with outward patience and internal repulsion. His fleshy grip made her bones crack. He too held his breath and grew red from the effort of squeezing her. He sputtered softly into her ear yet another, *"Mi hija,* why don't you come more? Your calls, your visits, they are your grandmother's life; they keep her alive."

She drove straight to the pharmacy to get the new medication her father had asked her to bring for Margarita. Clara had not known her grandmother was having stomach problems too. The *asquerosidad* of that house had depressed her. In two short years the place had gone from a worn, neglected home to a filthy warehouse for her grandfather's filing cabinets, full of papers he could no longer read, and broken office equipment. Despite the chaos, they still had all her porcelain figurines on display in the hexagonal lighted curio cabinet her grandparents had brought with them from their honeymoon trip to Spain. The figurines were supposedly hers, accumulated childhood feast day presents that Fausto had declared were too valuable to leave his house. She could look at them there.

The pharmacist was hesitant to dispense such strong medication without a prescription, but his hesitation disappeared when Clara declared that she would not be providing an insurance card; she would be paying cash. He explained that the syrup must be taken with food, in the precise dosage, and that driving and alcohol must be avoided. At the thought of her grandmother in her current state driving about town, Clara let out a little laugh.

It was hard to fault Margarita now, the way she was. But Clara could not help having the ugly feeling that somehow the situation was just. In a sense Margarita had been Fausto's accomplice in so many of Clara's confrontations with that man. "Please, Clara, do it for me, apologize. . . . Clara, you have no idea how you have hurt him, storming out of the house like that. He adores you. Call him, Clara. I am not well enough for this."

That Margarita, she knew how to invent the misunderstood good intentions behind *poor* Fausto's insults and insinuations, mostly about Clara's father, her mother, and her siblings, but if she refused to hear those, then also about her. . . . Yes, if Clara did not apologize, Margarita, in a proud gesture of solidarity, included herself and Alicia within the injured party. No, they all could not come to dinner. No, they all would have to miss graduation. Yes, they all had forgotten her brother's birthday.

She thought about her father, a man who had been at every

after-school game, at every PTA meeting, who waited up for all his children at night, yet who remained an absence in their lives. When Clara was at college, he called every week. But somehow they seldom managed a conversation. He waited patiently for Clara to come up with something to say, a story to tell. Sooner or later they reached silence. Clara listened to his breathing and imagined her father on the other end, staring at the lighted Touch-Tone keys. Sometimes he took his breath in suddenly as if he were about to speak, about to utter something important to both of them. But the air always came back out wordless. Eventually Clara ended the call. She said she had to go to the library or to work or to meet someone.

She wondered what Andrés's interior life must be like. Was it filled with long, fruitless silences, like his phone calls, or full of his parents' voices, assigning guilt, making demands, expressing frustration?

When she arrived at the house again, she left the car running in the driveway, guaranteeing an excuse for a quick exit. She handed the medication to Luz, who answered the door. Clara gave Luz the special instructions and asked her to take the bottle to Margarita, then drove away.

She had slipped Luz a little bonus. How that woman stayed on, with the way her grandfather treated her, Clara could not understand. Fausto was one thing. But to hear Alicia echo his complaints in words not her own always made Clara lose her patience. "Tía Alicia, don't speak that way about Luz. Don't you understand what a good person she is? Don't you see how hard it is to work here?"

Clara honestly hoped the medication would help with whatever new symptom her grandmother was suffering. She still remembered that first stroke. Clara had arrived to find Fausto on the prowl outside her grandmother's room in the emergency ward, hunting down her doctor, yelling at the nurses who would not authorize painkillers. Her father was on the phone trying to page the same doctor. The rest were gathered around the door holding their heads. Alicia was weeping Ave Marias in a chair. Clara went straight into the room with that no-nonsense rise to crisis she had learned from her mother. She found Margarita writhing on the bed, her eyes searching frantically about the room for something, anything or anyone, to relieve her pain. It seemed to Clara that when her grandmother saw her, Margarita's body convulsed, lifted itself off the bed for a few seconds, and dropped back into it with a moan. Clara held Margarita's hand. Margarita looked into Clara's eyes, trying to speak, trying to move, but her body would not obey.

"Pain, Grandma? *¿Dolor?* Is that what you are trying to tell me? Where?"

Margarita rolled her eyes inward, then stared back at Clara, opening her lids wide, locking her pupils on Clara's own, as if to insist Clara understand her.

Clara did. "Your head hurts, Tita?" A relieved groan from Margarita.

"The doctor is coming soon. The nurses are calling him. He'll prescribe something to take away the pain. Just a little longer."

In truth she had no idea when the pills would finally come. "Soon" was such an indeterminate word. Clara thought she could stand almost any pain for a set period of time, as long as she knew when that was. She could tick off the minutes, second by second, each a second closer to relief. But limitless pain must be desperate. Clara held her Tita's hand, talked in soothing tones; she does not remember what about, just that she fell into a rhythm, a song, whose beat her grandmother echoed with her hand every time Margarita squeezed.

After her grandmother had stopped speaking, Clara became interested in the family's history. She wished she had listened more carefully to all those stories her grandmother had so often repeated and could no longer tell. She pumped Alicia for the endless facts the woman held in her brain. To her regret she discovered that Margarita's claims—the family joke—were actually true: Margarita Irizarry was a direct descendant of the famous Spanish explorer Ponce de León. She talked to all she could find who knew the Pérez family in Havana and in exile.

When speaking of the Pérez Irizarry, people always focused on Fausto. In Havana they had spoken of his legal genius, of his generosity, of his "secret" sexual exploits, and later of his misfortune with his daughter. In exile they spoke of his unbearable arrogance, his drinking, his renewed wealth, his disagreeable and insulting judgments, his sexual exploits, and his misfortune with his daughter. Poor Margarita was always, in Havana and in exile, just *poor Margarita*—poor because of Fausto.

Clara's maternal grandmother had a theory as to why her in-laws' life was so disastrous. "Margarita just never stopped him. My Víctor told me to be quiet once in front of all his loud *dominó* friends, you know, like Fausto does. *¡Mira!* I turned around and dumped my Bloody Mary over his head, right there in front of everyone. Well, he never said anything like that to me in public again! 'It's better to get green one time than red many,' I always say."

To some questions Clara never received an answer from anyone. Not even her father could divulge information about her aunt's medical condition. No one except Margarita, Fausto, and the attending doctor knew the truth about that difficult birth.

Fausto

Clara, Clara de mi alma.

Fausto watched his granddaughter and his son drive away. It seemed his family always came in pairs—when they came, that is—or in force. By now not even Clara faced him alone.

That Clara would break his heart someday. She was constantly looking for ways to goad him, to contradict him. She inspected his every move. She disapproved of everything he said. She did not understand how deeply he felt for her, how much he wanted her to go through life knowing truths instead of *tropezando*, finding them out as she went along, like everyone else. His granddaughter was not like everyone else.

After everything he had done to show her she was his favorite, his chosen one! After the many times he had told her how she was *el orgullo de mi vida*, the source of pride to him that his own children had never been! After the trips to Europe, the guitar lessons, the French tutor! After that new car he had bought her for her graduation. After all that, she still did not understand his heart.

His own daughter was such a disappointment, often such an embarrassment. Secretly Fausto blamed Margarita. He was convinced her lack of will, her lack of *carácter* had made her cowardly and limp in labor. Hearing her moans, sensing trouble, he had pushed a nurse out of his way and burst in the labor room. "Push, Margarita. *¡Empuja!*" he had shouted at her.

"The baby has been stuck in the birth canal too long. It's not getting enough oxygen. I'll have to pull her out with forceps. I can't guarantee anything."

She should have pushed the kid through. By the time the doctor finally took the forceps and dragged out that limp, bloody blue thing Fausto knew. Margarita had given birth to their *desgracia*.

Margarita

Her granddaughter Clara, so well-meaning, so strong, so like her grandfather. She brought dominoes to play with her grandmother, and so Margarita could practice using her right hand again. She read to Margarita. She printed out headlines in big, bold letters, so Margarita could read them for herself. She could not understand Margarita's reticence, her inability to rise to the occasion. And Margarita could not speak to explain that she was beyond fictional stories and beyond factual tragedies and occurrences. How to explain to Clara what it means to lie expectantly, desirous of change, however small, anything to promise that her own story will have a redeeming ending?

She remembered the beginning of her life with Fausto. For their honeymoon Fausto decided they would go to the mother country. Margarita had never been to Spain. She adored the plane ride. She felt she had at last found a physical experience that matched the way she felt about life. It was all down there, small and far away.

The dry, hot air in Madrid made her skin peel—small price for the way it made her normally sticky, wavy hair smooth and slippery. Despite the hundreds of hot olive oil and avocado treatments her maids had applied to it at home, it had never before moved when she shook her head or covered her face like a lustrous blond veil when she looked down. She bought a little travel brush at the hotel store and brushed her hair at every fabricated opportunity. She felt gloriously beautiful. Fausto spoke to her as if he were an American movie leading man. He massaged lotion into her decomposing skin.

They ate at the renowned Mesón de Cándido, beneath the magnificent Segovia Aqueduct, where they were presented with the house specialty, *cochinillo neonato al plato*. These small baby pigs were so tender they could be sliced cleanly with the edge of a small plate, their bones as soft as human ear cartilage. They seemed to Margarita like mangled premature babies.

Fausto delighted in feeding her. He fed her *queso manchego* and *jamón serrano*. "Tita, try this chorizo, it's *el legítimo*, not that mishmash they try to pass for chorizo in the Americas." He fed her gingerly, as if the heavy, rich taste might damage her internally somehow if not introduced into her mouth with proper gentleness.

First there was Andrés, a son. Fausto was fat with pride. He threw a huge welcome home feast for Margarita and Andrés Fausto Pérez Irizarry. After sundown there were fireworks in the yard. Margarita and the nursemaid were hard pressed to keep the celebration from startling the baby. He gave little jumps each time a fiery rocket lifted off the ground. His resounding success with his firstborn renewed Fausto's zest for Margarita, for the woman he had at home.

Pregnant again, she was grateful that now he would be happy and leave her alone for a while. Then, of course, came Alicia. Then, of course, there was no great celebration. Then, of course, there was no more sex.

What would her life be now had she stayed at Torrecillas? How, if at all, would she have escaped *la Revolución*? If it were not for Fausto: "He's down from the Sierra. Pack two suitcases. Get the maids to sew whatever jewelry you have here into your underwear. We leave in two hours. An American client is flying us out in his plane. Margarita, move! Angela! Angela! Help her! Alicia's medications, Margarita, don't forget them. I'm going to the firm to get our property deeds. Those *cabrones* will be confiscating everything."

If it were not for Fausto, she told herself, she would now be one of those old, lonely women living in that man's Cuba, hungry for food, hungry for news of her exiled family. She would be writing letter after letter exposing every sordid aspect of her poverty, pleading for money, medicines, and photographs.

"Whenever you want out, Mami, just say the word," her quiet son, Andrés, had promised. But it was a word she would not say. Neither would Fausto, she knew; *enough* was not in his vocabulary. At last she was understanding something. Long ago, when the Cuban winter with its rains and molds swept in, she could escape with Andrés and his asthma to Lake Placid. There the chilly air would make her shiver and allow her son to breathe. She spent blissful days by the window without Fausto and without Alicia, watching her son, miraculously recovered, play outside. Indeed, at times she felt grateful for his asthma, since it mediated these escapes for her.

Recently an idea was growing sweet and juicy in her mind. Here they were, she and Fausto, together still. This illness had become in part her punishment, in part her revenge. Yes, she could look at it this way. Let him try to escape her now with some pathetic, greedy, low-class nurse with dyed hair. Margarita only wished she could die after he did, even if just one second after. That way every resting second of his life he would have her on his hands. No amount of J&B lunches, no amount of grandiose gestures to Cuban-American foundations that got his name in the paper, no amount of tragic role playing—the burdened husband, the disappointed father, the wise benefactor to all— could relieve him of her. He would never put her in a home, unless he could do so in secret.

Yes, Margarita thought, together *para siempre*. In many ways, she thought, this must be love.

Only Alicia worried her. As Margarita had become more dependent, Alicia had grown more self-sufficient. But she had also grown more and more obsessed with Fausto, with his clothes, his medications, his opinions, his whereabouts, the way she used to be with Margarita, instinctively letting go, day by day. She should not be left in Fausto's hands. What would her mother, Carlota, have advised? Have dared to do?

Margarita sat in her sala, where she could see her mother, even in the semidarkness of early evening. Alicia had found Carlota. Their papers, including all records of the various shipments Fausto had made in the weeks before the coup, had been confiscated at the airport. He, like many others, had suspected the government's ultimate collapse. He had discreetly sent off valuables that would not arouse too much suspicion, their paintings among them. No one could remember the receiving agent in New York; no one could remember a lot number. Even when one name sounded familiar, there were warehouses full of goods waiting to be claimed by persons unknown, some of whom would never make it off the island again to claim their lots.

Whatever else could be said about her mind, Alicia had an infallible memory. The four of them walked through warehouse after warehouse, looking for their possessions among endless boxes and wooden crates. After a week of daily trips to these huge storage buildings Alicia, then fifteen, suddenly stopped in the middle of yet another aisle and pointed at a tall wooden crate. "That's it! That is the crate I saw them make in the yard," she said. "Abuelita Carlota is in there." And so she had been. And so she was here now.

Now, thirty years after their last vacation on that stunning white beach, Alicia could still remember people's phone numbers for their Varadero beach houses, not to mention their Havana ones. Lately her mnemonic prowess had taken a different interest. Biography was the kindest way to describe it: the trials and especially the tribulations of anyone they had known before 1960. This archive was of course especially valued at the Cuban circle meetings, where Alicia was always much in demand. How she cherished the greedy attention from those women in pearls and hats, those collectors of clothing and furniture for poor Marielitos and other recent exiles less fortunate than themselves. At first, in her eagerness to please, Alicia stumbled over her words, but slowly, amazingly she organized her thoughts in an orderly sequence she was incapable of imparting to any other form of expression. Out came whereabouts, marriages, divorces, bankruptcy announcements, children, grandchildren—all garnered from the many newspapers, local and distant, to which Alicia subscribed. But her passion was for the deaths. She would lock herself in her room and lie tightfistedly, motionlessly on her bed from morning until dusk if anyone touched the obituaries at breakfast before she had a chance to devour them. She always saved this parade of the dead for last, the grand finale to deliver to her well-dressed audience. Alicia was their chronicler, their historical depository. They dumped information onto her, knowing that then they could safely forget it, that all they had to do to retrieve it was ask Alicia and out it would come in flawless, accurate detail.

For the duration of these briefings Margarita always walked away.

Theft

In the months she had not been able to move, Margarita had become a wondrous listener. She learned to hear not just the mangoes dropping in her yard but also much about people she hadn't known to listen for before. Breathing, swallowing, coughing, gas, sighs—all those bodily sounds that reveal state of health, state of mind, intentions, reactions. It became easier and easier. People forgot her dumb presence, as if she were a newborn and had forgotten their language. They held conversations on any subject, even about her, in her presence. Or excited by her apparent nonpresence, they spoke to her directly of whatever they needed to utter aloud but could not speak of to *real* persons.

Margarita liked these confessions; they made her feel more active in the world than she had felt before the stroke silenced her.

Tonight she lies awake listening to Fausto's stomach acids make his ulcer bleed. Even though they no longer share the same bed, his restless, stuporous tosses keep her awake. She sleeps in a hospital bed next to their old king-size one. Alicia has gone to her own room tonight. She means to punish Fausto for having drunk too much at lunch. This is just as well. Margarita does not like Alicia sleeping with Fausto. It also helps to have one less person's breathing to tune out in order to find that steady, monotonous silence where she can fall asleep.

Yet tonight something surprises her. The front door lock is turning. Yes, she is sure, someone has come in the house.

Quietly, very quietly Luz and her lover, Juan, open the front door. Luz has a key, of course, so the matter should be quite easy. Still, Luz is nervous. Doña Margarita has supernatural hearing. Luz sometimes thinks Margarita can hear her thoughts, her schemes.

At first Luz's plan was to wait. When Margarita died, it would be much easier to steal from the old man. He was drunk so often with a *quimbombó* here and a *quimbombó* there. Sad how a supposedly worldly man like that could not call a scotch a scotch. He could certainly whisper other much fouler words. But the old lady was taking a long time to depart, and Luz needed to send money to her kids. Their aunt certainly wasn't going to take care of all those extra kids for free for much longer. She couldn't get them out of the Dominican Republic, and if she went back, they all would starve together. Well, with this money she could certainly buy a green card or two.

The hallway is easy. All possible obstacles have been removed so that Doña Margarita can safely walk through it. When they come to the bedroom door, Luz is suddenly frightened. Even though the old woman cannot talk, she can still scream. Luz prays that she is asleep. She had placed a megadose of tranquilizer in the silver medication tray the old man insists the nurses use to dole out pills. But Alicia always takes charge of that last dose of the day, so Luz cannot be sure. Well, Alicia mostly cared that her mother got the medication at the right time, Luz thought. How could she possibly remember how many of each colored pill belonged on the tray? The old man certainly would not hear a thing with all that alcohol marinating his brain.

She would come to work the next day extra-presentable in case he called the police. But she doubted he would. The money must be unreported. Why else would a man who made such a spectacle of the paperwork and bank accounts he had to keep track of keep so much cash in the house? If he did chance to call the police, why would they suspect her? She was just that idiot *dominicana* who cleaned the house and Margarita's shit. She knew nothing about anything. Besides, even if they did, the old man knew better than to let them accuse her unless there were witnesses. She could talk. Luz knew he could not bear the humiliation if she told, not of what he'd done to her but of what he couldn't do. She would tell if he did not protect her, if he fired her. She certainly did not have any *vergüenza*; she couldn't afford any.

The door creaks slightly as Juan taps it open. He has a big knife. He would have liked to bring a gun, but they couldn't afford one. The room is dark. It takes Juan's eyes a few seconds to adjust. Luz, however, is used to this darkness. She walks right in, drops to her hands and knees, crawls to the bed, and begins reaching underneath it. Juan, who can now see, stands close to the door, guarding the two sleeping bodies.

Juan stares at the woman who sits reclined in the hospital bed. She is a white skeletal corpse dressed in a dark sleeveless gown. Her clavicular bones jut out from her chest as if they were trying to prop up her chin. Her translucent arms are marbled with bruises and veins. She sleeps with her eyes open, eyes that seem fixed on him. One of them winks at him. Juan looks at the face. It is smiling. The woman's body begins to jerk slightly, rhythmically. Her heavily ringed hands clang against the metal side rails on her bed.

Luz sticks her head out from under the bed. Juan backs up, trying to exit. But he forgets he has closed the door. It makes a loud, hollow boom as it stops his momentum. Fausto wakes. Luz ducks her head back beneath the bed and grabs a handful of bills from the cardboard box she has located. Fausto has turned on the lamp on his nightstand and is trying to rise from the bed.

"*Vamos,*" Luz says to Juan. There is no longer any point to secrecy. Fausto is charging toward them like a tipsy red bull. Juan turns around and simply grabs Fausto's hand in one hand and his shoulder in the other in an orderly's grip. He sits Fausto down on the edge of the bed. "*Si te levantas, te mato,*" he warns, and leaves the room. As he walks down the hallway, Juan can hear Fausto's curses and the raspy, gurgling sound of Margarita's laughter.

"Shouldn't we call the police?" Clara asks. She has accompanied her father on this, the latest of middle-of-the-night phone calls from his parents' house.

"*No, de ninguna manera,*" Fausto replies.

"Why not? Don't you want her arrested? Don't you want your money back? What if they come back?"

"She's right, Papi; they did threaten you."

"Don't be dense, Andrés. I'd have to say what I was doing with so much money in the house. I'd have to say where I got it."

"Fine. Clara, help Mami and Alicia pack," Andrés orders. "I'm taking them home with me."

Margarita rises from the chair where she has been listening. She walks slowly over to Fausto and loops her hand through his arm. Alicia, still seated, begins to cry a deep, inconsolable cry. Her lips quiver; her face turns upward; her hands rise and fall helplessly in front of her like claws, as if she were about to speak.

Fausto's free arm crosses his body; his hand covers Margarita's with a tight squeeze. He speaks: "I think it is clear. If I am not welcome in your house, they do not wish to come."

Margarita

Margarita had thought twice about alerting Luz and her lover. She had hoped they were on drugs or at least nervous enough to react violently. It would have made everything much easier.

After Clara and Andrés left, how she had wished the thieves might return. How she had prayed, sent out psychic messages, commanded Luz and her *querido* to come back and shoot bullets into all three of them *sin piedad*.

But in the morning they all were still here. She walked into the little dining room and found Fausto sitting at the table, his back to her. He was working on some papers laid out before him. He wrote in the large black print he had taken up since his cataracts had deteriorated. Margarita thought he was probably changing his will, yet again. Alicia was still in bed, where she would probably stay all day. It was her reaction to trauma—a stubbornly self-induced coma. Clara or Andrés would probably stop by tonight to cheer her up, to take her to dinner or to play cards.

Margarita placed her hands on Fausto's shoulders and leaned into him, placing her chin upon his head. He grabbed her hand, kissed it, and turned around to look at her. "Tita," he sighed, and gave her a smile, which she returned. Margarita walked to the kitchen and, without being asked, fixed him a scotch.

Then she went for a walk. There was no longer anyone to stop her.

Out the door, down the lawn stairs, up the street, went pajama-clad Margarita, waving a merry *"¡Buenos días!"* to astonished neighbors and strangers. They saw her traipse into the cement-strewn park without trees, the one with the primary-colored swings, that notorious hangout for hoodlums, drug addicts, and thieves. From there she could still hear her mangoes drop—those juicy sounds, like the watery thud of lifeless bodies falling to the ground.

JAMES LÓPEZ
Emoria at the Tracks

1.

Emoria stands ankle-deep in parched grass, its golden spikes scratching the webbed interior of her toes, as she looks down into the splintered and enslaved wooden plank and tries to imagine the number of identical wooden planks, weathered and rotting, that lie ensnared and arrested underneath these two iron rails, rusted and oppressive in their rigid stretch beyond the horizon, between this foreign dry plain and her home. She does not need to look up to feel the pitiless distance enter her eyes, to absorb that limitless horizon, that illusory black line that turns everything—every limit, every dream of escape—into two screaming, desolate plains, into two equally horrid and mammoth possibilities between which she feels increasingly insignificant and abandoned. Her legs, still youthfully thin and hairless, feel the hem of her skirt shift lazily in the lugubrious, humid breeze, no relief from the torrents of perspiration that enframe her face and leave streams and brooks engraved into the compliant fabric of her body. Her thin ivory dress has become a mimicking cotton skin underneath the burning eye of this sun, her body acquiescent and pliable for the irrational sculptings of heat to transform her into a salty pool hidden among these tall, thirsty weeds bowed before a sky scorched pallid, seamless, and faded. The black clouds that lie so far off that they cannot be real mock the reality of the girl, herself melting into this harsh, foreign soil, dissipating in this humid air, lacking even of the salty oceanic elements that compose her flesh and remind her of home, now threatened with extinction, with anonymous fusion into a temporary mud with this vicious, lonely dust. Against her own judgment (and simultaneously with the judgment of the young that challenges and does not allow its owner the vain luxury of feigned ignorance or frightened disregard) she lifts her head and confirms the insurmountable distance between her and the place of her belonging, follows with her charcoal-colored and prematurely old eyes that oak and iron umbilicus back through the stubborn, dead grass, through the invisible passageway that breaks the cage of earth and sky and leads back to home, now only a memory as fantastic as the possibility that anything exists on the other side of earth and sky, and up to the womb of her mother overburdened (yet why her as well, so young and entering the confusion of her own body in that murky and chaotic pool of pubescence?) with twelve other children, her siblings and half siblings, with Roque, the poor young brute who alone requires the diligence of two mothers, with her father (and only alone and powerless could such a thought enter her mind so that it could as easily wither and mingle with the dry stones that litter the track), consumed by a madness whose origins were as elusive as those of the track itself, and with her absence, which, she believes, still wanders quietly weeping through the house, following closely the dark skirt of her mother, asking, begging to ears distant and overburdened (yes, overburdened to madness as well) if she, Emoria, please, little Emoria, could be of any help.

The sun remains fixed in the perpetual noon that seems to dominate this place fit only for flies and accelerated decomposition within an air so saturated and heavy that its movement provides more burden than relief. Emoria stands motionless, which is still motion enough to blur the distinction between her tears and the perspiration that streaks her young face and forms salty pools in the recesses of her collarbones. In this land of no relief she feels the small paradoxical satisfaction of the track, which reminds her of the fading possibility that her home remains at the delta of this rigid, inorganic river while simultaneously, cruelly revealing the tangible solidity and external reality of this parched plain and the nightmare—miraculously out of view for the first time in six months—of her aunt's house, of that vicious slave driver for whom family is profit and Emoria beast of burden, a small, undeveloped ox destined to spend her impending womanhood upon her knees, whether by washbasin or on wooden floors, made to glisten with the sweet and still-unbitter sweat of her youth. Standing defiantly and anonymously alone, Emoria wonders if her labor is being missed back at that familial prison, if her aunt, above the stove she hasn't had to stand over for half a year now is cursing at that ignorant girl so full of ungrateful tears, whom she has rescued from that madhouse father and prolific mother making mouths they could not feed properly, all the while plucking the chicken with her bony hands, deprived of the maid she didn't have to pay, Emoria, that crybaby mule who knew only how to complain and mope in the midst of the work she was bred and destined to do. Yes, Emoria thinks, looking at the now-harmless rain clouds in the distance, perhaps that witch, that stony, bitter woman full of pretense, is having to work, deprived of someone to manage, deprived of the joy she shows in pointing her long forefinger toward some task, that shrill voice speaking in the European lisp she has acquired from listening to the radio, so unnatural to the rhythmic Cuban tongue she detests as she detests her family and her race and even this land to which she is so well suited.

Emoria feels the minute vibrations of a fly's wings as they resonate with the taut red skin of her cheek, feels even the pull like a raindrop on a tense canvas the creature's spindly legs relax their weight below her right eye, feels its murky breath dripping weightlessly onto her lips, and continues remembering—that task so integral to the despairing encroachment of adulthood yet so miraculously difficult to a child—remembering the yellow flowers on the bedspread she shared with Hortensia, her sister, and with Olga—divine and loving Olga, her twin—maybe gone, maybe still covering her round face with that floral cloth of night, remembering, remembering even against her own powerful will the waxed red mustache of her father as he sat (and had he ever really sat like that, with his legs crossed regally smiling at the sparse dinner table, laughing at Roque as the latter mauled his portion of chicken, swallowing skin, gristle, and, if not for their mother diligently watching, the bone itself—all tasting good to Roque, all sad and humorous and loving in the curled lip and small, grateful eyes of her father—if it had occurred, if it still occurs?).

Alone, she feels her body disintegrate, feels the muscle fall easily off her bones like stew meat, her interior bubbling and gurgling in lonesome escape from the horror of identity, feels the bitter herbs of memory pushing through her porous skin, dissolving and reducing her to an evaporating pool of reminiscence, her sole conjunctive element since she left home. Among the myriad tears rolling down her face, she recognizes one that carries within its substance the genealogical sorrow of her mother's tired hips and strained expression as she sent Emoria away to work in her sister's *chinchar*, to clean the pungent leaves of tobacco for sale to the factories, to strip away the dried dead meat of those broad leaves from their tender veins, its addictive blood staining upon her hands and impressing upon her nostrils that smell that so defines everyone in this section of earth, that smell that resides even now so far distant from the workhouse in the sinewy tissue of her young body, that flows as though from an endless spring in the saturated liquid of her tears and perspiration. She recalls the press of her mother's lips on her forehead and the rough palms of her father's hands on her hips as he lifted her onto the back of the truck carrying the portable factory, the new mother for whom she would now on be working. She remembers, like the cloudy nonreality of a photograph, her mother and father standing below the pecan tree in full bloom, Hortensia a full foot taller than Olga, the two sets of eyes not knowing whether to be envious or sad, Roque with the cord tied around his ankle, smiling because that has always been his primary expression even at funerals, Alfredo and the others so much older and foreign than her full siblings bidding her farewell with a detached silence and her knowledge that to them, to that set of children fathered by a stranger, she would hardly be missed, and even Papalote, that mongrel and foremost companion of Roque's, extending his oversize ears in curious acknowledgment of this ceremony of absence, of uncertain farewell. She recalls the cool ocean breeze of fall, which almost seems to soothe her overheated skull beneath this foreign sun, filling her nostrils then and restraining the sobs that were struggling in the back of her throat as the truck, that strange mechanical beast within which she had never ridden and seen only on rare occasions with the frightened awe of a child, jolted her full of the distress and longing of those helpless in the face of a reality over which they have no control. And then the disappearance of the house and of the familiar trees and clouds and noises that she had thought were the sole trees and clouds and noises of the world itself, beyond the horizon, past that point that as hard as she tried to recall could never be pinpointed, beyond that horizontal point into a world so foreign, if not for the contents of the cage, then for the alien nature of the cage itself, the new horizon like a new set of bars beyond which she could no longer be sure that home, that dusty daguerreotype, still moved and breathed as she hoped, hoped with the fury of the condemned, that it still did.

Beneath the weight of a heat too dense for her thin legs she sits beside the track and listens to the crackling of the dry grass, the sound of its dead vegetative body burning beneath the flame of her memory, engulfing all the dehydrated matter around her, burning in a solitary and immense holocaust everything, including herself, everything except the track that runs invincible like a foreign metal artery through this dying organic earth. In repose she feels better, as though she were finally resigning herself to the inescapable limits of this plain and could slowly melt into a pool of her remembrance without having to inflict the self-torture of reassuring herself of their reality, but understanding their fiction as the joy of this doomed memory, as a final defiant act against the white-hot sky that so ruthlessly murders in a swirling, combustible mass of confusion the tangibility of a past, the possibility of anything beyond the flammable decay and torturous present of this field.

2.

Out of the rippling earth, liquefied beneath the flaming air, Emoria remembers the evening when she was cleaning the dark wooden floors of the house as she did every Thursday while listening to the birds as they prepared for sleep, not susceptible to the insecure and timorous reality of night. On her knees with the brush, she watched the foamy swirls of water turn dark as they became saturated with the thick dust that would so invincibly return the next day, causing her to doubt the practicality of this repetitious and tiring work. She stood for a moment to relieve the pressure on her young knees, turning red on the uncomfortable floor, and looked out the window to see Roque return from the store a half mile away, to see the cord that ran by her feet to the leg of the kitchen table begin to shudder and move at the return of its human cargo. She felt both sympathy and humor at the sight of Roque, the same emotion she knew her father felt for his young brute son, an emotion so different from that felt by her siblings, that fear or indifference they offered him only because he was part of the family and they could not ignore him as perhaps they wished they could. He entered through the back door and walked by her, picking up the slack in the line as it bundled around his ankles as he approached the kitchen, greeting her in that incomprehensible grunt, that guttural profusion of sound that were his words and that contained within their clumsy syllables all the sounds necessary to convey his simple thoughts. As he disappeared into the kitchen, she returned to her knees, to the boring monotony of cleanliness only to be lost once again in the song of a mockingbird, her favorite of all the birds that lived around the house. As the minutes slipped away lazily, she became alarmed at the silence of the house, usually noisy and clamorous with the movement of so many occupants. Although the majority of the family had yet to return from the cigar factory, the silence seemed inordinately suspicious, mainly because she could not hear the nervous rattlings of her father in his insomniatic fidgetings throughout the rooms of the house. The noise her father made, had been making increasingly over the past year had become the only source of calm she felt, knowing that his hands were busy, that he was somewhere easily located, that the culmination of that irrational progression she had been witnessing but could not understand had not yet occurred, as in that dark cave of her unconscious she knew it would occur. In this place where *privacy* was not a word, she was left with no recourse but the realization that her father was quickly losing his mind. But the loss of his rational capabilities did not coincide with a loss in the qualities that made her love him so intensely with a love not shared communally among the household, the sense of tenderness he always carried even after he could no longer work, even after he did nothing but wander around the house with a rag, a towel, with anything within reach, swatting at flies, emptying the cabinets and washing the clean dishes again and again until sunrise, when Emoria would watch his peeling, water-soaked hands skin a banana and drop it whole into his bowl of grits, would watch him with incomprehensive eyes glowing catlike in the early-morning dark as he pulled the furniture away from the walls in search of any insect or cockroach to kill with furious passion, as he fought with the single-mindedness of the insane to keep his house free from the vile creatures that so easily penetrated those walls.

And the silence was not like a sound then but a vision enclosed within the window frame as the sun dropped below the line of thunderclouds in the distance, dissipating outward as luminous purples and glowing reds, filling the sky within that artificial box with an ominous panorama of dusky light and radiant color, lacking the sound of the explosion it portrayed, and filling her raw, soapy hands with a shrieking chill of silence, with the mute dread of her father's absence. She stood slowly and began to search the house. She remembers now the compulsion she felt as though led by a cord not unlike Roque's, its intertwining thread composed of love and responsibility instead of hemp, yet even more restrictive as she followed tightly his invisible footsteps throughout the house, through the kitchen left immaculate, through the back room—the only one with the curious metallic screens to cover the windows, a project of her mother's to relieve the influx of winged insects and the growing anxiety of her husband—on through her parents' bedroom, where he no longer slept since he no longer slept at all, and then through the room where she slept and where Roque lay on the floor facedown now in the deep sleep of those who cannot worry, still not expecting to find him but simply retracing his steps, the steps she knew he had made this afternoon, the steps she had not seen him make but now followed as though they were her own, feeling the invisible cord, the familial magnet that would lead her to him, that would lead her, she fearfully believed, to something different this time. She could sense it as though these steps were retracing the steps of a descent, a descent she was too young to understand fully but old enough to witness, to experience with the horror and despair of an adult. Her small feet continued forward, their bare red soles warmed by the imprints of his shoes as she followed his path back through the soapy corridor and out the door onto the front steps and the beginnings of the woods, the air swirling with mosquitoes, dragonflies, and gnats, feeling the humid breeze off the bay to the south, smelling the thick air on this low vegetable earth. The sky was still red, and the moon already visible yet liquid, as though covered by a translucent sheet of fine silk swaying in the same humid breeze or as though the very worn cotton of her dress carried within it a moon, as she would have herself protected and carried within her young, absorbent body her father's lunacy. Everything around her had suddenly become foreign as though her father's steps were carrying her into a different landscape, one of shifting liquid and chaotic organisms, one in which her own restrictive and monolithic body stood incongruously before a nature swimming in the blood of a dying sun, in the gaseous plasma of that crimson sky. And still she was pulled forward into the trees, feeling more distant from her home than at any time in her life though she was no more than twenty feet from the front porch, moving sure-footedly and beyond fear to the location of the fusion that she did not comprehend but craved, to that final understanding of her father's madness that, as she neared the end of these retraced steps, she felt she would comprehend fully, just as she had always comprehended fully the silent communication of tenderness they had always shared. Forward, maybe a hundred feet from the house, she began to smell smoke, feeling his footsteps become warmer and recent, continuing their descent. As she crossed beside a large bush, inextricably tied to the cord now, to her father's same mad, desperate steps, she entered a clearing lit in the glow of a torch, a small clearing flickering in a crude, primitive light, not unlike the magical light she had first seen in the movie house, its fiery origin set in the defiant left hand of her father. She saw him beastlike and rabid, with his shirt open, saw him like a man and not a father, saw him cursing while with his right hand he swung madly at the air, killing by the handful those insects that swarmed around his torch like specks of dust, infinite in number, undefeatable, saw his bare chest already covered with welts as mosquitoes sucked his mad blood, saw the torrents of perspiration run down the side of his head like rivers originating from within his soaked, disheveled hair, saw his teeth clenched underneath his red mustache, which had always been so carefully waxed and now looked like a twisted, overgrown bush, saw all this before she saw his eyes. Emoria remembers now the pupils like two gaping mouths fang-guarded, two mouths independent of throats, caverns without end or exit, two holes that held her frozen in the stifling humidity of the clearing. She remembers their vast emptiness, and she was overcome by a sensation that she could identify only as hunger, a hunger that originated not in the lean bowels of this man's belly, but a hunger primary and liquid that coated her father's brain, that had been seeping like a slow profusion of acid into his body, a hunger so possessive and uncontrollable that it had erased the tenderness that so glorified him in her mind. She remembers now that she understood at that moment that he was then capable of cruelty and violence equally above the comprehension and bounds of anyone or anything that she had ever known, that he was completely mad, and that within that madness lay the vengeance of love defeated, of tenderness and understanding denied, the vengeance of the insane when they realize that even they will not be immune in their insanity.

Emoria recalls arriving home filled with an exhaustion that originated within her chest, feeling the very spot like a lead weight beside her heart, feeling it throb heavily into her ears and eyes, the latter opened beyond their ability to distinguish anything clearly, only blocks of color and simple shapes that encircled the tunnel she had entered back at the clearing. She knew her mother was home, and Alfredo next door in the house he had built to keep watch over this asylum, sitting fatly upon his porch and committing his greedy espionage like a buzzard falling into the lazy, hypnotic circles that mark the beginnings of its vicious trance and descent upon injured flesh. Emoria could see herself, another simple block of color, standing frightened and not understanding what this other Emoria, the one still dreaming while awake, understood: that she was now marked, marked with a knowledge incomprehensible, a knowledge she had acquired from her father at the clearing, red and inhuman within the light of his crude torch, as he lashed out at the air itself with insurmountable rage, disembodied and magnetic, invisible yet present within the cavernous pupils of that lost madman (not a father, but a man, Emoria thinks, a man, she wonders in a way she had been physically incapable of back then). Those tunnels she had entered, that the Emoria who calmly bent down and began cleaning the floor planks again—not the Emoria who was still trembling like a child with eyes opened and blind—had entered left her now on this new floor, on this new surface infused with the soapy reality of a new knowledge, encircled in a slow cloud that, as it refined her sight to a pitch of pitiless and impossible clarity, filled her with rage, rage toward this new clarity, toward this new ability to see beyond sight, rage toward everything human and not human, rage even toward that other Emoria, the one blind and terrified, staring wide-eyed into those empty, mad pupils as she felt the warm sting of urine run down the inside of her legs.

On the floor Emoria looked up into the antique mirror and in its warped glass saw her father as through a filter of cellophane stretched taut and nervous, felt glued by her knees to those soapy planks, to the cold, wet floor of those tunnels. Emoria could see through those mad pupils, through those two dull, hazy openings in the glass, as though through an entrance or an exit she could not tell, at herself, at that other Emoria frightened and on her knees scrubbing the floor of the house like a little obedient child. As her father approached in the mirror, its glassy distortions swimming in the liquid medium of dreams, she discerned the sparkling edge of the kitchen knife, the one her mother used to mutilate chickens, its reflective light gleaming off the old glass. Yet the knife itself did not cause her fear, even as her father, still bare-chested and covered in perspiration, approached from behind and became larger, distended and more ominous in the warped glass, even as she could smell the musky odor he had acquired in the woods become more prominent like an angry fog enveloping her young body. Her fear arose from those two empty holes in the glass, those eyes that in the brief interval of her flight home had been filled, filled with a new presence she could recognize, a fear arising from that new identity that had never been a part of her or her father's secret communication yet now stood behind her, armed with that crude blade. A third person was among them, was inhabiting those two caves like a vengeful, rabid animal, a beast that thrived in the deceitful light of the mirror, that held her in hypnotic stagnation upon the floor. Her father was so close then that she could hear his irregular breathing, could hear the strained friction his thick palm made as it clutched the knife's wooden handle with increased pressure, but still she was trapped by the twisted image of the mirror, still she was frozen by the liquid atmosphere the warped glass emitted, as in a dream when one cannot move even as the earth itself disappears from beneath one's feet. Then, from where she still could not remember, just as the knife reared back and became larger in the mirror's reflection, she spun around on her knees and confronted the eyes of her mad father, looked deep into them, deep enough to see the new presence that had ended her and her father's unspoken dialogue, saw with horror into the new black mirror of those eyes, at herself, on the floor, filled with madness and rage, filled with the murderous violence only capable in the suicidal, saw herself, Emoria, in the eyes of this man, poised to kill this frightened child like a bothersome insect, like an unpleasant memory. She could say nothing to her father as she stared at herself in his eyes, could feel only sympathy toward him as she felt within herself the realization that she had seen what perhaps she should not have seen and had given birth to this new realization. With the desperation of those who watch someone they love die, with the longing to re-create, to connect with the memory of that communication, with the innocence she had lost, and to save her flesh from the Emoria she saw in his eyes she screamed, screamed like a frightened little girl, "Papa, no, Papa!"

When her mother entered the room, saw the knife covered in the greasy bubbles of detergent and Emoria huddled in her father's lap as he gently stroked her hair and she pressed her face against his bare chest, she dropped to her knees and began sobbing, screaming, cursing as though incapable of withstanding any longer the encroaching disorder that had overcome her home. She clutched the leg of the dining table and buried her head in the soapy water, mumbling and writhing so as to look like the only insane person in the room. Emoria lifted her head from the wet fur of her father's breast to look at her mother and then looked back at her father, whose expression had become blank, an ignorant and inauthentic remnant of that tenderness he had once carried so proudly. Still, Emoria could not move; she felt uncomfortable as though the vision she had experienced were still present, as though that madness, that rage that was now as much hers as it had been her father's had not left but been absorbed by everything around her, as though that unbearable clarity that had infused her mind, that had filled her with such fury were in repose but still volatile, like the knife cushioned by the soapy water or her mother prostrate on the floor beyond tears. It was in this state of uneasy calm, as the darkness of the night began to fill the room, that she felt Alfredo's heavy steps on the porch and his ignorant hands slam the back door behind him. He entered without shock at what he was seeing, as though he had known beforehand that this would be his chance to exert control. Emoria had not noticed until then that all her siblings were standing in the doorway in shock, staring dumbly, only Roque looking with curiosity as though he were viewing a foreign race engaged in a ceremony all their own. Olga stood next to Alfredo, and Emoria understood at once that it must have been poor Olga, frightened to death, who had run to fetch him, as though that grown man incapable of any emotion save greed were capable of resolving, much less understanding, any of what had occurred. Emoria, unmoving in the clutch of her mad father, saw with such clear vision that it frightened her, saw her family and the house itself, that table leg still clutched by her mother's hand as her father had clutched the knife, the cord tied around Roque's ankle in a simple bow knot that he did not think to untie, Alfredo confused although he did not understand what confusion was, saw the unreality of the situation as though it were removed from time itself, saw it and all the things in it as though they were plastic and inorganic, as if they were all connected by the faulty wire of a rotted, rusting machine. She was filled with such horror by this influx of knowledge, of insight, that as a reflex, she stared up into her father's eyes, which had not left her scalp, just as his large hand had not stopped caressing her hair, only to see the blank expression of a doll, the once-mad cavernous pupils filled like a hole in a dam where all the water had long ago spilled forth. It was then that Emoria felt more alone than at any time in her life, and she felt the rage she had experienced earlier when she was the one who had inhabited those now-empty eyes return and rise up within her, and with that rage her understanding became even sharper, so sharp in fact that she knew Alfredo's words before they even spilled forth from his clumsy mouth: "Enough, that's enough! This ends now!"

3.

Emoria places her hand on her empty belly, feeling the almost pleasant tickle of the dry grass as it presses against the backs of her legs, and thinks that it must be dinnertime at her aunt's house and how that old witch must be cursing having ever brought that ungrateful child out to her *chinchar*. The air has become more still and heavy, and the perspiration continues to drip methodically from her eyebrows to her cheeks, flowing down to the corner of her lip, where with the slightest flicker of her tongue she reingests it. Even though she has not moved in some time, the weight of the air and the heat it generates make her restless as though the sun itself were looking upon her with shame and resentment. Sitting close to the earth, her thin legs and arms becoming just other blades of yellow grass, she studies the track, the indentations and fractures in the old wood, the small shadows born of splinters and knotholes like pupils in the wood, like black eyes that repeat the strain of the immense steel and iron monsters they have supported. In a landscape scorched to pale homogeneity these planks maintain in their chipped skin and labyrinthine hived interiors the only proof of time, a proof the cold iron bars that strap them in place are incapable of providing. Emoria feels, while her eyes comb their rough skin, like such a plank or perhaps like a worm that may live within their crevices, so far away from people or their possibility that she joins with the secret underground of this wasteland, the one place left for movement. Never has she felt so alone or detached from physical presence, from proof that her thoughts exist tangibly and not in the hot and silky breeze of memory alone. She lies now full upon her back, as though hiding from the indiscriminate eye above, in conjunction with the pale weeds, parallel to the track as though in competition with its snakelike body to see which has carried the bigger weight. She turns her head and looks at the track as though she were looking at Olga in bed beside her, were engaged in sibling communication with one who has perhaps seen but not understood what the other has, as though in such proximity to a being almost identical to herself

she still lay forgotten and bathed in the shimmering net of solitude. Emoria awaits the train that never seems to come and lies
even closer to the earth as if to bring about a train of her own
creation.

Prone, Emoria closes her eyes to the vicious sun, forgets her
body in the new orange light, her eyelids serving only as translucent veils against this bright field of scrutinous illumination, and
constructs within the crooks and splinters of her memory, where
the light has yet to penetrate, the front porch of the house,
constructs it as though from nonexistent elements and with the
patience of immortality, on the day when she returned from the
fish market and found Alfredo smoking a cigar in the unpainted
rocking chair, her father's chair, sitting fat in the light of her
now-unscrupulous eyes, sitting on her porch at midday when he
would normally be at the cigar factory, the thick blue smoke
billowing from his mouth and nose like a human locomotive
pouring down upon the girl at the foot of the steps, bearing
down heavily now upon the girl lying receptively and prone in
this scorched field of memory and dead grass. She remembers
walking past him, alone an act of defiance, oblivious of his worn
face buried in smoke, oblivious of his grotesque grunts within
that helmet of tobacco, and into the house with eyes frantic and
searching for that which she knew was no longer there, search
ing for the body that was her only connection to a reality other
than this one, a reality not governed by the rigid laws of time
and the factory. She had become the sole protector of that
devastated shell, maintaining its sanctity, allowing it still to caress
her skull in an empty replay, an involuntary reflex of that communication that had once prospered, those large palms groping
her head like a physical reminder of the once-sublime connection that had transpired between young and old eyes bonded by
blood.

Standing in the middle of the living room, already itself infused with emotion and wrath from a few nights past, Emoria
felt the air melt and retreat through the screenless windows,
looked forward through the doorless doorway into the kitchen,
where her mother stood in her dark dress spreading outward

from her wide hips, emphasized by the stained cloth of her apron, one hand pushing back the graying hair on the side of her head, pulling the already taut strands into the enormous bun that decorated her large head. No words were spoken, as though the smoke from Alfredo's cigar had carried any potential words away in its ethereal wisps, as if with the removal of her father's presence she were now alone in the midst of that overpopulated house, her presence now a nuisance, a reminder of the madness that seeped forth from these walls. She saw her mother differently now, her prematurely old face contorted by ignorance, an inability to understand her own surroundings, as though she had become only an overworked machine or a photograph long abused as it tears and fades and transforms the expression of its subject from a smile to a demented, spotty despair. Emoria remembers that old mouth opening without teeth, its tongue as aged and tired as the body it inhabited, the wind that generated forth from it feeble and trembling as it weakly resonated through the air saying, "They took him." And still a long time passed silently, the mother in the doorway surrounded by the smell of the kitchen, the humid stench of boiling meat and salted beans, the fat rising in globules of sticky white foam to the top and sides of the pot, the air beyond her mother becoming thick and heavy, slow-moving, saturated and congealed so that her mother became interred within a gelatin of nonmovement, buried within that shaking, greasy mass of cooked food, atrophying like a cripple of the mind, and bloating like those deprived of thought or decision.

Everything around Emoria's small frame slowed down as though the earth itself were yawning, but within the expanse of its extended and distended breath she became firmly rooted and infinitely tiny, like an insect unconnected to time's enslavement, so that in its smallness, equipped with oversized and multiple eyes, she could see Alfredo's cigar smoke commingling with the fat air of the kitchen, could recognize their similar element, could see in the toothless cavern of her mother's mouth Alfredo's tobacco-eaten gums, could smell the sourness of his armpits in the stew's aroma, could taste the salty perspiration of her father's chest in the tears that now ran down her face, alone and transformed between two ignorances attached to a different clock that left her abandoned within this terrestrial yawn, imprisoned between her mother, the defeated, and Alfredo, the defeating. Still confused and unsynchronized to the movement of the house, she felt the door to the porch close behind her and smelled the overwhelming stench of Alfredo's cigar as his thick hands, spawned of a different father, touched her shoulder in a movement so revolting to her that she fell to her knees and crawled backward away from him, still so overwhelmed by her unattachment to the temporal reality of the house that she dared not speak for fear that her words would sound identical to Roque's incomprehensible grunts (now she thinks that perhaps that is where her true empathy for Roque was born, that perhaps he as well spoke the language of those outside time). On her knees, her mother's frame blocking the entrance to the kitchen, she stared up into Alfredo, looming over her like the cigar factory itself filled with the pungent odor of tobacco and sweat and urine, stared at and through him and saw the words that would emanate from his foul mouth forming syllable by syllable in the acidic furnace of his belly, and floating like vapor over her and into the thick air surrounding her mother's head; "You see, a house filled with nuts. He almost kills her, and she can't understand why he had to leave, as though we could afford to keep a crazy house operating on the money we make. She's crazy just like him. It won't be long before she's chasing roaches and talking politics with Roque. Hopeless. You'll all end up poor and crazy living off of me. We're cursed." And still on the floor, and still in slow motion, she watched as he disappeared in a cloud of blue smoke through the porch, only then to turn around and face her mother, to see what remained of that mass of tired bones, and met the eyes of a woman sick of living, saw her not as a mother but as a woman grown old. Emoria, staring into those eyes too clouded by suffering even to recognize the girl at her feet as her own daughter, was overcome by the realization that somewhere therein lay a small girl like herself and that within her, Emoria's, mind there was born an old, worn-out woman like her mother. No words were spoken before her mother turned around and disappeared within the white, humid vapor of the stewpot.

In the weeks that followed (and only now in the solace of the tall grass can Emoria recall those days with a snicker of victory) she withdrew into a silence that rivaled even her mother's muteness. Emoria, always having been the liveliest and most outspoken of her siblings and half siblings, spread a cloud of tense discontentment throughout the house and especially to her younger siblings, who still did not comprehend the disappearance of their father. This quiet rebellion began to disturb Alfredo most of all now that he spent inordinate amounts of time at their house, retreating to the bedroom with their mother, who, as Emoria quickly came to understand, in her defeated and almost unconscious way received orders on how to run the household. Emoria remembers painfully now her mother's eyes looming over the dinner table day after day, eyes like small metal disks that saw without expression, that hid like a mask any anguish or suffering underneath, that watched without joy her myriad of children, expressionless even toward Roque as he guzzled whatever food was placed before him and what remained of the other children's meals, eyes that after dinner, while the children cleaned dishes and reset the table, retreated to the porch and watched without joy as the sun, pierced by the tall pine and cypress on the horizon, burst into its cloudy rainbow of purple and red, eliciting only a sigh from those massive lungs rocking back and forth in the old chair. It was on just such an evening that Emoria followed her mother to the porch and sat in the stationary chair to her right and, as the old woman swayed back and forth like an overburdened metronome and the sky repeated its cycle of death, told her that she wanted to throw a party. Her mother stopped rocking in order to look at her little daughter, and in the fading light Emoria thought she saw tears forming small pools in the crevices surrounding those eyes. They sat for what seemed to be a long time before her mother, for the first time in so long, gave the hint of a smile, one born not only of joy but, Emoria imagined, complicity, and said it would be all right, it would be just fine.

Now, amid the utter solitude of this thirsty plain, Emoria reconstructs her house full of people, people consuming food, consuming music, consuming other people in the madness of dance, in the romantic briskness of a *danzón* or the buckling hips and sweaty brow of a *guanguanco*. With the repressed smile of her adolescent lips Emoria remembers Francisco, whose ability to dance was music in itself, twirling her throughout the house as though swimming in air, he, though Alfredo's age, the antithesis of the clumsy and vicious construction that was her half brother. She remembers Francisco's delicate, firm hand on her waist leading her to a separate world filled with music and exhilaration. She remembers in a burst of laughter his small mustache quivering as he said, "Girl, you can dance, but why are you pulling me so hard?" as she struggled toward the front door, where Alfredo stood without crossing the threshold, so that he could see, see with his hateful little eyes, Emoria dancing and the crowd having a wonderful time, he who had screamed and even broken a chair exclaiming that the party could not take place, that they could not afford it, that, with his sick, obvious hypocrisy, they should not have a party so soon after their father had had to be taken away. Yet there she was, in the flowering of her defiance, wriggling and showing off in the angry light of his glance. He turned, slammed the door behind him, and returned to his porch, where he sat the rest of the night simmering and consuming cigars like food. Emoria can only remember regretting that his poor young children, their faces pressed to the window of their bedroom, were forbidden from attending, forbidden from even tasting the plate of roast pork and yucca that Olga, her little sister, had taken to them after the party was over.

Emoria, long after everyone had gone home, had watched the sun return to life, felt ecstatic in her victory although not in an entirely vain manner, for that night she had seen her mother laugh and a small illumination return to her eyes, had seen a reduced portion of the happiness she had known before her husband's illness return, and had overheard—yes, even now by the tracks it hardly seems real, but then, in the dim light of the new sun, it was absolutely and joyfully real—her mother tell Esperanza that perhaps they should bring the father back and care for him at the house even if it would be a strain, even if Alfredo would lose his mind in anger. Then, as the sun broke through the trees of the forest, and as the minuscule breath of each individual bird turned into sweet music at the end of its hard beak, in the midst of that very energy that like light she felt enshroud her, she sensed, like a cloud hovering ominously in the distance, that rage return, the rage she had acquired in the forest clearing, that rage that could slow time itself, that rage that now emanated from her eyes casting a dismal light on Alfredo's sleeping house next door, and she suddenly envisioned within herself that bare-chested man overcome by rage in the forest now perhaps strapped in his own filth to a rusted hospital bed in a mental ward far away, and as the fog slowly lifted from the forest, she felt her victory become bittersweet.

4.

Emoria lifts her head from its pillow of dried grass as though awaking from a deep sleep; the magnetic pull of the earth conjoined with the heavy air makes her feel as though a large body were lying prostrate upon her. She struggles to her feet, rubbing her eyes in the still-ominous sun, its light like two compressed streams of fire aimed directly at her eyes, melting them like butter. She turns her head away to avoid the glare, once again fixing her eyes upon the track, which, as she tries to rub the oppressive light from within her eyes, vacillates in her mind as though it too, despite its permanence equal to the seemingly immortal yellow within the grass, were dissolving. Once again she attempts to look at the horizon, to provide for herself that small reassurance of the finite borders of this plain, at least to pretend that this plain ends, that the track arrives somewhere, that beyond the blue sky streaked with clouds, that sky she has come to see as the bilious canvas of a circus tent, still exist some familiar trees and perhaps the smell of the ocean that, to her, was the defining smell of home. Now, her eyes almost closed and her hand still protecting them from the raging light, she feels slightly ridiculous, once again like a little girl in the face of this vicious nature, no longer the hero she was in the protective blanket of dead grass. It is this little girl who finally manages to remove her hand and see through the gaseous spots of light that cloud her vision her father in the distance coming toward her on the track, he too banished to this desolate plain or perhaps, in the unreality of her vision, arriving to take her back over the horizon as though he had knowledge of the tracks' destination, that they would lead them both to home. He looks thin and gaunt, like the tall yellow grass that surrounds them, and pale in the light that consumes them both. He appears both far away and near, as though he were on just this side of the horizon, yet close enough for Emoria to see deep red stubble where his grandiose mustache had once been. He walks on the verge of falling, as though supported by invisible attendants, yet does not seem to get any closer. Emoria focuses and refocuses her eyes to see his features better, his lips thin and chapped, his white uniform fitting loosely, his feet clothed in drab blue slip-ons so different from his patent leather buckled shoes, which once resounded with such authority on the floor of their house. She looks again at his head, shrouded in the unholy halo of this sun, at his hair cropped short by clumsy, utilitarian hands, and at his forehead, graced with the presence of new, ignorant wrinkles. Emoria views all this with the detachment required of this foreign environment until she views his eyes, which are as blank and devoid of expression as the cold iron bars that strap the wooden planks of this track to the hot, torturous earth. Frightened, Emoria turns quickly away and finds herself confronted with another horizon, identical yet empty, comforting in its emptiness, and when she turns back, she can no longer distinguish between one direction and the next. It is once again the hot, burning, empty plain that greets her vision, and she is able to follow the track with her eyes as though they were the path leading to the front porch of the house on the afternoon when she and her mother stood at the top of the steps watching the remnants of the man that had once been the foundation and destruction of their home as he was led, each arm supported under the pit by an attendant in the manner of a drunk or an old, weak invalid, thin and sickly, walking like a child who had yet to learn how to place his feet correctly upon the solid ground, his cheeks sallow within that once-grand face left bare and undecorated by a razor in some foreign, unconcerned hand. Tenderly she watched the attendants help him place his feet upon the steps leading to the screen door and saw his thin legs, hidden within the oversized cloth of his uniform, buckle as though the steps were made of dough and not of the hard concrete that he had mixed and poured himself to grace his home with a respectable entrance. She looked up at her mother's face, already expecting to find her eyes once again filled to overflowing with the suffering and the unbearable incapability to understand the confusion and ugliness that surrounded her, as though the madness and humiliation that pervaded this house were congenital, bred like a disease born of deceitful and vengeful organisms. The puffy, thick skin that surrounded her mother's eyes mimicked the superfluous folds of her father's uniform as though both her parents had shrunk, no longer capable of maintaining their own skins, as though the muscle, bone, nerve, and energy that could produce a household full of children had decayed from within in slow, invisible decrements, had exhausted itself in contact with something deadly and indefinable. The attendants managed him through the door into the living room and through the threshold leading into the kitchen and placed him like an unwieldy parcel onto the chair by the small table. Roque was sitting across from him with a deck of cards, mindlessly shuffling and reshuffling them, the rope that attached him to the table leg bundled all around his feet and underneath his chair. He looked across at his father with those eyes slightly crossed and disconcerting, wiping with his wrist a thin stream of mucus emerging from his nostril, clutching the king of hearts in his hand, releasing only a small, high-pitched sigh to serve as recognition of his father's return. Emoria watched sullenly as her younger siblings, the ones not yet spending their days at the factory's wooden table peeling, deveining, rolling, packaging, and loading tobacco, came and caressed their father's head, kissed him, and hugged him as they would a doll, shrinking back to the doorway to watch in silence as he sat there, motionless, seemingly without the slightest recognition of his surroundings, his eyes blank and ignorant, fixed upon the grimy deck of cards in Roque's large hands being dismantled and reconstructed over and over again, like the surf, Emoria imagined, or the beating of her heart. She stood silently next to her mother, both quietly watching that old, strange man sitting across from Roque, the two of them a childlike, mindless counterpart to Emoria and her mother, caretakers by choice over a situation neither was capable of fully understanding. Emoria thought back to the morning after the party and felt herself become uncomfortable with the unreal symmetry of the situation, as though this entire scenario were taking place in some child's picture book, thought out previously and precisely like a play, and then she felt time slow down again, felt herself become detached from her surroundings like a drop of water as it separates from the moist canal of a leaf heavy with dew, and she looked out through the kitchen doorway, abandoning her father at the table, out into the living room, where Alfredo stood watching his stepfather and half brother Roque staring into empty space, his face contorted with thought and the grim wrinkles of connivance vibrating on his forehead. Slowly, as in a state of half sleep, Emoria watched as his face turned and his eyes met her own, felt frozen and connected to earth only by the sensation of her mother's dress against her elbow, and she understood beyond words what Alfredo saw sitting at the kitchen table, saw how similar his sight was to her own as though she were viewing the two mindless bodies at the table painted upon his pupils, and saw or imagined (even now in the sun's glare uncertain whether she had seen or imagined) a smile, broad and defiant, not born entirely of ignorance but of understanding, as though it were almost a part of herself smiling, form upon his fat, tobacco-ridden lips, felt that smile overcome her and quash that rage that had risen again within her at this new frightening communication, felt it wash over her in that state beyond time like a wave of fire or the cessation of her own heartbeat.

Emoria remembers the endless hours on the back porch, watching her father stare out into the woods, not moving except when, with the aid of her mother or older half sister Cuquina, she took him to the outhouse at regular intervals so he could evacuate the fluids his stagnant body accumulated over the motionless hours. The monotonous circle down the steps and through the yard and back again was like a clock to mark the featureless days. Emoria would clutch his cold hand, would lift his arm over her head, would scratch his scalp, would dig her fingers into his protruding ribs to elicit a laugh, only to be met with a cold stare or perhaps, on the rarest of occasions, the hint of a smile. Mostly his head would eventually drop, and with his chin resting against his chest, he would fall asleep until the hour arrived to take him again to the outhouse. Alfredo began making his presence known around the house again, ignoring the old man completely and, to Emoria's dejection, once again retreating to the bedroom with her mother to discuss the family finances. Likewise Emoria began to feel her motives become polluted; she remembers now how she began to hold on to her father as a tool to disturb Alfredo, to place herself and the old man in his way and remind him of the existence of this other presence, this other consciousness that infused those walls, that flew through the air like flies buzzing incessantly in their ears.

It was during this time that Emoria's mother decided to cook a large dinner and bring the family together, hoping, as she had confided to Emoria over the pots of yellow rice and freshly killed chicken, that the presence of so many familiar faces at once would rekindle at least a hint of the qualities that the old, sleeping man on the porch once possessed, that with the bustle of voices and children she would be able to recapture at least a shadow of the man she had married. Emoria remembers now with what concentration, bordering on madness, she worked in aiding her mother to light once again a small flame in her father's cold, dull eyes, even if only to recall and generate the madness that had caused such anxiety and premature anguish in her young heart. She sat in front of him for hours, kneeling, looking up as though in hurried, frantic prayer, at the dark sacks and bilious folds in his emaciated face, at the lips drawn and silent, reciting the names of his children and stepchildren, of the few relatives he had that she as well knew, of the men he would drink coffee with, smoking cigars and imparting upon them the stories of travel that she would never hear, telling them of a Cuba they had never seen before the onslaught of his insanity, reciting and repeating like a chant the names of hogs they had slaughtered, the dogs and cats numberless that they had imparted names to, even the cow that they once owned, of which he had been so proud that he had shown Emoria, a girl of six or seven, how to milk it so that it was a pleasure for the cow and not a burden or punishment, grabbing his limp hand like a teat now and pulling, squeezing just as he had shown her, trying desperately to cause a seepage of emotion from his dry, empty face. There she was, on the floor of the porch, clutching his hand, both of them asleep when her mother walked in, immediately shaken at that vision reminiscent of that night in the living room lost together in their exclusive oblivion, and shook her daughter's shoulder to wake her and get the old man ready because the guests were due to arrive very soon.

Like a world far away, as though she were constructing it from these wooden planks and the nails of her imagination, Emoria remembers the long table, pieced together haphazardly from the tables of generous neighbors, placed lengthwise and uneven and covered in a variety of cloths, where, Emoria remembers, the generations of her immediate family sat, her seven surviving brothers and sisters, of which she and Olga were the oldest, her six grown half sisters and half brothers, her mother's close friends, Esperanza and Pijuán, who had always frightened Emoria with her obvious black wig and ever-present umbrella and nervous twitch, and the great old man Máximo Gómez, who had once been a constant companion of her father's and had always been a dominating image in her memory, clothed as he was in a shroud of sweet cigar smoke, bellowing laughs that shook her weak, undeveloped ribs, now sitting at the table, still laughing and talking incessantly but diminished in her sad, nostalgic eyes, the great figure appearing both hopeful and awkward at a table inhabited by a family diseased and collapsing, sitting obvious in her mother's intent to generate new life from old, defunct experience within this, her second husband, dead as well, even though his continued heartbeat deprived her of at least the stability of widowhood. Looking up from her position at the table, her eyes level with its surface, looking over the unmatched plates and hands of varying ages, looking down almost as through a tunnel, perhaps one that she wished to recreate, Emoria saw her father, limp and staring at the table ahead of him, staring impotently and ridiculously at empty space from his position at the head of the table, dressed in the best clothes of a man who no longer existed, a man for whom those clothes would fit and not hang loosely about that decrepit frame, where the hair that Emoria had once found a place to hide her aggrieved face now protruded obscenely from the top of his shirt although it was buttoned to the top and adorned foolishly with a black tie. Shifting her eyes only slightly in her head, surveying a landscape broad and frightening in only the slightest of movements, she saw Alfredo seated next to him, the oldest of blood kin present, powerful and heir to the confusion seated around him, looking at the old man with the same unthreatened amusement with which he looked at his two youngest children, sitting on the floor, diapered and playing with a wooden box mounted on wheels intending to represent a locomotive.

Then her mother entered the room, triumphantly carrying the pots of yellow rice and chicken, disappearing and returning with yucca, plantains, salads of tomato, avocado, onions, and sardines, a huge gourd of homemade sangria and cider, and *batidas* of papaya, banana, and cantaloupe for the children, all so much of a narcotic, a fuel to engage the machine of remembrance and regeneration. And then the beginnings of noise, of lids uncovered and knives unsheathed, of mandibles engaged in rhythmic destruction like engines, of mouths full of food and exclaiming the delights of digestion, of throats full and gurgling like busy canals and lips swollen from contact with garlic and the swelling ecstasy of liquor. Emoria recalls the joy of so many bodies consuming without fear of running out, without single-minded concern for the individual plate and the dependency required of food, recalls the gluttonous bursts of laughter emitted from Máximo Gómez's throat as he expounded upon the celestial virtues of food and its primacy to the maintenance of a people's identity, recalls her childish joy at watching Roque place an entire leg of chicken in his mouth and return to his plate the bone missing the entire bulbous knob that was once a feathered hip, recalls almost with remorse the selfish joy emanating from the table, oblivious in its communal astonishment at the pleasure of eating, when Olga, her poor twin sister always the innocent and suffering witness, exclaimed, "Papa, what's the matter?" and everyone, mouths full but jaws silent, turned and watched as her father's eyes fluttered and closed and his head lurched forward onto the plate of yellow rice untouched, his face buried among chicken, grease, and fried plantains, sat and listened to the monotonous drops of urine fall from the edge of his chair onto the wooden planks of the floor.

5.

Emoria watches now compliantly as delicate drops of water rhythmically hit the planks below her eyes, each minuscule drop exploding upon the track as her thoughts had exploded into incoherent fragments of emotion, dialogue, and perception when, still oblivious of the gravity of the scene, she had heard Máximo Gómez quietly mutter to himself, in a manner devoid of all the buoyancy and optimism she had thought him to embody, the word *carajo*. She remembers now how she stood by silently, propelled into a world where speech was inadequate, as Alfredo stood and, lifting her father into his arms like a child, exclaimed that the party should go on, that her father, that man who had communicated with her and unknowingly condemned her to premature madness, was simply an invalid, and that there was nothing anyone could do. She remembers painfully the vi-

sion of her mother collapsing into tears amid the stoic silence of
her children—even Roque looking about in ignorant disbelief—
while Esperanza caressed her scalp and Pijuán clutched her umbrella, her face twitching uncontrollably. Now, while a thick
blanket of storm clouds blocks for the first time the vicious light
of the sun, Emoria is reminded of later that night after the plates
had been cleared by the guests and they had retreated to their
homes, and after the children, herself included, had been placed
in their beds, when she, while wandering throughout the house,
unable to sleep, overcome by the obsessive insomnia she had so
acquainted with her father, heard the deep growl of Alfredo's
voice behind the door of her parents' bedroom, and leaned
silently against it, and for the first time heard the name of that
distant aunt and of the hope that in her hands Emoria would be
able to attend school and be free of this torment and that they
should send the old man where he would be more comfortable
and well taken care of, and of a place called Quentuqui, and
never throughout his speech hearing her mother's voice, but
only the slow, steady drone of her father snoring, naked except
for a thick towel folded underneath his buttocks.

The fat, taut globules of water strike cold and heavy against
Emoria's skin as the purple and black clouds spread throughout
the sky like blood in water, blurring the distinction between the
sky and the earth. Earlier, she recalls, they sat harmlessly in
the far reaches of this strange dome, like a bruise providing only
the hint of annoyance, the appearance of pain without the
wretched discomfort of swollen, discolored skin, curiously foreign to the arid monotony of this plain. She watched as their
liquid bodies rolled over one another in an orgy of movement, a
bloated, humping blemish, gorged air and vapor, stretched and
sagging, as they unfolded to cover the sky and plunge the landscape into premature darkness. Watching the chaotic majesty of
these clouds, their ability to spread and reproduce spontaneously
as if they emerged from the invisible elements of the air or
converted them like a cancer from monotonous persistence into
uncontrollable violence, Emoria falls into a reverie, frozen into
the landscape of dead grass like a small tree, vulnerable yet rigid,

both insignificant and integral to the composition of this plain. She stands defiantly as the thin membrane of the sky opens and water gushes forth upon the earth as though it were the sky's turn to perspire, stands complacently as the cool water soaks into her dress, revealing the sensuous growth of the woman she is becoming, and watches in silent concentration the bursts of light that generate seemingly from nothing and as of yet cause no sound in the far distance. She looks down toward the track and watches the mud bubble, pop, and breathe from in between the wooden planks, watches the dry, thirsty sand metamorphose into living matter as though the remnants of life forced underground during the unbearable heat were now in the process of resurrection within this liquid medium, this marriage between earth and sky and the murky, damp copulation that blurs the distinction between them. It is from within this conjunction that Emoria looks out and can no longer recognize the horizon, can no longer see the limit of this cage, feels the illusory power of distinction enter her soft, wet skin as though within this strange merging she were becoming the only line, a vertical rod inhabiting both realms yet belonging to neither, her feet implanted within the thick, bloodlike mud and her face exposed to the light, abundant moisture of the sky.

In this wet, soothing conjunction, in this new monotony of mergence, Emoria feels transported once again, transported not beyond the horizon but within it, as though in her striking foreignness to the change occurring around her she were singularly dispossessed from the world and could look upon, with the lonely sadness and pity of an exile, that girl six months ago as she sat beside her mother looking across at an organism that only slightly resembled her father, lying naked and slowly atrophying into no more that a hairy, malshaped fetus, hearing the name of that aunt, her mother's sister, whom she had never seen, who ran a *chinchar* somewhere far off by the name of Quentuqui and who would make sure that she, little Emoria, would be able to attend school, hearing the words clumsily recited in the raspy, tired, and increasingly masculine voice of her mother as she had heard them uttered behind that very door by Alfredo a few nights before. She watched as her mother stared at the sagging cot across from them, stretched and creaking from the dead weight it supported, not even hearing or, Emoria thought, understanding what was being said, bathed in the dusty light of that Florida afternoon as it seeped from the small window behind them and illuminated the eyes of her half-dead father, opened and staring like a corpse and perhaps, Emoria had wished, hearing the bland yet catastrophic words being spoken to ears that had already heard them. It was that thought, the thought of those dead ears that had once so often understood the innocent ramblings of a young girl hearing now of her sale that caused the tears to begin flowing steadily and uncontrollably from her eyes as she looked up at her poor, defeated, and ignorant mother's face, and she continued to cry even as she watched the wrinkles on that face fill with the salty tears of old age as if those folds and crevices had been worn into place by uncountable tears and sadness. And the two women crying, sobbing beyond hope, clutching each other powerlessly, Emoria feeling the sagging, weak flesh of her mother's arms underneath the thin black cloth, feeling the lukewarm and moist cheek as it pressed against the top of her skull, yet still staring from underneath her mother's overgrown bosom at those dead eyes set deep in the skull like a cadaver, searching with all her strength for a response, an answer from her father before she would leave him forever, feeling the pained, desperate clutch of her mother's hands as they squeezed her small frame, as they tore at her flesh with a child's innocent desperation, yet still looking at the pupils she had once entered, trying to find an opening that was no longer there, becoming frightened within the clutch of an old woman that was quickly becoming hysterical and violent, but riveted to the grisly stare of her father's corpse, searching for life as she struggled from underneath her mother's grasp, finally leaving her to rip the mattress to shreds with her bare hands, as Emoria clutched the side of the cot and placed her face against her father's, feeling the faint, dusky breath as it slid like mucus down her cheeks mixing with her tears, and as she felt her very heart explode with anguish and desperation and only half listened to the mad groaning of her mother behind her, she met with that cold, dull stare like the bright, featureless surface of bone.

6.

The rain is becoming more opaque and confining; it encircles her as if in the collapse that is occurring the dome she envisioned only surrounded her own insignificant frame, as if the plain itself were confining itself to the isolation of her body. She looks around and sees only water and an implacable grayness, perhaps, she thinks, the color of nothing, and hears the whisper of groans that generate within her and that coincide with the small bursts of light that no longer illuminate the distance but, she thinks, emanate from her interior landscape and merely highlight the impenetrable gray net that surrounds her. She strains her eyes, and the plain is gone, strains her eyes with such force that she sees in the uncountable liquid mirrors that fall around her a small girl stoically erect in the hot kitchen of a home looking toward the back door, slightly opened, as two strange women talk in whispers, one bathed in tears and the other, tall and bony, staring over her at the girl in the kitchen. The girl is standing next to a small table, her feet playing with a large mound of rope, when, obviously startled by a noise, she turns to see a large, balding man clenching a cigar hungrily in his teeth as he supports a feeble invalid, dressed clumsily in oversized clothes, whose head dips and bobs as his feet mimic the act of walking, like a doll's in the unconcerned hand of a child. The girl yells, "Papa, I don't want to go from the house," and clenches the cold, limp hand of the invalid, who involuntarily pushes her out of the way as he is propelled forward by the other man. Watching the two men pass toward the front door, she notices peripherally a drop of blood fall upon the kitchen table. A flash of light, solid and incorrigible against the gray net, pours forth through the opening of the back door, and soon after the crying woman opens her mouth and roars, "Emoria," with such force that the iron rails of the track vibrate angrily. The slaps of the rain awaken within the girl another girl named Emoria, who shrinks backward, clutching the hot stove and screaming, "No, I won't go, I won't go," and sees another small drop of blood splatter upon the kitchen floor. Another rip of sound shakes the girl so violently she falls to her knees, burying them deep in the mud, and looks up at a large congregation of faces of varying ages that look consolingly and curiously at her, a chorus of confused faces that Emoria recognizes as her siblings and half siblings and that, terrified, her face pressing against the hot stove as if it were comforting flesh, sees one called Alfredo come forth and clasp her around the waist, lifting her up from the floor, and delirious Emoria looks at his smoky, sweaty face and says, "Papa, I don't want to go from the house," looks at that ignorant face and believes she sees a proud red mustache curled at the tips and gentle, understanding eyes that she can enter like a tunnel and emerge refreshed and sane, looks deep within those dark pupils and meets with another light, but this one steady and silent, and she falls upon the track clutching the cold iron, pressing her face desperately upon the warped, rotting wood and awaits hungrily the small circle of light that penetrates the surrounding grayness. Emoria feels her father's rough palms lift her into the air, into a smoking cloud of tobacco and stew meat, where she hears the explosion of another drop of blood as it bursts upon the mound of rope underneath the kitchen table. Then, carried through the air, Emoria hears the words drip from his lips, "C'mon, let's go," in a voice that was not her father's, and she strains against his shoulder as she strains against this track, her eyes following the light that sits amid the wet gray dome like a pupil, and over that shoulder like a cold metal bar she looks back at the kitchen table, stays riveted even as she passes through the back door and hears the hoarse ramblings of the truck that will take her away, listens to the all-consuming rip of sound that seems to accompany the circle of light that is rapidly approaching her on the track as she listens to the sound of bone being torn from bone, watching Roque, her brother, blood streaming from his lips, pulling the teeth from his mouth.

SERGIO TRONCOSO
Angie Luna

She asked me if I liked them. And what could I say? They were *wonderful*. Her breasts were round and white and everything you'd expect from a beautiful woman. I can't believe she *asked* me, as if I could have thought otherwise. I'd never been with someone like her before. I was terrified. But she seemed shy and even unsure about herself. I didn't understand that at all. What did she see in *me*? She had of course looked at herself. Everyone I knew had looked at her. I heard all the comments about her, wishful comments. But with me she was just playful and tentative. I kissed her, looked out the window of my mother's Buick Regal. She pressed against me and unzipped her skirt. *She* unzipped her skirt and laughed. My God! Did anyone do this in a car anymore? Next to an office park in the middle of the night? Only in El Paso. Jesus. It was very warm holding her. I loved holding her hips. She was soft in all the right places. Her perfume was all over me hours after I got back home. I couldn't stop thinking about her. And when we were driving back to Juárez, to her place, which she shared with her sisters, speeding down the Border Freeway through a gauntlet of amber lights, she was joking and her hair was all over her face and she was smothering me with kisses and I thought I was going to explode again, but I kept the Buick between the lines. Angie

Luna was something out of a Revlon ad. A remarkable woman. But why did she choose me?

She told me, after we were relaxing in the backseat, that she had had sex only once before. Only once. She told me that an older man, a semiboyfriend, had forced her to do it with him, pushed her down, taken off her clothes. She said she didn't mind too much. She said she sort of wanted to. She wanted the experience with an older man. She wanted to be ready for when she got married. Now she wasn't sure she would ever get married. Now *she* was the older one, but she didn't really act that way. She was shy, I tell you. I didn't know why, but I got angry. Maybe the East Coast did that to you. I told her not to let a man do that to her again. Ever. It wasn't as if I were trying to score PC points to "nail" her, as they said so crudely in Amherst. We were already completely naked, both of us quite happy. I told her it was terrible what he had done to her; I told her as vehemently as I could. She was way too shy for her own good. She became embarrassed, and I backed off. I told her it really wasn't her fault. But I also told her that anybody who did that to her was a fucking macho bastard. Was I going out of my mind? Mr. Goody-Goody. Where did *that* come from? That's what a college education did to you.

When I took Angie back to her house just over the Free Bridge, off 16 de Septiembre, I noticed that the streets were quiet and empty and shiny from the rain that had fallen earlier. Whenever I went to Juárez as a kid, with my parents for dinner, I had thought México was such a crowded country. Always packed and busy. A lot of sun and too much traffic. I almost never went to Juárez at night, and I had never been to Juárez at three in the morning. There was no one around. Angie said I could meet her sisters next week. They'd already be asleep by now. Three sisters alone in México. Probably all gorgeous. At the Popular she had told me that her older sister had left Chihuahua City for *la frontera* about five years ago. To get away from her father, who wanted her to be a nice little girl and marry one of his friends. Shit. Can you believe that? That sister left, got a green card, found a job in El Paso as a secretary with the help of a woman she met at Cielo Vista Mall. The first sister then offered to put up the other sisters if they also wanted to come to Juárez but told them they'd need to get jobs. And they did. What a life! They all had pitched in for a down payment and had just bought this little house, in a clean neighborhood. And they were still saving money. Their goals were to become American citizens, buy a house in El Paso, and learn good English. My Spanish was perfect, she said, except that sometimes I would screw up the counterfactual with weird concoctions. She said my parents had done a good job teaching me about my heritage. I wasn't a gringo yet, she said. She hadn't met my parents. I wasn't sure what my mother would think of Angie. Or maybe I was.

I saw Angie at the Popular again on Monday, after I had finished putting out the cotton briefs for boys, all colors, size six through twenty. I had already dumped all the designer jeans out, for the back-to-school sales. Joe was off my back. He was somewhere in the back room, yelling to a supplier who had brought in the wrong stuff. That's what you get when you don't plan your summer job: a frenetic boss who's under pressure himself and vents it on the stock boys. At least I had met Angie Luna there. That made the entire summer. In two weeks I'd go back to Massachusetts. She was coming down the escalator from the mezzanine bookstore and music shop where she worked one of the cash registers. God, she was a vision! She was wearing a tight black dress down to her knees so it wouldn't look like too much. Still, it was enough. She had Marilyn Monroe's body, with short jet black hair. As she rode down the escalator, she leaned slightly back on one foot, the fabric pressed against her thighs. I almost fainted.

She didn't kiss me, and I guess I didn't expect to kiss her, not in front of all the idiots in the store. It might even be a good idea just to be seen as "friends," and that's what we did. She asked me if I wanted to have dinner at her place next Saturday night, and I said that I did. I don't care what anyone else says: Women in their thirties can look great. I was having trouble breathing. She had on her confident look, the one she pushed like a shield against all the stares from the old men in the shoe department and the hungry male managers and assistant managers. The other stock boys just winked at her and asked her out brazenly and tried to get real close to her, but she didn't bitc. Up to this day I still don't know why she asked *me* out. Maybe to her I was an oddity. Born in El Paso but on my way out. Just as soon as I finished my B.A. in economics. She said, as we walked to the perfume counter of Estée Lauder, that she wanted to see me before Saturday. I was going back to school in two weeks, right? I said that I was. She said she wanted to get to know me better, to talk about what I was studying and how it was to live up there alone, without your family. I said that maybe we could see a movie, have dinner, spend a few hours just hanging out. She liked the idea. Before she turned around and went back up the escalator, she asked me if I was coming home for Christmas, and I said that I was. She smiled and winked at me and marched up the up escalator. Did she know how *fantastic* she looked just walking like that? She was really way too sweet for her own good.

"*Ese*, Victor, did you plug her, man?" the voice of Carlos Morales hissed from behind me. I turned around. The fat bastard was wearing a dirty white T-shirt, his coiffed hair almost to his shoulders.

"What?" I said. I wanted only to get away from him, so I started walking quickly toward a Dumpster in a corner filled with boxes of belts, dress shirts, polo shirts, and socks. He'd run back to the employees' lounge as soon as I started unloading this shit.

"You know, man. *No te hagas pendejo.*" He plunged his hips forward and swung his arms back in a motion more vulgar than I can ever describe, all the while grinning stupidly.

"Shut the fuck, man. What are you talking about?"

"You went out, didn't you? I heard about it already. From Cindy in Women's Wear."

"Yeah, so what? It's none of your business."

" 'It's none of your business,' " he repeated in an exaggerated, snotty whine. "What a *man* you are!"

"Shut up, *cabrón*. You better get your ass to work. Guess who's coming down the aisle." Joe was whizzing by the dress shirts, and he didn't look too happy. Just as Carlos was stacking four cardboard boxes up to his chest, Joe almost slid to a stop right in front of him, didn't say a word, but wiggled his finger in the fat boy's face, and Carlos twaddled after him. He glanced back at me, raised his arms in bewilderment, and pretended not to know what the hell he had done wrong this time. Damn. The whole store knew about us now. I was glad I was going to be there for only a few more days. Doña Leticia Jiménez, the softhearted battleax who really ran the whole place from her perch in Women's Lingerie—forty-two years of selling panties!—rushed by me as I emptied the Dumpster and gave me a thumbs-up and grinned. Shit.

By Wednesday I had already dreamed of Angie Luna twice: once on Monday, in that black dress, on the escalator and again the next night. A more complicated dream. We were in Central Park, in the Ramble. Doing it. I hadn't ever been to Central Park! I once read about it in a magazine, however. This woman was really getting inside my head. I told my mother I was going out with some friends, and she just kissed me on the forehead and told me not to drive too fast. She said she was going to send me back to school with a box full of *flautas*, some cookies, and a brick of Muenster cheese and tortillas, for making quesadillas. Did I have any requests for food? They might be going shopping later. I said that I didn't. As I was cruising down the Border Freeway toward the downtown bridges, I remembered how I had never really gone to Juárez in high school, not by myself. I always heard, mostly from my parents, how you could get pulled over by a Mexican cop who'd just want a *mordida*. If you didn't have enough money or didn't play it savvy enough, if you made him feel like the asshole that he was, then you might wind up in a Mexican jail, no one would know where you were for a while, maybe you'd escape only after you tasted your own blood. So I never went alone. That is, until now. It wasn't that bad. I'd never been stopped at all. Sure, the traffic up the bridge was a mess during rush hour or a weekend night, but you'd sit and wait until you got there, that was all. I knew where to turn, I started recognizing the main streets, Avenida Juárez, 16 de Septiembre, Avenida Lerdo. I had even been on Avenida Reforma with Angie one day, the big boulevard that takes you south, outside the city, deeper into México. We went to visit one of her friends who lived in a neighborhood where all the houses were freshly painted and neat but the streets were dusty, unpaved, full of swamplike puddles big enough to swallow a pickup. I wondered if my parents had always warned me about Juárez, their own hometown, because they really thought it was dangerous or because they thought I couldn't hack it outside *gringolandia*. I knew what to do on these streets.

When I finally got to Angie's house, it was just getting dark; the desert sun was just a faint crown of orange and yellow lights peeking out from the mountains. Angie had told me to be there by eight, and I was early. If I had waited any longer at home, my little brother might have taken off with the car. Anyway, maybe I could hang around and see what her house was like. I didn't mind. Angie answered the door wearing an apron and looking like a voluptuous version of Ozzie's Harriet. An apron over a sharp party dress. She said she was glad that I was early, gave me a real wet kiss right on the mouth, and told me her older sister would be back in a second. Rocío had gone to the grocery store. Angie told me to relax and asked me if I wanted a beer, and I said yes. She said she was angry with her little sister, who had promised to be there to meet me but had then taken off with her boyfriend and probably wouldn't be back until late. Her little sister, Angie said, was a problem. A couple of months ago Marisela had stopped going to nursing school. Now she had quit her job and was looking for a new one, and her *novio* would take her out dancing and drinking every week until the wee hours of the morning. Marisela did nothing around the house, and the two older sisters were having trouble controlling her, getting her on the right track.

Angie told me, as she was putting away a bucket and bottles of cleaning fluids, that they were planning a big get-together for Saturday. Could I still come? Sure I would. A couple of their friends would be over for dinner, including Rocío's boyfriend.

After dinner they'd sit around and have a few beers and cuba libres and maybe play the guitar and sing a round of old and new Mexican songs. One of the guys coming was an excellent poet at the Universidad de Juárez, and he might read some of his poetry. I never did any of that stuff at the Amherst parties I went to, except the drinking, of course, so I was a little nervous about being out of place. A Chicano *americanizado*. But Angie had always made me feel right at home, so I quickly forgot about my fears.

"*Oye, Victor,*" she whispered in my ear, catching me by surprise from behind as I strolled around the living room, "*eres un amor,*" she said sweetly, kissing my earlobe. I shivered.

"Angie. What if I got a room for Saturday night after dinner?" I said, having thought about this now for hours, my shoulders and back still sore from pressing against the Buick's door handles.

"*Perfecto. ¿En dónde?*"

"Maybe Motel 8 or the Holiday Inn. Something nice."

"*Muy bien.* You know, I'm going to miss you so much."

"Me too. I can see you *en navidad*, right?"

"*Sí. Ay, mi rey,* why do you have to go study in Massachusetts? *Te vas a poner triste allá tan solo,*" she said, stroking back my hair so gently.

"*Entonces dame algo para soñar en ti,*" I said coyly, finding everything I wanted in her dark brown eyes.

"*¡Ay, diablo!*" she said, and kissed me so softly, her lips lingering over mine and opening up into a chasm and taking me completely in. I couldn't believe what I felt. I took a step back to kiss her hand, but it was really to calm down so I wouldn't be completely horny the entire evening. Jesus, she was incredible. As we were about to walk out the door, Rocío stepped inside and said hello and asked us what movie we were seeing. I said we weren't sure yet. She asked me if I was coming to the Saturday night *reunión*, and I said that I was. I didn't think I was too articulate; in fact I thought I was stammering. If Angie was voluptuous, Rocío was downright elegant. Like an Isabella Rossellini: reserved, confident, playful. When Angie and I finally got into the Buick, I kept thinking that in a weird way I could understand why they had had so many problems growing up, with their father and his friends and whoever else had tried to dominate them. These sisters were resplendent in a rough and unforgiving world. But I didn't get the sense, from that first and very brief meeting, that Rocío was shy like Angie. The older sister seemed capable of being tough and even competitive. I now knew where Angie had gotten her own confident look, which she plastered on her face like a mask when she was at the Popular. What would have happened to the two other sisters without an older sibling like Rocío? In the cowboy country of Chihuahua City? Maybe El Paso wasn't that different from Chihuahua. Maybe here they just screwed you in English instead of Spanish. At least the sisters seemed in good shape now. At least here their father wasn't breathing down their necks.

We drove to the State Line, an expensive restaurant, at least for El Paso, which served steak and ribs and even *barbacoa*. Nothing here for a celery-chomping Yankee. I didn't mind blowing a big chunk of my paycheck on Angie; I really loved being with her. After last Saturday night I felt as if the summer had been more than just a terrible blur of time passing away, and it had taken just her touch to do it. We got a cozy booth overlooking the lights of I-10. The young waitress brought us water and our menus. I didn't know if I could just reach out and hold Angie's hand. While I was thinking about it and pretending to look at my menu, she scooted over to my side and kissed me on the cheek. Maybe she could read my mind. That thought seemed frightening to me and even more exciting than her holding me tightly in the backseat of the Buick. Finally the waitress came over and took our orders: barbecued baby back ribs and a Corona for me, and a Texas T-bone and a Dos Equis for her. There were only a few couples generously scattered around the restaurant. Once in a while you could hear the boisterous and arrogant laughter of a group of six businessmen in a faraway corner, some of them struggling to understand the Spanish of the big Mexican client they were entertaining for the day. I took her hand and kissed it and thought about why I had been born when I was, and not ten years earlier, and why the hell I was up in bucolic New England studying how to calculate the present value of projected cash flows and the like. The beer had just the right cold sting slipping down my throat, and I knew then I didn't want to be anywhere else in the world.

Angie told me that she had just been promoted to assistant manager of her small department in the mezzanine, so I made an impromptu toast to her success that made her eyes become even brighter and more loyal. I was really happy for her. She deserved every good thing she got. She said the new position just meant more work and just a few extra dollars at the end of the week, but maybe she could eventually move up even higher. She said she was a little apprehensive about some of the things she would have to know in her new position. She was afraid the other cashiers would be jealous of her promotion and would jump on her mistakes when and if she made them. Up to this point the manager in charge had been supportive and had told her she deserved a shot because she had worked so hard without ever being absent. But she did have to master certain skills. I asked Angie what these things were. She said the most difficult one was something called inventory accounting, something she had never had in school in Chihuahua. I laughed. She glared at me. For the first time I knew she wasn't just sweet and shy but also proud. I told her I wasn't laughing at her.

"*Entonces* what are laughing at?" she asked, still serious and stealing a pair of ribs from my plate.

"I just finished my second course in accounting. Got an A minus. I'll help you with inventory accounting if you want me to."

She smiled hard at me, in a friendly sort of way but still prideful. "Well"—she snorted—"as long as you teach me so that I can get an A because I don't want any A minus." This Angie girl was something else.

So instead of going to the movies, we drove east on I-10 to the UTEP library, which I knew was open until midnight. She had never been there before. I told her anyone could just walk right in, find a comfortable sofa overlooking the atrium, and read or relax. I showed her where she could get snacks, where the newspaper room was, and where she could make copies of whatever book she wanted. I found old editions of the accounting books I had used at Amherst and took her to the bank of conference rooms with chalkboards on the third floor. It was hard enough getting through the basics of debit and credit and assets equals liabilities plus equity without having the titillation of Angie's turquoise dress rubbing back and forth over her thighs every time she crossed her legs. I kept my focus, however. She seemed mysteriously captivated by the provisions for uncollectible accounts and merchandise returned. She asked whether these things might vary by store because she knew from experience that many customers would buy a load of goods on credit only to list fake addresses or return half of what they had bought the previous week. I said that the company probably had a rough idea of what these percentages were, and she could tell them if these numbers didn't really apply to the Popular downtown.

After a couple of hours we drove back to Juárez. I promised to help her a couple more times so that she would be ready to get the specific information she needed for her new assignments. When I pulled the Buick up to the front of her house, she slid closer to me, to the middle of the front seat, and kissed me and stroked my neck and chest until I told her I was going to rip her clothes off if she didn't get out of the car. Before she opened the door and stopped tormenting me, she whispered in my ear that I shouldn't forget the room for Saturday night. I could hear her black pumps clicking on the sidewalk as she walked to the front door, each click opening up and pinning back my heart to the wall of a blissful hunger.

The next day I finally got my airline tickets in the mail, and it suddenly dawned on me that I would be leaving next week. I had already told Joe that this would be my last week, and he had grunted a thank-you and told me to come back if I ever needed a summer job. Sure I would, I said, thinking that if I ever needed another mindless stint of time, I might instead opt for a temporary lobotomy if there was such a thing. I didn't bother to say good-bye to anyone at the Popular except Doña Leticia and the rest of the "girls" in Women's Lingerie, none of whom was younger than fifty. I had always liked their raucous free-for-all and the fact that these ladies could talk enough trash to make me blush and then turn on a dime and face a waiting customer with the most serious of faces. Angie Luna I didn't need to say good-bye to because I would be seeing her on Saturday. I'd also see her a couple more times next week so that she could get a good sense of accounting or at least enough for her to find on her own the answers to any questions that might come up. It occurred to me that I was teaching accounting to Marilyn Monroe's Mexican double and that somehow I should feel stupid about that. But I could never figure out where exactly the stupidity was in that situation. My mother, in another of her prolonged good-byes, was already hugging me and kissing me whenever I walked through the house, imploring me to write and telling me not to walk alone at night in Amherst and to make my reservations for Christmas with enough time to spare. My father didn't say much except to point out that he was glad I had worked all summer and saved money for school. He said they too would add to the pot before I left. I thanked him.

On Saturday morning I got up early and told my mother I was going over to Grandma's to say good-bye in case I didn't get a chance next week. I had breakfast with my *abuelitos*, who were always early risers, and then drove my grandfather to his favorite store, the Western Auto on Paisano Street. I think he was look-ing for a new lawn mower bag. He told me he'd walk back the ten or so blocks because his legs were getting stiff from lack of exercise. As soon as I returned to their house, my grandmother said she needed a ride to El Centro, a community center for senior citizens. She said they were in the middle of a food drive. As soon as I dropped her off, I knew I was free for an hour or two before I'd have to pick her up. I went back to their house and dialed a couple of hotels and motels on I-10, the ones I had driven by many times before. I had never really done this before, yet I didn't think it would be a big deal, and it wasn't. Last year I had gotten a credit card at Amherst from the tons of solicitations I always got in the mail, a Visa with no annual fee ever. I got room rates, checkout times, and finally settled on the Holiday

Inn next to the airport because it was convenient and probably nice. It wasn't the cheapest one, but I thought it would be worth it to be comfortable with Angie. I told the reservations desk that I was visiting relatives from out of town, made a one-day reservation for a junior suite, and told them I'd be arriving late today, probably around ten o'clock. No problem. Angie and I would spend part of the night there, I would drive her home whenever she was ready to go, and early on Sunday I would go back to the Holiday Inn and check out. Simple. As soon as I clicked the receiver down, I felt a great elation come over me like a gust of the desert wind that sweeps through Transmountain Road. I couldn't wait.

I finally took off in the early evening, after renewing my lease of the Buick with my mother. Be careful, she said, don't get too crazy with your friends. She didn't know I was going to my first Mexican party. The whole scenario made me a little nervous. All of a sudden I thought I'd forgotten my Spanish. I didn't know if they would just hang around, drink some beers, or dance. What music would young Mexicans dance to? I didn't know if I'd feel too young among Rocío's friends or if they'd think I was just a quasi gringo invading their territory. I wasn't a real Mexican, and I wasn't an American either. At least not at Amherst, where everyone just assumed I was the expert on the best place for Mexican food. I was more like a shadow playing both sides of the game. I didn't mind. I knew Angie would be there and we would have a good time. When I arrived at Angie's house, Rocío answered the door, kissed both my cheeks, and introduced me to a few people who were already sitting on the couch and on the floor. The other women kissed me on the cheeks too—I thought this kissing was terrific, for its immediate friendliness and sophistication—and one of the guys handed me a beer and scooted over so I'd have a good spot on the couch. Angie came in, I stood up, and she planted a big one right on my lips and sat next to me, her hand curled around mine. I was in a semistate of shock, smiling stupidly in the face of this unabashed, almost bohemian warmth.

It was unlike any party I had ever been to. The first thing that struck me was that this crowd was slightly older than I was, in their thirties. A few were at the university, as instructors; others worked in Juárez; only one other person worked in El Paso besides Angie and Rocío. Only Marisela and her boyfriend—she, by the way, was just as beautiful as her sisters, if only a little runty—were close to my age. Since I was six-three, I didn't really stand out, at least I hoped I didn't, and no one even bothered to ask how old I was. After the initial flurry of kisses I felt immediately comfortable being there. The other thing I liked was that they mostly sat around smoking and talked about politics and ideas, about the differences in American and Mexican cultures, about sexual politics and the differences between men and women, and even about sex itself, in an affectionate and open way, not in raunchy terms meant to shock or brag. Sure, I didn't like the smoking part, but even this seemed different from Amherst. You weren't a pariah if you did it, and if you didn't smoke, you didn't have that look of utter disgust. You just accepted it as being a part of this group of friends. There was also none of the paranoia of being checked out or the strange hope of checking someone else out. Just about everyone was part of a couple. This seemed the most natural thing in the world. It wasn't a roomful of lonelies.

Someone brought in a trayful of little tostadas topped with pinto beans and a tangy white cheese—they called them *sopes*—and there was a huge bowl of guacamole, extra-spicy, and another bowl of tortilla chips on the coffee table. More trays of hot food would just appear suddenly in front of the small group. Angie and Rocío kept shuttling to and from the kitchen without missing a beat of the conversation and laughter. After a while a friend of theirs, Fernando, walked in, and he was carrying a guitar that he started strumming and tuning before he sang a Mexican ballad, very softly at first, until the rest of us joined in. I felt a little stupid because I didn't know the words, but everyone was smiling and having a great time, and after the second verse I knew most of the refrain. Fernando sang for a while; one or two or three would join in; sometimes he'd just play without singing, letting us decide whether to join in or just listen to the guitar. I laughed a lot with Angie because she would keep whispering all sorts of things in my ear. We were both a little drunk. Everyone else was too. They only got friendlier with one another, arm in arm at the sound of their favorite *rancheras*, singing and swaying and declaring to the world that they were Mexican and proud of it. There were serious discussions about death and the purpose of life. We also laughed wildly, at the simplest things. One of them suddenly stood up, took out some papers from his coat pocket—he was the only one wearing a jacket, but no tie—and demanded silence and was greeted first with hoots of excitement and then with a quiet so unnerving I thought I could hear myself perspire in the alcoholic heat. He recited some of his own written words in a voice at once passionate and then vulnerable. Poems about love and affliction and not knowing exactly who you were. Poems about courage and even the wretched life of the poor. I saw Angie shed a tear, and others too, including the men, whenever something struck them deeply in the heart. Instead of feeling embarrassed, they were comforted and held by their friends, and I thought I was a part of them. After what seemed centuries of time gone by, Angie squeezed my hand and said we had to go. I stood up, kissed the women good-bye, and shook hands with the men. They asked me to come back, and I said that I would.

As we drove across the international bridge, I could feel Angie's head resting on my shoulder, her hand on my lap, her slow and warm breathing. I thought she might be falling asleep, but when I glanced down, she smiled at me and nuzzled my neck. I exited at Airway Boulevard and pulled into the Holiday Inn. Angie said she would wait in the car. When I came back with the room keys, she was combing her hair in the rearview mirror and touching up her lipstick. We drove around and parked facing I-10, right at one of the entrances to the main part of the building. Our room, on the second floor of a long hallway, was huge, with two queen-size beds, a small denlike area with a couch, a writing desk, a bathroom almost as big as my dorm room, and the perfect quiet we had been looking for. She said it was tremendous, and I agreed. She asked me if I minded relaxing and talking for a while, and I said that I didn't mind at all. I put the chain on the door, found a small radio and turned it to a jazz station from Las Cruces, and sat down with her on the couch. She had already slipped off her shoes, so I did too.

We talked about everything. When I would come back to El Paso, and for how long. How many years I still needed to finish my studies. Whether I liked her sisters, and how many brothers and sisters I myself had. If she could save enough money to buy a new car, since her old one was giving her so much trouble. How she would do in her new position, and with which allies and avoiding which enemies. Whether I wanted to come back to El Paso forever. I told her that I wasn't sure. She reached over and took my hand, pulled me closer to her side. We kissed and caressed each other until nothing seemed to matter anymore, not our distance from each other and not the futility of our love, which wandered far away into the deepest part of my mind. Her perfume enveloped me, took me in, and carried me up. I asked her if she still wanted to be with me. She asked me if I could turn off the lights.

I held Angie Luna for hours in that room, and I remember the different times we made love like epochs in a civilization, each movement and every touch, apex upon abyss. In the luxury of our bed we tried every position and every angle. I explored the curves on her body and delighted in seeing the freedom of her ecstasy. Her desperate whispers and pleas. I told her I loved her, and she said she loved me too. We lay in bed with our limbs entangled, in a pacific silence that reminded me of existing on a beach just for the sake of such an existence. I couldn't imagine the world ever becoming better, and for some strange reason the thought slipped into my head that I had suddenly grown to be an old man because I could only hope to repeat, but never to improve on, a night like this. I finally took her home some time when the interstate was empty, and the bridges seemed to lead to nowhere, for they were desolate too.

I saw her a few more times before I left for Massachusetts, but nothing shattered me like that particular night, the night of my first Mexican party and my first teary-eyed *ranchera*, the night when I knew nothing would stop us, and then nothing did. And I just slammed into that black wall. I came back to El Paso for Christmas, having written to her but having received only one brief letter in return. She had returned to Chihuahua; her sister Rocío confirmed this in the empty coldness of a desert winter. Angie had returned to take care of her ailing father when nobody else would. I had never bothered to ask Angie about her mother, and I felt like an idiot. Rocío said that indeed their mother had died many years ago, of breast cancer and its neglect. She told me not to feel guilty about it; most of their friends didn't know either. She told me that Angie had made the decision to go back to Chihuahua, freely and without any remorse. Rocío asked me if I wanted to stay for a drink. I told her I couldn't but only because I thought I was going to choke. She said she would tell Angie I had stopped by. I thanked her for being so kind.

ILAN STAVANS

The Kiss

For Jules Chametzky

Angels can fly because they take themselves lightly.
—G. K. CHESTERTON, *Orthodoxy*

Among the most meaningful scenes between Dr. Isaac Otaño and his twenty-one-year-old student Lucha Reyes began casually. It took place on an elevator, Lucha looking more worried than usual. He knew she had returned from her native town in Mexico less than a month ago. They said hello and walked together to a bus stop. She was angry. She could not, would not concentrate and was far behind in her readings. She cried, and Dr. Otaño knew her tears were honest. Apparently she had received a phone call from an almost forgotten neighbor in La Cordillera. Surprises break the paste of routine; they force the world to a standstill. With both tact and aplomb the caller notified Lucha of her mother's sudden death: two gunshots, one in the chest, another in her forehead. She had been with her not long ago . . . and now she was dead. Right away Lucha's suspicions fell on Jaime López-Benítez, the village governor and a member of the ruling party, who had won an election less than seven months before by a landslide; when the votes were counted, 105 long-deceased peasants had magically endorsed him, and if judged by the number of voters, La Cordillera as a whole appeared to be twice as big as it was. But while she was acquainted with his spiderweb, she had no substantial evidence against López-Benítez, nothing to prove him guilty. In fact, as Otaño quickly found out, only one clue had become available to her: A passerby claimed to have seen a governor's bodyguard wrestling with her mother outside a cantina, but it was improbable, if anything, because Lucha knew her mother considered the cantina the devil's own home and would never come close.

Otaño talked to Lucha for less than twenty minutes. Days later he meticulously retraced Lucha's subsequent actions. That night she suffered insomnia and found no appetite to eat even a slice of bread with coffee. She again used the phone to reach out to her past and got in touch with a stepbrother, who gave her more bad news: Earlier in the week López-Benítez claimed her mother and three of her friends, whom Lucha knew very well, had been leaders of an opposition guerrilla group budding up in the jungle. Villagers took his statement with disbelief, if only because no such guerrilla warfare had ever been heard of in the area; but he justified the deaths as "a merciless response to subversive hoodlums." Her mother's body had been raped, badly tortured, and dumped in a nearby river. The wake was poorly attended. No newspaper acknowledged her death.

The following afternoon Lucha showed up at Otaño's office. She knocked at the door, he asked her to sit down, and she did, delicately, crossing her bare legs. She claimed to have an announcement. Yes, she had come to, ah . . . Well, to say good-bye. She was to depart once again, though no specific destination was suggested.

It wasn't necessary for Otaño to inquire any further. He immediately recalled the day when Lucha had invited him to her family's modest apartment in Queens: tiny porcelain figures, Lladró imitations, behind glass cabinets; oil paintings of landscapes with reflecting rivers and mysterious mountains and sunsets; an imposing crucifix on a yellow wall; a tableful of appetizing foods; a shy, polite uncle, fifty-five years perhaps, apologizing for the modesty and nonluxurious habitat. Otaño, for unexplained reasons, smelled tragedy then. His misgivings, he now knew, were well founded. In his office Otaño saw Lucha tremble, shaken, notably in despair, and realized once again his deep admiration for her. A young lady of high intellect, he thought. Leticia Reyes Montes: Her name, unremarkable, trite, had appeared in his rosters, exams, and letters of recommendation, but people, including himself, preferred the more charming Lucha. The air in his office felt tense. He was about to observe that . . . . well, nothing really. A highly confident Brooklyn native, a forty-two-year-old achiever incarcerated in his role of erudite model, Otaño was about to choose silence. After three months of encounters in classrooms, hallways, elevators and at bus stops, she had surely given him the necessary tools to interpret her dismay. Her good-bye no doubt was perplexing. "Be well, drop me a note" would have been a formal response, but what she needed was support. "Don't do anything you could regret," he finally said, a lousy, pretentious statement with little relevance to her dilemma.

A forthright woman, of incredible stamina, of independent means and strong ethic beliefs, Lucha was returning home. Otaño considered taking a stronger moral stand. He thought of persuading her not to be distracted by banal circumstances. You ought to, you must, you should realize . . . But in all truth, nothing banal—not in her mother's assassination, not in the governor's infamous reputation—had occurred, and thus he decided to keep the sermon to himself. Obviously nothing could change Lucha's mind. She seemed possessed.

Several months before, when he first talked to her in his office during course preregistration, he had been already well aware, through whispers and asides from colleagues and administrators, of her angelic stature. In class in spite of her high intellectual caliber, she almost never raised her hand and only reluctantly agreed to participate in discussions. She had vision and courage. She was his student for only one semester, but Otaño and Lucha bonded automatically. A degree of excusable sensuality, and a small one at that, heated their physiques. Early on he had fantasized sharing a delectable night with her in bed, exploring themselves, sucking and swallowing. But it was inconsequential: neither of them was lascivious enough to make the first advance. Furthermore, her body appearance preoccupied her only superficially. Otaño knew, for instance, that Lucha had dated only once because she perceived herself as obese, ungratifying to men, although it was far from true. The word *acumen* sums it all up. Lucha would stop by Otaño's office after classroom sessions. They would talk about imminent assignments, about Flaubert's "A Simple Heart," Isaac Babel's "Story of My Dovecot," Baldwin's "Sonny's Blues," and "God Sees the Truth but Waits," a story by Leo Tolstoy, whom, Otaño won't forget to this day, she disliked as morally irresponsible and scrupulously manipulative. Who would have thought that immersed in her thoughts, Lucha indirectly used her literary passion, her classroom time, her imagination to articulate her own visit to hell? She emulated the heroes studied in Otaño's course (Raskolnikov, Emma Woodhouse, Jaromir Hladík) and dreamed of a fate similar to theirs. A student's mind is enigmatic, unpredictable, and Otaño, eternally self-possessed, impossibly self-congratulatory, was satisfied only in provoking detours, in signaling new routes in Lucha's mental labyrinth, never in exploring any particular rendezvous together.

She had hazel eyes, curly hair, dark skin, and was short. Time and again Otaño suspected distant similarities to Madame Bovary, and this comparison made him smile. As he saw her, hers was a hidden beauty, one that streamed out from an inner force. When she found out her teacher was of Jewish descent, she inquired, not without deference, about it: about his philosophy, about his vision of God. Readings, she wanted readings. Sometime in midsemester Lucha, before death overwhelmed her, had begun planning a vast summer devoted to books, and Otaño responded by recommending what he knew and was acquainted with: some Martin Buber and Kafka, a handful of biblical chapters (which, as a result of her orthodox Catholic education, Lucha already knew by heart), Anne Frank's diary, and perhaps an encyclopedia. Their conversations would religiously settle on reminiscences of Mexico, a tourist site to him, a place emanating enormous ambiguity to her, especially La Cordillera, with its petite church in its center, its grocery store in perpetual disarray, where she bought soap, soda, her uncle's tobacco and beer, and her own chewing gum, the unfinished municipal building. She both loved and hated her town and frequently dreamed of scientific devices to erase it entirely from memory. Once in his office Lucha told Otaño, not without a twist of sadness and magnified sarcasm, about a dear sibling of hers who needed to be hospitalized of a so-called self-inflicted knife wound. She also talked about an ancient rivalry between the governor and a handful of families; about ridiculous (*offensive* is perhaps the right term) offers to buy her mother's property; about bodyguards firing gunshots at her mother's house, a rustic, unassuming enclave in an otherwise economically lucrative milieu; about a rebellious plan by various neighbors to denounce López-Benítez's intimidating practices as corrupt, unconstitutional, and undemocratic, which resulted in their subsequent disappearances.

Otaño's memory can evoke Lucha in a state of extreme exultation. While she would talk about the swift changes apparent in her village, her facial expressions would go from ire to desperation. She wished never to discuss the topic of La Cordillera again, but soon after she was nowhere else.

She longed for a full assimilation in the United States, for a share of happiness in a home away from home. Crossing the border, at age twelve, when the alphabet was still an alien intonation in her mouth, had transformed her magically. Up until then she had never seen a dishwasher, and could not conceive of women voting, which to her eyes seemed a contradiction. Her English language was as clear as the second law of thermodynamics. She had crossed by foot. In her past was her father, an old-looking young peasant of strong religious faith, who had cultivated a small landholding together with two siblings and had died of alcohol abuse when she was a child, was difficult for Lucha to evoke. In her past was also (or so she hoped) her beloved mother, who had given birth to thirteen children, four of whom died before their second birthday. And in her past were the miserable conditions that had forced an uncle, Eduardo Matías, to emigrate first. After settling in a city Lucha always

called *Tshi-ka-go*, where he earned his livelihood delivering piz-
zas by bicycle, the fat dollars he received were big enough to
expand his dreams, so he had sent word that Lucha and her older
sister, Cristina, should buy two train tickets (the money arrived
in an envelope). He would wait for them on his side just five
days later.

Life in *el futuro*, as she loved to call her new environment, was
benign. Together with her uncle Eduardo and sister Cristina, and
after a period of prosperity and fragile happiness, Lucha moved
to *Nueva Iorq*, where the three opened a small restaurant for spicy
appetites, El Rincón de Odeón. Disoriented yet eager, she had
pledged allegiance to a new flag only a few months ago. With
conviction Lucha talked to Otaño about the opening of "her
Mexican mind" and about the discomfort her distant village
generated in her. She repeatedly mentioned López-Benítez.
"Since his election," she argued, "he has evicted many of the
village's families, buying their property for a few pennies. But
my mother refuses to sell." She added: "She has received two
death threats."

Otaño got acquainted with Lucha's immediate family when
he was invited to Lucha's birthday party at her Queens apartment. Her sister had married an Italian, had three kids, and was
hardly interested in her surroundings. Cristina's purpose in life,
clearly, was to live the present to its fullest potential. In spite of
his shyness, Lucha's uncle was utterly charming. He looked like
a hardworking immigrant capable of eclipsing suffering and fa-
tigue by thinking of what was once left behind. Lucha had told
Otaño that both her uncle and Cristina were responsible for her
upbringing; she also claimed to share little with them aside from
room and food. Her intellectual curiosity, her insights drove her
to other latitudes. She hoped to become a teacher.

But not until later did he realize the scope of Lucha's full
power and determination. Looking back, he recalls a prophetic
encounter during which the conversation switched, somewhat
mechanically, to an inevitable topic: justice. Indeed, he still remembers Lucha pondering philosophical subjects like enlighten-
ment and moral consistency. Could one be fully educated yet

refuse to efface, to eclipse one's own instinctual drive? Were human and divine justice complementary? At one point Otaño remembers her saying: "Civilization is instigated by night-mares."

What haunted Lucha wasn't only the nightmarish vision of her mother's decomposing corpse but the rape itself. In fact, the sheer thought made her vomit. Tears ran down her cheeks. Although, as far as Otaño knew, nobody was ever able to verify the true identity of the rapist, Lucha had no doubt within her. Besides, her mother's womb was sacred. It had brought her and her siblings to this life and light; it was the origin, a temple. Reliving in her mind, night and day, the scene of terror and shrieks in which her mother was penetrated was a form of tor-ture from which Lucha found no exit. She needed to react.

Uneventful months, no more than three, went by after her departure. Otaño frequently thought of and even imagined a bloody, confrontational scene in her La Cordillera with a nasty bodyguard, in which Lucha was badly injured. But the tranquil-lity of summer took over. He was through with the semester, ready to put aside all endeavors. Then, one morning, he saw Lucha back in New York, walking by on the sidewalk. He headed toward her, greeted her with warmth, and inquired about her sojourn, but she appeared resistant. Their dialogue lasted less than a minute. She didn't seem interested in anything more.

Until a couple of afternoons later, when a phone call came. The moment Otaño heard her voice he understood that Lucha's story had been precipitating itself toward its irreversible end. She put to use words like *desperate, abysmal*, and *painstaking*. She wanted to see him alone and in private. He told her they could; he was busy with a visiting cousin the next few days, but free over the weekend. No, she had to see him right away, that very evening. He agreed and suggested the nearby Café Classé, but she begged to see him at his place. Again, *en secreto*.

This last dialogue, in which Otaño mostly listened and Lucha talked, lasted several hours. It's superfluous to expand her ac-count beyond the most essential. Her journey home had lasted less than a week. Like Anna Karenina's suicide, it was planned intuitively. Since Lucha had not yet paid her full tuition for the semester, after she said good-bye to Otaño she declared a default and dropped out of sight. That left her with several hundred dollars, which she used for her plane fare and theatrical props. She worked extra hours at El Rincón de Odeón, washing dishes, sweeping floors, and cleaning toilets, a routine she had long abandoned. While orchestrating her strategy, Lucha evoked her mother's gentle smile. She talked to her through silences. She asked God to give her enough strength to rectify her mother's miserable death and the courage to perform her task in total anonymity; if anybody in La Cordillera ever recognized her, she would be forced to return defeated, ethically dissatisfied. The whole trip, by plane, train, bus, and walking, took her three days. She arrived exhausted and slept for thirty-six hours in a fourth-class hotel room, where she had registered under an alias, Yigany Lomelí.

Did Lucha carry out her entire plan? Otaño has no doubt. In spite of the enormous embarrassment she felt, the shame she underwent while detailing graphically, methodically, the course of her path, Lucha's voice never betrayed her. She had used a handful of theatrical props: makeup, a wig, cigarettes, sneakers, and a vast closet of Americanized costumes. Pretending to be an American journalist, dressed as a tourist, with camera, baseball hat, and all, she wandered silently at night around La Cordillera. She revisited what had been at one point her mother's property, now repossessed by the Ministry of Public Work. Her childhood house had been burned to the ground; stones and fallen trees were dispersed over the field; a merciless tractor had damaged it all. Lucha studied the latest construction sites and wandered around the municipal building until she thought she had memorized the governor's routine.

What happened next, in Otaño's view, was completely stunning. She requested a meeting with her mother's victimizer. At first López-Benítez's secretary took her for someone else, then apologized. She inquired the purpose of Lucha's visit to La Cordillera, to which Lucha answered that she was writing an article for an American newspaper about recent developments in the village, thanks in full to the governor's uncompromising vision. She was allowed to go in and, as planned, proceeded to befriend her target. López-Benítez employed several consecutive mornings in showing off his major achievements: an electrical plant, a still-unfinished highway, a three-star hotel. Lucha asked about the well-being of the villagers, and the governor delivered a brief speech, strictly political: People are better off, a young generation is taking control, and so on.

Lucha was coquettish. López-Benítez kept focusing on her naked legs. After an hour they separated. She returned to her hotel and spent the next hours alone, drafting a three-page manifesto on legal abuse and the need for justice. She used the jargon of old-time revolutionaries, a Ché Guevara rhetorical twist here or there, blaming the north for colonialism and accusing the governor of lawlessness. She invented a full-size guerrilla group, armed by foreigners, preparing a coup d'etat. She then sealed the letter in an envelope and addressed it to a nearby radio station.

Lucha claimed to have mailed the letter just before the seventh night, when she was invited to a private party at an exclusive villa. Drinks were abundant. López-Benítez got drunk, made everybody laugh, and in the end invited her to his office. Luck was on her side. It was late when they arrived. The streets were empty. In his car he placed his hands on her. She felt dizzy. She wanted to vomit. Her mother's image would not vanish from her mind. The man who had raped and killed her mother was now seeking his pleasure with Lucha. A few minutes into his office, her blouse and skirt on the floor, his pants unzipped, he said, "Kiss it." At that point Otaño heard her swear. The clock on top of his desk ceased its endless pace. In less than a minute, enough to accumulate the strength she had prayed for and required, Lucha assumed the little that was still hers in La Cordillera. She ceased being Yigany Lomelí and became, once and for all, her old self: Leticia Reyes Montes. In a single bite she sealed her past forever.

Governor Jaime López-Benítez died of two gunshots, one to his chest, the other to his forehead. He was found swimming in a pool of blood, castrated. A succinct communiqué received by a radio station attributed the crime to guerrilla warfare in the jungle.

Otaño sat silently while Lucha concluded her remarks. Once again she was visibly shaking, except that now she was terribly frightened as well. Where to go? She said she was beyond herself. She had become her own prisoner. "I've achieved the impossible. . . . I bit the dust. . . . I've cut myself loose from my roots."

Since then he has seen Yigany Lomelí once or twice on the sidewalk. They manage to exchange a smile of complicity, but little else. It's as if they didn't know each other.

VERÓNICA GONZÁLEZ
Through the Raw Meat

She was horribly affected by his death. Ridiculously so, since she had never actually known him. She could still feel the hundred tiny strips of meat inside her, and her stomach ached with all of it. She felt the softness of the wind blow up against her face, her arms, her bare legs. She attempted to replay the feel of the initial inexplicable and unavoidable attraction that had struck at her center. But she could only feel the water hit her, see a sky red beyond the thundering clouds, know the air was transparent between the drops that fell in the heat of that swampish August early evening, and then she cried, lugubriously cried, in that park, unwashed hair, pathetically staring through moist eyes at St. Zenobias and St. Luke, St. Bartholomew and St. Anthony of Padua rhythmically rising and falling as they shifted weight on the damp wood of the distant seesaws.

No, no, no. Like this:

It was raining. It was hot. I was sitting in a seedy park, where, by the way, I knew no saints played. And my hair was dirty. I'd begun to like it that way.

It was then that I first saw him. He appeared, only a little wet—his hair covered in a silver veil of tiny drops—and I followed him as he walked through water, as he proceeded with sullen eyes focused on the earth below. It was as if I were drawn up off my bench and made to follow him down Big Oak Street to Fragrant Pine Avenue. Past stores where merchandise would have, on a sunny day, lined the street, past bakery after bookstore after bank, to Quaking Aspen Road, where he walked half a block down, then into an ugly gated house, and I, after slowly passing by, turned back and stood in the now-pouring rain to stare mutely at the building's streaked facade.

I had been sitting in that park alone, feeling sorry for myself and wondering why I, in an attempt to ditch my past, had moved to this city where I knew almost no one, and he, that beautiful thin man in black clothing, had come out of nowhere. He was tall and had, I think, light hair. He had green, slitty eyes and lips and a nose and wore too long shorts and large thick-soled shoes.

I stood in the rain, and I knew where he lived, and I'd hang out in the park every day until I saw him again. Then I'd run up to him and stroke his thick (I think light) hair, look into his sad, downcast eyes—kiss—and whisper my name. That would be the beginning. It stopped raining, and I walked home.

Indoors I jutted my head out the window of my third-story room and spit at the heads of the old men on the stoop below. I missed. I really hadn't even tried to come close, but the gesture made me feel better. I was getting sick of them and the same beer-tainted questions they asked every day. Yeah, I was from California. Yeah, I didn't have a job. Yeah, I stayed indoors an awful lot, was awful quiet. Yeah, almost every time I came home, after finally venturing out, I carried with me packages (full of junk I didn't really want)—and I missed, hadn't even tried to hit.

I pulled my head in and read the letter I had had to reach around the fat one, who always wore a muscle T-shirt, to get. It was from my mother:

Another earthquake. The heat. My father and she had visited my grandmother. The psychics had predicted another, bigger quake on the twenty-fifth. The cats were fine, and so were my grandmother's eyes. The newscaster on Channel 9 had said the psychics were often right. There was in fact a fault line going right through the mountains where they'd said it would occur. And my mother, my beautiful, intelligent mother, whose mother, my father claimed, was a wannabe *santera*, seemed worried about these psychic predictions.

I felt something must be wrong for her, something must be wrong for her to fall under such influences. And I worried. But I didn't call.

Instead I jotted a short description of the one I had seen on a small piece of paper that I then folded and refolded. I didn't know his name, and I hoped it would work anyway. I lit a pink adoration candle and placed the piece of paper under it on a dish I'd covered with honey. I tried to remember the Hail Mary but couldn't. I wondered if menstrual blood really worked, and if yes, how it was that women tricked men into drinking the magical love-inducing drops. I might have to ask my grandmother.

My hair was still wet. I stood in front of the mirror and flattened it down on my head, then pulled it back hard until I felt my scalp hurt, and painted my eyes black. Black eyes and a fake mole by my mouth, and I looked at myself in the mirror until I was full with the altered image. There.

I walked one block down to Cock Tales, where I had agreed to meet my friend Eve. I ordered a cuba libre and tried to eavesdrop on the two women in the next booth.

I tried but couldn't hear, so I watched them laugh and sip and smile and lick red lips. When glasses were emptied, the taller one stood and held her arms out in supplicant indignation as her friend offered her money she wouldn't take. She fluffed her hair and strutted toward the bar, and the friend, still smiling, glanced my way. I imagined it an accusatory smile and looked away, pretending I had not been watching them. I took a large drink, and as my discomfort grew in the crowded bar, I more and more wanted to be alone, to be able to focus my thoughts on the one I had followed.

But I heard Eve's voice, and when I turned, I saw she was

surrounded by full glasses and laughing faces. She saw me, shimmied her bigness over, and gave me a dry peck on the cheek.

"You'll get used to it . . . everyone kisses in New York." The smiler waved at Eve. "How long you been here?"

"I don't know. Not long. I don't feel too well, though." I did my best to create a half smile that might serve to indicate an undefined ailment.

Eve ignored my encoded grimace. "Well, you look fine, very dramatic—is that new?"

I remembered the mole and was suddenly embarrassed. "Oh, yeah, the wonders of eye liner. Look, I think I'm gonna go after this drink."

"What's wrong? Listen, you have to start getting out. I wanted you to meet some people."

I could tell she was disappointed, maybe even a little disgusted, so I touched at my center and defined my self-created illness for her benefit. "You know . . . my weak stomach."

While I finished my drink, I asked some questions and learned some things. She'd been in New York only a couple of years, but she knew everyone and could offer layers of information to pile onto the thinnest of descriptions: tall, thin, long (I think light) hair, sad green eyes, ugly brown shoes. She'd known his brother, Jack, and told how he'd died in a fight. He, whose name she could not recall, was strange, never went out, had no close friends. He'd gotten worse since his brother's death. People said he walked with rocks in his shoes, as a penance for the death he felt he'd somehow caused. She asked why I asked, my Eve, who loves to divulge information in an urgent, uninterrupted straight line. I ignored her question, leaned slowly forward, and kissed her pink cheek. "I'll get used to New York; soon I'll be kissing everyone too." She frowned at my departure and threatened to call my mother to discuss my well-being as I walked out the door.

I would sleep in the glow of my pink candles. And I would follow him. Follow him again—my newfound avocation.

★   ★   ★

It was by following that I learned that he worked at the butcher's. There were several on my street, and he worked at the one farthest from my house, and I didn't eat meat, but I started going there anyway. I would order what I learned to order, and I would give the meat to the stray cats that lived in the park. They started recognizing me and would wait drooling in the early afternoon.

Then, after three weeks, he did too; he started recognizing me. And I knew that my magic had begun to work.

I'd heard his name—Edward—on my second visit, and I'd written it on a piece of paper and switched it with the description I had previously placed on the honey covered plate under the candle. I'd resurrected it out from deep within:

> Hail Mary, full of grace,
> the Lord is with Thee.
> Blessed art thou among women
> and blessed is the fruit
> of thy womb Jesus:
> Holy Mary, Mother of God,
> pray for us sinners now
> and at the hour of our death.
>
> Amen

and I'd recite it three times whenever I lit a new candle. I scrubbed my hair clean, dried it, then rewet it with my grandmother's violet water every day before I went in, and now I noticed he looked at me. Looked for a bit too long while I ordered what I heard other ladies order.

The next day it was the same look. And the next day it was the same look. That look, in combination with the smell and the wait in the too-crowded shop, made me flushed. He handed me the white-papered package, and I gave him the money I always gave in exchange for the meat and those, now noticeably too long stares, and my cheeks became red with the heat.

I loved him. I now knew I loved him. And all the way home I thought about our words:

"Half a pound of flank steak . . . please."

"Is this piece all right?"

"Yes . . . please."

It was something nearly concrete, and I manipulated the memory, replaying it again and again. As I walked, I brought him forward: Edward in his bloodstained apron surrounded by slabs of this beast and that and huge tongues and ripped-out hearts. I smelled his meat-soaked skin, and I saw him chopping and cutting with huge knives. I saw his fingers, always with some red, wrapped around the whiteness of my package as he handed me what I'd been waiting for, and I knew now that I loved him.

I didn't stop for the cats. I got the flank steak home, unpacked it, and sliced it into one hundred tiny strips, which I fried on the highest flame. The multitudinous worms sizzled, and their vapor settled in my pores. I went to my bed and sat with the still-hot pan on my lap and ate them slowly, counting as I went. And though my stomach began aching at number thirty-three, I kept eating and counting, and I knew that the cats would be mewling and pacing.

And then I dreamed. For three days I dreamed awake. And in my daydream I'd see Edward in his shop, exactly as in full wakefulness, always flanked by those dirtied large posters of St. Luke and St. Bartholomew, the patron saints of butchers. As in life he rarely said a word, only occasionally lifting those beautiful green eyes, catching mine, then letting them drop. In my dream I realized it was this that drew me to him: his aloneness, his silent, somber solitude. Then I would take control. I would stand, the ladies falling back and forming a circle around me, I in a white crinoline robe, and whisper to him:

> With the aching in my heart
> as I wait until tomorrow
> When I spy on your large hands
> make their way through the raw meat

With the mocking in my ears
of the ones who saw my
stares at smooth
Severance; the cleave,
As instructed by your saints

With the pain I felt inside
As you tore my things away:
my eyes and ears
and throat and heart
They were yours—to you I gave

And I settled for the knowledge
that you didn't know a thing
as I waited for a breath
of an air that held your scent.

                                        Amen

Then he'd look at me. For too long he'd look. Then, finally, he'd smile. He'd reach over with long arms, and he'd tear my things away and feed them to me slowly, slowly. And I loved him more. Then he'd float, up toward the ceiling, and his feet, freed of the thick-soled shoes, would drip blood from the wounds caused by the rocks. I'd catch those small drops in my mouth, where they tasted of wine, intoxicating with the thought of his liquid inside me. For three days I saw these images, over and over again—circular so that the end became the beginning—and each time I loved him more.

When, after three days, I rose from my bed, I'd decided. I lit my candles and washed my hair. I rewet it with violet water, then walked the twelve blocks to the butcher's, counting the tiny strips inside me as I went.

Today I will stop, I told myself. Today I will blow out the candles. Today I will stop believing in St. Anthony, whom as a child I'd used to find things: "Go get a sock. Tie a knot in it. You're tying St. Anthony of Padua's balls together. He'll be in so much pain he'll help find what you've lost." I would obediently tie his balls as my grandmother with the bad eyes gave me power over the world. Today I will stop using the sickly-sweet violet water she'd given me as a gift. Today I will call my mother, whom I've been worried about for a month. Today I will go meet Eve and her beautiful friends at Cock Tales. Today I will put an end to my own self-lacerating silence, and today, I told myself, Edward will be mine.

The shop was closed. My shop was closed. There was a sign in the window saying it would remain closed all the following week. How could they when I had decided that today? I must have stood there rereading for much too long because, because that nosy old bat with the black wig and white-powdered face came over and started in on me with that running, inclement voice of hers.

"They're closed, you know. For all next week they're closed."

"Yes, I see—"

"On account of Eddie. I see you in here every day, didn't you know? It's been closed since yesterday. You should have known. So much has happened in that poor family. It's horrible. Horrible."

"What?"

"Right off the Williamsburg Bridge. They found traces of blood on his shirt, under his nails, and on his feet, and they thought he was involved in something, some kind of crime. But of course they found out he was nothing but a butcher. It was mentioned on the TV two days ago, didn't you see? His uncle is furious . . . about the TV. He thought it only right to close for a while. Eddie was his favorite."

"What's that?" I wanted her to stop, to shut up, but I asked to be tortured, to have it drawn out. I realized she had probably been standing there waiting, waiting for just such an opportunity, someone to gossip to, and instead of telling her to stop, I begged her to go on. "What's that?"

"The church bells? Saturday afternoon mass."

"No—I mean . . ."

"Oh. Yes. Of course. His favorite nephew. He was a nice boy,

Eddie, strange, though, so sad, so quiet. His brother was killed while breaking up a fight between Ed and another boy a year ago. Now this. Their poor mother, all the tragedy has her wrinkled. She used to hum nothing but boleros before; now it's always tangos."

I walked away as she began to hum.

I thought about how he'd come to me in a vision, allowing me to drink from his wounds before leaving for good. I imaged the silver veil that had covered his hair the first time I saw him now lining the inside of his lungs, and a qualm inched through my insides. I slowly walked home without any packages and looked right past the old men on the stoop, who somehow knew not to ask questions. I went upstairs and put out the pink candles and lit a pure white one, and then I took out a black sock and tied St. Anthony's balls in a huge knot—and still haven't set him free.

There, there. Two lines of white space are enough time for mourning, especially since Eddie did not die. He is alive as I write this. But you must understand she was in a terribly romantic way when she told you her version. Besides, she wants your pity. Now the narration may proceed.

She arrived at the butcher's in quite a state. She embarrassed herself that day.

She ran into the meat shop wearing nothing but the cheap crinoline lining of a tackily fancy dress her grandmother had picked out for her. She rushed in with the words on her lips, and she couldn't control them, though in all fairness to her I should point out that a part of her tried. They were already shooting looks at her as she pushed her way through the crowded shop. She was a strange sight: unbathed and mad-eyed in the sloppily torn white lining of her grandmother's dress. She smelled bad too, the combination of the too-sweet flower perfume and a body in need of washing. And she was pushing people this way and that, almost knocked over the old lady with the white pancake makeup and matted black wig. The old lady screamed, then scowled at the girl's back.

Then, when she was right in front of him, she did it. She opened her mouth, a little too loudly exclaimed, "Edward!" and already she had gone too far, for how was it, he must have wondered, that this madwoman knew his name? He looked up from his meat and met her red eyes. "Edward! . . . I love you." She whispered the last part, but it was so silent that everyone heard. Poor Edward looked down, quickly dropped his eyes, and his uncle had to come from behind the register and ask her to leave. She wouldn't move at first, just kept staring at Ed, so the uncle gently shoved her a little, to get her feet going. Forty-eight eyes followed her out, and the old lady in the black wig elbowed her ribs as she moved slowly past. She stood outside the shop, to the side of the entrance, for almost two hours, not moving at all, only occasionally blinking and not uttering a sound. When it began to drizzle, she absentmindedly walked to the park, where she sat on the bench and, surrounded by nineteen stray cats, cried in the light August rain.

DANIEL COOPER ALARCÓN

The Economy of Virtue

The frayed tether is pulled taut, once resilient fibers un raveling with astonishing ease. It is made from the coarse hemp of maguey cactus that sprawls among the surrounding mountains, and its reputation is centuries old, durability unquestioned, the effects of wind and rain overlooked. The burro straining at the frail rope wants only to escape the heat and flies by plunging its diseased body into cool lake water just ten yards away, and as the last spidery strand releases, it jerks forward and plods into the water, soothed by the deceptively cool mud drawing it down, encasing its legs. There are shouts from the people chatting nearby, but the burro ignores them. Only when the mud reaches its chest does it begin to bray, a series of frightened cries that will haunt the man cinching the broken end of rope around his waist.

Ladies and gentlemen, never say, "A picture is worth a thousand words." Rather, a picture *needs* a thousand words.

A cockroach skittered across the tiled floor, bathed in thin light the color of diluted blood. She squashed it and looked at herself in the mirror, her tired reflection made sinister by the safelight, a surprise that made her reach out and touch the glass with spread fingertips. On her wrist the face of her watch told her it was one thirty-five in the morning; already she had worked six hours in the cramped, makeshift darkroom. The heat was oppressive, but she made only rapid concessions to it, now and then brushing a limp strand of hair from her eyes, then returning her attention to the scene she struggled to draw forth from the chemical baths.

It formed piecemeal: bits of the burro's large frightened eye and part of the priest's hand reaching for the as yet invisible bridle, his fingers working desperately—an illusion created by the waves of developer rocking in the dirty plastic tray. A similar tray containing stop bath rested on the toilet tank, and the bathtub was littered with unsatisfactory prints. Those with potential she clipped to the line that normally held the shower curtain.

A picture needs a thousand words.

The phrase certainly had not been any great revelation to her. Anyone who had ever looked through a viewfinder or spent an hour in a darkroom knew the camera was a notorious liar. But despite her disdain for the cliché, she knew she would spend a good portion of the next day in front of her typewriter, trying to set down how icy cold the lake water had been when it splashed up through the slats in the rotting dock. She had a photo of Rubén bent over the outboard motor, weeds necklaced about the propeller, but she did not have the fascination she felt watching his muscles define themselves under his T-shirt as he started the engine. It was erotic, but also a kind of wonder at the complexity and simplicity of the human arm and how it worked. She could photograph his smile, but not the singsong cadence of his native tongue or the charming slips he made in English. In the sultry afternoon the sounds of her old typewriter would drift like the chatter of birds into the heat-stilled *zócalo* as she tried to get it all down.

She wanted the reader to experience the cold metallic seats of the launch, the thick scent of gasoline as the engine caught, the hard impact of the boat repeatedly slapping the water, scallops of silver wake fanning out behind. She could no longer remember what she and Rubén said, only that they had to shout to be heard over the engine. Later, panning the other side of the lake, she saw them: a drowning burro, a thin, muddied priest trying to reach it, and a group of frightened onlookers anchoring the rope about his waist. In that instant she knew it was hopeless, but the professional in her took over, pushing the zoom forward in a smooth, skilled motion that uprooted the surreal tableau and brought it forward with incredible speed, depositing it on the glassy water next to their boat.

Every time the priest tried to grab the bridle, the burro tossed its head in terror, its movements working it deeper into the mud. The moment was coming; she took the picture.

"There is no fucking moment of truth, Iverson," her colleague Frank Hewitt used to say. "Just f-eight and be there."

If it had been Frank in the boat instead of her, he would have set the camera on autowind and held down the release. That was what separated them; there was no artistry to his photographs.

So absorbed was she in that compact window of lens it was a shock to see the burro fall heavily and sidelong into the water, until the gunshot reached the boat. The priest disappeared, then was pulled from the lake, his face caked with mud, eyes glazed with fear.

All this would be telegraphed by her typewriter keys to the tourists in the quiet square. If they knew the code, they might decipher a series of unsuccessful attempts to explain the value a Tarascan family placed on a fly-ridden burro. Much later, exhausted, she would have her thousand words. Unsatisfied, she would nonetheless dutifully file them and the photo via telex to Mexico City. There the text would be slashed, and if the photo ran, its cutline—her long afternoon's work—would read: "PÁTZCUARO, MEXICO—Father Pedro Cruz tries unsuccessfully to rescue a burro drowning in the muddy shallows of Lake Pátzcuaro. Moments later the animal was shot by its owner to spare it further agony."

After lifting the soggy photo from the fixer, she clipped it to the line and eyed it critically. It was perfectly timed; she had captured the decisive moment. Leaning back, she looked around the bathroom. Photos were strewn about in no order, scattered in a disjointed record. She grabbed a handful from the tub and shuffled them, trying to get the chronology right, pausing to massage her neck, sunburned and sore from the camera bag. It was time to quit. She was hot and tired, queasy from the fumes. The excitement of work was gone, and she knew that in the daylight the photos would seem lackluster. Leaning against the bathroom door, she held one of them up to the safelight and appraised it, then compared it with the enlargement she had made and was surprised to see details she hadn't noticed before. That was Mexico, she thought, so intricate, so outside the realm of representation. Janet closed her eyes and tossed the photos into the tub with the others, scattered, disordered, out of time.

Janet wrote:

In hard, pelting rain four campesinos walk single file in an uneven ditch beside a highway trellised about squat green mountains. They have already walked three miles, still five miles short of the cane fields where they hope to find work. If they are fortunate, it will be a ten-hour day of backbreaking labor. The rain caroms off their hats and threads rivulets around their arms.

"Let me have a cigarette, Ramón."

"You know what your doctor said."

"That doctor. What good is he? Ask Arturo."

Their white shirts and black trousers are dirty and patched, and the rain has soaked through the thin leather of their shoes. From their belts swing rusty scythes.

Silently Arturo curses Martín for reminding him of what he has been unable to forget. A year ago death claimed his young wife and left him a widower. Every day he listens to the voice of Dr. Gómez when she was first diagnosed: confident; reassuring; even jovial: "No one dies of pneumonia anymore. Your wife will be fine." Two months and a regimen of powerful antibiotics later, she slipped away, drowning in her own lungs. Now, at thirty-eight, Arturo works relentlessly during the week, spends his Saturday nights drinking and his Sundays hating every sigh Father Cruz makes behind the cold brass confessional grille. He says nothing, keeping his eyes fixed on the mud-slicked gravel.

On the other side of the highway the mountain breaks away sharply in a vicious tangle of scrub pines, cactus, and rocks. Above the men, to their left, occasional small farms can be made out through the curtain of rain, terracing up the mountains. They walk slowly but steadily, talking little, conserving energy. Martín's son, Miguel, thinks about the tamales his mother made and packed for them, sweetening the meat by baking it in banana leaves. But breakfast is still another mile away, when they reach the halfway mark.

To take his mind off the hunger, he thinks about the family's upcoming Sunday trip to Morelia. Every week they took the six o'clock bus, crowded among the other families, the babies crying and the driver's cassette tape blaring, and, depending on the number of stops, arrived close to noon. Then, while his father disappeared into some of the biggest, most beautiful buildings he had ever seen and his mother went to the market, Miguel would squeeze into the crowd of campesinos outside the Sony store (his father joked that the store had replaced the cathedral as the most popular spot in Morelia). Taking up a seat on the pavement with the others, he would look through the big plate glass window and watch the television screens. There were many screens of different sizes and shapes, and there were at least three screens for each channel. Although most of the boys his age liked to watch football or baseball, Miguelito liked to watch the American TV shows. Dallas was his favorite. He dreamed of having a ranch like that. He promised himself that someday he would turn his father's small farm into a magnificent hacienda just like Ehsouthfork. When his attention wandered, he noticed the city boys in their elegant clothes and mirrored sunglasses and the city girls in their short skirts. He felt confused, intimidated, excited, and angry. Later, as they returned home, just before dozing off in the crook of his father's arm, he wished for his own TV.

Miguel listens to the rain sizzle as the cars cut swiftly past on the adjacent highway and tightens his three-fingered grip around the machete (his fourth finger lost to the same blade in a moment of inattentiveness). They plod on, heads bowed so their hats can deflect the hard stinging rain, each man lost in a kind of vacancy, a willed numbness, also to shield the rain. From the corner of his eye Miguel sees jagged veins of white light throb in the sky. A moment later *thunder drums across the valley, echoing from mountain to mountain. Although he did not think it possible, it begins to rain even harder, so hard walking is temporarily impossible. Holding their ponchos over their heads in a makeshift tarp, they huddle together in the ditch.*

Miguel watches with concern as his father convinces Ramón to give him a cigarette. The doctor has told Martín his lungs are bad and he must quit smoking, but Miguel says nothing. Even greater than his worry is the happiness it brings him to see satisfaction slide over his father's face as he inhales deeply. Lighting the cigarette in the rain proves to be tricky business, but they accomplish it after several tries. They talk little or not at all, certainly not about the rain that makes their work possible.

"Will they have work?" ventures Ramón.

"They'll tell us they have none, so they can pay us next to nothing. But they'll work us. No question."

"Cabrones."

Miguel's father starts to commiserate but is stopped by a series of deep coughs that shake his body and lets the rain pound in. The others look on with concern as he coughs up phlegm and almost drops to his knees.

"Qué malo."

"He should be in a hospital."

Arturo and Ramón steady him while Miguel stretches out his hand, but Martín brushes it away and forces a smile. "It's nothing, just the rain," he says. On his feet, his arms draped over his friends, the rain streaming down, they laugh together.

I want a close-up of those hands, she thought. *Follow the forearms in from each side of the frame, Tri-X to contrast the thick black hair with the arms and the whitewalls with the rubber. Capture the change in skin tone in the fingers as he exerts pressure on the lug wrench. Hurry, quick, just before the nut loosens. There.*

Now the priest, standing shoulders hunched against the downpour that makes his features hazy, cloudy. A mood to fit the man . . . wait for it, wait, now as he turns—

"Please, Janet," Father Cruz said, raising his hand.

"I didn't think you'd mind."

"It's nice to be asked."

She shrugged, then thought better of it. This man was an important contact. "I'm sorry, Father, you're right. I should've asked."

The word *Father* was a hard one to get out, and it didn't sound right. After all these years it still carried contempt when she spoke it. . . . Janet was surprised by the self-revelation. Was her old antagonism with the church coming back to her? Because of the priest? She remembered how he had tried to save the burro on the lake. . . .

"Father Cross. That's too much. I like Father Pete much better. You don't mind if I call you Father Pete?"

He frowned.

"It'll grow on you, trust me."

Despite himself, Peter smiled. It was a nice smile, Janet thought. She liked how it fought against itself and lost, revealing a conspicuous gold tooth in front. She could tell he was self-conscious about it.

She bagged the camera against the rain and reflected that one of the drawbacks to being a writer and photographer was that you never stopped working. Even when the camera was sealed tightly in its waterproof bag, her eyes went right on taking pictures, framing them, asking, Color or black and white? How much distance to put between? Vertical or horizontal?

Below Rubén's feet, the rain created channels, eddies that crisscrossed and formed muddy deltas. Rain ran down the runnel of her back, soaked her blouse. It was all a bit ludicrous, the three of them standing in the rain because of their pride. This was no mountain shower, either, but an uneven rain that clattered off the car roof in staccato bursts. The sound reminded her of the summer a house had been built next to her parents', with the carpenters hammering away. Janet shivered. This was not the way she thought the day would go. When Father Cruz had agreed to meet with her, she anticipated an interview in a musty room, damp and dark. But then he asked her if she would like to visit the Eduardo Ruiz National Park.

Rubén wrestled the flat off the wheel, its treads packed with muddy mortar, and looked up at them exasperated.

"Señora, Padre Cruz, please . . . go back in the car."

"Too late now," Janet said.

Father Cruz just smiled, squinting into the rain. Janet could see he was shivering.

"Are you thinking about the burro?" she asked.

He was too startled to respond. Rubén stopped tightening the nuts and held the lug wrench immobile.

"We were on the lake, sightseeing," she explained.

Peter nodded, looking down at the muddy ground, where rivulets of rain cut into the road's shoulder. "Then you saw more than you bargained for."

"Watch your feet."

The car eased down and settled into its springs. Rubén hoisted the jack, tools, and flat into the trunk.

"That was very brave."

"Very foolish. That burro had more than one disease; it would have been dead in a year anyway."

When they had picked her up in the morning, it was six, and the plaza was still and cold, the only sound a steady scratching from an old Tarascan woman wrapped tightly in a rebozo and sweeping with a gnarled broom of bound willow branches. The stone benches of the plaza were wet with dew, and sleepy waiters were slowly taking the chairs off the outdoor tables.

Rubén's old Buick climbed laboriously up out of the low plaza toward the highway, past roadside restaurants that sold *pescado blanco* and handmade sweaters. The *camino* out of Pátzcuaro was beautiful, a boulevard bordered by stately old trees whose branches entwined overhead. The truck sped though their lattice of shadow, then slowed as Rubén maneuvered them gently over a set of *topes*. Soon the vista became so romantic, so cliché, so surreal, Janet said, "No one will believe me." She began to photograph: plowed fields, black and heavy with moisture; fog buoyed in the hillocks and mountain elbows. Ahead and to the left a campesino held the reins of two oxen, his arms extended in supplication, while the rich soil spilled over his bare feet. The road twisted, wound, bent, unwound, sometimes a semi trailer nearly pushing them off the road. Cutting through a marshy valley below them, a railroad track meandered. Cornstalks grew through the burned-out shells of cars. Children sold iguanas by the side of the road. A naked doll rested in the crotch of a tree.

The pueblos were white scars on the landscape, towns built along the old highway to Mexico City. Between them were abandoned mines with silent veins of silver and quiet, unattended apiaries like desk drawers stacked by the road, their hidden hives the only outside structures not covered with political advice for the upcoming presidential election. Riding in the back of a big truck in front of them, two men sat bundled up against the mountain wind that tossed the tall pines about between the skeletal legs of massive power conductors. It was then, as they rounded a corner, that they saw the thunderstorm sweeping toward them.

"That's a new record," Father Cruz said.

"Not bad in the rain."

Janet was embarrassed that they insisted on speaking English, even though she continued to answer in her broken Spanish.

"Okay, crazy people," Rubén said, "can we get out of this rain?"

As she turned to get into the car, she saw a group of campesinos on the other side of the road, about a hundred yards away.

"Coming, Janet?"

Looking through her lens, she concentrated on the men clustered in the vertical frame, their ponchos held over their heads in a kind of tarp, the men laughing and smiling. They had their hands cupped about a cigarette, and suddenly a match flared, exposing the creases of their leathery skin. *Poverty shouldn't be so picturesque*, she thought, but snapped the picture anyway.

★ ★ ★

"Tell me something, Father Pete. When you give a sermon like the one you're going to give today, do you sprinkle in a few jokes?"

"Jokes?"

"Yes, you know, like 'A funny thing happened on my way to church today.' "

"My job is not to entertain."

"I appreciate that, but you know, my major objection to organized religion is that nobody involved in it seems to have any sense of humor. Take the Bible, for example."

"What do you want? Jesus cracking jokes around a campfire?"

"Why not? He was human, wasn't he?"

Cruz allowed himself a smile. "This book you're writing, is it a theological tract?"

"That's right, the theology of tourism. The tourist as God."

"Whoever hatched this idea is crazy. We have no ocean here."

"No, but you have more lakes than any other state in the republic. State-planned tourism is Mexico's economic panacea: Cancún, Ixtapa, Huatulco—"

"Do you know what Cancún was like before 'seventy-three? *Selva*. Everything was flown in, and the city was built from the ground up. But here there are lives in the balance. Not everyone wants to work in a hotel."

"Some do."

"Let's just say I don't believe in trickle-down economics, especially where the water's bad. Have you ever been to Acapulco? Just go a few miles inland, away from the expensive hotels, and look at the misery there. And Acapulco has been a tourist town for over thirty years."

The car rumbled on, descending from the mountains to Uruapan. Ahead, walking single file in the ditch, were boys in tattered shirts and pants, some with sombreros, all with rusty scythes in their hands. The car passed, spraying them with dirty water. None of the boys looked up.

"You think the resort developers were just snowing me? You don't think a resort will bring in a lot of money, spur the economy—"

"Oh, sure. A lot of money. And it will all end up in the bank accounts of PRI officials. Those kids who cut cane for a living won't see any of it."

They were out of the mountains, the tires cutting through small bays of water sunk into the highway. On either side of the road, disappearing into the horizon, were orderly rows of squat trees that spread their branches like the ribs of old umbrellas.

"Perhaps we should get another opinion," Janet said. "What do you think about all this, Rubén?"

Rubén shifted uncomfortably in his seat and watched the road. "*Pues*, I don't think anything is ever all good or all bad. But you know, I have a cousin in Acapulco who hires out his boat. He never stops complaining about the tourists, the gringos. But he makes good money, takes good care of his family. Two of his children are attending the university. And I look at my friends here, especially those who are farmers. They live in a different century from us. I think they deserve a chance for something better. If it fails, it fails, but at least we had a chance."

Silence took hold of the car. "The countryside is beautiful," Janet said, thinking it an idiotic thing to say.

But it was beautiful. The vegetation had become almost tropical; rubbery leaves ten feet long depended from trees with ringed trunks. And the mountains, always the green, saddled mountains turning hazy blue in the distance.

"*Muy hermosa*," Rubén said.

On their right were a series of wooden stands and lean-tos where travelers could buy avocados and various fruits—apples, oranges, mangoes, papayas—bulging out of the dark interiors like brilliant impastos. They passed a long trough brimming with rainwater where a middle-aged woman washed clothes at one end and two boys watered their horses at the other. The horses, tired and dusty, bent low, extending their firm necks over the rotten wood and plunged their snouts into the insect-mottled water. Their manes trailed down in dirty braids; their thick, plumelike tails twitched nervously.

She looked out the window and saw a road forking to the left, marked by a sign with an ominous outstretched index finger: A

LAS CATARATAS. She could hear the muted sound of rushing water as they swept past, Rubén swerving around a group of horses proceeding down the road. Peter looked at them sadly. Then Uruapan came into view, clustered tightly in the valley and clinging to the surrounding mountains like grapes on a trellis. Janet was still not used to Mexican cities. To her the houses seemed gloomy and bland: one-story, unseparated, made of white adobe painted orange at the base, the roofs flat, sometimes covered with half sections of overlapping orange pipe. Rubén slowed and blew the horn at a group of shirtless children playing soccer, the rain giving their dark skin a wet sheen.

"The children seem so happy."

"They are happy, thank God."

That's what makes Mexico deceptive, she thought. The lack of desperation. It made you careless. Misery hid in beauty, and you dropped your guard, unaware that it was chipping away at you until you looked more closely.

"The only thing Mexico has going for it is the family. Its children."

"And the church," Rubén said.

"Is that true, Father Pete?"

"The people think it is."

"Do you think it is?"

He ran a hand through his receding black hair. "I'm less and less sure of that, but I think that's my problem. . . . It's not enough for me to help these people spiritually. . . . I can't just stay in a church while they starve or suffer. I need to help them, to see tangible results. . . ."

They were passing into wealthier neighborhoods. The houses had tall TV antennas and large cylinders of gas on the flat roofs, and some of the houses had gates. Even so, the city continued to appear ugly to Janet. It had preserved none of the colonial architecture that to her gave Mexico its charm.

"Have you set up programs to help them?"

"Of course. Food share programs, youth volunteer social workers, various education programs like how to preserve soil and grow better crops."

"And? Tangible results?"

"They get lost in the larger problems. It's like trying to bail out the *Titanic* with a sieve."

"So why don't you tap into the resort project?" Janet asked, her head beginning to ache.

"That's already happening. I'm mediating between the state tourism board and a Tarascan group opposed to the project. We've had to swallow our pride and accept the inevitable. It's a tricky business, knowing how hard to push."

"What do you think will happen?"

"I wish I knew. Maybe if someone could make the government representatives feel like they had someone to answer to . . ."

"You mean, make them feel the eye of God?"

"No, I was thinking of the eye of the camera."

Janet laughed, long and loudly. "Father Pete, you're amazing."

"You have to admit you're in a powerful position. You could really put this project in the public eye and not whitewashed the way the government would like."

"Who said anything about whitewashing?"

"Then you agree?"

"Agree to what? This conversation is becoming unpleasant, Father."

"Agree that these Tarascans and campesinos deserve a fair share of the proceeds. That won't happen unless there's some scrutiny, and that means the press needs to be involved."

She looked down at the wet floor mats as though they might have warned her and shook her head. "Let me tell you a story, Father Pete. I lived two years in Nigeria as a child. My parents were both teachers. It was social work, education—not unlike what you described earlier. My parents thought they were going to make a difference; they thought they were going to change people's lives."

"And of course they didn't."

"Not the way they thought they would. The kinds of changes you want aren't brought about by individuals. Certainly not by me. I'm just here to write a book and take some pictures. Nothing more."

"I see." He was quiet a moment, then said, "Why did your parents go back home?"

The car turned down a narrow one-way street leading to the central plaza and found it cut off by a stalled bus. Janet watched an election poster flap in the breeze.

"They got tired, Father. They just plain got tired."

Rubén braked, and they floated through a sea of pigs plodding forward stubbornly, snub-nosed, fat bellies like barrels assembled by drunken coopers, followed by a herd of thin, bearded goats with strange, strange rectangular irises, the car narrowly missing the last straggler, a lame female that hobbled out of the way, teats slung low to the ground. Rubén turned left, and they began the sharp descent to the national park. The car shuddered violently crossing a pair of railroad tracks, picked up speed passing the open-ended building that served as both tavern and depot—the men within hailing them with cheerful shouts and raised flagons of frothy beer—and swerved to avoid a taxi careening back to town. Beside the sloping road, Byzantine telephone poles leaned toward one another conspiratorially, as a steady stream of campesinos moved along the ditch toward the park.

"What's going on?" Janet asked.

"They come here to sell their wares to people like you."

Janet gave Father Cruz a sideways glance but said nothing. The car pulled off the highway onto a bumpy dirt road that led to a clearing bordered by five small, fragile kiosks. Inside one of them there was a pile of green coconuts that reached to the ceiling. As they stepped out of the Buick, a group of young men leading horses surrounded them. They all were speaking at once, and Janet was caught between the rumps of two horses that flicked their coarse tails across her bare arms, stinging gently, as if helping their masters convince her to hire a horse. Rubén had already settled on three, and before she knew it, the rest of the men went away, leaving two boys and three horses. Rubén, Father Cruz, and Janet swung up into the saddles. Two other boys lingered, arguing passionately that their horses were better, but the three horses were already plodding off.

The descent was steep and short and of little interest to the horses, which had made the trek many times before. When the three riders dismounted, Rubén motioned for them to move up the footpath with him. Here the park provided testimony to the fertile soil and heavy rains characteristic of the region. Stone paths took them past lush plants, natural fountains and cascades, a wide, meandering river, and banana plants with leaves wider and taller than any person. Tarascan women sat watchfully beside the crafts lining the paths.

"What's going on there?" Janet said, pointing to a kiosk overlooking the river where a small crowd had gathered.

Cruz took her arm. "Come with me. I want you to see what kinds of jobs tourism provides."

A young man, perhaps eighteen years old, stood on the roof of the kiosk. He wore red swimming trunks and a thin blue windbreaker. Forty feet below him the river churned itself into white foam. Another boy approached Janet as they neared the crowd. "C'mon, c'mon," he said in Spanish, passing an overturned straw hat before them. "Give something so you can leave with a clear conscience." She fished three hundred pesos out of her pocket and put them in the hat. Worthless, she thought, and was surprised that he seemed satisfied with her donation.

On the slanting roof the young man took off his jacket and tossed it aside. He was tall and thin with a head of thick, curly hair, and he tugged nervously at his swimming trunks. He shivered, and his ribs were clearly outlined against the quick rise and fall of his chest. After a final intense lobbying effort, his friend waved to him, and he stepped up to the edge of the roof and crossed himself. Standing arms at his sides, knees bent, he pushed out, out, out, bringing his arms overhead, palms touching each other, and there was a moment when he seemed frozen in the air parallel to the water. Then his body rotated, and he dropped soundlessly to the water, which opened and closed behind him in an instant, but Janet had gotten him at that moment when he hung suspended in the air. He surfaced and hauled himself out of the water without acknowledging the smattering of applause; while everyone watched him, one of the younger boys clambered up onto the kiosk.

"Luis," the boy yelled. "*¡Mira!*"

The diver looked up and shook his head, and as Janet prepared to take his picture, she saw his eyes widen. The air currents rustled, and this time there was a thud followed by a chorus of horrific astonishment. Janet took the photo, and when she looked up, she saw the boy lying in a shallow pool near the rocky bank. His small head lay turned at an impossible angle, and as she refocused the telephoto, she saw that his eyes were open and there was blood trickling out of his right ear. Water lapped over his nose and mouth.

Peter started forward.

"It's too late," Janet said, snapping another picture. "His neck is broken."

"You don't know that."

But as if to prove her right, the older diver lifted the boy in his arms, and the small head flopped backward, touching the boy's back. Janet snapped a vertical of this. When she looked up again, Cruz was working his way down the embankment. Rubén was staring at her.

"What did you think I do for a living?" she asked, her anger barely under control.

"Exactly this," he said, turning his back and walking away.

"Rubén, wait."

But he kept walking. Father Cruz signaled her to go on without him, and as she started after Rubén, she was surrounded by children wanting to sell her chewing gum, T-shirts, ashtrays. She brushed them aside. By the time she reached the entrance to the park, Rubén was nowhere to be seen, but there was a man in a ratty T-shirt who took her photograph with a Polaroid and then asked her if she wanted to buy it.

"No, thanks," she said, anxious to get away.

"Hey," he shouted after her, "you ruin my day. You ruin my day, you American bitch."

"You ruined your own day," she said, blundering into a cloud of mosquitoes. She slapped at them, ineffectually, agonized, and her only thoughts were of getting away, inside, away from these parasites, but as she ran off, they followed her, biting fiercely, and Janet could think of nothing else to do.

ABRAHAM RODRÍGUEZ, JR.

Babies

It was good fucken-shit, not that second-rate stuff. It was really good shit, the kind you pay a lot for, so I stared at Smiley for a while cause I got real curious bout whea the money came from.

"What?" he said, lookin at me while he rolled anotha joint.

"Whea you get the money, macho?" I axed him, an he started backin up into the riot gate we were standin in front of.

"Aw, c'mon, don't start."

"Me start?" I yelled, real loud, cause I knew it bugged him whenever I did that on the street an everyone knew our problems. "I'm not startin nothin, I juss wanna know whea you got the money, whachu been husslin."

"It wasn't no hussle, *muñeca*, juss chill out."

"Yeah, yeah, I heard that before, man. If the fucken cops come snoopin around the house for yuh ass again, Smiley man, thass it, we're through. I don't wanna fucken hassle with that no more."

"Shut up an, like, smoke."

I'm serious, Smiley got some real special shit, don't taste like tree bark. We smoked an hung out for a while, then Smiley went to the super to see bout maybe gettin some work, cause usually Smiley could get somethin to do, like plumbin or puttin up a ceilin someplace, an then we could have money for rent. The goddamn food stamps ran out. Now we're in some serious shit. I din't know before, but when I went upstairs with my friend Sara, I saw the empty book. I'll tell you somethin else we ain't got: food. I checked the frigerator an the bastid's empty; even the light bulb quit on us. It smells all mildewy in thea, an thea's some green shit growin in the egg tray. Clusters of dead roaches float in some dingy water at the bottom. Thea's a half-empty box of Sugar Pops. Dinner.

Check it out, Smiley don't really care bout food anyway. When we first moved in together, he knew I couldn't cook for shit, but he said fuck it, cause he wanted his favorite piece of ass with him. (Thass my sentimental Smiley!) Thea's no house-cleanin either cause thea ain't much of a house, juss a two-room apartment on the fifth floor that came complete with a mattress. (We washed it off first.) We got a small black-and-white TV, a love seat that smells funny an has a paint can for a fourth leg, an a old bureau we grabbed off the street that came with its very own roaches. (For free! Whea else but in America?) Thass all our furniture. We got a gray exercise mat we use like a dinin area on the floor, so when people come to eat, they gotta sit on the floor like Chinks or those Hindoos.

Sara hung out with me for a while until we finished the last joint. She has a radio. It's really her man's, but she carries it around anyway. She played it while we sat by the windows, cause it was spring an the breeze was cool an fresh. Sara is kinda dark, but she's Rican, with long hair. She's gotten a little fat, but then she had a baby bout two weeks ago.

"Whea's the baby anyway?" I axed, thinkin bout that little dark bundle I saw wrapped tightly in blue at Lincoln Hospital when she had it an I went to visit.

"It's around," she said tiredly, not wantin to talk bout it.

"Whea around?"

"I think Madgie's with him outside the bakery. Or maybe I leff him by the liquor store. I dunno." She shrugged like thea was a bug on her shoulder.

"Man, you gotta cut that shit out," I said, without too much conviction. "Yuh a motha now," I added, feelin it was the right thing to say an shit. "You gotta be responsible an take care of your baby."

"I know," she said loud, forehead all pruned up. "I know that! What, chu think I don't know? You think I treat my baby mean? He hangs out with me alla time! Alla time, dammit, he's thea, remindin me!" She lay back on our dinin mat. "Shit. Tell me I don't care bout my kid. I bet if you had a kid, you do better?"

I din't say nothin cause I knew she was all crotchety bout that kid. This always happens with her, so like always, I juss let her blow all her steam out. You could tell it was botherin her. Her man (not the one with the radio; he's the new man), the father of the kid, at first seemed hip to the idea of a boy, but then he got real pissed off. One night they were outside the liquor store an it was bout midnight. They were both drinkin, an they got in a fight. He wanted to know what right she had to fuck up his life. All he knows how to do is drink an stan around, he ain't got time for no babies, so what she come with this shit now for? She threw a half-empty bottle of Smirnoff at him, which really upset some of the otha winos nearby cause it was such a waste of good drinkin stuff. She got all teary an stood out in the middle of the street with the baby carriage.

"Fuck you!" she screamed, all hoarse. "I don't give a fuck!" An swoosh, a car passed bout three inches from the baby carriage.

"I hope you get kill, bitch!" he screamed back.

A big bus appeared, one of those new air-condition ones from Japan that look like bullets. It started honkin. She swung the baby carriage at it. Thass when I stepped in. I had been waitin for Smiley an saw the whole thing. I dragged her off the street to her house, whea I fixed her a drink. (Her apartment, by the way, is worse than ours. At least ours has a ceilin over the bathroom.) The baby was cryin like somebody stepped on it.

"Put this over his face an he'll shut up," she said, handin me a blanket. "It always works."

I took him into the bathroom, the only otha room in that

dump thass private, an I shut the door on him so his cryin sounded far-off an echoy.

"I'm so fucked up!" she wailed. "I lost my man, an here I am stuck with that—that . . . ohhhh, fuck that bastid! Mothafucka, iss all his fault! To hell with him! Who needs him? You think I need him to bring up the baby? I'll bring it up all on my own, who needs him? That prick. He better gimme money, ain't no way he's gonna walk out on me an not gimme money, I don't care if we ain't married, he still has to gimme money, that bastid. . . ."

"If you don't stop screamin, the baby ain't never gonna shut up an sleep," I said.

Her eyes got all wild. "Din't I tell you," she screamed, "to put a blanket over it? Put a blanket over the baby's head an it'll shut up!"

So much for the memory. She was lyin on the dinin mat like a corpse, her eyes cuttin holes in the ceilin. Everything was quiet now. When the joint finished, she tuned the radio to some house music.

"So whachu name the baby?" I axed, now that she had calmed down.

"Baby," she said. "It's called Baby."

I grimaced. "Thass stupid."

"Fuck you, juss whachu know bout babies?"

Okay, I know that I got leff in a carriage in the hot sun when I was a baby, my older brotha told me. He said my motha got drunk an forgot whea I was, an I hadda go to the hospital. I remember when I was three, my motha was with this man. She got drunk an put a hankie over my eyes so I couldn't see; then the two of them spun me around an around. They sped off in his Camaro, strandin me on Randall's Island for a long time. I got lost an walked around an cried a river, until cops saw me an took my hands an told me stories. They showed up in the Camaro an felt all embarrassed. A big Irish cop with a thick mustache got real mad. He noticed they were both stoned an gave them tickets. When we got home, my motha beat the livin shit outta me.

"It was juss a game," she howled. "You din't have to go fuck it up."

"I don't know," I said to Sara. "I'm juss fucked up." I got up, away from her. I din't wanna talk bout babies no more. I went to my favorite drawer in the bureau an got my stuff. Sara watched. She liked to watch me shoot up, though she never did H cause she said she din't wanna die. She juss liked to watch an ax stupid questions like if it was school an I was her tutor. I took out my kit but let it lie for a while cause I was still buzzin from the joint.

I hate it when people say I'm a junkie an shit cause it's really not true. I know I got it all under control, an plus I know I can stop anytime I want. (I did once, for three whole days, an then since I knew I could take it or leave it, I took it, cause I mean, what else is thea? Why shouldn't I feel sweet?) Some Hispanos been axin me whea I picked up such a habit, cause around 149th thea ain't no sixteen-year-old girls on H. The fack is, I used to hang out in the Village with this funky guy named Matt who used to do crazy shit like steal cars for a day juss to ride around. I met him through a friend in junior high. Me and him used to hang out a lot in that park with the big white arch thing whea he used to deal H to all the junkies who hung thea. I axed him what it was like to take H cause I seen him sniffin it, an he gimme a book to read: *Christiane F.* I read like four pages an said enough of this shit, I hate books.

He got mad an said I should learn somethin, but I wouldn't go near it again, so he said fuck it, I should learn the hard way then. He shot me full of H. I first felt like I was gonna throw up on him; my stomach was dribblin around, an my head felt like it was separatin from my body. I got real nervous until Matt told me to relax an not be uptight, an then I started feelin real good. The next day he shot me up again an made a joke bout that bein my last free sample. When that freeze hit me, I was on cloud nine, ten, eleven. I was free of everythin that bugged my head out, like my motha, who was out fucken like a dog in heat, or my bad grades in school, or my older brotha, who one day disappeared without even a fucken poof leavin only a pair of Pro-Keds on the kitchen table as a good-bye. Nah, I wasn't thinkin bout nothin at all, juss gettin more sweet H an takin more trips into that sweet nothin land.

I hadda keep shootin after that. One time I bought some real bad shit from some guy I din't know, a fucken Latin dude, an it was awful. I felt like if bugs were crawlin all over an I couldn't stop scratchin. That was the only time I ever got fucked up. That was a year ago that I turned on, I mean, an since then I haven't gotten the sunken face or the bags under the eyes or the circles neither. I look great. In fack, guys keep axin me out all the time, but I got Smiley, so I say nah. I'd only be like my motha if I said yeah.

Smiley's two years older than me. He's tall an sleek, with a sorta beard that feels nice. He smokes pot like a stove. He dropped out of high school to work in a car shop on Bruckner Boulevard. He lived in whass now our place with two otha dudes cause his father hated him an his motha din't really care bout nothin much. His father used to beat her around like a Ping-Pong. Smiley got sick of it, so one day, durin one of his father's drunken freak-outs, Smiley took a kitchen knife an stabbed him. Yeah, Smiley stuck him, an they threw him in Rikers Island for six months. I think thass one of the most heroic things I ever heard of in my life, which is why I really love him, cause he's so sweet an courageous. He met me one day cause one of his roomies, a thin kid with a bushy head an a face used to stompins, brought him to school to hang out, an he met me in the cafeteria. We started seein each otha an got it on. Six months ago he kicked out his roomies for bein slobs, an he axed me to move in. You betcha ass I did. I leff my nympho bottle-sucking motha on Cypress Avenue with her roomful of men doin rotatin shifts. She din't miss me.

For a little while thea were fluffy clouds an flowers an what they call "romance" on TV. I should end that whole story with one a those happy-ever-after things like in all great lit, but thea's always trouble. Last summer the cops busted him twice cause he lost his job an started doin some husslin. Once they caught him with stolen goods, the otha time he got fingered in a muggin. I tried to get him to stop, but then he has to get his smoke, an I need my H; I get real cranky without it.

My buzz faded out, so I lit my juice an shot up quick, cause Sara was gettin loud. (She always does when she gets high, always sayin the stupidest shit as loud as she can.) I juss floated away an only came back to the room years later when she mentioned Diana.

Check it out, Diana is this sixteen-year-old girl who's really preggos, like out to here. I don't know how many fucken months gone by. She's younga-lookin than I am an has a real pretty complexion, like an Ivory girl, skin dark an smooth, eyes bright, tiny red lips that pout, a nice narrow waist. The first time I seen her, when she moved in with her motha an sister, I said this one won't last. She din't. She got fucked fast enough by this guy everybody knows, named Freddie, who thinks he's all bad an acts like a beat boy. Now she's real big, an he's nowhere in sight.

"I know her motha," Sara was sayin, walkin around real fast. "I talk to her alla time, you know, she like, talks to me, knows I'm a motha too. She's a real slick lady, no shit. Works in Lerner's, that store? The one on Third Avenue, no shit, she sells dresses." She laughed hysterically for some fucken reason. I told you, she gets this way when she's on smoke.

"An like, she's a real decent, upstandin woman, she don't be hangin out with all these scums an shitheads. She got it all together. She really care bout her two girls, which is why issa shame bout Diana. An Marissa be fourteen nex month. Hope it don't happen to her!"

Yeah, Marissa, fourteen, wears black boots an skintight pants an waist cords an glossy lipstick an two huge plastic heart earrings. She's next. Nah, I don't think it's good for a growin girl to have a motha who works at Lerner's.

"Though I seen her yesterday, she was wearin a miniskirt with those—those wild panny hoses an shit with the designs on them? Shit, man. Her motha dresses her real good. She's really a motha, you know." She leaned real close to me. "She's tryin to get Diana to get a abortion."

"It's too late," I said, knowin Diana was too far gone for one. "Yeah, but she knows somebody who'll still do it, an cheap too. I told you, girl, I talk to her, she confide in me an shit! I tole her it was the right thing to do. Babies can be the death, man. I tole her I shoulda aborted mines. You know? I axed her if she wanted my baby, but she said nah."

I started laughin. That was really wild!

"I'm serious, *muñeca*, I really meant it, cause I know she's a good motha."

"An she said no?"

"Yeah."

"You really give yuh baby away to somebody if they take him?"

"Sure, why not?" she said, gettin up, as if I insulted her or somethin. "She can bring it up good. Give it a good home, an toys, an moncy, an shit." She wasn't facin me. "I don't wanna talk bout this no more."

"Okay," I said, feelin like I did somethin wrong. "You want some Sugar Pops?" I brought the box over from the fridge an dug deep into it, poppin the stuff into my mouth.

"Nah, I gotta go," she said, an poof, a kiss on the cheek an she was out the door, with the fucken radio too.

Talkin to Sara bout babies made me feel funny inside. It's like, I don't know, I think I could be a great motha sometimes, but then I think maybe I'm too fucked up to even take care of myself, an I don't know enough bout things an life, an maybe I'll juss fuck up the kid. Those otha times, when I think I could really swing it an be a good motha are kinda painful cause it gets like an itch, an it makes me wanna swell up right away. I guess cause I was thinkin bout it so much, an cause I was high on H, when Smiley came in late at night, I axed him bout babies.

"What about um?" he axed back, rollin a joint as he sat on our dinin mat.

"Do you ever think of havin one? One for us?" The thought made me all crazy. I hugged him, like I had a billion tiny worms dancin in my veins. He pushed me away, got real serious.

"You not pregnint," he said, angry. "You pregnint?"

"No, Smiley, I—"

"You better not get fucken pregnint, or I'm out the fucken door. You see that door?" he yelled, pointin to it. "I be out of it if you get pregnint. I ain't supportin no fucken baby. Thass that. No way. Be bad enough supportin me an you." He got up, lickin his joint shut. "You got enough H?" he axed before he went into the "bedroom."

"Yeah," I said, feeling like somethin got taken out. He saw my spression an kinda felt bad, so he came over an kissed me an picked me up like some baby an planted me in bed an kissed me again. "Now, we don't want no babies, okay?"

"Okay," I said.

An then we fucked.

The next night, I was sittin on the stoop with Diana. It wasn't like I planned it or nothin; it's juss Smiley wasn't home, an I decided to wait for him outside. I had been in the fucken apartment all day long, throwin up, mostly. Maybe it was the smoke an the H? I told Millie bout it, an she laughed an said, "Uh-oh," but the bitch vanished before I could get the story out of her.

Anyway, I was gonna hang out for a while an went downstairs. Thass when I heard cryin, soft cryin an sniffin. I looked down the hallway an saw somebody down by the otha stairwell that goes to the otha side of the buildin. It was juss the top of a head behind the handrail whea everybody puts their garbage. I walked right over, cause I'm a curious bitch, an saw it was Diana in a cute blue maternity thing that said BABY an had a arrow pointin to her belly. She heard me sneakin up an got all self-conscious. We weren't really close or nothin, juss talked once or twice, so I started yappin a whole lot, first bout the smell of the hallway, then garbage. I told her my top ten worst insects list (she cracked up), an then finally I got to ax, "So how come yuh down here cryin?"

Diana kinda sighed an rearranged her long hair with a toss of her head. She wiped at her face clumsily. "My motha an I had anotha fight about the baby."

"She still wancha get rid of it?"

"Yeah. She knows I'm seven months—" her voice cracked—
"but she don't care. She says she's gonna do whass bess for me if
she gotta break the law to do it, an she says she'll drag me down
if I don't want to. I juss wasn't inna mood for all that shit
tonight, so I juss ducked out."

"What bout your man, whea's he?" I tried soundin like a
therapist I saw on TV.

"I don't know. Freddie went away. I ain't seen him in six
months." She started to cry again, an I gave her a big hug. She
was tremblin a little, juss like Sara's baby when I first picked it up
from its crib two weeks ago an it looked like a tiny red prune.
We walked out to the stoop an sat thea for a while.

"You think your motha's gonna come down an getchu?" I
axed.

"I don't know. She'll send Marissa. She expected me to sit
thea an hear anotha sermon about what I gotta do, but I'm not
gonna, I'm not gonna kill my baby," she said firmly, her voice
gettin louder, "because it's mines, an Freddie's, an someday he'll
come back, an even if he doesn't, so what? The baby is . . . a
produck of our love for each otha, a part of us, you know?
Thea's a part of me in that baby, an if I let her kill it, she'll be
killin somethin of mines! I feel it, you know? It moves around in
thea. It does bumps an grinds an shit! It's juss waitin to be born.
I'm not gonna let her murder my baby!" she yelled, clenching
her fists as if she was gonna punch me.

"Don't get so worked up," I said, tryin to calm her down.

"Worked up? Don't get so worked up? You ack like this is
somethin trivial, like buyin *lechuga o tomate*! It's not, you know.
It's a baby. An it's mines, dammit, mines!"

"An how you gonna bring it up?" I axed, already gettin too
involved, but somethin happens to me when I get yelled at. "If
you have it, you gonna stay witcha motha?"

"No way. I know a friend who lives near Melrose. She's
gettin it ready. In a week I can go live with her."

"So what? How you gonna bring it up? How you gonna feed
it? You got money for that, or is yuh friend also a fucken bank?"

"She's gonna help me till I get on my feet," she said slowly, as if she was tryin to remember lines from a play.

"Yeah? An how you gonna get on yuh feet? You leff school?"

"I'm goin back."

"Takin the baby witcha?"

"Stop it."

"You'll need money for a baby-sitter. Whea's it gonna—"

"Freddie'll help," she said angrily.

"He's halfway to Bermuda by now." I knew that was cruel, but juss who the fuck she think she is yellin at me like that when I try an help?

"Fuck you!" she yelled. "Yuh juss like my motha!"

Thass when Marissa appeared in the doorway, wearin a polka-dot miniskirt with wooden sandals that clacked real loud.

"Ma says to come up," she said, a finger in her mouth.

"I'm not goin up thea. You tell—" The words froze in her mouth, cause juss as she turned to tell Marissa off, she spotted her motha coming down the hall.

"I'm not comin witcha!" Diana screamed, jumpin off the stoop an tryin to run away. This was when her motha put on some speed an grabbed her, pullin her to the stoop again.

"Let her go!" I yelled, tryin to untangle them, but I got an elbow in the face real hard from one of them. They both collapsed on the sidewalk, Diana yellin, "I hate chu!" an throwin punches like a demon. Millie, the daughter of the guy who owns the bodega next door, started yellin for the cops. Diana's motha was hittin back now, an hard, up on her feet while Diana rolled on the ground from the punches, getting soaked from a dribblin hydrant she slid under. Her motha started pullin on her real fierce while screamin bout respect. I thought she'd hurt her or somethin, so I lunged, pullin her away.

"Leave her alone!" I cried.

"Leave her alone?" her motha roared back in my face, her eyes real big. "Leave her alone? With you? She's my daughter! Do you hear? She's my daughter, not yours! My baby! An she's not endin up like you!" Her voice was hoarse, her arms flyin around like pinwheels as she gestured wildly at the crowd (which always forms at the first sign of a free show). "Buncha junkies an shits, you gonna save my daughter from me? I'm savin her from dirt like you!" She grabbed Diana again and started draggin her. "Less see you stop me, *carajo!*" She had completely flipped, her eyes bulgin, her hair a mess, her red blouse all torn up. She kept draggin Diana even though she screamed an swung out at her, her otha arm gettin scratched up from scrapin against the sidewalk. Two guys from the bodega came out an pulled her motha off, because Diana was movin funny, holdin her stomach.

"Oh, God!" she cried, louder than anythin I ever heard in my life. She wriggled an folded into a ball, clutchin her stomach. I bent over her, tryin to unfold her, me an Millie both tried, but we couldn't. When she looked up at me, her face looked horrible, all cracked inside.

"Oh, shit, get an ambulance!" I yelled, at nobody an everybody, while Marissa stood frozen to the spot, by the stoop, starin blankly as if watchin TV, absently pullin up on her designer panty hose.

It was a week after that that Sara gave away her baby. She got rid of it somehow, I don't fucken know how, I juss kept seein her without it, so I axed her one day, an she juss got this real idiot grin on her face like when she's stoned, an she said, "It's gone," an then she walked away from me with her blarin box, over to her new man by the liquor store, with the gleamin pint of brandy. I juss ran home to my H after that; I juss couldn't deal with it.

I don't know, I don't read much, don't watch news, don't care bout how many got fried in Nicaragua or wherever, but sometimes I get this feelin, an it's not bout politics, cause that guy Matt, who turned me on to H, was a real militant black motha who was always sayin the system hadda be overthrowed, an I think he's still sayin that from his sewer hole somewhere.

I don't got a head for that shit, you know? But this feelin I get. I look out my window an see it all crawlin by, see it all scribbled on Sara's face, stamped on Diana's torn maternity suit. I remember her motha's words, an they all seemed to hit me somewhere.

Shit, I even feel it now when I look in the mirror an see the circles under my eyes an the marks on my fucked-up arms: We're in some real serious shit here. It's no place for babies. Not even a good place for dogs.

I guess I can't pretend I'm alive anymore. Diana's baby was lucky; it died in the incubator. On my seventeenth birthday I dreamed I was in that incubator, chokin. Smiley woke me up with a cupcake that had a candle on it, yellow flame dancin nervous, like it might go out any second. He remembered.

Smiley noticed I changed a little, cause I wasn't so happy anymore. I juss wanted to take my H an cruise on my run an not botha. He even got mad cause I din't wanna fuck so much no more. I din't tell him I was pregnint, not even after four weeks passed.

I saw Diana on a corner, in shorts an Pro-Keds, all smiles, cause she was high, her eyes lookin like eight balls.

"Lissen," she said. "I was wonderin if like maybe you could do me a favor and shit? Can you like turn me on to some horse? I really wanna try it, an Sara said you'd turn me on. Whacha say, yeah?"

Somethin inside me popped. I'm not normally a violent person, but like a reflex an shit, I smacked her right in the face, hard. She fell back about three feet against a riot gate that rattled.

"Whachu do that for?" she yelled, blood burstin over her teeth from a busted lip. She was breathin heavy, like some tough butch. I juss stared at her, then went upstairs to my H. I felt bad for her motha. I felt like maybe her motha shoulda beat her up more. I wished my motha woulda cared that much for me. A good motha in life is a break, an nobody with a good break like that got a right to go lookin for H.

"Man, you out already?" Smiley said one night in surprise, going through my kit. "I thoughtchu had a week's worth."

Smiley din't know thea was a tiny baby inside of me, but I knew it. I also knew thea was a part of me in that baby, an a part of him, an zero plus zero equals zero. So I din't say nothin.

I got a abortion.

LISA Y. GARIBAY
Daddy

My father uses the same noise to call to my baby sister that he used with me when I was her age, twenty-one years ago. It's a sort of whistle, a forcing of air between the tongue and front teeth, and a repetition of the same note on two different scales. When I was younger, and even now, sometimes, when I remember that whistle or hear it called out by a bird, I feel for a few seconds all the security and trust I once invested in the man who was my father.

That is not to say that he is no longer my father or that he has passed away. He is still alive, healthy as far as I know at the age of forty-eight. I still regard him as my parent. But he and my mother have been apart for twelve years now. And he is married again to someone else. This is Marriage No. 3 for him. Maybe this time he'll get it right. I really hope that he does, because this marriage has produced one of the most beloved things in my life, my baby sister. Alexandra Isabella. It's a beautiful name. I don't think he was the one who thought of it.

When I first met Alexandra, she was just three and a half months old. I had returned home from school only a few days before my father's abrupt introduction to this little being, which he assumed I was immediately going to accept and embrace. Far from it. I was enraged, disgusted, and even frightened by her. It took me quite a while, several months at least, to get over the fact that I was projecting the resentment and disappointment I felt for my father onto the poor little girl, who was just as at fault for being born to him as I was. It took her to teach me that we are not to blame for the person he is. I love Alexandra dearly; she is intelligent, innocent, and beautiful. But I worry—a lot—about her future, expressly because of who her father is. My father.

I watch her when he comes through the front door and uses the noise to announce to her that it is he who has entered. I look at her face and cannot understand the joy contained within her expression at hearing that whistle come from him. Was I ever so utterly thrilled, so easily and completely sated? I cannot comprehend her smile, her laugh, and the entirety of her happiness. Then again, she is only a year old. She has yet to find out who my father—our father—is. She has yet to become conscious of his humanity, the overwhelming tendency toward imperfections that he harbors. She has yet to be let down by him to the point where she can no longer excuse it. I long to be her. I don't want to be disillusioned at my age, having been brought to this point of hindsight by his hand, the hand that brought to me wounds I still struggle to heal.

My father had his share of problems growing up. His family was not wealthy. My grandparents worked hard from the moment they were old enough to be able to support first themselves and later their children. They dedicated their lives to making ends meet, which left little time for anything else. My father has told me that he never talked much with his parents, never had an openly close emotional bond with either his mother or father. He, his sisters, and his brother grew up believing that feelings were to be kept private, never exhibited in public, and only admitted within the family when it mattered or when punishment was involved. He must have had to become very independent at a young age. Too young, perhaps. His inability to comprehend the importance of the bond between parent and child has manifested its ugly self in such an unignorable way that it can only be the result of an emotionally unstable childhood. A childhood like the one he gave to me.

The divorce and annulment between my mother and father became official in 1984, almost a year and a half after my father had left our house for good. I vividly remember the day that he went. Unnaturally I can recall it now without feeling much sadness. If anything, I am just sorry that it had to happen. It seems inevitable to me now, a day that had to come, and could have been much worse than it actually was. Of course this is the benefit of hindsight, so it is said, that blessed distance that keeps us from losing our sanity as we lose the perspective of subjectivity, of being a part of what was going on, and become more of an observer the farther away time pushes us from it.

That day was Sunday, March 7, 1982. Coincidentally that was also the birthday of my father's father. Of course we did not celebrate the occasion that day. Sundays had always had a very particular ritual about them in my immediate family. The ceremony of the day was different when my father was around; after that Sunday it changed forever. Like a script that had suddenly been revised to exclude a key character, calling for the rearrangement of text, dialogue, stage directions, even how all the other characters had to relate to one another, nothing was ever the same.

Every Sunday before that one, my mother would wake up, shower, and dress, then wake me, my sister, and my brother (in that order, descending, according to our ages) so we could ready ourselves for Mass. We would always be delayed by something or another that came up—mostly because of my father, who has always been and will never be anything else but late. My mother would certainly agree with me in saying this; she might even go so far as to say that he is at least a decade and a half late for his own funeral.

We were woken up as usual that Sunday by my mother, myself first and my sister a little while later. But before we could head to the bathroom and rinse the sleep from our faces, my mother said that we should go into her bedroom, that our father wanted to talk to us. My brother, however, was allowed to sleep in. I remember now that I knew then what was happening, that the screaming and the incessant arguing had led to this. I walked into the room under the oppressive weight of a complete dread of what was to come. My sister, fifteen months younger than I and therefore not much less conscious of what was happening, shuffled sleepily behind, clutching her white, stuffed unicorn with a purple horn. Unicorns were for many years her favorite animal, and purple her favorite color. My sister changed a great deal after my father left. A short while later the unicorn was left neglected and dusty on a closet shelf in favor of solitude, and her color of choice for everything from clothes to curtains changed to black.

My father was sitting on his side of the bed, the side closest to the door, where he belonged as the man of the house, ready to leap out of bed and out the door at the slightest hint of intrusion of trouble during the night. He was already dressed, although not in slacks and a starched, white, button-down shirt, as was his customary churchgoing outfit. While I did notice this breach of tradition, I can't remember now what it was that he was wearing instead. Sweats, probably, or jeans. He got up from the bed as my sister and I entered, and motioned for us to sit in his place. We both obeyed and waited to hear the worst.

Before the first sentence was out of his mouth completely, I was already in tears. My mother has always criticized me for being overly sensitive. During the times when I needed her to understand, when I was on the verge of emotional collapse and needed her comfort more than anyone else's, she, in her attempts to keep herself together, would lash out at me, call me "crybaby." She made things even worse with her jeers and insults and forced me into seeing things with such confusion and frustration that I am still affected by it today. In many ways I reacted by going to the opposite extreme of what my father had always done. My sensitivity was a response to him and the way he acted, lacking emotion and detached from any expression of anger, sadness, disappointment, or even joy that he might have felt.

He spoke to us softly, and I cannot remember whether he did

shed any tears, although I know the moment must have been hard on him as well. I do not doubt that he was being torn up inside, just as we were. My sister started weeping softly moments after I did, although I know she did not fully grasp what was going on. My father told us that he was leaving, that he would be moving out of the house and going to live somewhere else, that this was something he had to do. He told us he would always love us and would be there for us even though he would not be in the same house. Of course he had never been much of a support for us in the first place. But his presence had always been utterly comforting, and his being there gave things a sense of being complete.

The attachment a child has to its parent is almost illogical; in our case it was very detrimental in its unwavering loyalty. It was this attachment to my father that caused a great rift between my mother and me, when I would defend him in his absence from her accusations and put-downs. But it was this loyalty that kept me from growing truly to hate my mother for her misguided and misdirected hatred, which was nothing more than her own reaction to being hurt beyond comprehension and almost beyond repair. It is also this bond that allows me to forgive my father today, despite all that he has done, and to overlook the fact that he did not call or send any acknowledgment that he remembers that I turned twenty-one on April 17.

I do not remember in detail the words my father spoke to us, but I do remember that they were very carefully planned and that he asked us if we had any questions or any response to what he had said, as if we had just listened to a professor lecture us on biochemistry or the Civil War. I vaguely remember hugging him tightly, staining his shirt with my tears, and asking him not to leave. The memory skips here to scenes of eating breakfast afterward (we had Eggo waffles, which went down fairly easily), then to attending mass with my mother and sister and brother. Afterward we drove to my grandmother's condominium. I do not know whether my mother had called her in advance, but I remember clearly what she said when my grandmother opened the door: "He left me . . . he left me." My mother broke down at that point, and while she was being comforted by her own mother, my brother, sister, and I stood around them, avoiding one another's eyes and staring uncomfortably at the carpet and our leather Buster Browns.

The rest of the day is a blur. My mother's extended family, represented by the matriarchs who were my grandmother's sisters and their husbands, who sat demurely sympathizing and offering legal and financial counsel, assembled to discuss what had just happened. The women took turns looking after us, the only children present. I remember sitting at my grandmother's dining room table, being fed into placation and trying to understand their strange conversation, a mixture not only of words I knew and did not know but also phrases in English and Spanish. My brother, who was only four years old at the time, must have been much more confused than my sister and I by what was going on around him. My father had elected not to give him the same talk my sister and I had received. He felt he was too young to understand anyway. The three of us were treated with the same unintentional disregard by the rest of my mother's family that day. It was my mother who needed the attention, which we could be spared because of our youth and ignorance.

It is also said that children bounce back from these things much more easily than adults do. It is also a well-worn adage that time heals all wounds. My brother has suffered incredibly because of this lack of compassion and understanding at that time, a simple mistake that was made out of the best—though not well-thought-out—intentions. He in turn learned never to expect anyone to understand him, keeping all his feelings bottled up inside him. He also bears the ugly, indelible scars of never having had a father around for the most important years of his life. Two weeks and one day ago he tried to kill himself, although it was much more of a cry for help rather than a sincere attempt at ending his life. When I talked to him about this, several days after it happened, he said he was glad finally to let everything out. He is only seventeen.

I do not remember anything else I did at my grandmother's that day, or what time we finally returned to our own house.

But when we did arrive back home, we found that our father had left each of us a note on our pillows. I still have that letter, which I kept for years behind a framed photograph of my father holding my giggling baby self on his lap as my first birthday was being celebrated. The note had been written on paper torn from a yellow legal-size tablet, the kind that was abundant in my father's office at the bank that he was the vice-president of. I remember reading it and crying yet one more time, not completely understanding the full meaning of the words. I was saddened more that they had come from my father and that it was his familiar handwriting on the page that contained such an awful message.

I put the note away that night in the place where it remained for years afterward, behind the photograph, which I kept on my nightstand, where I could stare at it before I fell asleep each night. I didn't read the note again until at least seven or eight years later. It is only now that I can read it without being overwhelmed by the same sorrow it brought to me the day it was written.

Needless to say, my life was changed forever when my father left. I am unable to recall a single complete memory of anything that happened before that day. I have cloudy, uncertain, and scattered memories about what I might have done with my father while he was still at home: sitting on his lap, sipping from his beer can and watching football with him on Sunday afternoons; yelling good-bye to him on weekday mornings while he was in the shower and our mother was getting ready to take us to school.

I have more unpleasant memories of my father's being at home than I do good ones. They are the ones clearest in my mind. I remember the first time I ever cooked anything by myself, a spaghetti dinner for the whole family, my mother watching my every move apprehensively as she hovered two centimeters above my shoulder. It is the fighting and the screaming that took place between my mother and father afterward that I remember most vividly. My mother had told my father days in advance about this landmark event. Although it was not such an incredibly significant rite of passage, it was still something that a parent should have been excited about and should have sacrificed ass-kissing time with the boss in favor of witnessing.

My father did not come home that evening until almost midnight, well past my bedtime. I remember hearing his key in the lock, the creak and shudder of the front door, and then his whistle, ever so softly, calling me to see if I was still awake. The same whistle I can't forget today. I had waited for him, watching my mother grow more and more furious as the hours passed. The sounds he made coming through the door woke me out of a sound sleep, and I bounded up and off the sofa where I had been lying and scampered out into the hallway to greet him.

At around that time I had developed a very odd habit. Whenever my father would come home (often very late), I would run to meet him as he came through the door and throw my arms around his neck so he could pick me up with ease. But in that short moment before he could wrap his own arms around my back and bottom to lift me, I would run my hands down his neck and around his jawline, feeling if this man was truly my father or if it was merely some impostor wearing a mask.

I honestly cannot explain why I did this or how it became a routine for me. I also don't know what meaning it held. Why was I so preoccupied with the fact that the man coming home every night could have been someone pretending to be my father? Nevertheless, it was a nervous ritual that became more and more important to me as the tension between my mother and father grew. It still stands today as one of the most significant memories I have of my father's being around.

For approximately three years after my father moved out of our house, I prayed each and every night before falling asleep. I begged God to bring my daddy back to me. I wept silently, pulling layers of bedcovers over my head and holding the photograph from my nightstand awkwardly between my forearm and chest, and I clasped my hands together tightly. My brother told me the other day that he had done the same thing. For the longest time none of the three of us could accept the fact that he was gone for good. I would repeat my prayer over and over again until unconsciousness finally took over. The prayer began as a very elaborate sort of mantra that would lull me to sleep, and over the years it became shorter and shorter until I finally realized the futility of it and stopped doing it altogether.

Not surprisingly, my father did not fight for custody of us. He and my mother agreed to visitation rights, child support, and those sorts of things that were beyond my comprehension, and superficial to my grasp of the situation. There were many times when my mother refused to let us see our father, times when he had not sent his check on time or did not come through with the monthly tuition for our private Catholic school. Although he was highly irresponsible regarding these matters, it did not make me love him the slightest bit less. I forgave his every transgression. I just wanted him to come home.

His lack of financial support greatly affected our lifestyle, though. I remember one ordeal in particular when I was in the seventh grade and the principal of our school was forced to ask us not to come the next morning because we had not paid our bill in so many months. My mother ushered us into our minivan after school and drove us all over town for the rest of the evening, stopping at the homes of friends, relatives, and acquaintances. She left us in the car while she knocked on doors and asked each of these people with as much pride as possible for any money that they could spare so that we could stay in our school. Back then it seemed like an incredible annoyance to me. By no means was I capable of realizing what an effort it was for her, emotionally and physically, to reduce herself to doing this, not to mention the overall task of single-handedly finding herself responsible for three young children. But now I look back at that day and realize how much more of an extraordinary and supportive person—how much more of a parent—my mother was, and still is, than my father.

My father finally got around to calling me, three days after my birthday. He apologized for making me feel as though he had forgotten and claimed that he had been trying to get hold of me since the day before my birthday. He asked how I had been, and

I asked him the same thing. The conversation was strained. It was the first time I had talked to him since several days before I had left home to return to school, four months before. It was apparent to me that we did not have much common ground or much of anything to talk about to each other.

But then I asked about my baby sister. "How's Alex?" His voice got lighter, almost giddy. "Oh, gee, she's great. . . ." Then we began to talk. He described how she had started to walk by herself only three days ago (the day of my birth, twenty-one years ago). He chattered on and on about her developing ability to talk, imitating the sounds she made and her own interpretations of words and language. He chuckled and sighed when recalling particular things she had done. Talking about her, he seemed so much happier and more comfortable, more satisfied, than he had been when trying to relate to me.

I had to wonder, though, if it occurred to him that our relationship had become so tenuous, such a struggle to maintain. And, if so, whether he ever thought about why. I wanted to interrupt him during one of his anecdotes, cut him short as he detailed Alexandra's antics, and demand that he accept the responsibility of caring for her until the end. Unlike what he had done to my brother, my sister, and me. But I couldn't. I gripped the phone, held my breath, and listened to him laugh.

ARMANDO F. GUTIÉRREZ
Chinese Memories

"Pedro, take your shoes off before putting your feet on the couch!"

Pedro loved to lie back on the couch, spreading his body across it for the perfect fit it gave him. He would fold his hands over his chest and tilt his head slightly to the left to see the television screen. His body was perfectly still, and his stare was completely blank. It almost seemed as if his fifty-four-year-old body were dead.

But now Pedro sat up and removed his shoes at the urging of his wife, Emily.

"I always forget, dear," he responded sweetly as she smiled and turned away with a stack of old newspapers to recycle in her hands.

He put his shoes down and looked at her butt as she walked out of the room. "Still cooking after all these years," he whispered to himself with a slight accent as he stared at that compact item of eternity.

Pedro reclined once again on the couch and wiggled his sock-covered toes. His attention shifted immediately to the new twenty-one-inch television set sitting ten feet in front of him. A commercial was playing on the channel, and Pedro took the time to admire his recent purchase. *Not bad for five hundred dollars. That fine wood finishing and the details in the base. The shape of the screen and its almost perfect resolution. That picture Emily put over it could go, though.*

The picture over the TV was a large eight-by-ten framed shot of Pedro, Emily, and their two children, Brito and Cheryl. It had been taken seventeen years ago, the day they had gone to the airport to pick up Pedro's father, Octavio, from his flight in from Mexico. Emily's mother, Evelyn, had gone with them, and she had insisted on taking that photo of them in the airport parking lot. It was a cold day in Miami, one of the rare ones, and the cold wind was blowing right into Pedro's face, pulling at his gray fedora. Pedro hated the picture because he'd had to hold his hat down with his hand so that it would not blow away. It made him look odd, almost out of place in a picture on which the other three individuals were standing and carrying on normally.

A program started on TV. It was a tabloid news program called *The World Today*. Pedro transferred his attention to the TV screen and began to watch the sensationalist show intently.

"And here is your host, Raymond Chung," announced the deep, invisible voice that had been narrating through the show's credits.

This seems so tacky, thought Pedro. *Not another one of these bad shows.* Just when he had picked the remote control up from his side and was about to change the channel, he froze. The face on the man behind the desk was very familiar. It held him in complete fascination for almost a minute. Then, when he realized why he remembered, he jumped up from a lying position to a sitting one.

"Ramón!" he exclaimed. "That's Ramón!" He looked around the room and pointed to the TV as if other people were there watching.

"What is it, honey?" asked Emily from a distance.

"*Nada*, honey. Don't worry," Pedro answered, his eyes still glued to the face of Raymond Chung.

It had been more than forty years, but Pedro had not forgotten Ramón Chung, or Raymond, as he seemed to have changed his name now. In any other case Pedro would not have been sure that he knew this fellow, but the similarities of Raymond to Ramón were too striking: the same dark golden skin, the shiny curls of blue-black hair that spiraled across the flat head. It was the Ramón he remembered all right. Even the eyes were the same, a Caribbean blue that was impossible to forget. Ramón's English was perfect, though, much better than Pedro's, but Pedro knew they were contemporaries and Ramón could not have arrived in the United States before he had. It was Ramón all right, but this Ramón had changed considerably from the thin little peasant he remembered from his youth. With his proud glance and his straight posture, Raymond was dramatically different from the Ramón Pedro used to know.

"*¡Oye narra! ¡Vete a lavar ropa!*" the altar boys would scream at Ramón while the priest was too busy with his large wooden cross to hear them. Ramón stood at the corner of Vida and Amargura streets to watch the Easter procession go by. He wore tattered beige pants made out of unidentifiable fabric and a tight white T-shirt that accentuated the roundness of his tummy. He wore no shoes, and when he first heard the altar boys, his first reaction was to look down at his dirty feet. They were covered with mud from playing in the fields on the outskirts of the city and the dried mud's dark grayness contrasted with the golden brown color of his flesh.

Imbeciles. They all are just a bunch of imbeciles. Imbeciles was a word Pedro liked to use because his best friend had taught it to him after overhearing it from his parents.

"My mother and father were arguing in the kitchen, and I was sitting outside in the living room. I heard my mother scream 'Imbecile,' and then I heard a loud slap. After that my father came out of the kitchen and took me hunting pheasants in the mountains. I like the word."

Ramón had liked the word too. His reasons were different from Pedro's. He didn't have a father so he couldn't associate it with pleasant hunting memories. He liked the word because of what it implied. It was an insult. He knew it. At that point in his ten-year-old life it was the worst he had yet come across. It was power to him, power to attack those who injured him. But he knew he had to be careful when using it. He didn't want to get slapped the way Pedro's mother had.

The Easter processions in Trinidad were huge affairs. Everyone in the small town got together to walk down the twenty or so odd streets, chanting religious songs and remembering Jesus' miracles along with the stations of the cross. Pedro was in the procession with his mother, Hilda, and his father, Octavio. The three were dressed in their best Sunday clothes. Hilda wore a billowy purple dress her sister in Havana had made for her. Octavio wore a nice gray guayabera and a pair of his best pants. Little Pedro wore a long-sleeve shirt that was too big for him but that matched his gray pants. They all walked serenely, chanting from their prayer books and stopping from time to time to listen to the priest's short speeches. Migdalia walked right behind them. She wore a yellow summer dress that radiated in the afternoon Cuban sun. Her light cocoa skin made a radiating contrast with her baby blue eyes, which she had to cover with her hands every time the procession stopped because the sun bothered her too much.

Migdalia had decided to leave Ramón at home for this procession. Though she was a Catholic true and true, she saw how the other kids in the town taunted her son whenever he was forced to be around them.

"God," she had prayed before leaving the house without Ramón, "it's not his fault that he doesn't come to praise you. It's mine. I will confess this to Priest Suárez next Monday."

The procession had made its way to the Parque Martí, its final stopping point. All the miracles and stations had been finished beforehand, but Priest Suárez liked to stop at the park and give a little sermon, almost as if he were at mass. The members of the procession would separate and spread apart, filling the few park benches that were scattered here and there as well as occupying the green lawn that spread out from the base of the José Martí statue the priest was using as a stage. Children at this point would scatter about the park, running and jumping. A few would play on the cement lot behind the Martí statue. Adults would look after these young children, who did everything but stand still. Their thoughts would float to them and away from the words of the priest. In fact many of the onlookers wished that they could trade places with the children because Priest Suárez was always known for giving dry, blaming sermons.

The young Pedro was one of the kids on the concrete lot. He sat in a corner, looking idly at the other children. He had pulled his shirt out of his pants and was leaning back on his arms. The kids around him were playing baseball with a large wooden branch and a rock. They were yelling at Pedro, asking him to play, but Pedro did not budge.

"I'm tired," he responded.

"You're not tired," one of the kids said. "You just don't want to play without your little *narra*."

Pedro rolled his eyes and looked on. After a few minutes of taunting, however, all the children returned to their game and forgot about Pedro.

"Hey, Pedro!" called a voice from behind him.

Pedro turned to see Ramón walking toward him with a rusty and decrepit-looking bicycle.

"Where'd you get that?" asked Pedro as he quickly stood and brushed the back of his pants with his little hands.

"My father gave it to me."

Ramón's father had died five years after Ramón had been born. He had been a Chinese immigrant who had arrived in Cuba to work at the Trinidad sugar factory in the outskirts of the city. One day after work he had decided to walk into the hills of Trinidad's tallest mountain, Tope de Collantes. From a distance he had seen what looked like a woman picking flowers. As he approached her, he noticed that it was a naked woman sitting in a sea of yellow wildflowers, crying. She was embracing her knees and had her head stooped down and draped all around by her long, lacy hair.

"What's wrong?" he asked as he approached.

Migdalia had stopped crying and looked up at the Chinese man in his long white shirt and silky pants. Her blue eyes were the first things that had struck him.

"I'm no longer a virgin," she had said, holding back tears. Ramón's father had been struck by her honesty.

The bicycle had been given to Ramón when he turned four. His father and mother had decided to pool some of their earnings and get a used tricycle at one of the Plaza del Mercado stores. Ten days after Ramón had first ridden it, his father was forced to leave to Havana to work at another sugar mill because the one in Trinidad no longer needed him. Ten days after he had left, Migdalia received a telegram that said her husband had been hit by a car on the streets of the capital and been fatally injured. Migdalia had looked at Ramón the second she had put down the letter. His slanted eyes reminded her immediately of her husband, and when she looked at the blue pupils that lay within, she saw her painful tears reciprocated.

Five years later the bicycle was in a terrible condition. Metal shavings were coming off the body, and the two smaller back tires were almost empty of air. The seat had long ago fallen off and become unusable. It was now replaced with a very uncomfortable piece of wood.

"You can ride it first," Ramón told Pedro as he dragged the bike across the space between them.

"Thanks!" Pedro took the bike and, before sitting on it, looked at the boys who were playing baseball. A few turned to look at him, and he smiled slyly as he sat on the wooden plank. Pedro would rather play with Ramón on any day of the week before associating with those other brats.

"This is hard to ride!" exclaimed Pedro as his legs tried to propel the bicycle. "The pedals are so hard to push."

"It's supposed to be that way. It's a workingman's tricycle," responded Ramón.

A workingman's tricycle. This thing is impossible to move.

Pedro pushed the pedals along and dragged the bike with him. Ramón followed, avoiding the sneers from the baseball players.

"Hey! I think I'm making it gain speed!"

Pedro was moving a little faster now. Ramón was having a little more trouble keeping up with him. The boys playing baseball had stopped and were looking at Pedro. He was too much of a distraction to their game, and on top of that the lot was not big enough for both baseball players and tricyclists to coexist without meddling in each other's space.

As Pedro got farther and farther away, Ramón noticed that one of the small back wheels was wobbling. He looked at it for a bit and noticed how its flatness against the floor made it look like half a circle with a moving center.

Pedro's incessant pedaling allowed him to gain some speed, but control of the vehicle was not as easy as its acceleration. He managed to keep the handlebars steady, but he noticed that sometimes they went stiff, probably because of the rust, and it took a good yank to move them to another course. It so happened that when the back wheel popped off the bicycle, the handlebars also became stiff. The sudden shock and squeal of the metal rasping against the floor caused Pedro to turn and look back, ignoring the small metal fence that partitioned the lot from the statue of Martí. The tricycle crashed into the fence, and Pedro's shoulder crunched into one of the spaces between bars.

"Ow!" he screamed so loudly that the priest stopped his sermon to turn and look around the statue. Ramón ran toward Pedro and reached him first. When the priest walked over to him and noticed the bloodstain on his shoulder, he pushed Ramón away sternly and opened his shirt up. Some people had walked over from the seated processionists, including Pedro's mother and father. They had recognized Pedro's scream, and when they noticed the small white clavicle sticking out of his shoulder, they ran to him in a frenzy.

"Pedro! Pedro!" screamed his mother in tears.

"What happened, my son?" shouted his father as they all knelt around him.

Ramón stood on the outside of this circle, and when he felt a hand on his shoulder, he turned and squinted to see his mother standing behind him.

"I told you never to use that tricycle again!" she shouted as she grabbed his shoulder and shook him violently.

Ramón did not know what to expect, but before giving in to the wrath of his mother, he turned to see Pedro being carried away by his father. Pedro's face was crippled with agony, but his eyes were open and looking at Ramón. Brown eyes touched blue, and for twelve years this was the last time they would.

Pedro rubbed his shoulder now. The clavicle bone had long since healed, and there was no scar left from its protrusion. Raymond Chung was announcing another news segment of his show, this one about a mother who had given birth to her baby accidentally while sitting on her toilet. Although Pedro had not seen him since they met in Havana while both were trying to get out of the country—more than twenty-eight years ago—he recognized the man easily.

"Emily!" he called loudly with a slight accent that hispanicized the name. "Come here!"

Pedro waited for his wife to come, but in the meantime he rubbed his shoulder again, touching the bony presence underneath, and fixed his brown eyes on the blue ones on-screen.

DAVID RICE

The Circumstances Surrounding My Penis

Up to the age of eight I thought I was pretty normal. I was a healthy kid with too much energy, running around and playing with my friends and fighting with my brother. I couldn't complain much until my cousin's neighbor Lolita informed me that I wasn't normal because I had a "funny-looking" penis.

My cousins Javier and Jimmy were three and four years older than I was, respectively. They lived with Mama Locha, my grandmother, in Weslaco, Texas, about ten miles south of Edcouch. Weslaco was a bigger town than Edcouch, but most of the houses this side of the railroad tracks were no better than the houses in Edcouch. Mama Locha's house had indoor plumbing, like many houses in that part of town, but it also had an out-house.

It was a small outhouse, divided in half. One half had a toilet, and the other half had a shower. Each had a door that locked with a latch. Both the toilet and the shower worked just fine, but it was a little scary to use at night because there was no light and I had this fear of a spider or a snake or something, anything, biting my butt.

Lolita was Jimmy's age, and whenever my cousins wanted to play doctor or house, she was the perfect nurse or wife. She liked to do *manas*, and most of the boys in the neighborhood knew it. She was cute and actually real nice. She had this look in her eyes, the kind of look a woman gives you when she begins her hypnotic trance. Now that I'm older I realize that hypnotic eyes are very rare, but at eleven Lolita was a master.

Lolita's eyes could make you do anything. All she had to do was turn them on and you agreed to whatever she asked. And she wanted to look at my *pipí*. I know that there are other names: tally whacker, dingy whopper, thingy, and, of course the name that works for boys or girls, down there. When she told me she wanted to see my *pipí*, I was really blown away. But what really knocked me out was that she followed her request with a deal: "If you show me yours, I'll show you mine."

After a few quick seconds I said yes, but I told her she had to show me hers first. She nodded okay in one quick second. Lolita was a pro. It was as if she did this sort of thing all the time. I asked where could we go to do this, and she said the outhouse. She told me to go into the shower half first and she would wait to make sure no one was watching; then she would go in.

As I waited in the outhouse, I tried to imagine what it would look like. I had seen baby girls getting their diapers changed, but I knew that it couldn't still look like that once they got older. I heard her light footsteps approaching, and I stood to one side to give her room.

Lolita looked at me, and I said we had to hurry before someone tried to use the outhouse. My eyes focused on her hands as she unbuttoned her pants. She wiggled her body slightly and pulled her pants and panties down at the same time to her thighs. It still looked like what baby girls had! It just had this vertical line and nothing else?

"Okay, your turn," she said, pulling her pants and panties back on. I unbuttoned my jeans and unzipped the zipper, bringing down my jeans and Fruit of the Loom underwear down together. I looked to see what her reaction would be. I was hoping she would be amazed and say "wow" or "eeelooooo" or anything that would make her want to look at it more.

Instead Lolita had a puzzled look on her face. "Why does it

look like that? It's funny-looking. Why is it so small? The *pipís* of Javier and Jimmy don't look like that." I had no answers for Lolita, I lowered my eyes and looked at the drain surrounded by the cool dark cement. I began to pull my pants back on as she slipped out the door. I didn't see or talk to Lolita the rest of the day, and I didn't tell any of my friends about what I'd done in the outhouse.

After a few weeks I managed to put aside what Lolita had said about my penis, and I didn't see her that often anyway. When I did see her, she didn't offer to play doctor or house with me, but there were always other things to do at Mama Locha's.

A couple of years went by and I was in the fifth grade and no one had seen my *pipí* since that day in the outhouse. I was in the boys' room ready to pee and kept my eyes on the metal pipe above the trough that delivered the water. Looking at this pipe where I knew water flowed somehow made me pee a lot easier. I heard someone come in, but I didn't turn around, just kept my eyes on the pipe.

From the corner of my eye I could see it was Fidencio Fuentes, a kid in my grade. He stood next to me and began to pee as well. I could hear his pee, but I kept my eyes on the pipe. I could feel that he was looking at me.

"Hey, what's wrong with it?" he said, motioning his head and eyes at my penis.

I gave him a confused look. "*¿Qué?*"

"Your thing. Why does it look like that? It's got that red ring around it," Fidencio said.

I knew what he was talking about. My penis had a thin pink circle around the top of it, but I didn't think there was anything wrong with it. I looked over at his sticking out of his pants. His didn't look anything like mine. I shrugged my shoulders. "There's nothing wrong with it. That's the way it looks."

After that strange conversation I decided to use the boys' room only if the stall was available.

Two years later I tried out for the junior high school football team. I was a small kid, but my father was junior varsity quarterback when he went to my school, so I thought maybe I could play football and one day be quarterback.

Of course every day ended with a couple of laps around the track, and I ran as hard as I could so I could shower before the other players got there. I would quickly towel off and put on my underwear even if I was still wet. This way they wouldn't see my strange abnormal penis. The football coach said I was pretty fast and suggested I try out for the track team instead of football, which was kind of nice.

As I dressed to go home, I noticed the other players as they walked in and out of the showers. Not one of them had a penis like mine. One guy had a curved one, but no one made fun of him because he was one of the best defensive players.

After a couple of weeks of running the two laps like crazy, I decided to take it a little easier. I was still very self-conscious about my penis, but nobody made fun of me or asked me why it looked that way, so it didn't bother me enough to quit football.

When I was fifteen, my family moved to Austin, Texas, and I attended David Crockett High School. Crockett was a big school, close to twenty-five hundred students. Trying out for football was way out of the question, so I tried out for the gymnastic team instead.

After practice everybody hit the showers, not just the gymnastic team but most of Crockett's athletic teams: wrestling, track, soccer, basketball, and sometimes football.

So here I was at a new school that wasn't just Mexican-American students, it had whites, Afro-Americans, Mexican-Americans, and Asians. The school had everything. Now with this many students from so many backgrounds there was much to learn and see. One of the things I wanted to see was if anybody had a penis like mine.

There were all kinds of penises. Some looked like mine, and others looked like the ones back home. It didn't seem to matter what your skin color was—though I did notice more white guys with penises like mine than Mexican-American or the Afro-American. Hmm, this really puzzled me.

After thinking about this for weeks, I concluded that you're born with the penis God gave you, and that's that. But I was still a little self-conscious about my penis.

A few months later my best friend from Edcouch came up to see me. It was good to see him and I told him how it was strange to be around the white and Afro-American guys. I was so used to being around just Mexican-Americans all my life, and I was still getting used to my new surroundings.

He asked me if I had gone out with any of the white girls, and I told him that I didn't think they liked Mexican-Americans. He nodded when I said that. "Yeah, those white girls like it circumcised," he said. He put out his hands and pointed both index fingers, keeping the distance between his fingers about a foot apart as he told me what white girls liked. I knew by the common hands gesture what he was referring to, so I played along.

"Yeah, like those white guys have. Not like us," I said, laughing.

However, I didn't know what *circumcised* meant. Never heard the word before, but I knew that whatever it meant, it applied only to white guys.

Eight years passed, and I had become quite comfortable with my penis. I was in love and dating a wonderful woman who seemed to like my penis just fine. She made me completely forget Lolita's and Fidencio's comments.

One night as we lay in bed, my girlfriend began to play doctor with my private parts. She would take the head of my penis and lift it and let it fall down. She did this a few times and giggled each time it fell back down. She told me she was trying to see if it fell more to the right or more to the left. (Her findings were that it fell more to the right.)

She asked all sorts of strange questions about my penis. "Doesn't your tally whacker feel weird hanging there? [That's where I got that name, tally whacker, from her. She was from Arkansas, and she told me that's what they called it up there. But I think the name dingy whopper is just as funny, and I got that name from a crazy girl in Dallas.] Have you ever got caught in a zipper? Does it get cold in winter and hot in summer?" All I knew was that I had never got my tally whacker caught in a zipper.

She played with it for a couple more minutes and then, with a pleased voice, said, "You know what? I'm glad you're circumcised."

The small cocky grin on my face fell right off. I jumped out of the bed and shouted at her, "What did you say?"

She said nothing and gave me a confused frown.

"What did you say about my tally whacker?" Again I shouted.

Again she looked confused. "What? I said I like it."

"No, no, that's not what you said!"

"David, I said I like it," she said.

"No, that's not what you said," I said as I shook my head. "You said I was circumcised."

She looked at me and threw her arms up as if to say no shit. "You are! Why do you think it looks like that?"

Suddenly I became very aware of my funny-looking penis. "I'm not circumcised. I'm Mexican, and there's nothing wrong with it. It's just the way it is."

She shook her head. "I didn't say there was anything wrong with it, David. I told you I was glad that you were circumcised."

"I'm not circumcised!"

She stood still for a moment and looked at me with a small smile. "You didn't know you were circumcised, did you?"

I didn't say anything. I just looked at the legs of the bed.

"David, there's nothing wrong with being circumcised. It just means that when you were a baby, the doctor cut off your foreskin," she said. "Your parents probably told him to."

I couldn't move. I just kept my eyes on the legs of the bed. She put out her hand. "Come here." I walked over and sat next to her, and she put her arm around me.

"I thought only white guys were circumcised," I said.

She shook her head and laughed. "Sometimes you can be real dumb."

From that day on I picked up where I had left off when I was eight. Back to being a pretty normal, healthy kid with too much energy.

MICHELE M. SERROS
The Next Big Thing

I hated drummers. They sweat too much, are always in the back of all band photos, and eventually grow whiny with an undesirable paunch to match. Singers are just pretty boys with gigantic egos to make up for small penises and lead guitarists? . . . Puh-leez! Now bass players, bass players are where it's at. Leonard was a bassist, the backbone of the band. The minute I met him I knew I'd be moving out on No Talent Gary, leaving him to cry with that stinkin' twenty-year-old cat I never liked.

Angela had introduced Leonard to me at her party as a musician from New York. Angela is the best. Like me, she sells ads on the phone during the day, but come night, she too is a done-up, made-up party glamour gal. Unlike Gary, Leonard was on his way up. Leonard was going to be famous, successful. New Yorkers are *known* for success. And everybody knows what dangerous, mad moody creatures they can be, never to be tamed or predicted. I liked that.

Three days later Leonard soon became Lenny, as in Lenny, a nickname I gave him in full baby voice. He yanked that phone receiver out of my hands forever and filled his rust bucket of a van with my stuff and moved me into the band's house. The band's house. Does it get any better than that? We'd stay awake for hours into the night, listening to those rats climb inside his bedroom walls, bandmates in the next room: hacking up phlegm, downing Black Velvet, and debating *creative differences.* Leonard would whisper childhood stories about a fourteen-year-old him and some nasty neighbor lady, making me think he was a natural pervert. I fell for him even more. Those first fresh days we were too selfish to share time with others, worried that we would fall asleep early and miss out on each other's newness. We'd stay up late till twilight, laughing, talking, getting it on. We'd wake up way past noon in each other's spit and cum, bra straps, panties, and wallet chains strapped around our throats and ankles. I'd lay my head on his belly, looking at his guitar collection, while he'd tell me about all his crazy dreams and I'd reply with "Man, Lenny, that was some crazy dream. I read somewhere crazy dreams are the sign of a real creative person," and then with his eyes half closed, he'd lift his chin up and stroke his neck—all smuglike. One week later we announced to the band we were in love, and like all corny couples, we vowed to see the world together. Didn't matter I was just out of a job and he living hand to mouth 'cause his band, his band was the next big thing.

That was eighteen months ago, and now we are seeing the world together, at least Europe anyway. Lots of people think touring Europe is seeing the world; they forget about Asia and Africa and all those Latin countries in between. "The most important countries!" my tía Annie would say. And lots of stupid girls think touring with a band is "so cuh-uul." It is, the first time, the second time, and maybe the third. It's the time you start to dread pulling out that passport you know you want it to be the last time, your last tour. Somewhere something went wrong; something, someone got stale.

It was March 23, two days after the first day of spring, when I realized this had happened to us. The band had just played its last date in Holland, and we were leaving Amsterdam. Thank God, it is so dreary with its suicide gray haze of a sky. Thank God we were bailing out on that ugly-ass place; thank God for the big music fest in Valencia. I wanted sun, a tan, to buy a Lladro piece for Mama and a better choice of men; ones with Spanish accents, long black lashes, and *straight* teeth. I had grown tired of Dutch people, but most of all, I had grown tired of Leonard.

It was only the second week of the tour, and he was passed out again, in the back of the bus. Not from overindulgence of recreational drugs, partying, or liquor. I wish! None of that cliché "confessions of the band" shit they try to sell to suburban shamed punk rock kids or Midwest ho-dads in "rock" magazines. Leonard was just plain *tired*. He was always tired. Every part of his body grew limp after only a few weeks on the road. What a pussy. We still had three and a half months to go on tour. It was only the nineteenth show the band had played in a row with no days off. The itinerary promised a bunch of days off, but Gunter, the road manager, said no, we could sleep on the bus during the day if we got that tired. More nights and days of work meant more money, but it also meant less fun time with Lenny.

The curtains of the bus were pulled shut, making it that kind of depressed darkness. Hints of brightness seeped through the crack where the fabric just couldn't meet. I knew it was bright outside. It was already spring weather. I wanted to be outside, doing something, doing anything. But I wasn't doing anything, with anyone, for that matter. I was stuck in a stuffy bus with five musicians, two drivers, one tour manager, and a fat roadie, passing time, passing gas, passing by castle after castle, snowcapped mountaintop after snowcapped mountaintop—ugh! The only thing good about touring is the shows. The springtime music fests in Spain and Greece are the biggest.

I had my head on Leonard's belly and raised it to see what was on the VCR. The sound wasn't on, but I could feel a buzz of boxed activity and saw the contrast of movement on the bus's ceiling. It was an Italian skin flick (or is that redundant?), and everyone was hypnotized by the screen, waiting for another tit scene or ass shot. Z-Man, the roadie, was the only one not paying attention. He was searching through Euro fast-food trash looking for his shades. He looked my way, and I quickly looked down. I knew if I made any eye contact with him, he'd corner me for hours to try to make me believe about all the girls he could have had last night, all the girls backstage who lifted crocheted minis to expose crotchless panties. Yeah, right. He is so sad with his fat, ugly self. He's lucky the band lets him lug gear and heave back line for them or he'd have no life at all.

It was too late; his eyes had caught mine.

"So, Miss Linda, did you have fun last night? While your boyfriend and I were at the Weg, breaking down the stage till the crack of dawn? You just took off with everyone for the bars. Man, I wish I had the easy life and got to tour around Europe for free with *my* boyfriend."

"Well," I told him, "maybe if you gave in to your desires, you could and it isn't my fault the promoter didn't have his shit together to get a breakdown crew."

I hated Z-Man. I wasn't about to fall for his guilt trip pettiness. Anyone who has to give himself his own nickname is pretty pathetic. He just wants people to say, "Z-Man? That's an unusual name. What does it stand for? How unique!" I hid my head back on Leonard's stomach, hoping he would get the hint and leave me alone, but he didn't.

"Don't give me attitude just 'cause you're some groupie who made good," Z-Man snapped. He found his sunglasses, wrapped them around his eyes, and put the VCR on fast forward.

I ignored him, pretending I was falling asleep. What an asshole! Where does *he* get off calling *me* a groupie? He's the one kissing everybody's ass. He's the one who after every remark has to look over to one of the guys for approval as if maybe they'll think, *Wow, Z-Man is so cool, he should be in our band instead of being just the roadie*. Roadie, groupie, it's the same thing. But *I* am neither one. How could he even think that? I'm part of the band, in a way. I help with things, keep Leonard happy. There is a *big* difference.

I remember when I was fifteen and I first heard the word *groupie*. My Swedish pen pal Kat told me that her sister, Solvie, gave head to every member in Sweet. Kat told me her sister was a groupie and loved to brag about it. I didn't know what *head* was till I finally questioned Kat, and then her tissue-paper letters, *por avión*, educated me twice a month after that. Since then I never thought of sucking dick as a groupie thing. I mean, it was a full power trip. Kat told me that if I learned the talent correctly, it would get me the things mediocre girls could never have; attention; excitement; rock star boyfriends; trips to Europe. She was right. Kat is no longer the pen pal I swore I'd have for life. Once I mastered the craft through her detailed letters, I practiced my stuff on various hometown losers who anxiously unzipped their creased corduroys. I was set. I didn't need her or them anymore. I wanted men in big bands signed to big labels with big dreams, men, I thought, Leonard was like. I wasn't no groupie.

I looked up toward Leonard's face. His mouth was slightly open, and I could see his dark tooth. I remember when I first met him I thought it made him look tough, like maybe he had been in a lot of barroom fights or something, maybe fighting over some girl, and I wondered what he'd fight over for me. But when he later told me that he had killed the nerve as a kid playing kick the can back in Massachusetts, I tried not to let it bother me. It was little things like that that were making him less exciting, less intriguing, and less attractive to me.

Leonard's face started to scrunch up tight as though maybe he were having a bad dream. I should have woke him up 'cause I know how much he loves to talk about his dreams once he wakes up. I've grown to hate that. I've learned over time he now starts off with "Man, I just had the weirdest dream," and that's my cue to drift off till I hear "man, it was so weird," meaning he's done with his little amateur storytelling. Then I'll say, "Yeah, honey, that was *some* dream." *He* has become the worst dream imaginable, a nightmare. Not in the form of fangs or black lagoon horror. He has become mediocre. The worst image for a fledging rock star. I didn't want him anymore. I wanted to leave him so bad, but go where? I didn't want to go home early. And to what? Telemarketing? Angela wasn't even around. She's off in New Zealand with Monster Mongrel. If I lost my cool and suggested any discontent, he'd call me ungrateful and have my ass off that bus, QUICK. I'd be the laughingstock. Man, wouldn't Z-Man get a big kick out of that? Watching me get dumped off at some shithole airport in stinkin' Germany while he makes grand with the band in Greece and Spain, extra legroom from *my* empty seat. No way! There was no way I was leaving early. I could grin and bear it. Leonard the man with big dreams had now become Leonard the man with boring dreams and a damaged tooth with a history just as bad.

I stuck two of my fingers into his nostrils until Leonard's mouth burst out with air. I laughed. I woke him up but didn't get his attention like I wanted. He started to lean his body against the window. I wrapped my arms around his waist, pressed my lips against his crotch, and blew hard through his suede trousers. He frowned down at me and barked, "Don't!" He turned his back toward me and went back to sleep.

Man! What a drag. I looked up the aisle at the front seat and saw Joe laughing softly with a girl from last night. I remember seeing her come into the club with her arms wrapped around some guy, and now here she was with her body wrapped around Joe. His hand was carelessly lying on top of her left tit, and I wondered if he played with both of them all night. I overheard him say one time, "Man, if I was a girl, I would just wanna stay home and play with my tits all day." I wonder, could Joe really play with the same pair of tits all day long? Wouldn't he get tired? I wondered what he was like in bed. He never seemed to get tired. If only he wasn't the drummer.

We finally pulled into Valencia. After three days of ten-minute gas, piss, and shit stops I was so happy. I couldn't wait to take a bath and have some fun time with Lenny. But Gunter said no. He said we didn't have time to check into the hotel; we needed to go straight to the venue. We had to do sound check.

I almost screamed! "Sound check? Come on! Why do *I* have to go? Come on, Gunter, take me to the hotel." But he just ignored me, directing Jorg, the driver, through the narrow streets.

I put my arms around Leonard. "Come on, Lenny, make 'em drop me off at the hotel. We could both go. We could break in a new bed, get some room service. Please, baby, let's both go to the hotel."

But Leonard took my arms off him and said, "Come on, Linda, don't make it harder than it already is."

I knew the real reason why Leonard didn't speak up. It was because he was just a bassist. No matter how cool they seem, bassists really don't have much clout in a band, they're really just second up from the drummers. If I was with J.J., the singer, I'd have been in a bubble bath long ago.

I looked up and saw Z-Man looking at me.

"What?" I asked him. "Get ready to lug your gear, *roadie.*"

At the venue I recognized many of the touring buses from last year. Black Roses and Plastic Dolls were already doing sound check. I got out of the bus to go backstage. I immediately ran to the catering table to check out if the Ryder was right this time. I found a shitload of salami and Brie. So what else is new? I pulled out a bottle of OJ from under ice and poured some into a glass.

"Hey, don't you want this to go with that?"

I turned around and saw Marco from La Maquina waving a bottle of vodka.

"Oh, hey, Marco, you're playing here too?" I felt embarrassed. I must have looked so gross from the bus ride. La Maquina is *the* coolest band, and Marco is *hot.* Even though he was a singer with a big ego, I heard he did have a cock to match it. He always had a handful of sequined Spanish mamas fluttering around him, but this time he was alone.

"*¡Ay, que linda¡* Is that the greeting I get? It's been, what? Over two months since I saw you? Come here, sit down with me."

I let him add vodka to my orange juice, then nestled near him on a torn leather couch.

"Hey, why aren't you helping get your sound check ready?" I asked him.

"That work is for peons. Let the roadies or drummers take care of it. There's partying to be done."

Man, I liked his style. Leonard hated Marco. He always said, "When I'm not around, stay clear of that asshole; he's only trouble." When I protested, Leonard would reply, "Linda, he's

Spanish. What else do you need to know? Don't you know anything what *his* people did to *your* people? *I* even know that. They love to conquer . . . anything." I hated when Leonard pulled his junior college history crap on me. He's always been jealous of Marco's band. But he wasn't around right then; it was just me and Marco.

"Ay, Linda, your hair is even longer and what? Have your tits grown too?"

"Marco! That is so rude!" I crossed my arms to cover my chest. But he didn't care, and neither did I, really.

"Hey, come on, why you getting prude with me now? Come on, Señorita Linda, *que linda*." He put one hand on my breast and squeezed it lightly. I nearly died! I mean Marco is so fine. He was trying to get to me, and it was working. It had been so long since Leonard really touched me.

Suddenly I remembered the bus trip. I must have looked terrible. I excused myself, grabbed my duffel bag, and went to find a bathroom. Club bathrooms are the worst, but European ones are even grosser. I found one and held my nose as I went in. In my bag I found the purple satin padded bra Leonard had given me for Christmas. Ha! If Leonard wasn't interested in having me in it, maybe Marco was. After rubbing on some rouge, pulling my hair down flat, I went back to meet Marco.

He was still sitting on the couch, but now Gunter and Leonard were talking to him. They both looked pissed. Oh, man! Marco must have opened his big mouth and told Leonard what I had just let him do.

"Get your stuff, Linda, we're leaving!" Leonard huffed at me.

"Why? Why are we leaving, Lenny? What's wrong?" I ran toward him to hug him.

He didn't answer, but Gunter did. "We got booted from the bill. Assholes didn't even wire us. We drove all this way for nothing."

Oh, my God! I couldn't believe this! "Booted from the bill." How embarrassing! Oh, man, I didn't want to get back on that bus. I hated it. I wanted to go to more shows. I wanted to party. I wanted to stay in Spain. I wanted to be with Marco.

"The kids want wilder stuff this year," Gunter guessed. "Anyway, we'll meet you back at the bus." He and Leonard left to go outside.

"Wilder"? What did he mean by that? Wild as in the opposite of tame? Tame as in domestic? Domestic like "common" and common meaning *mediocre*. Fuck! How could I stay with Leonard and his stupid band?

Marco looked up at me from the couch and clicked his tongue. "Well, it's a shame you have to leave, Linda. We were just getting to know each other, like I've always wanted. My band still has a show to do and even bigger ones later." He brought his drink up to his mouth. I saw that his fingernails were dirty and that his knuckles had two initials inked in. Whose initials? Some girl? Initials are chickenshit. Once he got to know me he would have his whole *back* a mural in my honor, my name, *in full*.

"Oh, Marco, it doesn't have to be that way." I plopped down next to him and snuggled my face into his wavy black hair. He laughed, putting his arm around me, and just then I heard Leonard's voice.

"Oh, so this is how it is, huh, Linda? This is what it's all about! Okay . . . okay, well, at least now I know."

"Leonard, come on, what did you expect?" I looked up at him but stayed sitting on the couch. "Come on, Lenny, I'm bored with it. I hate the bus, the guys are driving me crazy, and . . . I'm really not into the music anymore. I'm sorry, I'm really sorry, but I wanna have some fun too, you know. I'm gonna stay. I'm gonna stay here with Marco . . . 'kay? Come on, Lenny, don't put the guilt trip on me . . . what did you expect?"

"Yeah, well, thanks a lot, Linda, thanks a fucking lot for letting me know . . . yeah, well, have a good one!" And he left to head for the bus.

"What a baby!" Marco laughed. He looked around and then added, "Well, hey, I'm gonna go see who else is here. You wait here, I'll be right back, but if I'm not, I'll catch you after the show."

Marco kissed my forehead, grabbed his drink, and got up from the couch.

From the doorway I watched Leonard get on the bus and get into the front passenger seat, cramming his head into a pillow. Jorg put the bus into first gear and headed out past all the other vans and tour buses while Gunter flung my suitcase out the side door.

Then I saw Z-Man. He was watching me from the far left back window. I couldn't tell from his expression what he thought. Was he happy I was finally off the bus? Was he going to stretch out his fat legs on my old seat? He looked sad, and I couldn't understand why. Did he really truly believe I *was* a groupie? What made him say that?

I suddenly felt so gross, really wanting a bath, but instead I did nothing as I watched Marco mingle away into the crowd.

ERASMO GUERRA
Last Words

Reynaldo had killed himself with an electrical cord he had hung over his mother's favorite front yard tree. My mother called with the news and said, "See *lo que pasa, Ernesto.*" Now everyone stops and turns to see me. I am late. I stand by my car and notice how little has changed. My family huddles under withered trees planted in this barren part of the cemetery. The young trees don't provide much cover from the brutal summer sun, but only the *viejas* sit under the canopy. The men find their own shade squatting by their trucks and beat-up cars. With legs apart, long-neck *birongas* ride close to their jeans where their cocks should be. They sip their beers and drag on their cigarettes, dropping the ash, and tossing still-glowing embers into the dry yellow grass that connects everyone. I hear Tía at the head of the canopy. She cries out for her son Reynaldo, and then everyone turns back to continue with the last words.

I remain by the car and watch Tío Joe sip beer with the rest of the men. He pulls out a smile and says, "Ay." I look at him, the other men, the canopy of women, unsure where my place is.

I wish Michael had come with me. I should have invited him. The afternoon Ama called about Rey, I had been waiting for Michael to get home from work. The sun had set. Traces of the pale pink sky came through the windows and lit the bedroom, where I sat on the floor smoking a pack of cigarettes Michael had left on the nightstand. I didn't invite him. I didn't even tell him about Reynaldo or how he died. I only said someone in the family had died and I had to come home. I wanted to come without him. Put distance between us. I had to see where I stood in our own dead relationship. But I want him now. I want someone who does not make me feel so alone.

I step from the car and walk to the family. The air thickens with the slow recitation of prayer. The words, low and heavy, trickle into a mumbled whisper. Everyone takes a breath of the damp air, and then another string of words slide into my ears. I never knew how to pray.

When I moved out of the Valley—moved to Houston because it was farther than San Antonio and Austin—I had enjoyed the first drive back home. I had sung along with each song. I figured a year away from the Valley, things would have changed. But nothing had changed. Ama still had her stories about the number of cousins married and settled with kids. "I told your *apa que* maybe you had a girlfriend now but didn't want to tell us." She had coaxed, "Do you?" Michael and I had recently moved in together. I told her about him. "Now don't go around telling everyone either," Ama had said, but I felt everyone already knew. Ama dropped her smile and talked little the rest of my stay. On my return to Houston I told myself it had been my last trip back home. Yet here I stand.

Apa appears from between two parked cars. I didn't notice him there: the thin pair of well-worn blue jeans, the pressed white shirt, and the stale-smelling straw cowboy hat. The cigarette gum almost drops from his mouth as he parts his lips to say hello. "Aye!" he says. "How was it?"

I shrug. There is nothing to tell about a six-hour drive from Houston: scattered towns, the highway, and miles of bad radio. Every song sounds the same now.

Apa offers his arm for a handshake. I ignore the stiffness and pull on his arm to bring him closer. I hug him. Test him.

"Your hair is getting long," he says.

"I'm letting it grow."

"I don't think your *ama* is going to like it."

I ignore the way he hands me off to Ama, as he always does. He uses her and she uses him to get things through to me. To straighten me out.

"Where is she?" I ask.

"She's up front with your *tía*. You know your *ama*." He smirks, popping his gum. "Always *en borlotes*. I don't know about her, but I hate funerals."

He spits out his gum into the dirt and takes out another piece from his shirt pocket and nervously drops it into his mouth.

"Your *ama* is really worried about you," he says.

"About me?"

"Well, you know. Houston. *Que* it's so big. She just doesn't want what happened to Rey to happen to you."

"I'm not stupid," I say, resenting the connection. "Michael and I—"

"You tell her," he blurts harshly. "I don't like to hear about those things. And I don't think you should go around talking about everything you do to everyone."

"I'm not talking to everyone. I'm talking to you."

"I don't want to know."

Apa looks ahead toward the canopy. Apa, who has never hit me, who has never cursed me, has never praised me either, has never held me, has never wanted to know anything about me. I never could say anything. Silently I take in the trees and, under their bare bone branches, those cloistered in the unforgiving heat.

The eulogy ends. People leave their shade to offer their respects to my cousin Reynaldo. Their movement whips up a dust-carrying wind. Narrow roads of once-rough caliche crisscross the cemetery, making rivers of pale white dust. Dark earth from the nearby field sifts through the rusting hurricane fence surrounding this desolate part of the cemetery. At the far end of the field a tractor plows the failed crop of summer melon, now rotting in the dirt.

Apa quietly buries himself with the drunks still leaning against their cars as I step into the slowly forming line, wrapping around to the back of the canopy. I watch Ama comfort Tía, slumped into the chair beside her. Tía mumbles. She remembers: "Reynaldo. *Hijo tan lindo*, such a nice boy."

"*Sí. Sí. Sí,*" Ama soothes. With a free hand Ama touches everyone who passes. "Thank you," she whispers. The people turn from them, take a last look into the casket, and then move on and out—away from it all.

"Your *ama* told me you were coming."

I turn around and find Angel smiling behind me. "A *marimacha*," Ama said to me as a kid, "Angel. *Esa muchacha* is nothing but a *marimacha*. A real tomboy. Don't be playing with her." Back then it had been a threat to turning out wrong, even if Angel did act like a boy. Back then I never understood a threat. Back then I felt I could live an infinite number of summers.

"Angel."

"Hey, you remember." She smiles.

"It's been a long time."

"When did you get in?"

"Today. Just now."

"Are you going to stay for *unos* days?"

"No. I'm going back home tonight."

"Houston, right?"

"Yeah."

"You see anyone up there?"

I think about what Apa had said. Telling Angel that I might not find my Michael when I got back home, that I might find, instead, the strange sheets of our bed, drained of desire and stale like a bag of forgotten bread, food for birds, myself on a couch, not wanting to sleep in that bed I had somehow made for myself, saying all that would be, as Apa put it, talking about everything I did to everyone.

"No. I'm not seeing anyone."

I give Angel the familiar answer that keeps the family safe

from embarrassment. Today, however, I feel a tangle of crows take flight from their usual perch in my chest and leave me like an abandoned field.

She blots the sweat off her upper lip with the inside collar of her dress. Angel, who was once the boy of the short summer hair, rough, scabby knees, and bare flat chest, now wears too much makeup and a tight black dress. She looks at me as if the sun were in her eyes.

"Yeah, your mom told me you don't see anyone."

"You talk to her?"

"Yeah, you know her. She likes me. Then she doesn't like me. I don't think she really likes anyone."

"I don't think anyone really likes her."

"Ay, your own mom!"

"Don't tell her."

"You think I would?" she asks, softening her voice. "But you know, she told me *que* you were gonna come. I thought I was never gonna see you again."

"*Ah que.* Yeah, right," I say.

I try to laugh it off, but I remember how Angel faded into the Valley.

I had been sitting in our tree in the orange grove that stretched along the back of the *colonia*. I hid there all afternoon to stay cool, out of the sun, out of sight from everyone. Angel came up the tree with the news about the two male teachers from La Joya shot in an onion field, hands tied behind their back, naked. The papers said the teachers had shared an apartment in McAllen, but everyone whispered that they were *maricones*. "You see," Ama had said, "they kill people like that. Nobody likes them."

Angel and I knew that we would die deaths like that one day. Die crazy and sad deaths like the teachers from La Joya. We made a pact, days before we both started the ninth grade, that we would never leave each other alone in the Valley.

I knew then that it would still happen. She would leave me or I would leave her. Why else would we need to say anything when we already knew about each other without ever saying a word about it? Maybe the news scared us both, but it has been so long and now everything reminds me of death that I can explain little of what I was feeling that day other than a sense that we were both doomed and kidding each other.

Angel dropped out of school when she turned sixteen. I graduated from high school and quietly slipped out of the Valley, as Ama and Apa had wanted.

Seeing her now, I doubt she will ever get out. She seems to belong. She looks like all my other cousins.

"Can you blame me that I don't come back more often?" I tease. "I'm surprised I'm here now."

Suddenly I remember why I am here, and things are less funny.

"Your mom tell you everything?" Angel asks.

"She said Rey had been sick."

"Sad, huh?"

"I never knew he had been sick."

"No one did. Until the guy he had lived with kicked him out *de la* house. I think he told Tía *que* he was sick. I think both of them was sick. They got *unos de los* tests, you know and found out they had that thing *de los gays*. Everyone says that was the reason Rey killed himself. My boyfriend helped bring him down."

I look at her as she wipes her forehead with the back of her hand. She looks away, squinting.

"He's here *también*. There. That's him."

She points to a thin guy standing under a tree with few leaves.

"*Lo ves*, you see him?" she asks.

"Yeah," I say, and turn to her. "I didn't know you had a boyfriend."

"Yeah," she says, her forehead still wet, smiling timidly as if to say she cannot help the heat. "He works with the firemen. They went out to Tía's in an ambulance. You know, none of them wanted to touch Rey because they knew he was, you know, sick. *Y* they left him up there for a long time. A doctor had to come to say *que* it was okay to bring him down. He didn't care."

"Who?"

"My boyfriend," she snaps. "He didn't care Rey was sick. He's wanting to be a nurse. He said he's gonna have to do that stuff anyway."

We come up to the front of the canopy, toward the casket. I want to stop talking. Not out of any deep respect but because I want to walk through unnoticed.

"Yeah, he and I are going to San Antonio in a month," she continues. "We're gonna move up there so he can go to school. Me, I can't wait to get out of here. I'm tired of this place."

I do not want to ignore Angel, but the veil over the casket flutters, and everything fades. I remember running off with Rey when no one else would play with us. The games with Tía's dusty black leather heels, the creamy red lipsticks, and fashion magazines of women on runways; Rey and I playing make-believe in his tiny tar-papered house that sat on four dirty bricks. I remember getting caught by Tío Joe and the long ride home. Ama and Apa. Mad. Spanish. He's your son, one of them had said. And he's yours too, the other one shot back. I remember how when we get home, they forget me with their own fight, but I run to my room crying as if they had slapped or hit me with a switch from a limb off the limp tree out back. I forget Angel and everyone else, and I lean in, to the casket.

The sores, purple with disease, cover Rey's face. I wonder, if like eyes, they will open and vent a long damning glare. Milky, thin lines of something bubble out of the crack between his chapped lips, and a thin burn runs down from behind his ear, along the edge of his jaw and across the bump of his throat. A band of deep scratches tear at his neck.

"*M'ijo*," Ama says, "*no te pones* too close."

"*¿Mande?*" I ask to make sure.

"*Que no te pones* too close," she whispers fiercely behind me. I feel her breath sharp as fingers ready to pull me back. "The señor at the funeral home said *que no era* safe."

"What's not safe?" I ask under my breath. "He is dead."

A thin, desperate light covers the sky. Everything looks pale, flat, bleached out by the sun. I steady my hand as I lift the cheap veil off the casket, and Tío Joe watches me blankly. Tío Joe, who caught Rey and me playing make-believe, grabbed us from behind our necks, squeezed tight tears out of our eyes. Tío Joe who thought up a name for his own son—Reynaldo: *La Reyna del Rancho*—turns slowly to walk away.

I slip my hand into the casket and feel the rough suit snag on my fingers. The suit does not fit him. It is old and loose, a deep brown with grass stains. How long did Reynaldo wait in the tree? Wait for a lover to take him down and bring him home? Wait for the parents to take him in? Wait for something to happen, for something to change, for simple comfort? It seems as if after he had put on the suit, struggled with the cord, and then been let down, the morticians put Rey into a casket like a carelessly arranged gift in a box.

I run a finger over the jutting bones in his wrists. The skin flakes between his fingers. I take a breath and brush my lips on Rey's stiff hands as Ama always forced me to do as a sign of love and respect for the dead.

"*Ay, mi'hijo,*" Tía wails.

I feel a warm hand on my shoulder, but when I turn around, it is Tía who touches me. I hold her trembling hand. Ama shoots a glance from her chair. I look away pretending not to notice.

"*Ay, mi'hijito,* I know *que* you are just like Reynaldo," Tía says.

I weaken when she says it. I feel my lips part to say something, to defend myself, but the cords tighten in my throat. I want to tell her that she is wrong. I am not sick. I am not weak. I am not dead. I am nothing like her son. The faces sharpen and the voices die and I say nothing.

The gears whine and the straps roll off and the casket creaks as it sinks into the ground. It settles in with a thud. Hands full of dirt shower the casket. Then the shoveled clumps begin to send up a rhythm of the caretakers doing their work. Tía takes off her wedding ring, and I hear it clink when she throws it into the slowly filling hole.

The scene shudders through me, and I feel a familiar shame as if I had been caught playing make-believe again, making everyone believe I am not Rey. I see the thinly drawn line I strung to separate myself from him. I see clearly how the place we called home, the faces we grew up with, and a simple rustle of leaves led him to his end. I am there too. In fact I am still there.

ANTHONY CASTRO
Soldier

He couldn't even look me in the eyes. That was when I realized that he was hurt. This "soldier" had been wounded but not physically. His pain was worse; it was emotional and not obvious to the naked eye. He was bleeding internally and would continue to do so until he reached a truce. Unfortunately the truce had to be made with himself, and his pride left no room for compromises. I sat and watched him negotiate with himself, his eyes darting here and there but never meeting my gaze. He ran one hand through his coarse dark hair, and in the other he clutched a forty-ounce bottle of beer. Although his eyes were constantly fleeing, he held a look of indifference on his face. It was as if he were constantly shrugging his shoulders, the way a child does when it doesn't know what's going on. And he didn't know. He didn't know that what he was trying to fight was larger than he was, larger than I was, larger than all of us.

The "soldier's" name was Tony, and he was a "small-time" drug dealer. We had met my senior year in high school and became best friends; he was a transfer student from Puerto Rico. I remember he had a lot of trouble picking up English, so he was forced into one of those English-as-a-second-language programs. He eventually dropped out of school after failing to make any progress. Months after he dropped out I remember seeing him around the way. He had changed up his act, though. He was no longer the "hick from PR." I guess he had finally assimilated because there he was on the corner in his gold chains, beeper, and hundred-dollar sneakers. As I walked past him, I guess he recognized me because he flashed a smile that revealed about four hundred dollars in gold dental work. I waved back and kept walking, debating with myself as to who had the right idea: me or Tony.

The next time I saw him was about a year later and I was on my Christmas break. He was on the same corner as the last time. The ground was covered with snow, and I was walking to the store with my head down, making sure not to step on any ice patches. I walked past the "spot," and I heard someone say, "Oh, you don't know nobody?" I looked up, and there was Tony in a black leather shearling coat, ski hat, black jeans, and matching black boots.

"What's up?" I replied.

He walked over to me and gave me a hug. He smelled of cologne and marijuana. "Damn, you just disappeared, huh?"

"Nah" I replied. "I'm in school up in Massachusetts, but I come home every now and then."

He just kept nodding his head and then threw in "That school shit ain't for me, I tried and nothin'. I'm doin' all right without any degrees, as you can see." He pulled a thick wad of money from his pocket and smiled that million-dollar smile.

"Yeah, you doin' all right, just be careful," I said, trying to put together a smile.

"Yo, it's all good," he replied. Then he struck the thinker's position and proceeded with "Yo, you ever think about making some quick money? You know, a smart kid like you can make a brother like me a millionaire overnight and not to mention put a little something in your own pocket."

I chuckled at his suggestion because I had thought about it before and I knew that there was a lot of money out there for the taking. "That's not for me; you know that, plus my family would kill me," I said to him as well as a reminder to myself.

"Yeah, yeah, I understand, yo, good luck with all that, but if you ever change your mind, you know what to do," he said as he winked and walked away. As I turned to go, I heard over my shoulder "Oh, next time you come down you gotta meet my little boy, money's gonna be the next Camacho."

I continued to the store wondering how long Tony's dream would last and whether I would ever get to meet his little boy. As I passed a storefront, I looked at my own reflection in the window and tried to picture myself in all black and gold. All I saw was my old dungarees and my light blue parka. I started to wonder whether I would ever start to reap the same kinds of benefits that Tony was enjoying. I threw on my Walkman and lost myself in the heavy bass.

It was May, and I had just returned from school. I was headed down to the park to play ball when I passed a familiar figure sitting on the park bench. It was Tony, but he seemed to have lost a lot of weight and a lot of luster. He looked up at me blankly and then looked back down at the ground. "Yo, Tony, what's up?" I said as I approached him.

"What's up, kid?" he replied.

"Damn, you don't look so good. What you been up to?" I asked.

"It's a long story," he replied.

He ran his hand through his hair, put down his beer, and began to talk. "Remember I said that I had a kid. Well, I was living with my wife and my little boy a little while back. Everything was cool; we were living fat. I had more money than I knew what to do with. But it was never enough for me. I came here with nothing, and once I saw the money that I could make, I would never be satisfied, but anyway. I had started selling weed. Then I moved up to pumping crack, and that shit was a gold mine. A gold mine. I had these fiends stealing for me, killing for me, doing whatever I said. I thought that shit would never end, but I was dead wrong. One day I was on the corner, doing my thing, when my girl came up with my little boy. She was on her way to Thirty-fourth to do a little shopping, and she needed some loot. I picked up my little boy and was kissing him when these crackheads ran up talking about I had better give them all my money or they were going to spray us all, beginning with my girl and little boy. All chaos broke loose as I tried to put my boy down and pull out. I don't know what I was thinking, but I knew that I couldn't go out like a sucker. One of the crackheads grabbed my girl, and the other scooped up my little boy. I didn't know what to do. He had my little boy around the waist and had a broken bottle to his face. The other one had my wife around the neck with the nine to her throat. I froze up. Then I realized that it was all over. I couldn't do shit. I dropped to my knees and gave them all the shit I had, drugs, gun, all of it. They broke out after that and let my family go. I picked up my little boy and tried to hug my girl. But she was hysterical and started to scream that she couldn't live like this. She pushed me away and tore my son away from me. I was left standing there alone. She ran off into the night. My whole life had come to an end in a matter of seconds. I tried to pick up the pieces after that, but I got no respect in the street or at home. It was only weeks before my girl left me and I had to move my operation. I don't know, kid. It's over. I ain't nobody."

So here we were. The ex-kingpin and the broke college kid. Basically at the same point, struggling in similar ways. The only difference between us is that I had foresight and I had a better sense of the overall picture. Tony sat there looking at his beer as if the answers were floating in his bottle. I felt for him, but when I thought about it, I wasn't doing much better. Maybe I'd be better off if I were ignorant and not aware of reality. What was the difference between me filling some college quota and Tony bridging the gap between the poor community and the rich drug suppliers? We both were being used for cosmetic reasons. I sat there with Tony all night; we didn't say much to each other. As the park crowd thinned out, Tony lit a blunt and passed it to me. I took a pull and sat for a little while longer. As I bounced my ball, I heard a mother call her son to go home because it was getting too late. I took this lady's cue and gave Tony five as I made my way out of the park. I looked back at Tony in the darkness and just saw his silhouette. It didn't look like him from afar, and the truth is it could have been any one of us.

RICARDO ARMIJO

Drizzle of Moths

"Begin at the beginning," the King said gravely, "and go on till you reach the end: then stop."
Lewis Carroll, *Alice's Adventures in Wonderland*

When the little clown wearing the huge flapping shoes started his three-minute routine, I turned down the radio. Somehow I thought that without the DJ's shrill voice I would be able to see him better, although it would have been difficult to improve my view as I was the first in the long line of cars waiting for the green light. The young clown juggled three colorful balls and, while juggling them, added three bowling pins. He twirled a plate at the end of a stick balanced on his nose and finally threw himself on the pavement in a contortion act. On the other side of the wide avenue, a woman, perhaps the clown's mother, swallowed a torch and spit fire like an angry dragon. Under the afternoon sun the cars waiting in the opposite lane seemed eager to leave and get wherever they were going. Still on the pavement, the clown child crossed his legs behind his head and walked like a lame spider, without paying any attention to the heavy traffic that zoomed by, filling the air with honks, revving motors, and exhaust fumes. The driver in the car to my right looked at me, and together we approved the child's performance, and the passengers in the bus behind us stuck their heads out the windows and cheered him with whistles and exclamations of awe. You had to see him. The boy knew perfectly well what he was doing, with his gaze set in concentration and his lips tight inside the red smile splitting his powdered face in two. Even the pedestrians at the crosswalk watched him enthralled, and there was more than one who risked being run over to see him better.

What distracted me was the huge black bird that flew slowly above us and disappeared between the gray buildings. How strange and suddenly how beautiful it was to see him flapping his wings slowly, so comfortable among the TV antennas, the billboards, and the dirty air. I could not remember the last time I had seen one—and one so big, for that matter—or the last time I had raised my eyes to look at the sky. Immersed in that mixture of flapping wings and clown stunts, I reached out to the backseat and from my purse grabbed a coin for the clown, who had disappeared as if by magic and was probably passing the hat among the cars at the back of the line. The bus driver began to beep his horn insistently, and some of the pedestrians waved their hands wildly at me. At first I didn't know what was going on. I was just waiting for the clown, my arm stretched out through the window and the coin ready to be dropped in the boy's hand, which would touch me a few seconds later. Then, half dazed, I realized the car was moving. The man to my right looked at me with an expression of horror and took off, disappearing into the torrent of cars speeding by. It wasn't until then that I felt the shape under the car, a shape that for a second resisted the weight of the car and then succumbed with a crack of weak bones. Of course I screamed and slammed on the brakes.

Sensing something was wrong, the clown's mother dropped her torch and ran toward me. The driver and the passengers pushed one another out of the bus, and the pedestrians ran across the avenue, evading the cars that zipped by at full speed. When I was finally able to free myself from the seat belt and get out of the car, all sorts of people had already gathered and watched morbidly as the red pool formed around the huge shoes, which stuck out from under the car like those of a grotesque mechanic.

"You killed my child," the mother said, panting kerosene by my side. "What do I do now?"

"I—I . . . didn't see him . . ." I mumbled the best I could. "I swear to God I didn't see him."

"We didn't see him either," one of the passengers said.

"And we were sitting much higher than she was." A second came to my rescue.

"You killed my son," the woman said a second time, raising her voice. She put her hands inside her apron pockets, raised her eyes, and said out loud to the sky: "And now who will help me?"

"¡Yo!" everybody in the group yelled. "¡El chapulín colorado!"* They remained silent for a moment, looked at one another with wild eyes, then exploded in laughter and patted one another on the back while recalling memorable episodes of El doctor Chapatín and El Chavo del Ocho.

In the midst of the celebration the driver stopped laughing and turned somber. "A little more respect, ladies and gentlemen," he said gravely, glancing sadly at the boy's body. "No death, regardless of how small, should be taken lightly."

"I agree," said a woman in a red hat and dress, who had also stopped laughing. "We need to call the police."

"The po-lice! The po-lice!" everyone in the group chanted.

"The police are not going to do me any good," the mother said. "They are not going to replace the source of income that I just lost." And she looked at her son with tears in her eyes.

"I know, ma'am—" I started to say, but she faced me squarely.

---

* *El Chapulín Colorado*, an immensely popular slapstick comedy show from Mexico, was viewed throughout Latin America during the seventies and can still be seen in some Spanish TV channels in the United States. The formula line used to invoke the show's hero—El chapulín colorado—was: "¿Y ahora, quién podrá ayudarme?" ("And now who will help me?"). El doctor Chapatín and El Chavo del Ocho are two of the show's other characters.

"Who is going to reimburse me for the lost business?" she said, fixing her gaze upon mine. "You?"

"The poor woman is right," an old man with a cane and derby hat said while he walked fraily toward me. "The right thing to do in this case is to come to an agreement. Offer her a sum, miss."

"But—but—" I protested.

"Offer her a sum." He interrupted me softly.

"Give her one hundred!" someone in the group yelled.

"One hundred and fifty!" yelled another.

"Two hundred!" the woman in the red hat said excitedly, raising her finger as if she were bidding in an auction.

"But what's going on here?" I cried out. I rummaged through my purse, looking for a Kleenex I had put there that morning, but couldn't find it. Seeing me so upset, the old man pulled out his handkerchief and offered it like a condolence.

"No, thank you," I said dryly, and continued searching.

A young man raised his hand and moved to my side. "Miss," he said as if he'd known me for years, "I think one hundred is enough. Take it, it's for your own good. You don't know how these people are."

"A filthy one hundred dollars?" I yelled, breaking down in tears. "Is that what your son's life is worth?"

"If you want to give me more, I certainly won't object," she replied while checking her fingernails.

I yanked a bill out from my wallet and threw it at her feet. "There's your blood money," I said, tears streaming down my face. "And if you think his life is worth more stupid little papers, then take all of these." I pulled out all the bills I had with me and threw them on the pavement.

"Hold it," the driver said. "The original agreement was for one hundred dollars, not a cent more." And with no shame whatsoever, he picked up a bill and slipped it into his pants pocket.

Two or three in the group reacted but, being the cowards that they were, stopped because none of them wanted to take the first step. Seeing his opportunity, a boy crouched cautiously and tried to grab another bill, but the old man's cane stopped him. "That's *my* bill, son," he said, slowly reaching down for it.

"We also have a right to that money!" another two or three yelled, and they threw themselves on the pavement.

"This is not getting any prettier," the mother said when two or three more joined the others on the pavement. "I'll take my hundred, and that's it." And she tucked a bill inside her bra.

"We also want our share!" the rest of the group demanded, and threw themselves on the pavement to fish for whatever they could with their dirty hands.

"One moment, ladies and gentlemen," the driver said, but no one listened to him. They were too busy thrashing on the pavement, kicking and biting and snarling like dogs fighting for a piece of meat.

"One moment!" he yelled at the top of his lungs. When the disheveled group finally settled, he said: "Please. Ladies and gentlemen, there's no need to fight. There's enough money for everybody, but we need to devise a fair system."

He asked the woman in red to lend him her hat and then placed his own bill inside it. "Now," he said, "with the exception of the compensated party, those who grabbed any amount please return it and we'll divide it in equal parts."

There was a general rumbling in the group. Those who hadn't gotten anything agreed immediately and cheered; those who had been able to grab a small sum but less than what they would have wished for offered some resistance but in the end returned the money they had pocketed. But the two who had gotten a good deal—the first young man and the old man with the cane—refused flat out.

"It is not fair that only a few be privileged," an anonymous voice complained.

"Yes! Yes!" another shouted in agreement.

"Return what you have stolen!" the crowd yelled angrily.

The people surrounded the two traitors and began to march around them. "The people united will never be defeated!" they chanted, brandishing their fists and turning like a huge cogwheel. "The people united will never be defeated!"

The two men raised their guard, ready to defend what was rightfully theirs, but when the circle began to tighten menacingly around them, they had to search in their pockets and place the money in the communal hat.

"Do we have an accountant in the crowd?" the driver asked, satisfied with his performance as a union organizer. A thin man wearing glasses stepped forward and bowed respectfully.

"Please count," the driver ordered, and handed him the hat full of bills. "And make it snappy, because the light is about to change to green." He turned around, opened his arms, and addressed the group as if giving a public speech: "Now, let's count how many of us are here." He pointed to the old man, who was standing by his side. "Even though you don't deserve it," he scolded him, "you are *número uno*." He then pointed at the person next to him:

"Two," that person said.

"Three," said the blonde after him.

"Four."

"Five."

That way they reached twenty-two, accountant included. "Twenty-three," the driver said, pointing at himself. He then said to me: "Are you in, miss?"

I shook my head and looked to where I didn't have to witness the disgusting transaction, but my eyes encountered the pool of blood around the huge shoes, so I looked back at the group.

"Three hundred and forty-two bucks," said the accountant, who had put on the red hat and held the wad of bills in one hand while with the other pushed his glasses farther up on his nose. "Divided by twenty-three persons, let's see . . . one, and we have eleven, we bring the two down; one hundred and twelve over twenty-three . . . , six, and we have, let's see, thirty, eighty-six, no, no, eighty-seven: sixteen dollars and eighty-seven cents. Rounded up to the immediate inferior, that makes eighty-five. Each person receives sixteen dollars and eighty-five cents, and we have forty-six cents left over."

"Those are yours as payment for your valuable service," the driver said, and snatched the bills from the accountant's hand.

He took a couple for himself and began to distribute the money, but seeing that with so many large bills he wasn't going to be able to, he asked if anybody had change for a twenty.

"I think I do," the old man said, searching in his pockets. He pulled out a handful of coins, counted them, and they made the exchange.

The driver gave him his part of the deal. "You're forgiven, my dear sir," he said, and they both bowed respectfully. Then with the coins the driver began to distribute the money.

"Please, let's make a line," he said when the group bunched before him. I moved away a few steps, so that the sickness that marked the faces of those who were orderly getting in line would not rub off on me.

The clown's mother approached me. "We are okay, miss," she said. "Don't you worry. I'll handle everything." And she tried to touch my shoulder.

"Don't you dare," I snapped, and moved away from her.

The passengers who received their part returned to the bus and sat in their seats to wait in silence for the rest to finish. As they were being served, the pedestrians left in small groups and crossed the avenue and, while dodging the cars, chatted animatedly about the details of the tragedy.

Before leaving, the old man approached me. "See how everything worked out just fine, miss?" he said, smiling. Then he added shyly: "Although I admit that I tried to take advantage of the situation. But I'm only human and thus fallible. Please forgive me." And he bade me farewell with his derby hat.

When he finished, the driver took the hat from the accountant's head and returned it to the lady in the red dress. She took her time putting it on. When she finished, the driver embraced her, kissed her on the mouth, and they both walked to the bus as if they were an old couple. He helped her get on the bus and boarded it himself with a youthful hop.

"All aboard!" he yelled as he hung from the door.

The only ones remaining were the mother and I. And the boy under the car.

"Everything is fine, miss," she said. "Get in your car and leave."

I didn't move. "But what about the boy?" I asked, not knowing what else to do.

"Don't worry, I'll take care of him. Now hurry up, the light just changed to green."

The torrent of cars that had been moving stopped and gave way to the torrent that gushed opposite them. The air received a new batch of honks, revving motors, and exhaust fumes.

I clutched my purse and returned to the car. I tried to evade the body, but it seemed every maneuver I made would finish squashing the poor boy. Amid the dust and the smoke I saw the mother pick up her son's belongings and leave in a hurry. I stuck my head out the window and begged her to help me, but the bus and the cars behind me started to beep their horns, drowning my plea.

"Hurry up, lady!" the driver yelled angrily from his window. "You're holding up the traffic!"

I took a deep breath and stepped on the gas pedal. My upset nerves made driving difficult, and the car stalled a couple of times before it began to move smoothly. The back wheels raised slightly with the shape of the body, and the last thing I saw in the rearview mirror were my dry tears, the woman getting smaller and smaller between the heavy traffic, and, against the gray sky with no clouds or birds, the stream of smoke coming out from behind my car.

DEMETRIA MARTÍNEZ
Mark

The alarm had not gone off, but I managed to pry myself awake. Six A.M. The brown stucco wall was scribbled with light. I sat up, uncertain whether to head out early to the newsroom. Julie's eyes were shut hard as she watched her dreams. As I looked at her, my throat quivered. Then I remembered. After the party we had gone home and made love. Her small breasts were engorged. They had moved in my hands like goldfish.

Later she had gotten up to make some tea, and as I half slept, she held my hand, gently massaging my fingers like worry beads. She finished the tea and turned out the light. Whatever her old griefs are, they visit during her time of the month. She has learned to make good out of the ease with which tears ooze like a balm.

No doubt it was "the baby" she mourned. Not our son, Eric, who had gone off to Harvard, but a faceless girl who died in the womb at four months. That was two years before Eric was born. No name, no burial marker, no ritual. "Disappeared" at the hands of masked doctors following protocol. Weeks after the ordeal Julie and I were embracing on the couch when we felt a wetness, a cruel signature of milk.

She let out a cry that terrified me. Because that same cry was locked inside me, its dark wings seeking an escape. But I've always been better at solving than feeling, at least when it comes to grief. I know it's not fair. I act as if I'm being strong, but it's Julie who does the work for both of us every time she goes into the dark and places a flower at the tomb of the unknown.

Anyway, that morning after the party I reached over and kissed her on the hair. I ran my hand along her bare stomach. Julie is small, compact, except for some added flesh on her abdomen. She has never tried to work off those extra pounds even though she believes in cholesterol the way some people believe in the existence of a God. Those pounds speak of duty done, death and rebirth, a six-foot-tall kid who once lived inside her as comfortably as he now occupies a dorm room. Julie views her body, whatever its imperfections, as she does historical sites. There are parts you don't renovate. Period.

She didn't budge, so I got up and showered. I had dreamed about the Gulf War—or at least I thought I had—and this made me perversely happy, to the point that I wanted to go to work. Strange, isn't it, how a dream you don't even remember can wring feelings out of you that you thought had dried up? Operation Desert Storm. That unforgivable war made me love journalism like nothing before or nothing since.

Months before the war Kuwait was like an obscure gene that excited only a handful of experts. Then, overnight, the rest of us became literate: surgical strikes; collateral damage; human remains pouches. Televisions hummed; people watched missiles fly like footballs. The business page reported a record number of pizza sales.

Each day on the plaza protesters walked in circles, battered ships beneath sails of banners. The one I liked best was HOW MANY LIVES PER GALLON? During my lunch hour I studied them through the window of the Plaza Diner. I hadn't felt so alive in years, perhaps not since Vietnam, when I had threatened to set myself on fire to protest that war.

I wrote against the Desert Storm. Each published editorial felt like a Molotov cocktail I used to throw at police cars. At long last

I had something to hate. I hardly needed to eat or sleep; that's how thoroughly hate nourished and sparked me.

Photographs that major newsmagazines had refused to run—or that had not been released over the wires—began to surface. There was that grisly image of an Iraqi who had tried to escape the bombing; he looks like a mummy except he's wrapped in tar instead of cloth, and he's still seated in a truck, mouth cracked open in a scream.

It was one of the few times the cameras had snagged something human in the mangled concrete and steel of that war. I fought with the newspaper's higher-ups to get that photograph run. But it was not to be; they said they would lose subscribers, this was a family newspaper.

With nothing left to fight for, depression took hold of me. The troops returned from the gulf. During the war outrage had been my best friend. Then it exited quietly, leaving me to sort out the meaning of all that had happened on my own.

I left a note for Julie and got into my car. Images from my dream hovered in my peripheral vision, but when I turned to look, they moved. I had to settle for the vague, happy feeling that one day soon my hatred, not to mention my writing skills, would be fine-tuned in the face of another catastrophe. A war maybe, or an environmental disaster. When you're stuck behind a desk all day, anything will do. Sad, isn't it? A man has maybe thirty good years left on the planet, and the only real enemy he's made is boredom.

I parked in the lot, then pushed through the revolving door of the newsroom. I was surprised to see Emma Sánchez there, filing a stack of photographs.

"They're not making you come in this early, are they?" I asked.

"Oh, no. I just felt like it. I mean, I thought about what you said and came in and copied my clippings. Who do I give them to?"

It looked as if a late night had left dark dents below her eyes.

"Me. I'll pass them on to the editor."

I followed her to her desk. She gave me a brown envelope.

"Thank you, Mr. Newman. I know there will be others far more qualified for the position, but I appreciate your notifying me about it." Emma's voice was stiff. The party's democracy of booze and soft lights was over; she had switched roles like gears. I remembered I was her superior. I felt guilty.

"We're all on a first-name basis here," I said, tossing a paperweight from hand to hand. I had picked it off her desk. I stopped to examine it. Inside the glass mound was an image of the Mexican painter Frida Kahlo, with the muralist Diego Rivera's face seared across her forehead. Emma was wearing matching earrings. I set the paperweight back down on her desk.

"Here's a fax for you, Mr.—Mark. It was sent about half an hour ago."

Her voice momentarily leaked childhood, like the voice of an adult on the phone with a parent. She was one of those women who, when it comes to men, quickly settle into feeling superior or inferior. My first-name invitation, however superficial a token of equality, had unnerved her.

The fax looked interesting. It announced that some protesters were going to sit down on railroad tracks outside Santa Fe. A train carrying toxic wastes to sites along the U.S.-Mexico border was expected to pass through at any time. Representatives of church groups would be there. Evan Little Bear, on behalf of a coalition of Pueblo Indian activists, planned to make a statement about desecration of sacred land and increasing rates of cancer.

"Looks like the Peace Train Ten are going to hit the tracks again," I mumbled. "Make a copy of this, will you, and put it in the state desk basket. That Little Bear doesn't quit."

"No, it was never in him to quit," Emma replied. I looked at her questioningly. "After that train didn't stop last year, after he lost his leg from the knee down, he started a master's degree in environmental biology."

"You know him?"

"In college. We took a Southwest lit class together. I'll have this fax back to you in a minute," she said, glancing down at the paper. It was clear she was trying to protect Little Bear from the merciless train of reporters' questions. I wanted to say to her, I'm not like them, but it would have been absurd.

"Thanks. Give me any related stuff that comes across. And welcome on board."

I went to my desk and switched on my computer. The green-black screen made me think of bulletproof glass. I looked around. Reporters were beginning to huddle at their computers, deleting yesterday's certainties. By day's end new headlines would rise, a precarious skyline.

"Here's the original," Emma said as she approached me, "and another fax. It's hard to read. Something about the Santa Fe archbishop endorsing the actions of the Ten. Let's see. 'There will be an exorcism of the train by Father Gil Sandoval . . . rosary to follow, sponsored by Catholics for Justice.' " She held the piece of paper up. The periods had dilated like pupils.

"Sandoval's my parish priest," she added. "He picks his battles carefully—and only when he's sure he's not going to embarrass the archbishop."

"What church?"

"St. Anthony's. On the West Side. Although I haven't gone for a while."

"See if you can get a contact person to send the fax over again. This Sandoval could be worth talking to."

"I have to walk to the body shop this afternoon to get my car before it rains," Emma said. "Somewhere in that mess is the diocesan paper. It has an article about the church. I'll clip it for you."

"Thank you. Excuse me, but where do you get your car worked on? I'm looking for a new mechanic."

"Jaramillo's. Over by the Banana Republic. They're really good. Besides, you have to trust an outfit that gives away free rosaries to hang from the rearview mirror."

"That's the stuff of consumer reports for sure," I said, grinning. "Listen, why don't I drop you off later today? I've got to get some estimates for work that needs doing on Julie's car. You can give me the clipping then."

"It would be a big help. If it's no inconvenience."

"None at all. We'll beat the traffic if we head out at a quarter till five."

"I'll be ready."

When it was time to go, I gathered my papers together in my bruised leather briefcase. Inside I carried a picture of my son, his blue eyes flickering in the blast of a flashbulb, burlap brown hair. For a long time I thought he looked only like Julie, but later I would see both her and me in there, fifty-fifty, sharing our life sentence in his person.

"Here are the files you asked for," Emma said. I couldn't help noticing that she wore true colors, true red, true blue; in that blasted fluorescent light, it soothed the eyes to look at her. She shone like a stained glass window.

"Good. I think that wraps things up for me."

"It doesn't look like we're going to get much of a storm after all. I should have just walked. I'm taking you out of your way."

"Not at all. Besides, this is the monsoon season. It'll hit soon enough."

We pushed through the revolving door. A wind had picked up, and the air had a rich, rusty smell to it. Clouds had gathered in a wreath; sunlight spilled over the edges. The stucco walls of nearby houses and offices took on a gold cast, seemingly lit from within like *luminarias*, votive candles inside brown paper sacks that line our streets on holidays.

A short distance from the car I pressed a red button on my key ring; a whistle was followed by the click of doors unlocking.

"Nice car," Emma said as she opened the door.

I had bought the car when Eric left home. It was nothing but an expensive toy, a shame. It had a sleek black interior. It was animallike, bones and muscle bound in leather; its parts moved and hummed on command.

"I don't know what possessed me when I bought it," I said, shutting the door.

"Oh, most likely money. I know what happens to me when a few dollars come my way. It's off to the sales racks."

Jaramillo's auto was just a few blocks away. I pulled into a parking lot. Emma went into the office; a man working in the garage gave me the information I needed. Afterward I got back into the car and waited. When Emma did not reappear, I felt deprived, a feeling as faint but identifiable as bird tracks. A melancholy sweetened with nostalgia was filling me, but I was at a loss for words to say what it was about her that brought forth these feelings. It was as though I'd landed in on another planet; no guidebook offered telling phrases.

"I hate to bug you again, but could I bum a ride home? The battery's kaput." Emma's small hand gripped the door where I had rolled down the window. A gold band rested on her pinkie.

"Sure. I've got nowhere to go."

"I need to take care of one last thing," she said.

"Take your time."

The way I had dealt with exotic women in the past was to flatten them. Three dimensions to one, a page out of *Playboy*, a marvelous sexual fantasy. In this way I kept them at a safe distance. Emma turned around. She was magnificent in her blue and red Guatemalan shirt and matching pants; she carried herself like a queen. Hard as I tried, she would not flatten out. And this frightened me.

For months I had not looked forward to going home to Julie. But I'm one of those men who're just smart enough to fool themselves with abstractions when particulars are too painful, so I blamed the institution of marriage and recalled the days when Julie and I lived together.

We had rented a small flat in Boston. I free-lanced. She painted. Later we protested the war together. We surrounded ourselves with artists and activists who spoke of love, revolution, ecstasy—words that flowed like the attributes of God from the mouths of monks.

Sex was great. It made for continuity when assassins' bullets at home and news from 'Nam shattered time. All the words used to justify the war were like evil lyrics above the tambura drone of sex.

At our wedding a Unitarian minister read from *The Prophet*. The words weighed so much more than our decision to marry, which had been made in an almost offhand way. Marriage was a ticket whose stub would come in handy when children entered the scene.

I watched Emma as she talked with a mechanic who stood behind a glass counter filled with rearview mirrors. Emma's chin moved up and down, a gavel with which she controlled the terms of what I assumed was an argument. I caught a glimpse of her hands, multiplied in the mirrors, a vision of Kali. For a moment I sensed in her an ability to destroy whatever she touched, and this intrigued me.

Wind, embroidered with leaves, gusted upward. A few teardrops of rain rolled down the windshield. I rolled up the window on the passenger side. Julie's history society brochures were strewn about on the floor. I had tossed them there to make room for Emma; now an urge to rescue them overwhelmed me.

For weeks Julie had worked at the dining room table, expensive drawing pencils arrayed like silverware. For the brochure cover she had sketched the buttressing of a church. It could have been any church in northern New Mexico.

Gathering up the brochures, I prickled with sadness; she had worked so hard on them. I tried to go abstract again—by considering humanity's ceaseless efforts to create things that were both beautiful and useful, but that thought hurt too.

"Sorry that took so long." Emma set her book bag on the floor of the car and climbed in. Bag, bracelet, and anklet, cut from the same Guatemalan fabric, united the peninsulas of her body under a single flag.

"Is everything okay with the car?"

"Oh, I don't know. I always ask a ton of questions at car places so that they think I know what I'm talking about. It's Greek to me. But look. Another rosary to show for my troubles."

She opened her fist, revealing a swarm of yellow beads.

I muzzled a laugh with a tight bow of a smile. I had no idea whether Emma took religion seriously.

"Do you want me to stick these things in the glove compartment?" she asked, fanning herself with brochures that had fallen on the dashboard.

"Please. It's unlocked."

Emma opened the glove compartment. A map of Massachusetts slithered out. The paper was so worn it was hard to tell roads from wrinkles or counties from candy stains.

"You're from Massachusetts?"

"Yeah. We lived there up until about three years ago." I started up my car. "Boston. I worked at the *Globe*. We got tired of the hassle, the commutes. Now, you'll have to tell me where I'm going."

"Do you know the West End? The area around the Good Luck Bar?"

"Not as well as I should."

"Get onto Acequia, and go straight for a couple of miles until you hit Lupita's laundry. Then hang a right at the light."

I pulled up to the edge of the parking lot and adjusted my rearview mirror. When the road cleared, I pulled out, but not before realizing I had forgotten to release my emergency brake. The scent of jasmine had distracted me; it smelled sweet, cheap, exactly like what Julie used to wear, tempered with a bass note of patchouli.

Sweet, sweet Julie. She unfolded and folded our days like her white kitchen towels embroidered with the days of the week. She had no taste for surprises. How I envied her knack for happiness. But not always. The contentment in her face was at times hideous; her smile and her eyes looked as though they might melt together like chocolate bits in cookie dough.

I had high hopes that the Gulf War would embitter her; she would critique my editorials with flashing blades of eyes; she would blow into cups of black coffee and hold forth in the night. We would war against the war, stopping only to sleep or make love.

Instead she just grew sweeter, quieter. One day I had to go out to the plaza to interview a priest. I was in a hurry when she stopped me and handed me an umbrella. "If you don't take this, it will no doubt storm," she said.

I took the umbrella and shut the door without even a thank-you. Julie's pink and wrinkled voice frightened me. My wife was growing old on me in the worst way. War raged, but she acted as if umbrellas and regular exercise and understeamed vegetables held the answer to life's chaos.

"So you came here from Boston," Emma said.

"I applied for a job here. Julie had come into an inheritance. Things just fell into place. Then your house, your ancestors' house. The owners decided they wanted to sell. After years of turning down who knows how many offers."

"By the way, that was a great editorial you wrote. About the need for affordable housing. Do you think the proposal for the Adobe Manor housing project will go through?"

"Yes. I think there's enough guilt left in this town. But the project will end up on the far reaches of paradise. Not in my backyard."

"Maybe it's better that way. If the manor ended up near the plaza, you know who'd get the apartments? All the folks who think it's their karma to move to Santa Fe and who end up waiting on tables."

"Sounds like a story we should do. Tale of two cities."

"I guess I was thinking of the third city. The Chicanos and Indians who used to count on those jobs, especially high school—whoops, there went Lupita's. You'll have to go around the block. Hang a left at that light."

"This could be your story, you know. If you land that internship."

"Okay, slow down here. Go left at Evangel's hardware."

In front of Evangel's a group of men talked and drank Cokes. They had exquisitely sculpted faces, seemingly fired in the kiln of some pre-Columbian god. Next door women buzzed in and out of the Cut 'n Strut. I slowed the car down. Pigeons flew up from under my tires.

"This is mostly a Mexican area, isn't it?" I asked.

"Yeah, with large contingents of Guatemalans and Salvadorans. And lately people from Peru and Colombia from what I've been able to tell. It's a regular UN. And just as contentious.

Everyone knows the *real* way to make salsa or pronounce certain words. I love it. But differences have a way of disappearing when *el aguacate* rolls around."

"*Agua—?*"

"The border patrol van. Color of an avocado, sort of. Okay, there's the entrance. Turn right after that sign into the parking lot."

"Adobe Acre Estates?"

"Yup. The Santa Fe mystique for those of us who can't afford it."

Pinkish stucco walls, fake *vigas*, and metal stairs all overlooked asphalt basted in motor oil. I had the feeling one good storm could strip the building down to a heap of plywood and cinder block, the remains of any Las Vegas motel.

"There's Mrs. Sandoval at it again. She's got the cleanest windows of anyone," Emma said. An elderly woman dried her windows with crumpled newspaper. Sunlight ricocheted off the luminous glass.

Emma puckered her eyes. "You can leave me off here."

"Let me drop you off by the building. It's no problem."

"Would you like to come in for a cup of coffee?"

Emma's eyes twinkled with horror. Her words had skidded ahead of her intentions. And I was not going to make it easy on her by kindly refusing the invitation. More than anything now I needed to talk; I needed to arrange thoughts like blocks, then knock them all down. This was the kind of play I missed most in my marriage. Sex could not take its place.

"That'd be nice. I could use a cup of coffee."

"Park anywhere near the stairwell."

We got out of the car. The moist air smelled like a meaty broth. It still threatened to rain. I needed rain. The day, despite auspicious beginnings, had hardened into a dull mass. I needed rain to loosen the caked soil of the day.

We walked up three stories; the stairs rang out like bad plumbing. "I can never find these damn keys," Emma said, tugging them out of her book bag. "Lot of good they'll do me in an emergency."

A tear gas dispenser the size of breath freshener hung from her key ring along with a laminated St. Jude holy card. "Never hurts to hedge your bets," she said. I was not sure if she was referring to St. Jude or the tear gas.

"Have a seat. Hope you don't mind instant."

To this day I'm not sure why that apartment buzzed with an eerie familiarity. I looked for clues on posters tacked to plywood walls and in paisley patterns of mismatched furniture. Splendid odors of garlic and cilantro blossomed like springtime as Emma lifted the top of a Crock-Pot. I sat down on a lumpy couch; I was certain that if I searched its folds, I would retrieve coins and crayons lost in childhood.

"Holy Ghost. I almost lost these beans." Emma stood behind a yellow nook that divided living room from kitchenette. "Oh, well, a few burned beans will lend a meaty flavor."

"Are you a vegetarian?"

"Not by choice. Animal tissue costs a lot these days. Besides, they're finding too many funny things inside the extra lean."

She set some mugs down on the nook, beside a statue of the Santo Niño de Atocha. The Christ Child on his throne braced cookbooks with help on the other end from a Franciscan friar cookie jar. The Santo Niño had raisin eyes, a chipped nose, and a dreamy Buddha smile.

"How do you take your coffee?"

"Heavy on the milk."

"Care for a drop of Kahlúa? I picked up a couple of bottles at the border, and now I'm stuck with them."

I was looking through an anthology of Chicano poetry that was heaped on the coffee table with a September *Vogue* and various treatises on the curative powers of vinegar, aloe vera, garlic, and the like.

The kettle shrieked.

"Kahlúa sounds good. You know, this place has real character."

"Nouveau poor," Emma said. "Just what my middle-class parents dreamed of. They work their way from the barrio to the 'burbs only to have their offspring hunting for bargains at Goodwill and the Price Hub."

"So you're the pendulum generation?"

"You could say so. But we're not rebelling against our parents the way you guys did. We're just sort of bumbling, vaguely pissed off that we'll never do better than our parents economically, ever. You folks have it made."

She settled into a chair. I blew on my coffee. You folks. The American dream shriveled in the vinegar of Emma's remarks. She sounded just like my son.

"You know, if you get that internship, your income will more than double. You're working, what, twenty hours a week now?"

"Yes. For the health insurance. Otherwise I'd do ten and volunteer somewhere."

"What exactly are your ambitions in life, Emma?"

"To work at a job where I don't have to wear hose and heels. Beyond that I'm not sure. I know I could be good at something if I applied myself. My father says this is only a stage. But stages have a way of getting long as bridges. Before you know it, you've crossed over your whole life on one."

"So how many years ago was it that you moved here?" Emma said. We were on our second cup of coffee. We had successfully accomplished a round of small talk about who was who in the newsroom.

"About three. We just packed up our things and headed to Santa Fe."

"You and everyone else. Boom times."

"Us white folks are still invading, huh?"

"Hey, some of my best friends are white folks," Emma said.

I smiled. I had seen such humor break the ice at gatherings of white liberals and Chicano and Indian activists. It allowed whites their guilt and minorities their anger, while leaving energy to fight for common causes.

"Jeezuz, look at that." I walked over to the picture window. A rainbow had alighted on the west mesa. A cloud passing overhead caused the light in the room to shiver.

"This is why I moved here. That light." I turned to Emma. "You're lucky to get such good light in here. Our house is kind of dark. We're planning to add a skylight to my workroom."

"You take much work home?"

"No. I'm experimenting with some fiction." Some aloe was growing on the windowsill. I pinched off a tip and rubbed the slime on a paper cut on my ring finger. I had crossed over into intimate territory, talk of creative life outside work.

"You write fiction?"

"On the side. Like a lot of reporters. Frustrated novelists. I've been away from it for a while, but I'm getting back in. I've made a vow not to take any newspapers into my room once the skylight is finished."

I didn't tell her that for ten years I had dreamed of quitting journalism and going back to free-lancing; this would give me some time to concentrate on my own writing.

"I guess a novel's a tall order for a town backlogged with similar requests," I said. "The problem with reporting is you spend so much time trafficking in facts you forget they reveal only a fraction of the truth. If you know what I mean. Plus, all the psychobabble in the air. It's ruining the English language. I used to write poetry. But now no sooner do I feel something than my mind interrupts with an explanation. I can't sustain a flow of imagery."

Too much Kahlúa. This was not the right time or place. I went over to the nook and stirred sugar into my coffee as if to rid myself of some bitter taste.

Emma must have sensed something was not right. She got up and opened the door. It was getting more humid. The breeze smelled of baking apples. "I bet that writing room will be just what you need."

"I hope so," I said, returning to the couch. "By the way, I wonder if your ancestors' ghosts are hanging around. I hear creaking in the walls now and again. Adobe shouldn't creak."

"You Anglos. Those aren't ghosts. They're spirits. You're not imagining things. My great-grandma had santos everywhere. Especially of St. Anthony."

"Finder of lost things."

"You're Catholic?"

"Post-Catholic."

"As in ex-Catholic?"

"No, more like a graduated one. Advanced degrees in guilt. None of the bells and smells. The church blew it on birth control and women. How do we know they've got it right on heaven and hell?"

"You're missing the point."

"What point?"

"You should be filling that pretty little house of yours with santos."

"I love the way Chicanos around here talk about their saints as if they were human."

"Well, they're not quite gods. Sometimes they come through for you, and sometimes they don't. But they're like family. You want them around."

"I have a Lady of Guadalupe collection, all sorts of things. Miniature plug-in altars. Dashboard magnets from the fifties. Refrigerator magnets. Let's see. Some carvings by a *santero* from up north. Does this count?"

"Mmm, I'm not convinced."

"It's an Anglo thing. You wouldn't understand. The less we believe, the more we collect. Put it behind glass. And if we get up too close, try to ask some questions again, we fog up the glass with our own breath."

Emma had gone over to check the Crock-Pot again. "Hey, these beans are about as ready as they'll ever be. I need a guinea pig. How about it? You'd pay ten bucks for a bowl of these babies at Santa Fay's."

She pulled some tortillas out of the refrigerator. On the counter was a tall black radio tuned to the college radio station. They were airing an old clip of a speech by Martin Luther King, Jr.; he was calling for an end to the Vietnam War. Then I remembered: the Tibetan temple above a Mexican restaurant in San Francisco. How I had sat at the feet of the Buddha after fleeing cops' clubs. They had knocked off my glasses and ground the lenses with their heels. I could not see to fight, so I ran. Once inside, I let myself cry for the first time in years, the war years. My defenses had been stripped; I could not see my way through the madness.

"So will it be red or green or Christmas?"

"Oh, yes, beans sound good. Red chile's my favorite."

She ladled beans into large mugs and took a seat. I told her about Eric, citing his various successes at Harvard. He was considering going into law or medicine. It was frightening to see him living up to my wildest expectations. When Julie and I married, I had wanted a girl because I figured I would be less likely to try to mold such a vastly different creature in my image. I pushed Eric hard during high school, trusting that one day he'd forgive me. I'd seen too many of his friends hanging out on the plaza until all hours, looking like war refugees in their battered clothes and black shoes. Trust fund babies. I wanted Eric to earn his way.

"If everything had worked out, I would've graduated from Harvard about four years ahead of your son."

"What do you mean?"

"I was accepted but couldn't afford to go. Financial aid packages have shrunk too much. I couldn't land a summer job. Everything seemed to go wrong. I guess it just wasn't meant to be."

No, goddammit, Emma, it was *meant to be that you go to Harvard, but the system screwed you, and people like me can afford to send their kids in your place.* How I wanted to say this to her. I was ashamed of having boasted about Eric. She got up to heat some more water. She had put me in my place.

"You're only . . . twenty-two years old?" I could have sworn she was much older. Her features wavered as my mind rearranged them.

"Close. I'm twenty-three. An old soul, though. How old are you?"

"Forty-eight. Listen, Emma, thanks for the dinner. I really should get—"

The light in the room shivered again as lightning scored the sky.

"It's still early. Stay, please."

I looked down at the floor, but it was too late. We both saw it, a tightrope stretched out between us like eternity. The rain pounded like fists on the hard earth. Emma safety-pinned her living room drapes.

CATHERINE LOYA

We Don't Need No Stinking Maps

I. Oxnard (1978)

We never do listen to music on the car radio. We listen only to Dodger games, but that's okay because the music would interfere with my reading, and besides, I like Vin Scully's voice. And I like baseball because for one thing, I play, and well, the players aren't bad to look at on TV, so clean-cut and wholesome, the way me and my mom like them. And they could play catch with me on dates at the park, under the yellow lights. This would be a much better date than eating pizza, or dancing to Village People, or going to the drive-in even.

My little brother, Eddie, is sitting in the back of our yellow, wood-paneled Buick station wagon. I'm surprised he hasn't had to throw up, sitting backward and all. He's kneeling on the seat, waving at people and pressing his nose up against the glass, like a pig. He likes the attention.

"Teresa, go back there and calm him down. Why don't you two sing?" Mom says to me. So I climb over the middle seat and join Eddie in the back. We like to sing on trips even though we don't know any songs; all we know are TV songs. So we sing the themes from *The Brady Bunch*, *Mary Tyler Moore*, *Happy Days*, *Laverne & Shirley*, and *The Love Boat*. I teach Eddie the words to the Beach Boys' "California Girls," which I learned at a slumber party last week.

Then for a joke Dad says, "Sing Spanish! Sing 'La Cucaracha,' the cockroach song. You know it." We laugh. This has to be a joke. He knows we don't know Spanish. He's always bugging us about Spanish. Just when I begin to roll my eyes and sigh, Eddie starts to sing.

"*La cucaracha, la cucaracha. Ya no puede caminar porque* some guy stepped on him and squashed him and now he's dead and bleeding brown cockroach blood."

Eddie knows what a cockroach looks like because he's killed them at our house, even though Mom yells at him to stay away. They crack like eggshells. We run out of words real fast, so I join Eddie making faces at the passengers of other cars, sticking out our tongues occasionally.

"Honey, which way should I go?" Dad asks Mom suddenly. She has no map. She never drives over Riverside County lines, only to the triangle of three different K-marts and occasionally to San Bernardino to visit her sister. Yet he asks her for help, counting on woman's intuition or divine guidance. She is the one who never misses church. Or maybe she saw a sign.

We are in Los Angeles now. I know this because I have memorized the way to Dodger Stadium. I know all the places along the way: the ice skating rink, the Quiet Cannon Salsa Night Club, the rich houses on the hills by the golf course, where I wish we could live. In Los Angeles we always take the Golden State Freeway to Dodger Stadium. Dad learned real good after he and Mom got lost in Watts coming home from a Dodger game. I was just a baby in the backseat of his '66 Buick.

But we're not going to a Dodger game today. We are going to Magic Mountain. My stomach is already churning, waiting to ride the curls of the roller coaster, Colossus. Usually summer vacation we go to Disneyland, but somebody got the idea to go to Magic Mountain from a commercial, so the four of us piled into the station wagon this morning, a station wagon even though we're only two kids. We're Mexican, not like those big

Irish and Italian families at my school, Our Lady of Perpetual Help.

Mom thinks Los Angeles is a long trip from Riverside. She has packed water, Cokes, and an ice chest full of fruit, even grapes. Really, we aren't supposed to eat grapes because of the Boycott. I heard that somewhere. Maybe TV. But Mom must not know anything about it because she still buys them. I peel off the grape skins, stick them to the door, and roll several grapes around in my mouth until they feel like tongues. After a while I crush them in my mouth; juice drips down my face. Mom winks and says, "Enjoying yourself?"

"Honey, which way did you say?" Dad asks again. She points left, with her left hand; the small diamond wedding band glistens in the sun, lights the way, away from the Golden State Freeway. Suddenly we are on a part of the freeway I have never seen before. Long after we have passed the buildings downtown, their gray shadows follow me, plastered on the rear window. The buildings bleed into one another, all colors, and my eyes grow large, taking it all in, and I think, *Someday I'll probably work in one of those important buildings*. I know they are important because they are so big. No one important ever worked in a dinky building. I'm so excited thinking about my powerful future and the roller coaster, Colossus, that I tell Mom we have to go on that ride first. And "No, I ain't scared."

"Not," she says.

On the way I keep dreaming of french fries and hamburgers. I am hungry. The ride is taking a long time. Too long.

"Hey, Dad, when are we gonna get there?" I ask.

"When we get there," he says.

Twenty minutes later we are near the ocean. Even though I can't see it, I know the smell. It's that large stink of a pier, same as Newport Beach, where men with rough faces, dirty, sell silverfish from wheel barrows. We drive closer to the ocean, and from the car I can see blond girls wearing bikinis, strutting confidently between the cars. For a moment I wish I were grown, like them, or at least a teenager. I want the long blond hair that combs glide through easy. I already got the tan skin; I just need the blond hair. But that will never be, so I wish for a body like theirs.

We are at the beach, on a narrow highway on the edge of California, following the curvy line of the ocean. I didn't know Magic Mountain was by the beach.

Mom rolls down her window and lifts her head into the breeze. I do the same thing, sitting behind her, mimicking. Suddenly I get the urge to bury myself in sand. I would lie down and let Eddie dump bucketfuls of dry, cold sand all over me, all the while, the sun beats down hard, baking me into a woman with hard mounds that fit good in a fluorescent pink bikini. My mom will never let me wear a bikini, though. "A two piece is for *cochinas*," she says. I know she means that a two-piece is for girls who don't get all As on their report cards. I got to cover up my body like it was something worth money. So instead of the body I don't have yet, I begin to think of the thrills of the roller coaster.

"Hey, Dad, do you have any idea where you are?" I ask, just to make conversation, but he ignores me. "I think we're lost," I continue. "Mom, do you think we're lost?"

"No, Mija, your dad knows where he's going. He was in the Marines. He knows how to get around. Don't you?" she asks him.

He grunts, tilting his head toward the radio. The Dodger pregame show has just begun. He is not listening to us. I retreat into my book, get lost in its pages, although the sweat on my thighs is making my legs stick to the seat in a very uncomfortable way.

Thirty minutes later I begin to think that maybe Dad needs help reading the signs, so I close my book, put on my wire-rimmed glasses, and read every sign along the way. OXNARD. "Hey, Dad"—I interrupt Vin Scully—"you worked in the fields, what's that over there to the left? Look. Look," I say, pointing a finger out the window.

"Strawberries," he says.

"How did you know that?" Eddie asks. "You can't see the strawberries from here. I don't see no red."

"They grow very close to the ground," Dad says.

"What's over there?" Eddie asks.

"Where?" Dad says.

"Those trees all in lines way over there?"

"I think those are—I don't know. I'm not sure," Dad says, kind of sad. "Hey, honey, remember when I asked you to point to the freeway we should take, how come you pointed to this one?"

"What do you mean, 'this one'?" Mom asks. "Do you mean to tell me there was more than one freeway? I thought there was only one freeway through Los Angeles, like in Riverside. Where are we?" she says, suddenly worried.

"Santa Barbara. We're almost to Santa Barbara," I say.

"We're supposed to be on the Golden State Freeway, north," Dad says. "That's what the TV said." Dad lets out a long sigh, as if he were blowing out some bad feeling.

"You better stop at a gas station and ask," I say. "I hate to be lost."

"And I want to get to Magic Mountain one of these years," Eddie says.

"Dad, do you want me to tell you where to get off at the next gas station?" I ask. "I really think we should before we get more lost."

"We can't be *more* lost because we're not lost. We're not lost," Dad says, in a strange voice. "We don't need to ask for help."

"Why not?" I ask, confused. "We've never been here before. Maybe at least we should get a map. Yeah, Dad, I think we need a map. Why don't you have a map? Don't you know it's important to have a map?"

"I don't need a map! I don't need directions!" He sighs and says, "Don't worry, Mija. I know the way. I meant to show you the ocean. You've never seen this part before. We'll go to Magic Mountain tomorrow. We'll stay in a hotel tonight." Mom turns her head to him and gives him one of her looks, a look I can't quite comprehend.

Dad reaches for the radio and lowers the volume. Silence. "Let's just see where the road takes us." He starts to sing, in the altar boy voice he is so proud of, sings the only song he knows all the words to, "Cielito Lindo," Beautiful Sky. "*Ay, Ay, Ay, Ay, canta y no llores. Ay, Ay, Ay, Ay, canta y no llores. . . .*"

Ay, ay, ay, ay, they sing but don't cry. Ay, ay, ay, ay, they sing but don't cry. That much Spanish I know. I crumple into the vinyl seat, covered with electrical tape, close my eyes, dream of the white roller coaster curves and fast dips, and remember how we got here.

II. San Francisco (1984)

He woke early, dressed, then knocked on my door before the alarm clock sounded. He had to pull me out of bed and push me into the shower. It was only after this awkward awakening that we slid onto our bicycles, plowed through slivers of dusty morning light, and rode the shortcut through the trees across campus. When we arrived at the train station, Ben insisted on locking the bikes to a faraway post.

"Can't we just lock the wheels to the frame?" I ask. "It's Kryptonite. The lock, I mean."

"Teresa, you want to have a bike when you come back?" he replies, and continues to lock his bike.

I knew what he was thinking: *She's from California. She doesn't know any better. She's not from New York City, like me.*

So I lean my salmon-colored bicycle, or pink actually, pink, the color of cheap T, G & Y nail polish, next to his black-framed racing bike and lock it to the post.

I follow him to the window, where he purchases his ticket. When it is my turn, I smile at the clerk and mutter, "San Francisco, round trip." This much I know to do.

When the train stops, Ben climbs aboard first and picks our seats. I know that he has chosen the side of the train that offers the best scenery. That's the way he is. He plans things out.

"I want to sit by the window," I say.

"Are you really going to look out the window or not?" he asks.

"Look out the window," I lie. Really, all I want is the sun.

He frowns and says, "Fine," giving up more easily than I expected.

I nestle into the window seat, lean my head against the warm glass, and let the humming stillness of the train soothe me.

"Here," Ben says, handing me a Walkman and two cassettes. "One is Jefferson Airplane and one is Jefferson Starship. Grace Slick is on both. Listen."

We are on our way to Golden Gate Park this morning. Every year Grace Slick gives a free concert in the park because she lives across the street or something. Ben really wants to go. He's been to a lot of concerts. Has seen Paul Simon in Central Park, Bruce Springsteen, The Who. I've never been to a concert. Don't like music that much. But I slip the headphones on anyway to be polite and choose Jefferson Airplane. The woman's voice is husky and strong, like the mariachi women on my grandma's radio. "Lola really knows how to belt them." That's what my grandma says. And the small woman whose man voice comes from some deep spot, dark within her, reminds me of Grace Slick. Still, I put the volume on mute midway through the first song. I don't like this music, and I wish I could read instead. I look out the window but can't see anything past Ben's reflection. All I see is the wild tangle of blue, red, green lines of the BART routes. He has pulled out the BART/MUNI map to plan our way to the park: which bus to take, which direction to walk, what sights to see, what neighborhoods to avoid, and where to eat at the end of it all. We don't know the city that well. We live at school, in the dorms at Stanford.

As the train screeches to a stop, Ben grabs his backpack, clutches it to his chest, and advises me to hurry. "If we hurry, we can catch the bus to Market Street. Come on."

I follow him because he knows. I follow him because he is New York and I'm not. And he *does* know because as soon as we reach the bus stop and join the tail end of the line, the bus arrives. "Wait on line. I just want to check the map again," he says.

"*In* line." I correct him silently, the way he is always correcting me. I let him because he is prep school and I am not. I see him walk to the map behind the Plexiglas. I wonder how the map could tell him anything; the Plexiglas is scratched, yellowed, cracked from the sun, and stained with graffiti. Even from where I stand, I can see the black marks, the graffiti. "Sad Girl y Flaco" it says, "P/V." *Por vida*. For life.

We stand in the aisle of the bus, holding on to the aluminum poles, rocking left, rocking right, trying so hard not to touch other people's bodies. As much as he can, Ben has put his body in front of mine—a curve, a cover, a church, for that which must be protected. Still, in the V of my elbow, a woman's hair brushes my skin, sends tingles through my body, sends me dancing the graceful dance of sure feet, liquid torso, slim shoulders. My body still.

We file off the bus, and in the cool morning shadow of skyscraper, we take the escalator down once, then twice, down to Muni. Standing under the fluorescent lights, I ask, "What bus do we take?"

"The J," he says.

"The J?" I ask

"Toward Haight-Ashbury," he says.

"Oh. Okay," I reply, as if I know what he's talking about, as if I have a picture in my head the way he does. I don't. All I can see is the color green.

I never rode a bus in my life until I met Ben, until he got me under his wing. Ben considers himself an expert on the New York City subway system. He has that on his résumé. His mother doesn't know how to drive a car and walks to the grocery store every other day, dragging a cart behind her, even in the snow. My family—we always had cars.

I carry my backpack on my lap, hands draped over it for protection against theft. I feel my eyes, usually an open caramel brown, slit to a glare. But soon we emerge from the underground tunnel; the yellow light pours in through the windows, carries us, like water, to the surface. And there I see the colors of San Francisco: rose, sherbet, lime, baby blue, lavender—birthday cake flowers. I want to eat them all or at least live behind their windows.

"We have to walk to the park now. Only a few blocks away," Ben explains. He grabs my hand gently, with feeling. I look down; his freckled hands grasp mine. I see his pale fingers between my own brown ones and slide gracefully out of his grip.

"What's wrong?" he asks.

"Nothing," I say.

The sun beats down cold. Only the glass made the sun warm. *This heat is not like the desert*, I thought, *not like where I'm from*.

We walk toward the park, toward the thousand shades of green, past the arboretum, past bicyclists and baby strollers and skaters until we reach the stage where Grace Slick will perform. We are here too early. Too early. Only a handful of people have arrived, staking out the choice seats, spreading their blankets and lawn chairs inches from the high stage. I look around. No Mexicans. Just me amid tie-dyed T-shirts, Birkenstocks, and clove cigarettes.

Ben leads me to a place not too close to the stage and spreads out his army blanket. I sit down cross-legged and take out a book to read. He takes out his map. My legs begin to itch already.

The sun streaks across the pages of my book. I can hardly read. I am concentrating hard on each line, the whiteness around each word. The glare.

Slowly the grass fills with squares and rectangles of color, blankets, and people until only narrow green veins of grass remain. The band has arrived. A man in crusty jeans, a faded T-shirt, and a blue bandanna tied around his head sets up the instruments. Nothing interests me but my book. I suddenly feel claustrophobic, even though we are outside. The music is about to start, and still, I feel no excitement. I have no expectation that the music will carry me away. And I know that's what Ben wants—wants his music to carry me away in an endless ripple of emotion, wants me to be a part of his world, wants me to like the things he likes.

A bumblebee hovers close to my hands, near the margins in my book. The bee scares me because I have never been stung, and I know that some people are so allergic to a bee sting they die. But they can never know they are allergic unless it stings them. And this scares me, this absence of logic. I watch it cautiously, follow it until my patience finally collapses. "Goddammit. Go away!" I say out loud.

"What's wrong?" Ben asks.

"It's this bee. It won't leave me alone," I say, trying to dodge it.

"Just be still. It'll go away if you don't bother it."

"What do you think I've been trying to do? It won't leave me alone."

Ben reaches out for it with his left hand, tries to snatch it out of the air. Misses.

"What are you doing?" I ask, frowning in disbelief.

"I'm trying to kill it."

"Don't do that. It's just going to get mad. And it's going to come back and sting us."

Ben's hand reaches out again to snatch the yellow thing out of the air. And misses.

"Please stop. You know it's going to sting me and not you! Please," I plead. The words fail, so I grab his hands to hold them down, but he shakes himself loose from my grip, and he grabs my wrist, hard, before dropping it.

"You want it to go away or not!" he says. At that he claps his hands together hard and this time crushes the bee in his hands. "Why are you so afraid of this?" he asks, holding his hand out to me. There, in the middle of the softness, lies the limp, flat insect. "You have such strange fears," he says. "And so many." I examine the bracelet of red fingers on my wrist. He pauses for a moment and starts again. "It's the Catholic in you. You really have to learn to take control of things. You can't just have faith. Life's about control." His voice, always too loud for public places, carries over my slim shoulders.

I fold myself up like a towel. Retreat. Stare at the stage. Twist my long brown hair. And then I feel the warmth. The hippies have been watching us. I feel the heat from their eyes, and suddenly it is my eyes that are hot. Burning. I want to leave. I want to leave and find a warm place to read and watch colors.

The words form solidly in my mind, steady as a song. "I'm leaving. I'm leaving." I gather my things—sunglasses, book, rubber band for my hair, suntan lotion I don't need—and pack them away in my backpack. The zipper zipping must sound of finality because he startles himself.

"What are you doing?"

In the inches between us I lay the words, deliberate as a fork on the table. "I'm leaving."

Grace Slick steps onto the stage, greets the audience. I stand, stretching to my full height.

"Where are you going?" he asks. "The music is about to start."

"I'm leaving."

"What's wrong?" he asks in a voice that sounds more like a boy's than a man's. Desperation. This is always how it is. He plots, argues, pleads, builds his case. And me, quiet. I turn my back. One step. Two steps. Three steps.

His words collide in an awkward attempt at emotion, ropes to bring me back. "You don't know your way home!" His words, clear, echo to the strum of the bass guitar. Still, the stares, the heat of the stares, penetrate me. The dirty laundry. Four steps. Five steps. "Come back here now! I mean it! You don't have a map!" The stares devour me. But all they see are khaki shorts and the Day of the Dead T-shirt. Not me. I turn around, look him in the eyes. A part of me is folded, still, but I manage to say it, without tears, between clenched teeth and a tight fist at my side: "I don't need a stinking map!" I turn away, not sure if he will follow me. Six steps. Seven steps. Grace Slick begins to sing, bellows. A throaty song emerges from the slim blackness of her clothes. Her words, like ribbons, satin colors, search for me in the crowd. "Don't you want somebody to love you? Don't you need somebody to love?" I walk away. Eight steps. Nine steps. With my neck straight, I push through the crowd, navigating a route through the slender spaces. I push through the colors, find my way out from the heat of their bodies. I walk to the edge of the park. There, finally, I take a deep breath and begin my mantra: "I am not lost. I am not afraid to be lost."

I stop for a moment, gather my face, and look for the friendliest of eyes to tell me where I'm going. A woman about my age, dressed like me in shorts and a T-shirt, passes, and I stop her: "Excuse me. Can you tell me how to get to North Beach?" North Beach because I suddenly feel my hunger and decide to get Philly cheese steak and cheese fries and a giant Coke, not diet. I know the place is on a corner, somewhere in North Beach, across from a bookstore shaped like a triangle and down the street from the Al Capone Triple X Strip Joint. That's what my body is telling me to do.

"You want to take Muni?" she asks.

"Oh, no. I want to walk. Just point me in the right direction."

"You really should take the bus. It's pretty far, and it'll take a long time to walk there."

"That's okay. I have all day." The minute I say this, I know she is right. Still, I'm resigned to walking. I'm so afraid to get on the wrong bus and end up nowhere.

I memorize what she has told me. Visualize street names and mark every mark in my mind. Each step I take, all I can think of is Philly cheese steak. Philly cheese steak. It keeps me from crying.

The sun feels warmer, and I even have to pull out my sunglasses and tie my hair up in a ponytail, high up on my head. And after a while, after stopping in front of so many slim Victorians to study their colors, shapes, and lines, and after squinting my eyes to look past reflections and into the windows, I don't feel so afraid. My knees relax; my whole body becomes a supple ripple of flesh, a flag atop a hill. I stand in a place whose name I don't know and follow the curves and hills and peaks of San Francisco with my eyes.

The sidewalk in Chinatown inches slowly, with an unfamiliar rhythm, as I walk past windows of shiny duck skin, rows of steamed pork buns, Nikon cameras. I feel I am about to become lost and wonder if this is really the right way to North Beach, as I trip over stalls filled with California oranges, broccoli, and cilantro.

The crowd is thick with tourists and people from the neighborhood, all probably on their way to Sunday dim sum. On the fluid border between Chinatown and North Beach I begin to recognize buildings. The Wells Fargo Bank with the red, Chinese-style roof. I remember the ATM, Little Joe's on Broadway, the smell of garlic. But what a relief to see the twenty-foot gangster on the marquee of the Al Capone Triple X Strip Joint. Yes. Without a doubt that is the marker. And just up the street, on the corner, to the left, is the Philly cheese steak place. Not a restaurant. No name. Just a grill looking out onto Broadway, a counter against the wall, and five greasy vinyl stools. I slip in, order my meal, and eat quietly in a shaft of sunlight.

III. New York (1988)

How was I to know not to wear cowboy boots in the snow? He didn't tell me. When I asked him what I should pack, all he said was "sweaters." When I asked what else, he said, "A coat."

"What kind of coat?"

"Down would be good. Do you have a down jacket?"

"No. What is that anyway, some kind of ski jacket?"

"Yes." That's all he said.

So I packed my black cowboy boots, thinking they would keep my feet warm. But the snow has seeped through to my cotton socks, has made the leather soggy and soon to be hard. My poor boots. My Tex-Mex two-step sex boots. Leather. My boots, the ones I dreamed of for months and spent a whole paycheck on, are ruined. Not to mention dangerous. I have been careful to step slowly. The snow crushes beneath the heavy heel of the sole with each step.

Early this morning we took the subway from Manhattan to Brooklyn. We didn't even have time to eat breakfast together. Scott has an interview for a judicial clerkship with a federal judge, a good, liberal, Jewish federal judge. I don't. So, instead of staying in the house all day, his house, his family's apartment, I am supposed to explore New York on my own. I have never been to New York. No one in my family has ever been to New York. Not ever.

We emerge from the subway tunnel, trudge up the icy steps, holding hands. I don't feel his skin through the leather gloves on my hands. The gloves belong to my roommate. She went to school at Harvard and knows snow in a way I never will. We move, in brisk steps, through Brooklyn streets, and the novelty overcomes me. "I've never been here before. I've never been here before," the words rhythmic, like a train. I follow his shiny dress shoes because he has been here before.

Scott leads me to an icy bench in front of the federal courthouse, and under the slim brown trees he unfolds the subway map again. "All you have to do is backtrack the way we got here and get back on the subway in the opposite direction. And to get to Bloomingdale's, you just get off here," he says, pointing to some thin black lines I can barely see. Thin, thin as thread. "You get off at the fifth stop. Count," he says, "one, two, three, four, and you get off at five."

"Couldn't you just highlight the whole route for me in yellow or something?" I ask.

"Don't worry, it's easy. All you have to do all day is stay on the blue lines and the green lines. And then, after shopping, if you want to go to the Met, you just get on the Lexington Avenue subway and exit at Eighty-sixth, then walk west, which is toward the park. Here," he said, and handed me a fistful of tokens for the subway.

"Got it," I say, even though I really don't. I would rather figure things out myself over coffee and eggs somewhere.

"And then I'll meet you at five at NYU. Okay?" he says. He must see some look cross my face because he says, "Don't worry. You'll do fine," and hugs me close to him, rubs his chin on the flat part of my head. "You should really get yourself a hat," he adds.

I watch him climb the steps up to the courthouse, the hem of his tan overcoat swinging as he disappears through the doors. I turn, thrust my hands into the pockets of my borrowed wool coat, and head back to the subway, retracing our steps so carefully, not bothering with scenery. I concentrate only on my destination, the other side of the water.

As the subway jerks to a stop, I examine the letters on the window of the train before I get on, once, twice, three times, not trusting my ability to read. I get on, and I stand in the aisle, facing the windows, holding on to the poles, and watch the reflections of the women surrounding me in the windows. They all are wearing beautiful long coats, forest green, red, navy, purple, coats to match the colors of their hair. I suddenly feel like a raggy outcast for not having a coat to match my hair and my skin. This coat matches my roommate's hair; chestnut, she calls it. Still, fear pulsates through me. I fold my arms over my purse, which is strapped across my chest like a gun, under my coat.

At the fifth stop I disembark, not even knowing the name of the stop or the streets. I have a blind trust in the directions that he has given me. I just wish I had had the sense to write them all down. Unfortunately I have no paper.

The stores don't open until 10:00 A.M., so I begin to look for a place to eat breakfast, a Denny's maybe. I walk a few blocks. The streets are already busy; the flow of traffic on the sidewalk is deliberate and steady, hungry in a way that seems unfamiliar. I don't see any Denny's. I want to figure out where I am before I get too lost, so I stop at the first breakfast place, Mykonos, which also has a good bargain painted on the window in Christmas colors. The balloon above the reindeer's mouth reads: "$2.99 Breakfast Special, Three eggs, toast, bacon, coffee, and orange juice." The long, narrow restaurant is lined on both sides with rows of red booths, divided by planters filled with plants. Even from the window outside I can see the vinyl booths shine with grease. *Mmm. Looks good*, I think, and enter with anticipation. I am hungry.

I open the door, walk in, and slither into an empty booth. There aren't many. I take off my coat, wrap it in a ball, and lay it on the seat next to me. As I take out the map, I run my fingers over the paper, smooth and knowledgeable as an ancient face. I slowly unfold it and spread it out flat on the table in front of me. *It's not even beautiful,* I think, *not like a painting.* The map, blurred and incomprehensible, sits before me. I do not even want to try. I push the map away, not bothering to fold it. I stare at it with contempt, the way I would stare at a man who uttered such a challenge, a man who would say, "You can't control me. Don't even try." I sighed, feeling the veins in my neck knot themselves into tight fists of frustration. *How could he abandon me?* I thought. I am angry at him for making me do this, for making me find my own way through this megametropolis. I am thinking, *Fuck him. Fuck him,* when my food arrives. With deliberate satisfaction, I cut through the ball of yolk with the edge of my fork.

When I finish eating, I push away the plates and spread the map out on the table, smoothing it with my fingers. First, I figure out where I am. I can't. I'm lost already, and it is only breakfast time. I have another meal and at least one snack before I can relax and depend on *him* again. I curse the lines. It doesn't matter that each subway route has its own color. What do colors mean to me on this map? What is red? What is green? What is blue? Nothing.

Somehow I manage to comfort myself with the thought that I could find the neighborhood and then slip into a matinee and be safe, in the dark, with yellow popcorn the whole afternoon. The thought motivates me, and I look at the index on the other side of the map, find Bloomingdale's, because it's the only New York store I ever heard of, and then run my finger down to the Ms for Metropolitan Museum of Art. Good thing it is not Monday. That's one thing I have learned from the fancy schools I've been to: Museums are usually closed on Mondays. It occurred to me that this was a fact my mother would not know. The last thing I find is NYU, which I know is somewhere near the Village.

I slip scraps of paper out of my purse to write down the addresses and directions. I find each place on the map and then write down everything, as if I were writing directions for a child. I don't write down "east" or "west" because who knows about that? All I know is left or right, up or down. East, west, north, south—those all are relative things. I write it all out in narrative form, as if I'm playing some game: To get to Bloomingdale's, walk out the door, and then turn left. Walk about four blocks (four big blocks) until you get to Fifty-ninth Street. At that street, turn left again, and walk two blocks until you get to Bloomingdale's. I did that for each place. And then I made out a schedule.

Bloomingdale's was a bust. All stores are the same. But I did buy a hat. Wool.

As I descended into the darkness of the subway tunnel, I felt as if I were descending into some unfamiliar part of myself. It wasn't the darkness, but the music from the saxophone, the city music slithering through the slim spaces between the people, that confused me: the fusion of tenderness and danger; the fusion of mystery and difference with the familiar. To ride the subway alone this way frightened me. I know I am a grown woman, but I have a Puerto Rican friend at school who grew up in the Bronx. Even she protects herself on the subway. "Dress ugly," she said. "If you look too good, you will definitely be a target."

I spent the day at the museum and ate a chili dog from a sidewalk vendor. I spent most of the time in the part of the museum with the impressionist paintings. I can't stand artifacts. It's like looking at old dishes. Anyway, I felt so cosmopolitan being there.

Later I got back on the subway and got out in the Village, walked around a little until I found a movie theater. Finding my own way in the world was too much trouble, and I felt frustrated and tense from having to watch my back and look for streets and from keeping all these mental images in my head all day. I ended up slumping in a red velour chair, plunging my hand into a bucket of popcorn, sipping cherry Coke, and wondering how come I couldn't find a man who would treat me like the woman I am. My temples throbbed as I tried to exorcise the map's lines out of my head.

IV. Los Angeles (1990)

I drove past the Cafe Tropical on the corner of Sunset and Parkman in Echo Park. Overnight the building face had changed its color, from the deep Halloween orange to white. So often the color alone had marked my safe return home, like the tree trunk in a game of chase. All change should happen like this, swiftly, men scaling ladders in the moonlight, slapping on white paint in the night. An orange the color of jungle birds and birds of paradise. Cafe Tropical, my marker. "I live just up the hill from the orange building on Sunset," I say. Cafe Tropical, my morning time hangout. Cafe Tropical, next to the Silverlake Lounge, where only once was I brave enough to peek through the heavy canvas curtains that shielded the open doorway. I saw Latino men dancing cheek to cheek, pelvis to pelvis, knee to knee, bodies in zigzag modern art shapes. I couldn't hear the music.

I told Carlos to meet me here, but he's like me. He has no *Thomas Guide* and a bad sense of direction. He's not from here. He just drove down for the day to audition for a gig at Kachina Grill downtown. Kachina Grill, Friday happy hour hangout for corporate types, serves nouveau Mexican food, red tortilla *taquitos*, spinach tortilla chips, black beans with goat cheese, and Budweiser.

Women fall in love with him easily. I'm not sure why the others do. It is probably his music or his exotic dark skin or his long Indian hair. His is something of a wild and exotic intelligence, not a cultured exotic, not a school- or museum-cultured exotic. It's his music, his fingers that give him the illusion of intelligence and deep thoughts. That much I have figured out.

I like him because he knows every version of "La Llorona" and has sung me "La pistola y el corazón." He never went to college but calls himself Chicano anyway.

My house is up in the hills. I knew he would never find it. So I told him to meet me here at the Cafe Tropical. After his appointment he called and asked where he should meet me. "My house," I replied, and made a mental list of embarrassing things I should probably hide. "But you know what, my house is really hard to find. The streets curve, and there are no street-lights. Why don't you just meet me at the Cafe Tropical? All you have to do from downtown is get onto Sunset and then drive west toward the ocean. You don't even have to get on the free-way. You can't miss it; it's an orange building."

"So it's on Sunset?" he asked.

"Yes," I replied. "The Cafe Tropical. There's a Laundromat across the street. You'll get to the corner, and on the corner closest to downtown there is a Korean hotel for businessmen, and in that same complex there is a foot doctor. Now you can't miss that because there's a giant sign with a happy pink foot that rotates. The other side of the sign is an unhappy brown foot on crutches. Just go one block past the foot doctor to the Cafe Tropical."

"An unhappy foot?" he asked.

"Yes," I answered, a little surprised because it sounded as if he were writing it down, spelling it in his head, "an unhappy foot." "It should take you only about ten minutes. I'll be waiting for you."

"See you soon, Teresa," he said, in a voice with just the slightest hint of promise.

"Oh, wait a minute, wait a minute," I said. "Do you have a map? Just in case you get lost?"

"A map?" he replied blankly.

"Yeah, a map," I said.

"I don't need a map. I'll be there in ten minutes."

I went to the bathroom to brush my teeth, just in case, put on lipstick, Indian Sugar, and headed out the door to the car.

At this time in the late afternoon, I did not recognize any of the regulars. I am part of the yuppie, *café con leche*, greasy crois-sant, and *L.A. Times* in the morning crowd. I order my *café con leche* and take a seat at the back table near the black oven. I pour sugar into my coffee straight from the container, first a T, then a C, then a heart. I always do this for good luck. At first I am so excited all I can think to do is sit and wipe the lipstick off my front teeth and watch the steam from the coffee let out long, slow breaths, like a song.

I look at the Guatemalan and Mexican masks hanging on the walls—the devils, the birds, the dogs—and wonder where he is. Fifteen minutes have passed. I have been sitting at the window that faces Sunset Boulevard and watching the cars' headlights click on, preparing for twilight.

Twenty minutes have passed. I think that he must be searching for the color orange. Suddenly I remember I told him to look for the orange building. I forgot to tell him that the building used to be orange, and now it's white. I forgot to tell him what color to look for.

All the houses up in the hills are neutral-colored, modern, sleek: white, gray, beige. But the houses down here, next to the Tropical, next to the Silverlake Lounge are dangerous colors. Colors that don't have names in English. It is all my fault. He doesn't have a map. He doesn't know what color to look for. He is lost on Sunset Boulevard. I pull my Walkman from my purse, slide in his cassette, fast forward to the song he wrote, his "Mexican Song," he calls it. "Allegría." Happiness.

V. Oxnard (1992)

The sun casts a warm hue over Ventura County, where the eucalyptus trees filter the light into a shade of gold that makes every color brighter, richer with the texture of memory, like a romantic California painting. I have left the grayness of the city behind me, driving to Oxnard on El Camino Real, Highway 101, to meet a man. Over all the hills that curve through the range of the Santa Monica Mountains, I have pressed the gas pedal to 70 mph just because I want to get there fast. I want to be there now, with the wind behind me, sitting in the red vinyl booth at our favorite restaurant, Cielito Lindo, drinking a beer and listening to the songs he picks from the jukebox.

Once I drive down from the hill and into the flat agricultural valley, I can't go as fast as I would like to go. I have to control my speed a little. The plywood fruit stands mark this stretch of highway. They mark the land in a way that a green sign with white lettering never could. Strawberries, melons, pistachios, grapes are my markers. This is where Alex works. He's an Irish-Mexican-American lawyer who represents farm laborers and learned to speak Spanish in college. Like me. Alex goes out into the fields, stands over the bent workers, and asks them if they have bathrooms and water, all the while looking at their hands, red from strawberry juice. He tells the men that cutting the strawberry vines with a short knife is an unlawful work practice and that they will hurt their backs and that their employers are breaking the law by making them use these knives. But they mostly don't listen to that part. He gives them his card and tells them to come to his office on B Street in Oxnard if they have any problems.

Usually we meet at his office downtown. But this time, since we want to be in one car, we agree to meet at his house first, which is right on the beach in Ventura. He thinks I will have a difficult time finding it, so he tells me to take the Sea Crest Boulevard exit and to call him from the pay phone at the Shell station. He says this, and my eyes crinkle into a smile, realizing that he is like me—or at least he understands me.

I like him because his taste in music is as wide and broad and warm as a plaza filled with sunlight, even if it is only an imaginary plaza I've never been to. He teaches me to listen to his music. *Sones de* Veracruz; huapango; *huasteca*; Cuban bolero; mountain music of Peru; Cuban rumba; Haitian merengue; Mexican *gustos*; Senegal salsa; Puerto Rican *cumbia* and Brazilian funk. Music moves him. Alex doesn't dance well, but he overcomes his stiffness with a lot of heart, and I love when he twirls and spins me because it feels like a wonderful ride. Tonight we are going to visit all the bars along Oxnard Boulevard, the farm worker bars, where mariachi bands play for cheap and wear psychedelic outfits and big cowboy hats. Tonight I will wear my cowboy boots, and I will fit in even if I don't belong.

I pull into the Shell station and park next to the pay phones. I put in a quarter, dial his number, and say, "I'm here," but really, I'm thinking, *I'm safe*, safe, like the tree trunk in a game of chase.

DANNY ROMERO

Crime

On his way home from work Libertad waited at a
stoplight. Out of the corner of his eye he saw Mr.
Charlie drive up behind dark sunglasses. Two screws sat in the
car. They waited to turn in the direction Libertad was taking
down the boulevard. This was the only way to the subway. He
thought he saw one of the screws lean out of the car window to
get a better look at him, but Libertad did not turn in their
direction to see for certain. He felt their eyes on him as he
crossed in front of them. He kept on his way, as nonchalant as
possible, trying to recount the contents of his shoulder bag and
wrestling with the urge to run.

The siren sounded for an instant. A voice over the loudspeaker
said, "Hold it right there. Punk."

Libertad halted.

The voice said, "Turn around."

Libertad turned and saw the lights atop the car spinning,
flashing, red and blue. *What's this crap?* thought Libertad. A
spotlight turned on him, blinding. "Get on your knees," said the
voice over the loudspeaker. "Keep your hands where I can see
them."

Libertad did. He tried to shield his eyes with his hands out in
front of him.

"Where you moving to so fast?" said a second voice from the brightness.

"You weren't trying to get away from me, punk?" said the first screw over the loudspeaker.

"Let's see some ID," said the second screw.

"You speak English, punk?"

Libertad was silent for a moment, trying to shield his eyes from the spotlight shining in his face. "Hey, man," he said, "what's the problem?" He reached for his wallet.

A revolver was cocked, a certain click-click, turning the cylinder, a fresh cartridge now before the barrel. Libertad froze.

"Wha'cha doing, punk?" said the first screw. The loudspeaker crackled.

"I'm getting my goddamn ID," said Libertad, not moving. "It's in my wallet."

"Dumb-ass motherfucker, you move again an' I'll send you back across the border. Dead. Punk." Again the loudspeaker crackled.

Sweat trickled down the middle of Libertad's back. He had never been across the border in his life. When he was younger, all his friends went to visit family or for smuggling. They brought back fireworks and switchblades. It used to be $100 for a pound of grass, $150 for a kilo. They bragged about the pussy and the one dirty theater where for $2 a person could watch cheap sex acts. He remembered summer nights when he was a teenager, when he and his friends walked through the streets, tossing quarter sticks of dynamite, M-1000s they were called. Not much later Frank and his brother Clown were shot and killed outside a liquor store by the screws responding to reports of sporadic gunfire. The media reported the screws had acted in good faith. Libertad wished he had an M-1000 with him now.

"I have to get my ID," he said.

"Go ahead," said the second screw. Again there was the sound of a revolver being cocked, a certain click-click, turning the cylinder, a fresh cartridge now before the barrel. "Slowly."

Libertad reluctantly brought down his right hand, still holding the left one up, and reached back. He closed his eyes; it was more comfortable. The backs of his eyelids stung. He tilted his head downward.

"Uh, you think you could turn off that light, please?"

" 'Please' even," mocked the first screw. "We're videotaping this punk," he went on. "You're on *Candid Camera*. Ha-ha-ha. We're doing a little training film." The second screw laughed nervously. The first screw said to the second screw, "You know, I hate these punks that complain."

"You know it," said the second screw.

The spotlight burned on Libertad. He brought his wallet out. He opened it and removed the first card out of the plastic window insert. He held it out in front of him.

"Hey, you do that real good," said the first screw. "What else you do real good? Ha-ha-ha. Punk."

It sounded to Libertad as if the screw still stood near the car. His ID was torn out of his hand from the left side. The spotlight blinked once, twice, then flashed back on again. The first screw laughed loudly.

"Check this out," said the second screw. His words trailed back over to the car.

Libertad could not hear their words. He imagined they were looking at his picture. In it he was four years younger. He had gone to renew his ID on the day after his birthday. At a party a few days earlier he had met this woman and spent the next seven days with her drinking, screwing, and swallowing Valium, 50 mg at a time. The Valium kept him so hard that week, he joked to his friends, that the wrinkles on his face had been stretched taut, and there was the reason he looked so much younger in the photo. And there was the reason he looked to be in a stupor.

Laughter came from the squad car.

On the boulevard the traffic was heavy as usual, traveling east and west. One hot rod, from the sound of it, roared down the street, the occupants screaming out, "Hhheeeyyy, sssuuuccckk-keeerrr . . ." as they passed.

Libertad had his hands up all the while. His knees ached on the uneven concrete surface of the broken sidewalk. He thought for a second that the sun was out but realized it was the heat from the light. Libertad wondered if this was how his brother had ended up. Was this what happened that night three years ago when he left work and was never seen again? Did they stop him and have him kneeling in the street?

Three or four times this month Libertad remembered scenes such as this as he traveled on the boulevard. He had always considered himself lucky not to be that person in the street, but as he knelt there now, he guessed it had been only a matter of time before he was rounded up also.

He heard one screw, keys jingling, walk over to him. "When did you get out of prison?" asked the second screw, now standing nearby.

"Why are you stopping me?" asked Libertad.

"Shut up, punk," shouted the first screw from over near the car.

The second screw said, "You fit the description of the suspect."

"What suspect?" asked Libertad.

"You don't worry 'bout that unless you're him," said the second screw. "When did you get out of prison?"

"I've never been there," answered Libertad. He wondered if he was carrying anything suspicious in his shoulder bag. It still lay near him, he thought.

"What have you been arrested for? Punk," shouted the first screw.

"Drunk in public," said Libertad. He heard the first screw reading off the ID information into the two-way radio. Libertad hoped his name came up clean. A person never knew what might happen. People had identical names and outstanding warrants for arrest. Mr. Charlie did not keep good records. They could take you in on fines already paid, time already served.

The first screw said, "L-i-b-e-r-t—"

"Any major crimes?" asked the second screw.

"—libber-todd, I guess . . . I don't care what the—"

"No, I haven't," said Libertad.

"—yeah, you know, the street in the ghetto part of town—"

"How many times you been arrested?" asked the second screw.

"I don't know," said Libertad. "Too many times, I guess."

"—this says he's thirty, but he looks older . . . Pancho Villa mustache motherfucker . . . looks like someone hit him in the forehead with a bottle or something . . . Frankenstein . . . dope fiend . . . you should see him . . . we'll check it out."

The second screw walked back over to the car. The two screws spoke too low for Libertad to hear them. The keys jingling walked up and stood near Libertad. "How long you been using?" the second screw asked.

"Hey, I don't do that," said Libertad.

"You know the routine," said the second screw. "Put your sleeves up."

Libertad brought his hands down and pushed his sleeves up.

"Any tattoos?" asked the second screw.

"No," said Libertad. He held his arms out in front of him so the screw could check for needle marks. "I don't do that," repeated Libertad. There were cars honking on the boulevard.

"Wha'cha have in the bag?" asked the second screw. "You got a bomb in there?"

"Just books and paper," said Libertad.

"You wanna open it up," said the second screw.

Libertad felt on the ground in front of him for his bag. He heard another car drive up and stop. Two doors opened and closed. Libertad opened the bag slowly and held it out. Another car drove up and stopped. One door opened and closed.

"What about that little pocket right there?" asked the second screw. "You wanna open it up too."

"Pens. Cigarettes," said Libertad. He opened it and held it out. On his left side he could feel pedestrians moving past him. He wondered if it might be someone from his work. "That's all," he said. He heard two car doors open and close. One car drove off.

"You got a gun or a knife on you?" asked the second screw. He stood closer to Libertad on his right side.

"No, I don't," said Libertad.

"Stand up," said the second screw. "Spread your legs and lace your fingers together on top of your head." The screw kicked his legs farther apart. He stood behind Libertad and began to pat him down. Two pairs of footsteps walked over to them.

"What are you doing around here?" asked a new voice.

"I work over on the next street," said Libertad. The second screw was feeling his coat pocket. "That's a book," said Libertad.

"Take it out," said the second screw.

"Why don't you go back to where you came from? Punk," said the first screw.

Libertad took the book out of his pocket and held it out. "I was born in this country," he said. The second screw took the book out of his hand, then felt the pocket to make certain it was empty.

"Why did you start walking away so fast when you saw us back there? Punk," said the first screw.

"I just got off from work," said Libertad. "I'm walking to the corner to catch the subway."

"You read that shit," said the second screw. He dropped the book to the ground.

Libertad stood in the middle of a circle of the three men, eyes closed, hands on head, fingers laced. "I just want to catch the subway," he said.

The first screw said, "We don't want to see you around here no more. Punk." He walked right up to him and stood rock hard against Libertad. "Get out of here. Punk," he said. They all three walked away.

Libertad opened his eyes by accident. They hurt. "Can I have my ID?" he asked, eyes closed again.

"This your current address?" asked the second screw.

"One-nine-four-zero East Seventy-third Street," said Libertad. "I work just over on the next street."

"Telephone number?" asked the second screw.

"Five-five-five-four-three-six-nine," said Libertad. "At work it's Q-Z-five-three-three-eight-one."

He felt his ID brush off his face as it was thrown at him. He could hear the three men climbing into the car, doors opened, then closed. He noticed for the first time their engine was still running. They gunned it; there was laughter. The spotlight went off. Libertad blinked his eyes open, trying to focus his vision. The car drove off. Libertad still blinked, on his knees and groping for his belongings.

Abuela Marielita

My daughter doesn't want people to know that I came through the port of Mariel, so she tells them that I came by way of Spain in January 1980, four months before I actually arrived *en los cayos*. In the beginning Gertrudes and Miguel didn't care; the first year it was fine to say that I came on a boat, not a jet, something I've never done. I used to like to tell people about the nice young man who took me and the others on his speedboat, such an enchanting boy, so happy that the guards had found his aunt and uncle, his only family left in Cuba. He said he didn't care that we others weren't *parientes* of his, as long as Chelita *y* Tatín were on the boat, although he had tried to find a sister of one of his neighbors, her name was Ester Ramírez, but that's all, just three people were on his list. *Ah, que muchacho más bueno.* He had been in Mariel Harbor waiting four days when his *tíos* were brought to the pier, imagine, not knowing if they would be able to go and all. I rode on the bus with them though I didn't know them at the time, of course. I was staying with my cousin's son and his wife in a section of the house I used to own before the revolution, and Jorgito, that's my *prima*'s son, was making arrangements to get on the list to leave. Well, if they were leaving, I wasn't going to be of any use to anyone. My mother died when I was pregnant, and her only living brother went to Santiago with his wife's family. I didn't have any *parientes* left in *La Habana*, so what did I have to stay for? My daughter was in Miami, and my son, José Angel, died as a young man in Playa Girón, I had no reason to stay in Cuba at all. Oh, I wanted to be with my daughter so much; *pobrecita*, after so many years, she didn't have anyone in Miami. It's true that Miguel's family is very large, but that day Jorgito said that I had to decide right away, and I did. I slept on it and prayed to the Virgins (both la Caridad del Cobre and Nuestra Señora de las Mercedes—one of my namesakes) to help me, and they did. In three days some guards came to the house to get me; by then Jorgito *y* Lola were gone, poor things, God knows where they ended up. I gave him my daughter's address, but I've never heard anything from him. I believe his wife had some family in Tampa, but Gertrudes says that's very far from Miami, although I know it's still in Florida because I found it in one of my granddaughter's books when I was cleaning her room. Well, anyway, after the first year or so there were so many of us here, and it was not popular to help Marielitos anymore. Things got very bad. One day I was darning some of my son-in-law's socks in the Florida room toward the rear of the house and I heard a big boom! My heart almost stopped; I thought it was a bomb, but it was the front door that was knocked down. Right in the middle of broad daylight there was this big empty moving truck parked right on the lawn and two men standing there ready to steal everything in the house. *¡Qué descarados!* I yelled at them, and they just calmly got back into their truck and drove away. Of course I was very frightened. That's when Gertrudes and Miguel decided to move from La Pequeña Habana out to Westchester. That's also when they told me not to say anything about being an exile from Mariel. My daughter won't even let me speak about it in front of my grandchildren, Marcos *y* Graciela, either, though I'm sure *la niña* knows something because she was already talking when I arrived, but even she doesn't say anything. She speaks nonstop English anyway; I can't hardly understand her sometimes. The little one, Marcos, has no idea, of course; he'll be six soon.

My *yerno*, Miguel, owns a glass store on Flagler Street, the

Cristalería Siboney, and Gertrudes works in an office for the county—a very good job with benefits for her, Miguel, and the children. I go to the Cuban clinic for the doctor because her insurance doesn't cover me, but I don't mind because I see so many of my friends there, especially now when I go every week for my *terapia*. My wrist feels much better. I twisted it while pulling Marcos away from the American man's dog next door. The dog had the ball Marcos threw over the fence in its mouth, and the child was trying to pull it out and through the fence. Well, the dog wanted to play too, but children can be so bad sometimes; thanks to God, the boy is fine. After that Miguel put up a wooden fence that blocks the view of the other neighbors' yards, a shame because Josefina and her husband have such lovely gardenia bushes and the neighbors' patio to the rear of us, the Lópezes, has banana and papaya plants that remind me of my own patio in Cuba. When I was newly married and my mother was still alive, I used to grow *jazmines* and dahlias in the court-yard; I haven't seen any dahlias here, though.

The new house my daughter and son-in-law bought has an apartment in the back; actually it's a little room, but I guess for one person it's fine. A few months after we had moved here and all the neighbors got to know us (and not know too much about me, of course) the room was rented to an older señora. She kept me company sometimes during the day, while I took care of the children, and Lord knows I could use Ofelia's, that's her name, help. *¡Ese Marcos es un ciclón!* Gracielita is no saint, either. *Pobrecita* Ofelia, what a kind soul, she couldn't take care of her-self after a while, kept falling down and not being able to get back up, so her sons, God forgive them, put her in one of those hospitals where they are supposed to take care of old folks. She was only six or seven years older than me, and I'm seventy-two. She was such a good listener too.

I meant to talk about Yamile, and maybe I steered away from the subject at times, but forgive me because I'm an old woman. Yamile came through Mariel also and moved into the *cuartico* behind the house after Ofelia left. She was very fat for such a young woman, so my daughter didn't notice that she was pregnant although I could tell by her look almost immediately; it was the look of a woman with child. Miguel wanted to evict her when he found out, but when Luz came, the baby, she slept almost all night, so he could not complain too much; besides, with the windows closed, you can't hear a thing anyway. Gertrudes doesn't like Yamile and treats her very rudely, something I lament very much because I have come to care for her and the baby, poor things. At first Gertrudes did not mind that I was talking to Yamile, although sometimes she made little comments about Yamile and her being on welfare and only working part-time at the *farmacia* near us. But then again, she couldn't say too much because Yamile always pays her rent on time and in full. She doesn't know, of course, that I give her a little hand with my food stamps ever since they gave me more. I never told my daughter that I get sixty dollars and not forty dollars—I'm always here when *la cartera* comes; we have a woman to deliver the mail, isn't that something? Nice girl. Plus, whenever they give out cheese or powdered milk, I always give Yamile some. She needs it much more than we do, and my grandchildren don't eat that cheese. They like the store-bought wrapped squares better. Anyway, Miguel has his own business, which is doing well, and my daughter makes a good salary. I shouldn't even be taking the stamps, but my daughter says they pay taxes for them and we might as well take them. I don't say anything about it anymore.

Yamile has been living here almost a year now, and Luz is just a little doll. I spend a lot of time with her now that both of the children are going to San Bernardo's. To me, Luz is like my own grandchild because I've been with her since birth. Yamile leaves her with me in the mornings when she goes to work. Most of the time the baby just sits and plays in the crib while I prepare the dinner or fold the clothes. She doesn't talk yet, so we haven't cut her hair; it's long in the back but kind of thin on top, *angelita*, she'll look better when it all grows in. In the morning when it's still not so hot, after everyone's gone, Luz and I go to the patio to hang up the clothes. She watches from that baby swing Marcos used to love so much. My daughter was throwing it out before I stopped her. I hang the clothes because I really don't

like to use the clothes dryer. It's so much better to sun the things
and let them blow in the breeze; they smell so much nicer too.
Gertrudes finally stopped fussing about it when Miguel said that
they would save on the electricity. They spend so much already
with the air conditioners on from the time they walk in the door
until they leave the next day. I always turn them off (they have
five!) when they're gone and open all the windows; I don't even
sleep with the one in my room on though my daughter can't
understand. The fan is really just fine for me; I tell her that the
air conditioner gives me a sore throat. The children know how
to turn them on, and it's the second thing they do, after they
turn on the television, the minute that bus drops them off and
they run through the door. I only like to watch my *novela* in the
evening; it's the same one my daughter watches, so I can watch it
on the big screen. I'd really rather listen to the radio during the
day, though. It seems that the television is on almost as much as
the air conditioner sometimes, and of course, *la niña* has her own
little color TV in her room. Marcos is starting to ask for another
one, so my son-in-law promised him a color set for his birthday
if he brings home a good report card this term, I don't understand, but I don't say anything, because he is their father and I
don't want him to say that I meddle, like I heard him say one
time when I was going to bed. Anyway, Luz and me, we hang
the clothes together, and sometimes I'll sing to her, she's such a
happy baby. I'm enjoying her much more than I did Marcos
because I was always worrying about what Gracielita was doing
the minute I turned away, what a child, that one, always into
everything. I'm sure half my gray hairs belong to her.

It was a very hard thing for me to find Yamile in the condition
she was in when I went to take her a plate of food from Marcos's
fifth birthday party. They had set up the patio with rented chairs
and tables and there were trays and trays of *pasteles cubanos* filled
with *guayaba, queso y carne*; sandwichitos of sweet ham with jelly
and cheese or a creamy meat paste—I love those. And they
ordered a huge blue and white sheet cake with those little robots,
the cartoon ones that Marcos watches all the time; he has them
all over the house. His parents got him a piñata in the shape of

one of them; oh, what does he call them? Something of *el universo*, I don't remember now, but he even had a costume for that fiesta the North Americans have in October. *Bueno*, I'll remember it later. There was music, and all of the neighbor families were invited, even the man from next door. Miguel said we had better invite him or he would call the police about the music, which was way too loud because Gracielita and her *amiguitas* would change to an American station and turn up the volume whenever they got the chance, though they never did dance to it anyway.

There were so many people there besides the neighbors' children and kids from San Bernardo's. There was Miguel's family from Hialeah, all of them. Even a first cousin of his that came via Mariel, but he didn't say anything to her, imagine, not even hello. There were a couple more North Americans too from my daughter's job, though they left right away after we cut the cake. Probably got bored talking to themselves; the neighbor man left early too. It was already in the evening when people were serving themselves more *arroz con pollo*. By then it had cooled off, and oh, there were tamales too, and I made a big aluminum tray of potato and chicken salad. I spelled Marcos's name on top with pimento slices, but he never saw it. He was too busy riding around all afternoon on the bicycle that Miguel bought him or running in and out of the house showing friends the new game tapes he got for his TV even though Gertrudes told him not to bring kids into the house. They didn't stop until they broke one of her Lladro figurines; she has a whole *vitrina* filled with them. It took me three pots of café to serve everyone, it's a good thing Ofelia left me hers, so I only had to wash one right away to make more for the last two people. Everyone seemed satisfied, either rubbing their bellies, sipping espresso or going back for more food, so I thought I'd check in on Yamile and Luz.

The music was still too loud, but I could hear the baby. Luz was very little then, maybe three months. I could hear her crying above all the noise. Gertrudes was talking with Estrella from across the way; poor woman, her son killed himself with drugs, only sixteen years old, a sad thing, really. Hemm, *ah sí*. I think

Miguel went for more ice or beer or both, though I can't imagine what was taking him so long; he slips away a lot lately, but I've learned to bite my tongue about it. Marcos was playing *computador* with his friends, and Gracielita was shut up in her room with two or three girls. They were talking on the phone when I checked in on them; I don't like it when she locks that door like that. Anyway, she did something that upset me very much. She's gotten such a mouth since starting school at San Bernardo's. I asked *las muchachitas* if they wanted any more soda, in Spanish, of course, but Gracielita answered me in English with that face she puts on whenever she's acting up, and they all laughed. All I could understand her saying was something about me being a Marielita, but I'm sure it was worse than that. I would have slapped her right then and there, but my daughter doesn't believe in that, so I called her a fresh and shameless girl, and they kept right on laughing. Such disrespect! I was so angry I just wanted to shake her, but the only thing I could do was close the door hard behind me. Marcos saw me in the hall and called out for more soda, so I brought some back for him and his friends. None of them said thank you. Gertrudes asked me if the children were all right when I walked past the living room. I said yes and went to my room to get my fan; my face was on fire! I took an extra tranquilizer from my drawer and remembered Yamile and the baby; her room shares a wall with my bedroom.

Well, when I passed the living room to go to the kitchen, Gertrudes asked me for more café, and I told her I would get it in a few minutes. She said she wanted some now with the cake she was eating, and I told her to make it herself or wait for me and walked right on by to the kitchen for the chicken and rice I left in the oven for Yamile and then back to the table in the yard and got some salad and a few *pastelitos*. Of course Gertrudes would wait, but I could see through the sliding door that she was raising some fuss about it with that conceited Hortensia; she's always talking about Spain, trying to catch me up in the lie, but I always say I can't remember the names of places in Madrid. Anyway, I got together a nice heaping serving for Yamile, and I decided to put a big piece of cake on a separate plate because there was so much of it left. It had much too much meringue—even for me—and the children didn't like the pineapple filling, so more than half the cake was left even though there must have been close to a hundred people there at one point or another. I figured I'd bring Yamile cake later, so I took the plate which had those *universo* robots printed on it—the napkins, cups, and paper tablecloths all matched too. I managed to save one of the cake decorations for Luz, I felt it in my pocket against my waist; then, hands full, I walked around to Yamile's little room behind the utility shed where the washer and dryer are.

Angel of God, to remember that poor girl with that whimpering baby, ay, it just breaks my heart. It's always very hot in that part of the house, and there wasn't a single breeze. *Pobrecita*, she only has two windows in that little room and facing the east, so all she gets is hot air. She was drenched and fanning herself and the baby with a piece of cardboard. Luz was kicking around and bright red. I could tell that her sheets were all sticky too. I noticed that there was a plate of bread and I think *mayonesa* on the table next to the crib. But that's all! Yamile got up right away and told me to sit, but I put the food before her and made her stay put. She always calls me Doña Soledad; she's the only one who's ever called me by my first name. Almost everyone calls me Mercedes, but I have always liked Soledad because it was my mother's name, and it reminds me of her; my full name's Soledad de las Mercedes Pérez y Pérez, not including my husband's name—Aguirre. Yamile's eyes were full of veins, and she was in tears when she asked me what more she could do with Luz. I asked her how much she had fed her already; poor thing couldn't nurse because of the gland medicine she takes. She showed me two bottles that were still dirty with milk. I reached over and picked Luz up, feeling the dampness of the mattress and the baby clothes, and realized that I had never seen her drinking water. I turned right around, bouncing Luz on my hip, and called out, "What that baby needs is water!" Yamile's thin eyebrows arched up while I went on. "You young people never ask the old ones anything, because you know it all already." She was smiling and crying at the same time, and then tears fell from my eyes too while I prepared a fresh bottle of water. I held Luz close to my bosom as she drank while Yamile was eating the food from the party and watching us.

VIRGIL SUÁREZ

Salvation

"Hear that?"

"What, Rafa?"

"The thunder dummy, what else?"

"No."

In the distance thunder rolled.

"Hear it now?"

"Yes," said Sonny in the dark of the small bedroom he and an older brother shared.

"Storm's coming."

They listened to the rain falling on the banana leaves outside by the window. It hadn't let up all night.

"Is he gone for good?" Sonny was referring to his father.

"Nah, he'll come back." His brother, Sonny knew, was only saying his father would return just to cheer him up. This time he was gone for good; their father had said so himself.

"He said he wouldn't."

"Wanna bet? Cowards always come back." Every time Sonny thought he'd fall asleep, Rafael broke the silence and spoke. His voice sounded so far away.

"I don't feel well," Sonny said.

Thunder broke again in the distance. . . . The rain had come in the afternoon, Sonny remembered, when the clouds gathered and turned the color of lead. He watched the sky from the patio where he had gone the minute his father started to shout at his mother.

They argued about the same thing: When was his father going to stop coming home so late? Sonny's father had one addiction: gambling. Rigo spent all his time and money at the fighting cock pits in Matanzas.

Sonny stood in the patio among the empty clotheslines and nervous chickens in their wooden milk bottle crates turned into cages, among the rusty bicycle frames and mildewy box spring mattresses and discarded stoves, among the pungent smells of chicken shit and gasoline and oil. Sonny stood in the rain and cried. The rain fell at an angle, so the roof ledge couldn't serve as shelter. The water felt warm as it soaked his short-sleeve shirt and torn pants, which were made out of flour sack jute.

Sonny leaned against the lime wall and remembered what his older brother Brito had told him once: A man didn't cry, and if little Sonny was a real man, he wouldn't be crying like a girl all the time, like his sister, Kenya. He stood in the rain and remembered, and for some reason all he was able to recall were the bad times when he'd heard or seen his father, during violent moods, hurt his mother.

Now the fever ran high. Sonny's brother, who thought Sonny had peed on the bed again, felt the high temperature on Sonny's sweaty skin that night when they couldn't sleep because of the thunder. Sonny's flesh burned. Immediately Rafa, as Sonny called his brother Rafael, the last older brother to remain in the house, rushed to their mother's bedroom, woke her up, and told her about Sonny's fever.

Gris Manteca awoke in a panic.

She was a big-boned woman with large hips, but that night she sprang from her bed as swiftly as a cat might jump from a windowsill. Then she ran to the bedroom and felt Sonny's forehead. Her hands felt cold to Sonny. The heat on her boy's forehead and loins alarmed her. For a brief moment she was lost and confused, standing there in the dark of the boys' room. The boy's testicles had swollen to the size of lemons.

Alone, she didn't know whom to turn to. It was raining hard outside, so hard that the drops hitting the tin roof of the tool shack next door sounded like the gallop of horses. Death was coming for her boy, she thought, riding on Her black stallion. Then she thought of the only person in the barrio who could help her. Josefa, the healer, the *curandera*, the medicine and herb woman. *La yerbera*, as people in the neighborhood called the ancient apothecary. But Josefa was too old to make house calls, especially so late at night and in such bad weather.

But time was too important, and Sonny's mother couldn't waste it on what ifs. Her mother had told her once that high temperatures can be lowered by bathing the boy in ice-cold water and alcohol. Home remedies passed from one generation to another, but she didn't want to deplete her chances.

What if . . . Josefa indeed was the only one who could truly help her.

She wrapped Sonny in several sheets and blankets and towels—anything she could find—and took her delirious son, delirious because she could see the high fever burning in his glazed green eyes. Heavy-lidded, the boy made quick, jerky movements, as if convulsing, with his arms and legs. He uttered some kind of nonsense spoken too softly for her to be able to decipher.

As a bird flew, that night Gris with her son held tight to her bosom flew out of her house and took Sonny to see Josefa. Guilt strapped around her legs. She couldn't move fast enough. As she walked, she felt as if she were walking in knee-high mud. Years before, when she had gotten pregnant with Sonny, she had come to see Josefa about getting an abortion. The last thing she needed then was another child. Kenya wasn't even a year old. Josefa said she couldn't help Gris because of a change of heart. Gris came in through Josefa's door and sat down on a *taburete*, a wood and cowhide chair. She started to cry so hard that Josefa had to make her some special *tilo* (linden flowers tea) to calm her down.

"I don't know why," Gris said, "God doesn't like me."

"Nonsense!" Josefa had said, then cleared her throat. "If God didn't like you, he wouldn't let you get this way so often."

"Rigo doesn't care what happens to me."

"Everybody in this crazy town knows what kind of man Rigo is. But yet you continue to sleep with him."

"He's *my* man."

A clear, gelatinous fluid ran out of Gris's nostrils and hung over her upper lip: snot. She had cried like a child. Too bad Josefa couldn't help her then.

The boy was too heavy for Gris to carry. She struggled uphill and tried her best not to stumble and fall.

It was the kind of mean night even dogs feared. Usually the dogs in the neighborhood barked at every passerby, but tonight they hid in their doghouses. She hated those dogs because their owner let them loose and they barked at her whenever she went to the bodega to buy food. Those damned yap-yaps!

She rushed by in silence, and silence was all she heard except for the sound of the rain falling everywhere. The drops of rain fell hard against her skull and shoulders and arms as she hurried up the darkened street. That son of a bitch, she cursed at Rigo. One day she was going to kill that bastard. Cut his balls off, she thought, and feed them to the dogs. From one mean son of a bitch to another.

The road to Josefa's house was muddy. Barefoot, Gris took her chances and tried hard not to trip. Her heels sank into the mud, and twice she lost her balance and fell, knees first, against the pebbly surface of the path. Nothing would stop her—not even the rain—from reaching Josefa's house.

Lightning flashed.

Josefa's place wasn't really a house but a shack built awkwardly on termite-ridden stilts. Slanted, it stood to one side of the hill behind the city's dumping grounds. The closer Gris came to the place, the more the sour smell of rotting things choked her. With the end of a blanket she covered her nose and mouth and tried not to breathe in that awful stink. She covered her son's face.

Gris reached the porch steps completely out of breath. The floorboards of the porch creaked under her weight, giving her the impression that they would split open and that she would fall into the rat- and vermin-infested cellar of Josefa's shack. On the door she knocked so hard she scraped her knuckles.

Josefa opened the door. She was holding a candle close to her face. The yellow reflection of the flame illumined her black face and made her eyes look like moons. Cataracts blinded Josefa.

"*Oh, mi santa Josefa*," Gris said. "*Ayúdame, mujer*. Sonny's very sick."

"Calm down, *niña*," Josefa said, opening the door wider to let the mother and child in. See, Josefa thought, it wasn't a cat scratching on the door to be let in. Faculties intact, faculties intact . . . she was old but not *that* old. Changó be her guide.

"I'm sorry to bother you this late—"

"Come," she said. "Bring the child to the back room."

Sonny's mother followed the glow of the candle to a back room that smelled faintly of jasmine.

Though Josefa was short and skinny, her shadow, thrown against the walls by the candle's flickering flame, looked tall and elongated. She walked slowly, her free hand stuck deep in the pocket of the robe she wore. Her feet—or was it her slippers?—made a scratching sound on the floor as she walked. Nobody knew how old Josefa was; rumor had it she was over a hundred years old.

In the dark the walls took on a completely different appearance. Josefa lit more candles as she told Gris to place the boy on the floor in the middle of the room.

"Remove all the sheets and blankets." Josefa spoke with compassion. "Bring the boy out into the open. Gently. Let him breathe."

Gris did what Josefa instructed. She placed little Sonny on the wood floor. So that he could be more comfortable, she bundled up one of the blankets into a pillow and placed it under his head. Sonny's eyes were closed; sweat covered his delicate face and forehead.

"He's burning up," his mother said.

"Remove his clothes too."

Gris told Josefa about the boy's swollen testicles. "I'm afraid, Josefa. If I lose—"

"Hush now."

Clothes off, Sonny lay still on the floor. Gris caressed his face as if rubbing would bring the temperature down. She was no longer paying attention to Josefa but praying for her boy. The Lord have mercy on her baby; he'd always been such a delicate boy.

Josefa opened a cabinet behind her and rummaged through drawers. She was looking for the right herbs and plants from which to make the potion she would rub over the boy's stomach. His being was being depleted; a mantillalike darkness had fallen over it, was pressing it. Something cold too had taken over his warmth. Sonny's belly was swollen and taut like the skin of a drum. She could only guess from the outward position of the boy's belly button what the problem was. The boy must have touched the aura of an animal killed by a *santero* for sacrificial purposes, done with bad intentions.

As Josefa took leaves and powders, mashed and mixed them with her fingers in a small gourd, and added several drops of melted goat's fat, she asked Gris if the boy had behaved differently at some point in the day.

"He plays for hours in the backyard," she said. "I don't know. I've been having troubles with my husband. Sonny hears us and thinks his father is going to leave us for good."

Josefa stood over the boy, wiping her hands on a towel she kept on a hook by the side of the cabinet. The ointment was ready. She explained to Gris about Sonny's coming in contact with a dead animal that had been sacrificed with ill intentions, used to cause harm.

"Tell me he's not going to die."

Josefa didn't answer. The boy would not die, but he would never be the same. From the minute she rubbed the ointment over the center of his being, the boy would change. His spirit would no longer be the same but summoned from a distant place, from another source. But Josefa, having been a mother herself, didn't want to disillusion the mother of the child. She carried the gourd, knelt, and placed it at the child's feet.

Josefa found blood on the boy's skin, rubbed it off with her fingertips, and showed it to Gris. "This is not the boy's blood," Josefa said, then noticed that Gris's knees were bleeding. Josefa gave her a towel to wipe the blood. The ointment, she knew from what she had learned long ago from her mother and grandmother, must not be contaminated. It had to be pure.

The *curandera*'s dark hands were wrinkled; her skin resembled that of a dry prune. She started to rub the oily substance outward from the boy's belly button. Once she reached the boy's temples, she stopped rubbing, spread his arms and legs out, and rested her hands over his heart. She put her ear to his chest. The boy had a strong heart, she thought, for its beating sounded like the thud-thud of rocks falling into a dry well. Josefa put her mouth on the belly button and blew into it as if she were inflating a paper bag. Sonny squirmed then. His hands and feet jerked.

Gris saw the tremor of the boy's eyes behind his eyelids.

"Hold him down," Josefa told his mother.

It was then that the mother felt the temperature decline. His skin broke out into a sweat. He opened his eyes and looked around, not scared or startled, but as if he'd lived in the room since birth.

Josefa moved away from Gris and the child, back to the cabinet, where she wiped the oil off her hands, opened the middle drawer in the cabinet, and removed a bottle of lotion. She uncapped the bottle and poured lotion over her hands. Then she began to shake her hands, sprinkling the lotion all over her body.

Despojo, Changó, a cleansing of the spirit.

Sonny's spirit was purified, no longer taken over by the aura of the dead animal.

"Take him home and let him sleep," Josefa said. "In the morning mix a pinch of this with water."

Gris accepted a small envelope from Josefa. In the bag, Josefa told her, was a special kind of herb that would help protect the child from further harm.

"What do I owe you?" Gris asked.

"Ten pesos," said Josefa.

Sonny's mother asked for Josefa's forgiveness, for she didn't have that much money with her. Josefa told her not to worry, that Gris could bring her the money when she had it.

"The boy is no longer lost," Josefa said.

"How was he lost?"

"No aim. No direction. In his weakness he became susceptible to bad spirits."

Gris and Sonny spent the night in another bedroom in Josefa's house. The storm passed in the early-morning hours. The sun broke through the clouds. Gris awoke to the crowing of a rooster. Next to her Sonny was sound asleep. She picked up the boy and walked out of the room. Josefa was nowhere in the house, so Gris left. How she would ever repay the *curandera* Gris didn't know, but Josefa had saved the life of her son.

YSA T. NÚÑEZ

Broadway

The courts were packed. Black and brown boys shooting hoops. They ran their fastest and dribbled under their legs, behind their backs, and up into the basket. If they ever missed; the end of the world. Sweat ruled the hour like a medal imprinted in the bare backs, bare chests of each and every boy trying to prove that he was a man. Their bodies collided and rubbed against one another as the ball darted back and forth. Their curses resounded above the hip-hop blasting from the boom box. After every layup each boy readjusted his falling shorts or jeans, which exposed more than the amount of crack of ass required by the style.

Girls at the bench or at the handball courts wore baggy blue jeans, extra-large T-shirts, and black high-top sneakers with shoelaces untied. Their hair was painfully tied up at the top of their skulls with scrunchies or rubber bands, and the rest fell down in kinky curls or pseudoperms, all covered with much gel. Their fingernails were recently sharpened and covered with bloodshot red polish to match the lipstick. Occasionally they shouted threats to the little brother or sister about what Ma was gonna do to them if they didn't quit playing with the broken glass bottles in the playground. And leave those needles alone.

Ana watched her man. Every turn, every flexing of his muscles, every jump and every fall, she watched. His huge black eyes were quick and sharp—guarding, watching every movement in order to get his hands on the ball. The muscles in his legs strained as he bounced back and forth, and his arms reached high in the air until he roughly blocked a throw and became the owner of the ball. He ran as fast as he could, dodging the bodies with expertise. As he approached the basket, he dribbled behind his back, made a full turn, and stepped forward to lay it up. The soles of his British Knights were worn and lost their friction. He slipped and came crashing to the ground onto his knee. The ball rolled off the court. He quickly scrambled to his feet and ignored the blood gushing from his left knee. His team surrounded him. Are you all right, man? He was fine.

She left then to save him further embarrassment. No man likes to have his woman witness his weakness. Snatching Carlos from the swings, she made her way down 138th Street. It was a sunny day with the kind of heat and humidity that made her skin feel as heavy as a fur coat. Not that Ana had ever worn one. In Harlem this weather meant tons of *tigeres* out on the streets chillin' with their buddies and always on the lookout for some "business." It meant boys playing football on their blocks until sunset or till they broke a car window. It meant girls sitting cross-legged on the steps of every building or the front of every car, looking good and being "ladies," which meant not running around. It meant a parade of brown faces walking every which way to the rhythmic sounds that consume the streets anytime you put that many Latinos in one spot.

Carlos was kicking and wailing and hanging from one arm, wishing to be released so he could continue his tantrum on the ground. He begged. Let's stay just a little bit longer, Mami, pleeeease. No! The Mister Softee truck came into view. Here's an ice cream. Shut up. Ma had refused to baby-sit him, so Ana would have to bring him along to her appointment. He was a very hyper child, running away from her all the time, trying to cross the street, crying for the simplest things. She didn't believe that terrible twos theory. He was like his father: restless, indecisive. He wanted this; he wanted that. Carlos, get away from that dog.

As she walked down Broadway toward the train station, she felt eyes on her. Male eyes, occasionally accompanied by a quickly whispered and much-unwanted compliment to a chosen part of her anatomy. She walked on briskly with her eyes focused straight ahead and Carlos almost dangling from one arm as he tried to keep up. She wore a green bodysuit that hugged her "handful" breasts and thin waist, dipping at the top in a V shape to expose just a little cleavage. Her black jeans were two sizes too large. Thanks to her black belt, they barely hung at her hips. They gathered around the ankle and would drag on the floor if her black high-tops hadn't been in the way. Huge looped earrings hung from her ears, almost touching her shoulders. Fake gold. She stopped at the corner bodega to buy a pack of Marlboro Lights 100s. She made her way to the door through the small walkway lined up with fruit and vegetable stands on both sides. A couple of old ladies arguing about the yam were in her way. The yam was rotten or something. Carlos, as he was being shuffled through the crowd, bumped straight into a couple of carton boxes and tripped over the entrance door. He was used to it. Life was hard for the little people. Julito DeChamps was blasting so loud that she almost had to shout out her order before the lady behind the counter got it. Holding Carlos in her arms, she struggled her way back out. Down at the train station she walked past the beggars. No, she didn't have any change. None of the turnstiles was working, so people had to line up to place their tokens in a tall black box by the token booth. It looked like a huge piggybank. Instead of the token, she placed a quarter in and rushed through the gates to the platform. They couldn't tell the difference. A token saved.

She sat on the benches to wait and placed Carlos on her lap. She lit up a cigarette and began to relax. She really wished Ma had baby-sat Carlos, but it had always been that way. A new boyfriend came along, and Ma forgot the rest of the world. Ma was heads over heels over some Puerto Rican. As if she hadn't been the first to warn Ana about those men. Not that their men were much better, but at least they weren't lazy, Ma always said. The only time she had enjoyed motherhood had been when she was playing house with Pa. She got tired of that soon enough. Pa was quick to raise his voice and lift his hand whenever the food wasn't ready and set by the time he got home or when his shirt wasn't ironed right. He never actually hit her, though. He never seemed to notice Ana most of the time except when, as a toddler, she forced her way onto his lap. Occasionally he'd watch her with something like fondness in his eyes, which would quickly turn into pity and finally into scorn. She wasn't a boy, and he could never forgive her that. She didn't even try to be like a boy. She missed every ball he ever pitched at her and dropped every ball he ever threw her way. On purpose, of course. She had never cared to please him. On Sundays Ma would dress her in ruffled pink dresses for church that never allowed him to forget. He'd been living in Florida with his new wife and their two sons ever since the divorce. Probably the only Dominican down there. He'd married a Cuban woman who made him go to Miami and taught him to hate Fidel. Ana called every once in a while to say hello. She always forgot to ask about the boys.

She looked down at Carlos. His head reclined in between her breasts. His eyelids were heavy with sleep. They kept shutting on him, but he'd stubbornly snap them back open. Maybe she should leave him with Maritza while she went to her appointment. She still had about an hour before she had to be there. Maritza worked at Macy's during the summer, but she would be coming out early today. She was a little shorter than Ana, with wavy hair down to her shoulders. She always wore slacks and blouses with shoes and her hair hanging loose or in a ponytail at the back. Her glasses always on her face. She was a college girl. She went to Fordham during the year. Really smart. Ana always wondered whether she could've gotten into Fordham, or to City at least. She could've been a lawyer or something, maybe a secretary. She looked at the bright side: She helped out the statistics. One more dropout. She knew it wasn't really her fault. She looked down at Carlos, who had fallen asleep and was drooling all over her hand. Except for his lips, he had all of his daddy's features. She imagined him a fully grown man dressed in a white gown waiting to begin surgery on his patient, or in an office presenting his new architectural project to the board, or running around preparing his next trial. Finally she gave up. She imagined him at the basketball courts, playing from sunrise to sunset. Only taking a couple of breaks here and there to do some "business." He wouldn't use it, just sell it; he'd be just like his daddy. The 1 train came, and she put out her cigarette and snapped back into the rush of people.

Down on Thirty-fourth Street the sidewalks were crowded with businesspeople on their lunch breaks and permanent shoppers searching for a sale. She walked into Macy's with Carlos waking up in her arms and was relieved to feel the cool air in the store evaporate the sweat from her body. Maritza worked in the men's clothing department. She'd be glad to take care of Carlos, she said. As Ana waited for Maritza to change and punch out her time card, she stared at one of the shoppers. It was a lady with red high heels and a black, sleeveless minidress that wrapped tightly around her figure. It must've been an expensive material. She cried out "expensive" in the way her hair was elegantly pinned up, in the way she gracefully strode from one side to the other, in the way her nails clearly were freshly manicured, in the way her makeup covered her face with just the right amount of everything a woman could wear on her face, in the way she seemed so comfortable wearing all that gold, and mostly in the paleness of her skin. She walked right past Ana in order to approach one of the salespeople. Her perfume smelled expensive too. She began to speak to the salesperson, who immediately recognized her. Her voice was deep yet very feminine. She went off on what seemed like a half hour soliloquy. Ana was always impressed by the way white people talked. They sounded like TV or movie stars. So proper and shit. They used words Ana had to look up. The lady wanted to purchase new tennis shoes for her husband. The last pair she had bought him two months ago were too worn now. It was very important for her husband to impress the boys at the club. You know how men are. Those old shoes didn't protect his feet right, and he'd be in pain halfway through a match. How mortifying.

Ana thought of Shawn, her man. She understood exactly what the lady meant. Tennis or basketball—the point was that they had to impress the boys. Only Shawn couldn't afford new sneakers every two months. He was probably still at the courts, wiping the blood from his knee every ten minutes. She knew he thought of her. He thought of Carlos. He was in the "business" because he wanted to provide for them. No one would make him work at some factory making minimum wage for the rest of his life. He'd already done that to support his ma and his sisters. His father had died after twenty-one years as a janitor. Your typical heart attack. He had preached honest work to his kids all his life. Then died leaving behind nothing to show for his hard work but a worn corpse, which there was no money to bury. Shawn's ma had to borrow from the relatives.

With Carlos safely in Maritza's grip, Ana started toward the exit. She heard him wailing. Mami, come back. He would throw a tantrum for the next half hour because he wanted his mami back. Maritza knew to buy him something. He'd shut up.

The waiting area was packed. Strangers learned each other's life stories within an hour. There was nothing better to do. A homeless man clenching a paper bag was sprawled motionless in a chair. One would think he was dead if he didn't snore so loudly. Women sat limply in their chairs as their three or four kids chased one another around the room yelling. Whenever one of them hurt himself, he'd come crying to his mother until he regained sufficient energy to go back into the battlefield. A woman sitting by the entrance caught the arm of one of her offspring, pulled him toward her, and spanked him. He crouched in a corner crying as she cursed under her breath. She then concentrated on catching one of her other two boys. She wore dirty blue jeans that were too tight around her plump waist and a white T-shirt that had been washed too much. Her brown (once white) sandals seemed to be overwhelmed with pain from carrying all that weight. Her hair was uncombed or had been disheveled by the day's struggle. Her name was called, and she got up. Her knees cracked from the effort. She walked over to the next available desk, where an impatient lady in a red suit waited for her. Without looking up, the lady began to read out questions from a sheet of paper. The woman stared blankly. *No hablo inglés.*

Ana watched from her seat. She walked over to the desk and offered to translate. They went through all the questions while the lady with the suit wondered to herself why these people didn't learn to speak English. This was America. When done, the fat woman thanked Ana nonstop as she complained about those Americans. Maybe she didn't speak English, and maybe she was poor, but she was still human. She gathered her three kids on her way out of the office and yanked them by the arms into submission. Ana returned to her seat and lit up a cigarette.

The wait was always eternal at the welfare office. Ana imagined that when she went to hell, this is what it would be like. And she didn't doubt that she'd go to hell. From what Father Manuel made it sound like, most people were going to hell. Her sin was premarital sex. Ma had always warned her, but when Shawn took her to his empty apartment and started unbuttoning her clothes and begging her to go a little farther, how could she say no? She only pushed him away when it hurt, but it was already too late. He held her afterward while she sobbed. That Sunday she went extra-early to church. But God wasn't fooled, and Carlos had already invaded her body. Ma had wanted her to get rid of it. Not only was she pregnant, but she was pregnant with a black man's child. Ma was very adamant about lightening the race in the family and according to her, Ana had set them a couple of steps back. Carlos was *morenito* but with fine features, so it wasn't too bad.

Finally her name was called. Ana Mendoza. She walked over to the last desk on the right. A woman in her forties wearing a rainbow bright blouse waited for her. Her posture was painfully straight, and her auburn hair was burned out from the dye. Ana sat down and attempted a smile. No smile was returned. The questions began. Ana had heard them all before and recited the answers without thought. Single . . . nineteen years old . . . one child . . . The woman stared with scornful eyes and yawned occasionally. The room was hot and full of smoke. Ana's clothes were sticking to her body, and she was dying to smell her armpits, just to double-check. She crossed and uncrossed her legs and thought back to the basketball courts. Maybe with her next welfare check she would buy Shawn a pair of Nikes. He never bought anything for himself, not even a big gold chain; everyone had one. She'd get him and Carlos a pair each. Carlos always wanted to wear clothes like Shawn. He would be just like his daddy someday.

TERESA ORTEGA
Soul Secrets and Bean Lore

Do you know those days when everything in the world is too hard? I'm not talking about every day, which is bad enough, but the extra-bad days: the sad, bad, lonely days. The nights of giving up.

A truly bad day will announce itself to me with a sacred occurrence. On a bad day I can hear my soul speak, making demands on me with all the grace of a pent-up chihuahua.

It has a simple message, and it's this: "Go eat some beans."

If you have not seen your own soul before, you should know that it's no bigger than a nugget, a splinter. Usually my soul hides deep in the middle of my chest, and for the most part it doesn't bother me one way or the other. By all accounts I've had good luck. Because despite its diminutive size, when a soul decides it has a quarrel with you, you're better off taking its instruction.

So on this bad night, following a long, bad day, having heard the familiar but insistent request for beans, I obediently head for my yellow kitchen. I appreciate my soul's need for a snack.

I go to the large white built-in cabinet and reach for a can of refried beans. I open the can left-handed, which means with some difficulty, and dump the beans into a little pan to warm them. Then I get the ready-made burrito-size flour tortillas out of the fridge and place one in a cast-iron skillet slick with butter.

The tortilla's delicate surface rises ever so slightly as it heats. Tiny puffs of air form pockets, browning in the sizzling butter; I see the moon's face, darkened with rings.

What is the exact color of beans? I do not carry any authority on the subject, yet I have looked innumerable times past the crooked wooden counter of a burrito stand into a steaming pot of pinto beans, and I believe there is no single color that can describe the leguminous, molten body that gathers from boiling and then mashing beans with onion, spices, and fat. The red, the orange, the brown, the white are all mixed together, so that you never know where white ends and brown begins, when the turn of a wooden spoon will bring a delicate pink from the bottom of the vat, when streaks of red will form over the whole, or when the beans will suddenly mass into a brown clump resembling earth. The mixing of colors is what makes it a Mexican dish, just as the Mexican people range across many hues.

Have you been in the courtyard of an old Spanish mission? In Southern California, where I was born, there were at one time twenty Spanish missions running up and down the length of the state. Years ago, standing in the lush central courtyard of one of the still-operating Catholic missions, surrounded by thick palms, red hibiscus, and gigantic stalks of birds-of-paradise, there, amidst a tropical Eden, I witnessed a sinister conjunction of hues as the shadow of a cross from atop the mission tower fell across the adobe courtyard, a dark slash against the orange-pink Indian brick. The heavy faith of the Spanish conquerors must once have entered this land as unexpectedly. Contemplation of that strange landscape might have afflicted me had not the unanticipated mixture of color, rosy sienna cast across pale terra-cotta, engaged my appetite irresistibly by reminding me of beans.

A craving takes you like that, fiercely, so we may approach our own joy without hesitation. It's the least tangible regions of the body that tend to edge out of our control. Sudden laughter, the spot where hunger growls insistent, a physical sense of our lovers' pleasure, random swings of courage: places where the soul comes through like a phantom to touch the world with us.

If this were breakfast I was making and not my soul's short order, there would be rice too, Spanish rice fried in bacon grease and drizzled with fresh salsa served on a hot plate full of beans. But the task before me demands attention. The tortilla is done, and I turn to the metal kitchen table waiting behind me. I lift the tortilla carefully out of the pan that I'm carrying in my gloved hand and place it on a heavy fired-clay plate. Then, quickly grabbing the beans off the stove, I half pour, half scoop the beans into the steaming center of the tortilla. No cheese, no salsa, no sour cream (god forbid), only beans. Next step is to fold the whole thing up into a thick bundle. My offering now waits complete, a genuine bean burrito.

There's a secret to feeding the soul beans. As you might guess, it can't be fed through the mouth but requires a more subtle means of intake. The eating, the ingestion, the incarnation, the bringing of another entity into oneself.

Pick up the bean burrito and hold it against your cheek.

Close your eyes.

Maybe not every soul remembers. If you're from the eastern part of the United States, where the closest tortilla factory is a full five states away, perhaps the aroma of frijoles will not penetrate to your soul. But if you're from the Southwest—from Yuma, Blythe, Flagstaff, or Tucson; from San Antonio, El Paso, Demming, Taos; from San Diego, Barstow, Needles, or Los Angeles—you know about the restorative power of beans.

You feel clutched against your face the warm, heavy weight in your hand like all the comfort you've ever known: a soft breast, a generous belly, your girlfriend's thigh cradling your cheek. The poignant smell brings back your best memories.

I remember the Mexican jumping beans my parents bought me for ninety-five cents at a highway stop in southern Arizona. I took the beans out of the red plastic box they came in and watched them jump up and down on my hand, tirelessly, for the next 234 miles. Finally they fell on the floor and rolled under the seat, lost. A happier time then: my parents silent in the front seat of the car going toward Texas, me alone in the back with my beans and a lot of time, nothing but staring and the long flat space of the desert. To be a child again, wise days, just looking.

My soul eats beans, memories, loving the savor of time well spent.

ANDREW RIVERA
A Day of the Dead

Felipe bounced the ball twice, felt the grain of its cheap rubber surface against his hands, concentrated on the chipped backboard, the rim twisted from all the fools who slammed and hung, Felipe included, twisted back into place, eventually, by the janitor, orange paint long gone, replaced by rust. The chain was gone too. He let the ball drop from his hands, just a hint of a shove from the fingertips, heard the smacking of rubber and air hitting asphalt, felt the ball rise toward him, grabbed it. He sniffed, then wiped his nose on his sleeve. He flexed his knees.

You play too much ball, the voice said. It came from the other side of the fence.

Dead, Felipe thought. Already dead. He squeezed the ball, and his fingers seemed to melt into the grain.

Too much ball, the voice said. The chain-link fence rattled aimlessly.

Felipe ignored it. He did not listen to ghosts. Instead he concentrated on the free throw, tried to block out the noise of the crowd, cheering him, yes, but in their enthusiasm providing a distraction, one that could cost them the game. Felipe bounced the ball again, felt Magic's familiar touch on his shoulder, not saying anything but just letting him know he was there before he went to the line; Felipe bounced again, caught A.C.'s eye and nodded yes, mirrored Rambis's grin, smiling just as much at his white-boy hair and Clark Kent glasses as anything else, took a deep, heavy breath and could almost taste the dirty smell of hot asphalt, no, of excitement, anticipation, of the knowledge that it is there within reach and that one needs but to uncurl the fingers of the hand to touch, to possess and that the moment of possession will fulfill everything, will be the last perfect moment of need even as need evaporates, that it will be all.

Felipe took his shot. It bounced off the rim, came back toward him, bounced past. He looked around the Forum, tried to catch Jack Nicholson's eye. No one was there. It was just a schoolyard.

The voice whispered something that Felipe couldn't hear. Felipe sighed. Eventually the ball stopped bouncing.

"Felipe," his mother called, her voice tugging, sharp and soft. "Felipe."

The one thing about living across the street from the schoolyard is that your mother always knows where to find you.

Saturday, his mother's voice: These things meant nothing to Felipe, and they meant everything. It was, he remembered, his turn to take the graveyard tour; Old Pete, his grandfather, wanted to visit his wives. Felipe hopped the fence, careful not to tear or dirty his clothes, trotted across the street, and slipped the ball under the porch. He heard the kitchen door behind him slam shut, a noise as final as the look on a face when all pretense is dropped, when the reason for living is gone, a moment that Felipe didn't know, but could implicitly, understand. Felipe García, reporting as ordered, he thought, playing with the memory of a movie he'd seen the week before. The ball slid into the shadow, but not before the faded words that crisscrossed its black-orange surface came into view: *property FHS*. He wondered, briefly, what it would have been like to be on the team rather than just having stolen the ball, to be in the real school rather than in the continuation school across the street where they kept fuckups like him, losers on their way to the army if they were lucky, jail if they weren't. Sixteen and a half and already a loser for life. He heard the screen door screech open again, and he stood.

"Are you going like that?" his mother said.

Felipe looked down: cutoff khakis, white T-shirt. They were ironed, creases sharp as steel running down his legs, across the lines of his shoulders and down his arms. He looked good, he thought. "Like what?" he said.

"With that thing in your hair," she said, and she gestured at his head. Her arms were white from baking for the women's committee. He could, he thought, smell the cinnamon, the sugar, the hot grease that reminded him of the stink of the church, with its candles and dankness.

Felipe raised his hands, touched the black hairnet that covered his head. "No," he said. He took it off, patted his hair back into place with his hand.

She shook her head. "He's waiting for you," she said.

"Who?" Felipe said.

"You know who." She shook her finger at him. "Don't go picking up any of your friends."

"Which friends?" Felipe said. He grinned, thinking she was playing.

She paused at the door, then turned. He noticed, for the first time, the white in her hair that did not come from a hand coated in flour. Her eyes were red-rimmed and tired. "You're like your father," she said. "Just like your father."

Felipe shrugged, felt his face go rigid as if it were a mask, cheap and plastic like the Halloween mask he'd worn as a child, its exaggerated features effacing his own. He watched his mother turn and go into the kitchen, saw her stumble and nearly trip on the half step from the porch to the house, then pause and wave him over. Her lips were cool and soft on his forehead, the apology implied, and Felipe felt himself relax. She spent too much time baking for the church, he thought, wasting their money on candles for ghosts, wasting herself saying rosaries to a god who didn't seem to care, her fingers nimble on the wooden beads that Felipe could half remember from his childhood, that seemed to have been in the house for as long as he had. He shook his head and walked to the garage. Ghosts are to be ignored, he thought. Ignored and forgotten.

Felipe was never sure how he got drafted into the graveyard tour or even why it took place. There were other grandchildren, ones with better cars who liked the old man and whom he liked as well. And why bother? The old man rarely showed any emotion, never cried, seldom bothered to get out of the car. Felipe always got the feeling that he would rather be off somewhere else, drinking, or watching a ball game with all the other old men, red eyes hidden beneath dark glasses, faces heavy, impassive. Someone, and he couldn't remember who, his mother, perhaps, but someone had said once that he'd worked them to death anyhow, his wives, the first two, at least, women for whom death might have seemed like a chance to sleep past daybreak, a respite from the predawn ritual of tortilla making, the soft pap-pap of their hands unbroken but for the sound of their own breaths, women who were bowed by babies, by work, by being mother and wife and so much more; the first two wives, but not María, María, who was too smart for that; María, the seamstress, who would tell him to fuck off when he yelled, who would trade him slap for slap when he got drunk, María, who sang with the mariachis, her voice hard and fine, hair dyed bright red well into her fifties, María so full of life until the plumber ran her down, him late for the job, her crossing the street, the shopping bag loaded with piecework she'd brought home still in her hand, its contents scattered like leaves in the wind, her body tossed onto the sidewalk she'd been rushing toward, her head down, twisted and ripped with one arm flung awkwardly across her eyes, as if she hadn't wanted to see or be seen, and bits of fabric lay soaking in the puddle of blood that had been her. Old Pete, Viejo, saw her when he walked to the corner to buy a paper, curious as to how the Dodgers had done the night before. He hadn't followed the Dodgers since. Felipe pulled up to the curb, got out of the car. *What's the difference?* he thought. *I blew the shot anyway*. A rematch, though, would have been nice.

His grandfather's house smelled. Felipe noticed it even as he knocked on the door, the smell of age and decay and something else, something that was close but that couldn't be named, not yet. He knocked again, nervous, aware of the tilt of the porch, of how the whole house seemed to tilt at an odd angle, of how the once-bright yellow paint was now faded and drab. He was in the wrong neighborhood. No one had seen him, and the chances were that no one would bother him, just picking up an old man and giving him a ride, the old man who moved so slowly through the neighborhood, calling people by other people's names, the old man who had collapsed in the street where his wife had died, paper crumpled in his hand, and who had to be helped away, the newsstand owner holding one arm and some homeboy with the other. As long as Felipe didn't show anyone any disrespect, he should be okay. Still, he was nervous. He was too far from home. He knocked again, the peeling, flaking paint rough under his knuckles.

The door lurched open. Old Pete stood there, wet eyed and shaking. He smiled. "M'ijo," he said. He reached out and placed one withered hand on Felipe's shoulder.

"You shouldn't do that," Felipe said. He felt the hand heavy on his shoulder, heavy and light at the same time, as if it would float away. Felipe wrinkled his nose. His grandfather smelled faintly of piss. "You shouldn't just open the door."

"Come in, M'ijo," his grandfather said, ignoring him. "I'm almost ready." He lifted his hand from Felipe's shoulder, and Felipe felt briefly a feeling of relief. The smell did not go away. Inside, the parrot, Zapata, squawked. Felipe stepped inside. One of the windows was broken, a piece of cardboard taped where the missing pane should be. The floor inside was slanted too.

"There are crazy people around," Felipe said.

"I know," Pete said, and he smiled.

"Being old won't protect you," Felipe said.

"I know," Pete said as he struggled into a heavy sweater. "I'm not afraid of you Chicanos."

"It's summer," Felipe said, noticing the sweater. He poked at the cardboard, decided not to ask how it had been broken.

"That's what you call yourselves, right?" Viejo's fingers shook as he fumbled with the buttons. It was one of those Mexican sweaters that the old people wore, dirty white with odd designs; he'd worn them for years. Felipe had had one when he was younger. He'd wanted to dress like his grandfather then.

"You'll be too hot."

"Chicanos." Pete shook his head. "You're Mexican."

"Chicano," Zapata squawked. He spread his wings, stretched himself erect.

"Shut up," Pete said.

"What?" Felipe said. He rocked back and forth on a loose floorboard.

"Not you, the parrot," Pete said. He walked over to the cage and draped a stained white towel over it. "Go to sleep."

"Pinche Pete," the parrot squawked.

Pete laughed. "María," he said. "María taught him that."

"I know," Felipe said, and he smiled. "Let's go." The smell of the place was starting to give him a headache.

"Yes," Pete said. "Let's go." He began to walk toward the door. Felipe watched, surprised. He'd never noticed that his grandfather shuffled before.

Aware of the eyes that followed him, Felipe drove slowly through the gates of Forest Lawn. Felipe wished that María had been buried in San Fernando with the other two, but his uncle Michael had paid, and he had wanted her here, in Forest Lawn, in the section that he had reserved for himself and his wife. There were only three plots. Pete would go somewhere else.

"Go straight," Pete said. He had put on his black sunglasses.

"I know," Felipe said. "I've been here before." He wanted to laugh. He thought that Pete looked like the Mexican Ray Charles.

"Turn here," Pete said.

Felipe shrugged, said nothing, and turned.

"Park here," Pete said.

Felipe pulled over, then walked around to the side of the car where Pete was struggling to get out. He reached down and grasped Pete's arm, but Pete pulled away. Felipe shrugged and stepped aside, watched as Pete used his cane as a precarious lever and lurched to his feet. They walked, picking their way among identical plaques, Pete careful to avoid stepping on them and Felipe not caring, until they came to María's plaque. Pete sank down, using his cane for support, and sat on the ground beside her. He sighed and placed his hand on her plaque, then leaned over and kissed the cool white stone. Felipe looked away.

"I forgot the flowers," Pete said. He sounded as if he were going to cry. "I always bring flowers."

You never bring flowers, Felipe thought. "I got them," he said. "I put them in the car." He just wanted to go home.

Pete did not reply; he simply shook his head slowly back and forth. Felipe was surprised; he'd never seen his grandfather act this way.

Felipe looked around, then walked back toward the car. He stopped, looked back to see if Pete was watching, but Pete was looking down, disconsolately patting María's plaque and muttering to himself. Felipe knelt and lifted a fresh bouquet of flowers from the grave beneath his feet. They were orange and white, and he lifted them to his nose and sniffed. They smelled of nothing. Felipe glanced down at the grave from which he had taken the flowers. "John Lopez," it read. This must be the Mexican section, Felipe thought, and he smiled. His uncle Michael had tried all his life to be white, bought his plot in the whitest graveyard he could find, all without knowing that when he died, they would stick him with the other wetbacks. Felipe glanced back down. Born February 7, 1978. Died February 11, 1978. Felipe shook his head again. A baby. He wondered at what would make someone, sixteen years later, return to lay fresh flowers on the grave of someone who had been alive for five days, whose time had amounted to little more than a few shaky, trembling breaths, a few cries, and who never could have known what killed him or even that he was alive. A waste of money, Felipe thought, but he knew that it was something more than that. He looked up again. Pete was still muttering away, his hand moving up and down, occasionally patting, then occasionally stroking María's plaque. Suddenly Felipe hated his uncle, and he didn't know why. He walked back to María's grave. His grandfather's back seemed small and frail, the sweater sad and weak.

"Here," Felipe said. "They were in the backseat."

"*Gracias*, Ramón," Pete said. He took the flowers and held them to his nose. "So sweet," he said. "Your mother always loved these."

"She's not my mother," Felipe said. He wasn't even sure which one of the wives was his grandmother.

Pete began to hum. " 'Besame Mucho,' " he said. "She always loved that song."

Felipe shrugged. It was getting hot. He decided to find somewhere cool to sit.

Felipe was tired. He'd been hanging out the night before, drinking beer with Ed and Serge in Ray's garage, getting high on some cheap weed Ed's brother had sold them. He was thirsty. He shook his head. What a way to spend a Saturday, he thought. He wondered how long it would take before he was hassled by someone, asked what he was doing, why he was here. *It's not me*, he would explain. *I want to leave. They wouldn't listen*. He walked aimlessly.

The statue in front of Felipe was strange. It was of a young man, tall, and for some reason Felipe thought that he should know him. He read the plaque at the base of the statue. "David," it said. David. The young man of the statue stared to his left, his face hard, stoic and passionless. He reminded Felipe of the faces of the Aztec gods painted on murals in his own neighborhood. Empty. He wondered what it was like to look like that, to be so clean, not to know what it was like to live with an apology on your lips, not to feel the weight of your head and shoulders as they hung and slumped, not to have to remember, constantly, to lift them, not to have to look out of a scowl, to be of something, someone. Felipe turned his own head to the left, lifted his chin. It didn't work. He felt the same.

Felipe looked around. Some sort of service was going on about fifty feet to his right, a bunch of people in suits and dresses, some crying, some as empty as the man before him.

He felt conspicuous. He didn't belong.

He saw a wrought-iron gate set into a bright red brick wall before him, open, and he ducked inside. His face felt hot, and his temples thumped gently; he rubbed them. "Fuck," he said aloud. "Fuck fuck fuck."

"Watch your language," a voice said. "This is a cemetery."

Felipe turned around, then looked behind the hedge from which the voice had seemed to come. A man, his face as brown as Felipe's, looked up at him. He pointed a large pair of clippers at Felipe. "You shouldn't be in here," he said.

"The gate was open," Felipe said.

The man stared at him, then turned back to the hedge and took a few desultory swipes at it with the clippers. "This is where the rich people are buried," he said.

"Here?" Felipe said.

"Yes," the man said. "They spend a great deal of money to be dead away from the poor people." He laughed.

"How much?"

"What does it matter?" the man said. "They're still dead."

He stood, and Felipe saw that he was short, shorter than Felipe at least, and that he had a small potbelly. He wore green coveralls, and a small patch above his left breast read "gardener."

"My grandmother is buried here," Felipe said.

"In here?"

"No," Felipe said. "Out there."

"Good," the man said. He took another whack at the hedge. "I'd hate to think that one of us was foolish enough to be buried here."

"Yes," Felipe said.

"Me," the man said, "I want to be cremated. Cremated and dumped in the water so I give all the people around here the shits." He grinned.

"Yeah," Felipe said. "That would loosen them up some."

The man laughed. "Are you hungry?" he said. "I have some lunch over here."

"Yes," Felipe said, "thanks." The thought of eating in a graveyard did not bother him.

"Good," the gardener said. He set the clippers in his wheelbarrow, pushed it out of sight behind the hedge.

They sat on a small stone bench and split a couple of cheese sandwiches, a thermos of coffee, and a bag of sour cream and onion chips. It was cool in that part of the cemetery, the grass wet and well watered, the sky overhung with trees, and high walls casting shade on the ground.

"I want to be buried somewhere where I can see the sky," the man said. "I want to be free."

"Me too," Felipe said. He wondered if the man had any other sandwiches. "Me too."

"Not here."

"No."

"It isn't home," the man said.

"No," Felipe said, and he felt that this was true, but he wondered then where home was. He'd never lived anywhere else.

Another man appeared at the garden gate, his arms crossed. "Paco," he said. "You done with the hedges?"

Felipe froze. The loudness of the voice startled him, coming as it did amid so much quiet.

The man set his sandwich down on the bench and stood. "Almost," he said. He did not have to add the "sir." The tone of his voice did that.

The other man said nothing, and Felipe took a chip and placed it in his mouth but did not chew. He felt it dissolve into nothingness. "Get on it," the man said, and he disappeared, suddenly no longer standing at the gate.

Felipe stood. "I have to go," he said.

"Yes," the man said. He looked away.

"My grandfather."

The man said nothing.

Felipe nodded, then hurried to the gate. He passed the humil-
iating statue and was halfway to the car before he remembered
that he didn't know the man's name. He was sure it wasn't Paco.

"Where were you?" Pete said. He was sitting in the front seat
of the car.

"I was walking," Felipe said.

"We have to see the others," Pete said. His voice was small.

"I know."

"They're waiting."

"I know," Felipe said.

Pete stared at him for a moment, then lapsed into silence.
Felipe started the car and pulled away from the curb. He looked
in the rearview mirror as he pulled away, saw that the flowers,
orange and white, were back on John Lopez's grave.

They stopped for lunch at a taco truck. Felipe listened idly as
his grandfather talked with the man in the truck in Spanish, not
understanding, they spoke so fast. Two wetbacks, he thought.
He bit into the burrito, swore silently when he burned his
tongue on the hot insides. Felipe held the burrito out from
himself as he ate, careful not to drip on his clothes. He whipped
his hand back and forth when he was done, throwing off the
grease that had leaked onto him, then wiped his hands with a
napkin and threw it on the ground. He looked up, saw that his
grandfather was staring at him.

"What?" Felipe said.

"Who taught you that?" his grandfather said.

"Taught me what?" Felipe said. He noticed a fresh grease
stain running the length of the old man's shirt.

"To eat like a pig."

Felipe shrugged, looked away. He wondered if the man inside
the truck was listening.

"Is this your Chicanismo?" Viejo said.

Felipe shrugged again.

"Chicanos. Flower stealers and pigs," his grandfather said.
The man inside the truck laughed.

"You ready?" Felipe said.

"*Vatos locos*," his grandfather said in a deep, gravelly voice. "Zapata would piss his pants from laughing."

Felipe shook his head. His grandfather turned and began speaking to the man in the truck again, about him, Felipe assumed. He wished he could understand them. Felipe leaned back against the truck, felt the heat from its side seep into his back, felt the sun on his face, and he closed his eyes. The ruttering of his grandfather's Spanish sounded softer that way, the truckman's occasional grunts more melodic. Felipe felt as if he were in a dream. The sound of a car door slamming startled him awake. He had not heard the car pull up. He opened his eyes quickly. It was police.

There were two of them, big, one black and one white, both with heavy mustaches, the black of their uniforms seeming ready to swallow him. They were walking straight toward him. Felipe glanced down at their hands. He was safe. If they had wanted to hassle him, their hands would have been at their belts, rather than swinging freely from their sides. Felipe nudged his grandfather. "Let's go," he said. He did not have a license. His grandfather's hand idly waved him away.

"Two burritos," the white cop said. He stood on the other side of the old man, legs spread as if to straddle the earth. "I'll buy," he said to the black cop.

The black cop laughed, then turned to look at Felipe. Felipe looked down. His grandfather rattled on. Felipe could see nothing but the tips of his own shoes. The ground beneath them was black, sticky, like the basketball court across from his house. He heard the white cop laugh at something he hadn't heard, assumed that they were laughing at him. He wished he'd stayed home. He was glad he'd taken off the hairnet.

"Come on, son," Pete said loudly. "Drive your grandpa home."

Felipe looked up. His grandfather was smiling broadly, and as Felipe watched, he turned to the cops. *No.* Felipe thought. *No.*

"Too old to drive myself," he said.

The white one ignored him; the black cop nodded, then turned his back.

Felipe felt his grandfather's arm snake through his own, and they walked back to the car. He opened the door and helped the old man inside, surprised at how frail he suddenly seemed and how willing he was to accept this. Felipe walked around to his own side of the car, careful not to look back at the cops, aware that they were watching him. He settled into the seat, paused before starting the car. "Are we really going home?" he said, hopeful.

"*Pendejo*," his grandfather said. "We're going to San Fernando to see Elena and Juanita."

Felipe shrugged, started the car. He sneaked a look in the rearview mirror, saw that the cops were intent on their burritos, eating as he himself had eaten moments before, food held away from the body. "Why did you do that?" he said.

"I hate cops," his grandfather said.

Felipe was pleased finally to drive through the wide iron gates of San Fernando Cemetery. He hated driving the freeway, cars blasting past on either side as he kept to fifty-five, afraid to go any faster because of what he'd heard of the highway patrol, always happy to pull over a Mexican. He hated his grandfather's insistent complaints, telling him that he was going too fast, that he was going the wrong way, that the radio was too loud. He parked carefully, avoiding the overhanging trees and the bird shit they would leave on his mother's car. They walked slowly toward the graves, side by side, Felipe holding his grandfather's arm. Somewhere Felipe could hear the whine of a lawn mower, but he was unsure if it was coming from the cemetery or from the new subdivisions just beyond the gate. Felipe wondered how anyone could live so close to the cemetery, to all those dead people. He would not have liked the constant reminder.

"This was a different place once," his grandfather said.

"Really?" Felipe said. He was trying to avoid stepping on graves. He felt different here. Death was different here.

"We used to come walking here, Elena and I," his grandfather said. His voice was quiet, as if he were talking to himself. "She loved to look at the hills."

Felipe looked up. There were mountains beyond him, a stark red-brown against the sky. They seemed unreal. "You went walking in the cemetery?" he said.

"Around here, idiot," he said. He pulled his arm away. "No one walks in a cemetery."

"You said here," Felipe said. He stuffed his hands in his pockets. It was getting cold.

"I was glad I could bury Elena here," Old Pete said. "Glad when your father paid to move Juanita here."

And where'd my father get the money? Felipe thought. *Dead in prison at thirty-one.* He said nothing.

"Help me down," his grandfather said. They were at the grave site. Felipe held his grandfather as he first knelt, then lurched into a sitting position. He stood then and folded his arms, waiting.

"Juanita was just a girl when she died," his grandfather said. "Not much older than you are."

Felipe was surprised. "But you were married," he said.

"We did things differently then," his grandfather said, and he sighed. "I'd like to go home now." He held one hand up for Felipe to grasp.

"We just got here," Felipe said.

"I'm tired. I want to go." His hand shook in the air, fingers splayed, waiting for Felipe's grip, his fingers almost begging, if fingers could beg.

"But you haven't talked to them," Felipe said. When he bothered to get out of the car, his grandfather always spoke to his wives, one at a time, telling them all that had been going on in his life, how the Dodgers were doing, new words his parrot had said. He never spoke of one to the other, as if he didn't want them to know. Or perhaps he was just being polite. Felipe did not know.

"I don't have anything to say," his grandfather said. "It was all too long ago." The hand dipped a bit, then rose, more insistent. His head was down.

Felipe reached out, grasped the outstretched hand, then leaned over and helped his grandfather to his feet. Above them the hills loomed, red and raw, hard, cold. *So old*, Felipe thought. He felt his grandfather put his arm around him for support.

"I've lived too much," his grandfather said. "I'm being punished for living too much, too long."

He was crying, and Felipe watched as a tear ran down his coffee brown face. It dripped, soaked into his shirt next to the grease stain.

"Don't cry," Felipe said.

"Do you know, I can't remember the sound of Juanita's voice or the look of her face or the way her toes felt when she tickled me in bed. I remember none of those things," his grandfather said, and his face seemed to drop, the skin too loose to support the emotion. "I remember the thing, the moment, but I can't remember the feel of those things."

"No," Felipe said. He didn't know what else to say.

"Or Elena," his grandfather said. "Or María." He rummaged through his pockets, pulled out a gray, dirty handkerchief. "I wish I could remember those things."

"Yes," Felipe said.

"All those mornings, all that time," his grandfather said. "You think you have all the mornings in the world, but you don't." He blew his nose loudly.

"No," Felipe said.

"I would do anything to remember," his grandfather said. And there were other things, other moments, things that Pete remembered with his body, felt, but that were remote, things that he could never speak of: the spot on her shoulder where he would lay his head at night, the other's laugh, deep and from the gut, that he could feel wash over him, cleansing, the brush of another's lips against his own, unspoken then and now gone.

Felipe put his arms around his grandfather, felt his frailness sag into his arms, felt the weak heaves that his chest struggled to make as he sobbed. *He's getting me dirty*, Felipe thought, and was ashamed of himself. He closed his eyes, wrapped his arms tighter around the weightlessness, and he held the old man, not knowing that this is in fact how we die: the half-remembered touch of flesh on flesh; the gentle whisper, the sinking thought, the indiscriminate fading of what we are.

Three things:

An old man walks, head down, angry that his wife sings and dances. She follows, castigating him. He loves her. She loves him. That is all that can be said, other than that he is a fool.

A hawk swoops low over the hills. Is it beauty or just a bird? How do we tell?

A cloud lolls by, its shadow darkening the mountains. Is it the breath of God? Or just a cloud?

Existence is story, part lie and part parable. We spend so much time sifting through our memories; it serves only to show how much life has already dribbled through our fingers, how many stories have gone untold. Let me tell you one.

The woman lies on the sidewalk partially; her feet touch the asphalt of the street, the skirt hiked up higher than she would allow were she alive. She still has the bag in her hand, the one she held before her as if it were a shield. The car struck her anyway, the bag split, and the bits of the piecework she brought home to sew for extra money dance across the street, blown about by the wind as if they were leaves in the midst of fall, blue, green, yellow, bits of orange, a lavender that she'd found particularly lovely the night before, when she'd held it up to the light, still capable of finding beauty in a bit of cloth despite the pain in her eyes, the ache in her fingers. She is a broken doll. You know this part, but here is something more. Later, hours later, her grandson will find one of these bits; he'll trap it beneath his shoe, and it will flutter in the wind, and then he'll lift his toe, a barely perceptible movement, a movement so slight that even he is hardly aware of it, as if the body and the mind had split, and it will float away, and it will be this moment—not the blood caked on the sidewalk, not the memory of his grandfather's stricken, unshaven face, not the knowledge that she died alone, her life frozen into a moment of terror—it will be that fluttering bit of cloth, so anxious to be free, that will make him cry. This is the real story.

An old man's back is bony and hard. There's not much life there. Felipe clung to what there was, hoping for a bit of comfort perhaps.

CARMEN G. ROSELLÓ
Green Apples

Late at night the sister can't sleep, so she stays awake, staring out at the darkness through her dirty little window. In
this part of the world the sky is crowded with stars that clump
together. She tries to ignore the smell of cow dung and imagines
that she is a space traveler. But the smell wins over, and she is
back in a car, cheek pressed firmly against the cold glass.

The sister was reading *Little Women* for the fifth time that day
in the old house. Her legs dangled off the armrest of the rickety
chair where she sat. Soon it would be time for her to leave Jo and
Amy and eat dinner with the family. The father didn't allow
reading at the table, and the few times that she brought the book
into the kitchen, he slapped it out of her hand and told her to eat
alone at the dirty table next to the sink. That day she was sucking
on a strand of curly hair as she read the book. Jo was tapping
away at a typewriter in her attic. Suddenly out of nowhere came
the father, screaming, "Go help your mother set the table." He
tore the book out of her hand and ripped it in half. The sister
cried out as the chair creaked, but the father ignored her. Some
of the book's pages were under the father's bare foot, getting
crumpled by his ugly toes. Her wet curl stuck to her cheek as she
ran downstairs to the kitchen.

The sister salvaged the two halves of the book and kept them for traveling. The missing pages described Beth's illness. She didn't miss them that much. In the car she could read until about an hour after the sun set. The sky turns a deep pink, then a purple as the sun sinks back behind the mountains that are covered with cactus and nopals. Sometimes, as the sun set, clouds would pass over it and the sky would be really dark purple like a grape, and then, as the clouds passed, the sky would be pink again. This is also the time to eat dinner, so the mother gives them little tortillas filled with cheese and meat.

The car is gray, and the inside seats are a nappy velour that marks the children's faces when they sleep on it too long. Each person makes his own space in the car. The sister sleeps on the right side of the backseat. She has an old torn-up Sesame Street comforter, a pillow, and a pile of books that she sets down at the foot of her seat. The brother has only a blanket, and he bunches it up to the corner of the back window to make a pillow. At night he shivers because the father turns on the air conditioning to stay awake. The sister spreads her blanket out and covers his feet, which poke tiny and dirty into her side of the seat.

For entertainment the sister has learned a way of controlling the things that are outside the car. She pretends she has a magical power. The sister likes to fix her eye on the occasional trees or stranded cars that she sees on the side of the road. As she sees them coming, she stares at them, slowly rotating her head to the right; they move slowly toward her, but as her head turns more to the right, the object comes faster and faster, and always, with a snap of her neck, it is gone; she has passed it.

Eventually, though, the children are asleep. In spaces made with blankets and pillows, the children dream with the colors of the sun beating into their closed eyes. The noises and smells aren't from the outside. The sister sleeps deeply and falls into her dreamworld, with a slow jolt. She dreams of floating against the dry wind that pushes their car back and makes it shift and sway when passing big rigs. She dreams of the dark rivers that appear in the distance under the hot sun. When they wake up, the children compare their dreams in hushed tones in the backseat, passing dreams between them like marbles. The brother dreams monsters most of the time that come out in the light of day. They live in bushes and at the sides of the roads. The sister takes his dreams and makes them into funny stories so the monsters stop being scary to the brother.

After a long draft of driving, the father pretends to close his eyes as if he were sleeping. The mother gets mad and yells at him, "Do you want to kill your family now? Is that what you are doing?"

The father laughs and taps the mother's back with his hand. He drives with his hand draped over the mother's seat, so at night, when the daughter lays with her head against the window, she can see her father's hand. She feels scared sometimes, like when she stares at it too long. She begins to feel the hand will move and grab her.

"We'll stop at a motel then and sleep and take a bath, and everything will be all right," the father whispers.

The mother turns her head away from the father and stares at the side of the road.

The sister imagines that her father is truthful, that everything will be all right after they are at the motel, and leans forward anxiously, looking to the road ahead for signs of one.

They stop at Los Huespedes Hotel. The manager's office is a little shack that faces the road. Behind it is a row of squat compartments. The buildings are faded, and the doors, painted red and green and white, have metal numbers hanging on them by nails that stick out crusty with rust. The mother goes into the office to ask for one room because she is in charge of the money. Leaning on the car is the father, who beckons to the children to get out of the car. The car makes soft ticking noises. The sister is always afraid that the car will not turn on again once it is turned off. She sits on the hood of the car, its warmth creeping softly into her behind and spreading down the back of her thighs. It is windy outside, and the breeze pushes the sister's hair into her face so she can see nothing except the strands of black that block her view. Then the father talks.

"Do you know why we're doing this. All this traveling?"

The sister looks up lazily at her father. "No, why?"

The father puts his stubby index finger to the dusty hood of the car. He draws a line with his finger. "Sometimes to get from here to here," he says, dragging his finger down his line, "you have to go here first." He drags his finger all over the hood of the car and then pokes the sister softly in her ribs. She laughs. The sound of the breeze picks up her laugh and carries it over the roar of the eighteen-wheel truck dragging past the motel.

"Do you understand, daughter?" the father says quietly.

The sister nods her head solemnly, and the mother comes out of the manager's office, with paper and keys in her hand.

The family trudges to the room.

"Children," the mother says in a tired voice, "please take a shower; you've been playing in the dirt for the last three days."

The brother looks down at his shirt, spotted with food and dust from the road, and slowly trudges to the bathroom. His hair pokes up from the back of his head from leaning against the car's backseat too long.

"Did you hear your mother?" the father says to the daughter, who sits on the hard motel bed. The sister picks at the nubby orange bedspread while the mother speaks. She has a big ball of fuzz rolled in her hand when her father speaks.

"Yeah, I heard her," the sister says quietly.

The children are hesitant because their smell is too familiar. Late at night, under her blanket, the sister can smell her young sweat. It is beginning to be like the smell of her mother, who tries to cover it up with perfume but not so salty. The sister takes in deep breaths and smells herself in the shell of her blanket until she falls asleep. When she takes baths, the smell of the strange soap at motels keeps her awake all night.

The brother comes out of the shower dripping water all over the dirty floor of the motel room. The mother is afraid that the brother will get athlete's foot from the floor, so she scoops him up in her arms and throws him on the wide bed where they all will sleep. He laughs and giggles as the mother tickles him. The father is looking at the daughter, waiting for her to get up and go into the bathroom.

The sister washes her hair and sees the long snakes of brown water make way down her belly. Her hair is too thick and picks up too much of the dirt that flies in the air. The mother will not cut her hair because she will look like a boy. She closes her eyes and imagines that she is at her house. It is a big house, and she has an older brother named Bob. She can hear the people in the next room talking, but she can ignore them and be at her house. Her mother, Beth—no, Jo—is downstairs cooking turkey, and her father is at work; he sells insurance—no, he is away at war, like the dad in *Little Women*. The people next door flush the toilet, and she feels the cold water stream down her back, giving her gooseflesh.

The family lies in the room, shivering under starchy white sheets, listening to the air. "We can never sleep here," complains the brother.

It is not like a car; they stretch out their limbs, and cheeks press to pillows that stay cool for only a little while. Not like the windows of a car at three in the morning. It takes longer to warm a mirror, so hot cheek is pressed to cold window for a long time before both cheek and window are the same temperature.

In the morning the family climbs out of the bed onto the frosty floor, which jars them into the day. They fumble into their clothes quietly, and the mother packs their sleeping things into a bag that she finds in the closet of the room.

"This way we can get to our sleeping clothes easier."

The father opens the door, letting in the heavy sunlight of the outside, which intrudes into the room like vast white space. The children leave the room and stand in the parking lot next to the car.

The warm sun feels nice after the cold of the air in the motel room, but the sister is tired of being outside after five minutes of waiting for the mother to check out. The wind moves briskly in the morning, and it sometimes overwhelms the sister, who takes huge gulps and finds herself suffocated. In a car it is different. She asks to sit in the car while the father packs their things in the trunk. She sits inside clean and silent.

The sister pulls the blanket around her legs and pulls her knees to her chest. The blanket smells like her; she is ready. Her father's bustling in the trunk, his shifting of suitcases sound noisily at the belly of the car. She listens to the hollowness of his movement and wishes she were somewhere in a house with her brother Bob.

The family moves fast past the visage. Neil Diamond will play until the tape reel thins and snaps, and then comes Kenny Rogers. The father talks about moving to Peru, maybe driving there. The sister covers her ears. She can still hear him because he is in the front and can turn down the radio. The mother has brought apples from the manager at the motel, and the brother chews noisily next to her. In his corner are toy soldiers that venture into the sister's corner. She gets angry and hits him. The mother twists in her seat and smacks the sister. The sister slips the blanket over her head and pretends she is sleeping.

That night the mother and father fight. They whisper, but the voices are so close. Sometimes the father rolls down the window so he doesn't have to listen to the mother's voice. The cold air rushes in, and the children shiver under their blankets. They can't say anything to the father because they are supposed to be asleep. The sister slips her cold right hand between her warm thighs and then her cold left hand between her warm thighs. The father rolls up the window.

The sister reads *Little Women* the entire next day even up to when the sun is cradled against the hills and the dingy windows cannot suck in any more light. The mother grabs the torn pages from the girl and says, "Don't ruin your eyes."

The father says, "Let her read. These kids get real bored sitting in a car all day long."

"Okay, then you deal with it when she goes blind."

The sister puts her book at her feet, pulls the blanket over her head, and falls asleep to the quiet hum of the car. That night she dreams of being Beth and lying quietly in a bed while Jo puts cold towels on her forehead. She is sick and dying, and she can feel what she thinks is her soul pressing against her chest, pushing to get out. The car makes a sharp turn and wakes the sister up. The harsh overhanging lights of a gas station blur her vision.

At the gas station people stare. They know from the way that the sister walks awkwardly for a few seconds, from the way the mother rummages around in the car for garbage, from the way the father spreads a neat map over the dusty trunk that they are travelers, gypsies. The sister walks into the gas station bathroom. She pulls up her shirt and examines the tiny breasts that are pushing their way out of her skinny chest. They ache terribly sometimes. It gets so bad that she has to push her knees against her chest to make them flat. They don't hurt so much that way.

She pees, then leaves the bathroom, walking into a tiny cloud of gnats. They float together as if they were connected, but they don't really go anywhere, just hang around outside bathrooms at gas stations and bus stops. The father finishes pumping the gas, pays the dark-skinned man, who looks at the sister with a strange smile, and the family gets in the car.

The mother drives this time, so she stays awake by telling the family stories. The brother sits with his arm wrapped around the front seat, holding the mother's shoulders. The sister presses her knees against the back of the father's seat because it is too crowded with his seat pushed way back into her space. They both have really long legs. Sometimes the father sleeps in the backseat and lays his head on the lap of one of the children. The sister never sleeps, though, because the father's heavy head crushes her lap. The mother tells stories of when she was small and lived in Peru, mostly stories of when her mother was still alive and made her pretty dresses and took her to nice parties. The sister hates dresses and hates her mother's stories, so she covers her ears. She thinks that the mother is talking to her, telling her to wear pretty dresses as if she could ever be pretty. It is easy for the sister to tune out her mother's soft voice. She wraps herself tightly with her blanket and presses her hands to her ears. Then she hums old commercials to herself until she falls asleep. Sometimes if the father is awake, he calls to the sister, who leans up to his seat and listens to his whispered stories. She can never see his face because he doesn't turn, just talks into space. His stories are better because they're about running away and riding motorcycles.

The brother says he has to go to the bathroom. It is very dark outside, and the mother stopped telling stories and now drives with the look on her face that she had when the father told them they were moving. The father is sleeping, snoring actually, and the mother tells the brother to hold it for just one more hour. He sits back quietly. He is afraid of bushes and likes to go to the bathroom with nice clean toilets with seats and paper. The sister stares at her brother, whose face is streaked shiny with quiet tears.

"I'll tell you a story," she says. "Once there was this little girl who lived with an evil mother who put a curse on her and died. The curse was that the girl could never pee. Well, the girl got really famous and so she got on *Real People*, and then, when she was on it, Skip gave her a green apple. Suddenly she started peeing and peeing and the studio audience got flooded out and the streets got flooded and the girl floated to China with Skip cuz it was his fault."

The brother begins to giggle, and then, as the sister joins in, the brother laughs harder and harder. The mother in the front seat hears nothing and keeps driving. The two children laugh until finally the brother asks the mother to pull over so he can go to the bathroom.

"You want to go to the bathroom out here?" the mother asks.

"I have to go real bad," says the brother between giggles.

The mother pulls to the side of the road into a gentle incline. There are bushes and cactus there that look like people standing around watching the cars go by.

"Go behind the cactus," says the sister. "You'll be safer."

The mother opens the door, letting in the cold air of the outside and letting out the brother from the backseat. He grabs the mother's hand, and they both run against the wind to the cactus. They disappear.

The father stirs. "Where are we?" he asks.

"Nowhere, Dad. Go back to sleep."

The father obeys, and the sister sits back and waits for the mother and the brother to pop out from behind the cactus. It is a long time waiting, but they finally appear, the mother looking tired and the brother looking satisfied.

When the brother gets back into the car, the children pretend to be eggs. They curl up at the foot of the backseat and pretend they are waiting to hatch. The sister gently places her books onto the backseat. They can wait a long time, and it is quiet except for the air outside. But they don't hear that anymore. Heads pressed against their knees, they listen to the rhythm of their breaths.

Contributors

Ricardo Armijo ("Drizzle of Moths") lives in Chicago, Illinois. He was born in Nicaragua and has made his home in the United States since 1980. He has published both in Spanish and in English, mainly in small literary magazines in the United States and Latin America. He has two unpublished collections of short stories: *Spider in the Petals* (1992) and *Tiempo de sobra* (1994), of which his story here is part.

Anthony Castro ("Soldier") grew up in the Bronx. He is a graduate of Amherst College and lives in New York.

Daniel Cooper Alarcón ("The Economy of Virtue"), a native of Wisconsin, worked as a newspaper reporter before studying creative writing with Patricia Hampl, Grace Paley, and Sandra Benítez at the University of Minnesota. He is currently an assistant professor of English at the University of Arizona. His fiction has appeared in *New Chicana/Chicano Writing 3* and the *Wisconsin Academy Review*. His book *The Aztec Palimpsest*, is forthcoming from the University of Arizona Press, in Spring 1997.

Lisa Y. Garibay ("Daddy") was born in 1974 and grew up in El Paso, Texas. She currently lives and writes in Hollywood.

Verónica González ("Through the Raw Meat") was born in Mexico City and raised in Los Angeles. She attended the University of California at San Diego and received a scholarship to New York University's creative writing master's program. She teaches at Medgar Evers College in Brooklyn.

Erasmo Guerra ("Last Words") is a New York City writer who grew up and has lived most of his life in Texas. His story included is an excerpt from a novel in progress.

Armando F. Gutiérrez ("Chinese Memories"), a Cuban-American from Miami, he works in the Hollywood film industry and is currently developing a screenplay.

Vivian Leal ("Mangoes") is a Cuban-American born in 1965 and raised in San Juan, Puerto Rico. She holds a B.S. from Georgetown University and an M.F.A. from the University of Massachusetts at Amherst. Formerly an assistant editor of *MELUS*, she lives with her husband and daughters in Clifton, Virginia.

James López ("Emoria at the Tracks"), a Cuban-American, has lived in Santiago, Chile, where he finished a master's with a dissertation on the Mexican poet and activist Homero Aridjis, and now resides in Miami. One of his stories has been published in the *Massachusetts Review*.

Catherine Loya ("We Don't Need No Stinking Maps") was born and raised in Riverside, California. She graduated from the University of California at Riverside and Stanford Law School. She lives in Denver, Colorado, and is a student in the creative writing program at the University of Colorado, Boulder.

Demetria Martínez ("Mark") won the 1994 Western States Book Award for Fiction with her first novel, *Mother Tongue*. She is also a coauthor of *Three Times a Woman* (Bilingual Press). A former reporter for the *National Catholic Reporter*, she lives in Tucson, Arizona. Her story included here is an excerpt from a novel in progress, *Mexican Rubies*.

Ysa T. Núñez ("Broadway"), a native of the Dominican Republic, lives in New York City.

Teresa Ortega ("Soul Secrets and Bean Lore") has been published in *Lambda Book Report, South Atlantic Quarterly*, and *Sinister Wisdom*. A Los Angeles native, she is currently working on a novel titled *Birth Memory West*.

David Rice ("The Circumstances Surrounding My Penis") is the author of a story collection, *Give the Pig a Chance* (Bilingual Press), from which the story included in this volume comes. He is from the Rio Grande Valley and was raised in Edcouch, Texas.

Andrew Rivera ("A Day of the Dead") was born in Los Angeles in 1965, received his B.A. from California State University in Northridge, and is completing his Ph.D. at the University of Wisconsin in Milwaukee, where he lives. His fiction has appeared in the *Quarterly* and the *Northridge Review*. The story in this anthology is part of a novel in progress.

Abraham Rodríguez, Jr. ("Babies") is a mainland Puerto Rican raised in the South Bronx. A guitarist and a graduate of the City University of New York, he is the author of *The Boy Without a Flag: Tales of the South Bronx* (Milkweed Editions) and *Spidertown* (Hyperion).

Cecilia Rodríguez Milanés ("Abuela Marielita") was born in New Jersey, of Cuban parents. She is the author of *Marielitos*, from which the story in this volume comes. She teaches multicultural literature and writing at Indiana University of Pennsylvania. Her work has appeared in a variety of literary journals.

Danny Romero ("Crime") was born and raised in Los Angeles. He has taught at Temple University and Lincoln University in Pennsylvania. His work has appeared in *Drum Voices Revue, Green Mountains Review,* and the anthologies *Mirrors Beneath the Earth: Short Fiction by Chicano Writers* (Curbstone) and *Pieces of the Heart: New Chicano Fiction* (Chronicle Books). He lives in Philadelphia.

Carmen G. Roselló ("Green Apples") is a teaching writing fellow at the University of Iowa Writers' Workshop. Her stories have won awards at San Jose State University.

Michele M. Serros ("The Next Big Thing"), a performance artist, was born in La Colonia and raised in El Río, both communities of Oxnard, California. She is the author of *Chicana Falsa and Other Stories of Death, Identity, and Oxnard* (Lalo Press). Her work is featured in the PBS documentary *United States of Poetry*.

Virgil Suárez ("Salvation") was born in 1962 in Havana, Cuba. In 1970 he traveled to Madrid, where he lived for four years, and then moved to Los Angeles. He has a B.A. from California State University in Long Beach and an M.F.A. from Louisiana State University. His books include *Latin Jazz* (William Morrow), *The Cutter* (Ballantine), and *Welcome to the Oasis and Other Stories* (Arte Publico). He has coedited two anthologies: *Iguana Dreams* (HarperCollins) and *Paper Dance* (Persea).

Sergio Troncoso ("Angie Luna") was born in El Paso, Texas, the son of Mexican immigrants, and lives in New York City. After graduating from Harvard, he was a Fulbright scholar to

Mexico and received two graduate degrees from Yale, where he now teaches a summer course. He has published stories in *American Way, Hadassah* magazine, *Blue Mesa Review,* and *Rio Grande Review,* and has finished a novel about a moral murder.

Select Readings

Acosta, Oscar "Zeta." *The Autobiography of a Brown Buffalo*. San Francisco: Straight Arrow Books, 1972.

————. *The Uncollected Work of Oscar "Zeta" Acosta*. Houston: Arte Publico Press, 1996.

————. *The Revolt of the Cockroach People*. San Francisco: Straight Arrow Books, 1973.

Anzaldúa, Gloria. *Borderlands/La Frontera: The New Mestiza*. San Francisco: Spinsters/Aunt Lute Foundation, 1987.

Augenbraum, Harold, and Ilan Stavans, eds. *Growing Up Latino: Memoirs and Stories*. Boston: Houghton Mifflin, 1993.

Colón, Jesús. *A Puerto Rican in New York and Other Sketches*. New York: International Publishers, 1982.

Fuentes, Carlos. *The Buried Mirror: Reflections on Spain and the New World*. Boston: Houghton Mifflin, 1992.

Fusco, Coco. *English Is Broken Here: Notes on Cultural Fusion in the Americas*. New York: New Press, 1995.

Galarza, Ernesto. *Barrio Boy: The Story of a Boy's Acculturation*. Notre Dame, Ind.: University of Notre Dame Press, 1971.

Gómez, Alma, Cherrie Moraga, and Mariana Romo-Carmona, eds. *Cuentos: Stories by Latinas*. Latham, N.Y.: Kitchen Table/Women of Color Press, 1983.

Gómez-Peña, Ernesto. *Warrior for Gringostroika: Essays, Performance Texts, and Poetry*. St. Paul: Graywolf Press, 1993.

Gómez-Quiñones, Juan. "On Culture," *Revista Chicano-Riqueña* 5, 2 (1977): 29–42.

González, Ray, ed. *Currents from the Dancing River: Contemporary Latino Fiction, Nonfiction, and Poetry*. San Diego and New York: Harcourt Brace, 1994.

———, ed. *Mirrors Beneath the Earth: Short Fiction by Chicano Writers*. Willimantic, Conn.: Curbstone Press, 1994.

———, ed. *Muy Macho*. New York: Anchor Books, 1996.

Kanellos, Nicolás, ed. *Short Fiction by Hispanic Writers in the United States*. Houston: Arte Publico Press, 1992.

Lewis, Oscar. *La Vida*. New York: Harper & Row, 1966.

Medina, Pablo. *Exiled Memories: A Cuban Childhood*. Austin: University of Texas Press, 1990.

Moraga, Cherríe. *The Last Generation*. Boston: South End Press, 1993.

Ortíz-Cofer, Judith. *Silent Dancing: A Partial Remembrance of a Puerto Rican Childhood*. Houston: Arte Publico Press, 1990.

Paredes, Américo. *With His Pistol in His Hand: A Border Ballad and Its Hero*. Austin: University of Texas Press, 1958.

Perez-Firmat, Gustavo. *New Year in Cuba*. New York: Doubleday, 1995.

———. *Life on the Hyphen: The Cuban-American Way*. Austin: University of Texas Press, 1994.

Poey, Delia, and Virgil Suárez, eds. *Iguana Dreams: New Latino Fiction*. New York: HarperCollins, 1992.

Rieff, David. *The Exile: Cuban in the Heart of Miami*. New York: Simon & Schuster, 1993.

Rivera, Edward. *Family Installments: Memoirs of Growing Up Hispanic*. New York: William Morrow, 1982.

Rodríguez, Luis G. *Always Running: La Vida Loca: Gang Life in L.A.* Willimantic, Conn.: Curbstone Press, 1993.

Shorris, Earl. *Latinos: A Biography of the People*. New York: W. W. Norton, 1993.

Stavans, Ilan. *Bandido: Oscar "Zeta" Acosta and the Chicano Experience*. New York: HarperCollins, 1995.

————. *The Hispanic Condition: Reflections on Culture and Identity in America*. New York: HarperCollins, 1995.

Thomas, Piri. *Down These Mean Streets*. New York: Vintage, 1979.